Jo Carnegie writes features for *Heat*, among other publications, and has interviewed stars from George Clooney, Justin Timberlake and Will Smith to Posh and Becks and Jordan. *Naked Truths* follows her début, *Country Pursuits*. She lives in London and Cardiff.

For more information on Jo Carnegie see her website at www.churchminster.co.uk

Also by Jo Carnegie

COUNTRY PURSUITS

and published by Corgi Books

NAKED TRUTHS

Jo Carnegie

CORGI BOOKS

TRANSWORLD PUBLISHERS
61–63 Uxbridge Road, London W5 5SA
A Random House Group Company
www.rbooks.co.uk

NAKED TRUTHS
A CORGI BOOK: 9780552157339

First publication in Great Britain
Corgi edition published 2009

Addresses for Random House Group Ltd companies outside the UK
can be found at: www.randomhouse.co.uk
The Random House Group Ltd Reg. No. 954009

The Random House Group Limited supports The Forest Stewardship
Council (FSC), the leading international forest certification organisation.
All our titles that are printed on Greenpeace approved FSC certified
paper carry the FSC logo. Our paper procurement policy can
be found at www.rbooks.co.uk/environment

Typeset in 11/13pt Palatino by
Kestrel Data, Exeter, Devon.
Printed in the UK by
CPI Cox & Wyman, Reading, RG1 8EX.

2 4 6 8 10 9 7 5 3 1

To Emma Messenger, my ideal 'ideal reader'

CHELSEA, LONDON

Guinevere Road

No.1

To
Soirée

№	
Nº1	Rowena
Nº2	Caro & Benedict
Nº3	Velda & Saffron
Nº4	Stephen & Klaus
Nº5	Velda's Studio

NAKED TRUTHS

JULY

Chapter 1

Saffron Walden peeled open a mascara-clogged eye. High above, a dusty lampshade dangled precariously from a peeling ceiling. Where was she? Saffron blinked and tried to focus. Her head pulsated unpleasantly, and fuzzy snapshots of last night danced through her mind. Oh God, it was all coming back to her now: she should never have let Fernando talk her into buying that last round of tequila slammers.

Saffron groaned loudly and struggled to sit up. As the duvet fell off she caught sight of herself in the cracked mirror opposite: alabaster white skin, small pert breasts, and a mop of peroxide blonde hair sticking out like it belonged to Worzel Gummidge. The remnants of last night's Amy Winehouse-inspired eyeliner were streaked halfway down her cheeks.

'You look like shit,' she told herself, which wasn't strictly true. Twenty-four-year-old Saffron Walden had an effortless cool that made her look cutting edge no matter how monumental the hangover.

'You look pretty good from where I am, *cariño*,' crooned a voice lustily. Saffron turned to find the glorious tanned physique of Fernando stretched out beside her. He was a beautiful Mexican barman she'd met in a club and been dating a whole six weeks.

Saffron looked round the bedsit distastefully. 'Have you never heard of a Hoover? This place is a shit hole.'

'I thought you liked it dirty,' he breathed. Despite the pounding against her temples, Saffron resisted the urge to giggle. He'd clearly been watching too much cheap porn recently. Fernando smiled back at her, and looked pointedly downwards. A large bulge was forming like a mushroom cloud under the duvet.

'I'll give you something to look happy about,' he said, suddenly pulling her on top of him. As he started grinding his hips against hers, Saffron could feel his erection burrowing underneath her like an over-excited ferret.

'I feel like crap!' she protested.

'Shut up.' Fernando kissed her, his tongue working into her mouth. He smelt of sweat and sex, mixed in with the faint tang of alcohol and aftershave. As his hands started running expertly over Saffron's body, she started to respond.

'Mmm . . .'

Miraculously, Saffron's headache was starting to disappear. Fernando wasn't the sharpest tool in the box, she reflected, but he *was* a bloody good shag. He looked up from enthusiastically sucking her left nipple. 'I told you I'd make you feel better,' he murmured throatily. One hand slid down and roughly pulled her legs apart.

Succumbing to the moment, Saffron sighed happily and reached for the bumper box of condoms on the bedside table. Her jaw dropped. 'Fuck me!'

Fernando groaned theatrically. '*Yeah*, baby!'

'Not you, idiot!' Snapping her legs together like a vice, Saffron grabbed the alarm clock. The red digits glared back accusingly: 10.10 a.m. 'Shit, I am so late for work!'

Disentangling herself from Fernando's amorous grip, she tumbled from the bed in a heap of long limbs. Her lover watched in disbelief as she retrieved a minuscule G-string from the floor.

'Baby, you can't leave me like this, my balls are gonna burst!'

But Saffron had already disappeared into the bathroom.

Exactly thirty-seven minutes later, Saffron flew through the doors of Valour Publishing, a gleaming modern tower just minutes away from the designer heaven of Bond Street in central London.

'Late again, Saff?' called out the cheery cockney security guard on the front desk. Saffron rolled her eyes as she rushed towards the lifts.

The middle doors opened to reveal the welcome form of Harriet Fraser, laden down with exquisitely wrapped parcels. Harriet beamed at Saffron. 'Just on my way up from the post room. I think Catherine's been sent another Cartier watch.'

The mountain of packages started to slide, and a small pink box fell out of Harriet's arms. 'Oh cripes!' she gasped, but Saffron had dived into the lift and caught it. The doors slid shut.

'Ouch, that hurt,' Saffron winced, clutching her head.

'Big night?' Harriet's eyes twinkled.

'Wasn't meant to be. Do I smell like a brewery?'

'Nothing a Polo mint can't cure. I've got some in my desk if you want.'

Saffron exhaled loudly and surveyed her wild-looking reflection in the mirrored wall. 'I can't believe I bloody overslept again. Catherine's going to give me such a bollocking.' Her face dropped even further. 'Oh

God, I've just remembered – I was meant to be doing a phone interview with Stella McCartney at 10 a.m.!'

The lift door pinged, and the doors slid open on to the fourth floor. As they got out, Harriet turned to Saffron, who was looking distinctly green round the gills. 'Don't panic,' she said kindly. 'Catherine's still at her editors' breakfast, and Stella's PR called. She's been struck down with some bug, so the interview's been rescheduled for next week. I've left a Post-it note with the details on your computer.'

Saffron grinned at her. 'Dearest H, where would I be without you? In fact, where would any of us be without you? I can't believe you've only been here six weeks.'

Harriet's cheeks went pink. 'Really?'

'Totally! And the other day I overheard Catherine saying to the art desk that you're the best PA she's ever had. You're like, a million times better than that useless old trollop Miranda. She only applied for the job because she thought she'd get to shag loads of male models.' Saffron snorted. 'As if!' They reached the office doors, and Saffron glanced through the porthole window. 'I've got to go and change in the loo. I had to make an emergency dash to Top Shop; otherwise everyone will know I'm a dirty little stop-out. Will you cover for me?'

'I haven't seen you,' said Harriet, smiling.

'You're a star!' Saffron placed the pink box in Harriet's arms and rushed off down the corridor towards the ladies.

Harriet watched Saffron go, flushing with pleasure. They really liked her! When she'd applied for the position at renowned glossy magazine *Soirée*, she'd never thought she'd get an interview, let alone the actual job.

Her father, Sir Ambrose Fraser, hadn't been able to

understand why she wanted to leave her quaint little cottage in the gorgeous Cotswolds village where she had grown up. 'Leave Churchminster? To move to London? What the bloody hell for?' he had bellowed during their weekly Sunday dinner at Clanfield Hall.

Her mother, Lady Frances, had been more understanding. Harriet had been through some life-changing experiences in the past few years. As well as going travelling, she had been very involved in organizing the Save Churchminster Ball and Auction. The event had been put on to raise funds to buy a piece of the village under threat of development, and it had been a roaring success. It made her realize she really was good at something.

At the age of thirty-two, with no real career track record apart from occasional secretarial duties for her father, Harriet had known life was passing her by. So when the job as *Soirée* PA/events coordinator had been advertised in the Media *Guardian*, she'd immediately sent in her CV. Two weeks later she'd been offered the job.

Sir Ambrose had retired to his study and refused to speak to her for three days. But thankfully her mother had taken her side. 'Churchminster will always be here, darling,' Frances had told her as they'd walked arm-in-arm round the grounds of the Hall one fresh spring evening. 'This job opportunity won't.'

So six weeks ago, at the start of June, Harriet had packed up the Golf, put her beloved Puffa waistcoats in the attic, and left. Driving away from the little cottage she lived in on her parents' estate had been dreadfully hard, especially when they, along with Cook and Mrs Bantry, the housekeeper, had come to wave her off.

Blinded by tears, Harriet had reversed over Sir Ambrose's foot by accident and nearly crashed into a ditch. Then halfway down the M4, she had been gripped by a sudden terror. It had taken all her strength not to come off at the next junction and flee home. What if she wasn't right for London, and *Soirée*? Everyone had seemed so stylish and together when Harriet had gone for her interview. Where on earth would her Laura Ashley wardrobe fit in?

To her immense relief, the team had been a down-to-earth lot, who were so pleased to have someone efficient after the disastrous Miranda that Harriet was given a hero's welcome on her first day. She enjoyed working for the editor, too, the formidable Catherine Connor. Tough but fair, Catherine set high, exacting standards, and Harriet was relishing the challenge of meeting them.

As well as managing Catherine's diary and making sure the office ran smoothly, Harriet was in charge of organizing *Soirée*'s famous autumn cocktail party. This year it was being held at the Natural History Museum. Harriet had been thrown in at the deep end, and was rushed off her feet liaising with florists and caterers, lighting people and guest lists, but she'd never felt so alive. Most nights, she would turn down invites from Saffron to go to one launch party or the other, and return to her rented garden flat in Fulham, exhausted but happy. For the first time in her life, Harriet felt like she was achieving something.

The only downside was that her love life was still so barren she made Ann Widdecombe look like a wanton harlot. She'd had one date, a picnic in St James's Park with the brother of an old school friend, but it had ended up being a complete disaster. Hugh Bonneville-Thorpe-Radcliffe was fresh out of the Priory, having suffered a mental breakdown from his high-pressured job as a city trader. After two hours recounting every excruciating detail of his therapy sessions, he'd unexpectedly tried to mount Harriet's leg. She still hadn't managed to push him off by the time a nearby gardener had turned his hose on them, before frogmarching the pair out. Harriet hadn't seen Hugh – or St James's Park – since.

Despite the mortifying experience, Harriet *knew* there was a man out there for her. South-west London was teeming with jolly, well-built men striding around purposefully with cricket jumpers tied over their shoulders. One of them had to be her Mr Right; she couldn't rely on the brooding Heathcliffe types in her romance novels for much longer.

But for now there were more pressing things to think about. Pushing the swing door open with her foot, Harriet entered the office. Music blared out from the stereo in the corner, while several staff tripped across the office on their way to a cup of tea and a gossip in the kitchen. Harriet remembered the first time she had walked in: it had looked like a cross between *Ugly Betty* and *The Devil Wears Prada*. Racks of expensive clothes had stood everywhere, while clouds of perfume and glitter billowed out from the beauty desk. All around there had been noise, and people laughing and talking loudly into their phones or shouting across the office about something. At that moment Harriet had felt like she'd stumbled on a really fun party, and she'd never wanted to leave.

Manoeuvring her way around the crate of Moët that had been sent from yet another PR company, Harriet deposited the parcels on her desk. Almost immediately the phone started ringing. With a smile she snatched up the receiver.

'Good morning, *Soirée* magazine!'

Chapter 2

Catherine Connor was preoccupied as she strode through the office doors half an hour later, having finally escaped her breakfast meeting.

She had always dreaded editors' breakfasts; they were just an excuse for most of them to show off their latest Chanel handbag, or get one over on a rival: 'Such a shame Keira dropped out of your cover shoot – did I tell you we've got her for our Christmas issue?'

To her discomfort, Catherine had ended up sitting next to her arch-rival Isabella Montgomery. Isabella was editor of *Grace*, a monthly glossy that tried to be like *Soirée* but was nothing more than a collection of uninspiring features and advertisements. Small, pin-thin and with shiny blonde hair blow-dried daily at Nicky Clarke's Mayfair salon, 43-year-old Isabella hid a vicious character behind her red-lipsticked smile.

'Cath-a-rine!' she had cried, when Catherine had entered the private dining room at the plush Wolseley hotel in Piccadilly. No one would have guessed that just twelve hours earlier Isabella had been naked save for a pair of thigh-length PVC boots, and riding her latest conquest to an early grave. He was a 71-year-old multi-millionaire German count, with the unfortunate combination of an over-ambitious libido and a pace-maker. Isabella liked money, power and sex – in that order.

'I was just discussing *Soirée*'s plummeting sales figures with Fiona! You poor thing, you must be having a *horrendous* time.'

Fiona MacKenzie, the Australian editor of *Teen Style* magazine, had rolled her eyes behind Isabella's back. Though no one would dare say it to her pinched little face, Isabella Montgomery was about as popular in the industry as Ozzy Osbourne at a vicar's tea party.

Isabella never passed up the chance to undermine Catherine; it was an open secret that she had got down to the last two for the *Soirée* editorship, and had been so sure of success she'd organized a congratulations party for herself. The day after Catherine got the job, a picture of a furious Isabella, sitting amongst dozens of open champagne bottles, at a party no one turned up to, was gleefully printed in several newspapers. The champagne sponsors had demanded compensation, and Isabella's employers at the time had given her the sack. It had taken two years of arse-licking and giving blow jobs to the right people before Isabella got offered the *Grace* editorship, but her reputation had been tarnished. Jealous of Catherine's success, Isabella somehow blamed her for all her misfortunes, and had had it in for her ever since.

Catherine had raised an elegant eyebrow at Isabella's latest jibe. 'They're hardly plummeting.'

Isabella had arched an over-plucked eyebrow back. 'But they *are* down, darling, aren't they? I read something about it in the Media *Guardian* last week.' A smug smile had flittered across her lips. 'Slippery slope and all that. You must be beside yourself with worry, especially with Sir Robin Hackford at the helm now.'

21

Sir Robin 'Hatchet' Hackford was the chairman on Valour's board of directors. A ruthless businessman, he had acquired an unrivalled reputation for driving profits up, usually by slashing budgets, cancelling expense accounts and laying off staff, regardless of their track record or length of service. His appointment at Valour six months earlier had set quite a few cats amongst the pigeons. Sir Robin presided over the board from the company's plush Bond Street office, but despite this Catherine, and the other editors at Valour, had yet to meet him. It was well known that the 62-year-old didn't mix with common employees, and preferred to let his own minions do his dirty work. Catherine thought he sounded like a complete arsehole.

'Of course, we're safe as houses at *Grace*, as we don't have to worry about circulation like you do,' Isabella had breathed. 'Our advertisers wouldn't like it if we got too big; one doesn't want to lose one's exclusivity. Clearly not something you've worried about . . . though I suppose now it could come back and bite you on the bottom! Oh dear.'

She'd looked around her to see who was listening. 'I hear Valour's board aren't happy at all with *Soirée*'s performance,' she'd added loudly. 'Have you spoken to them at all yet, darling?' She'd taken a sip of mint tea, ice-blue eyes looking innocently at Catherine above the bone china cup.

Luckily Fiona, sensing war was about to break out, had dived in and changed the subject. Ten minutes later, Catherine, not sure she could stop herself pouring the remains of her tea all over Isabella's head if she stayed, had made her excuses and left.

As much as Catherine hated to admit it, Isabella's words had touched a nerve. Over the past twelve months,

Soirée's sales figures *had* been declining. The only consolation for Catherine was that they weren't alone. The whole monthly market was suffering. Nowadays women were increasingly turning to the internet to get their news, fashion and gossip. Catherine had always wanted to work in glossies because they delivered that once-a-month, quality, luxurious treat. The anticipation was part of the pleasure. Now those times were gone, and the once-hallowed stamping ground was under siege. Especially as the price of *Soireé* had gone up – one of Sir Robin's first implementations. Catherine had protested to senior management at the time but it had fallen on deaf ears. It was an added pressure she didn't need, especially as magazine closures were becoming more frequent.

There was a tentative knock on her office door, rousing Catherine from her thoughts. Harriet's head popped round. 'Can I get you anything? Tea, coffee, sparkling mineral water?' she asked brightly.

Catherine flashed a brief smile. 'I'm fine, thanks, Harriet. But can you get on to that lunch booking at the Ivy? I'm taking the Fashion Council lot there next week.'

'Already booked!' answered Harriet, and discreetly disappeared back behind the door.

Alone again, Catherine leaned back in her chair and sighed. It hadn't been a great week so far. The day before she had found out that *Soirée* had lost another major advertising campaign, which would leave a big dent in their revenue. Was it an omen? Catherine shook her head. She was getting way too jittery, and Isabella hadn't helped.

Despite telling herself this, Catherine couldn't shake off her unease. It would have been nice to have had someone to talk to, and assure her everything was OK, but her own boss, *Soirée* publisher Adam Freshwater, was away on yet another holiday with his family. To add to her unease, when she'd bumped into the normally friendly chief executive, one of Valour's board of directors, in a restaurant last week, he'd barely been able to meet her eye before rushing off, mumbling something about his sea bass getting cold. A clammy knot materialized in the pit of Catherine's stomach. She was getting a very bad feeling about this indeed . . .

With her air of confidence and mantelpiece of 'Best Editor' awards, 35-year-old Catherine Connor was the archetypal successful career woman. Getting the *Soirée* editorship had been her defining moment, a mark of just how far she'd come. First published in 1865, *Soirée* was Britain's oldest and most prestigious glossy magazine. In the nineties it had floundered under a directionless editor, but that was before Catherine arrived and revived the title. Tough and demanding, she had nonetheless won her staff's respect and loyalty with her hard work, vision and dry sense of humour.

Along with the accolades, Catherine Connor looked the part. Tall and leggy, she had shoulder-length chestnut brown hair, cut by the top stylist at Charles Worthington. Her strong, chiselled face was saved from being too masculine by indigo-blue eyes framed by long eyelashes, and a full, cherry-red mouth. For all the labels gracing her wardrobe, Catherine favoured functionality over frippery, and wore minimal jewellery, light make-up and well-cut trouser suits. High heels were a different matter. Some women were born to glide across rooms in them – unfortunately Catherine wasn't one of them. A tomboy by nature, she still found it hard to walk in anything more than three inches, and often padded round the office in her stockinged feet.

A seemingly good 'catch', Catherine was not married, nor was she in any relationship. In fact, apart from an ill-judged fling – with an Italian financier who had erectile problems – two years ago, Catherine couldn't remember the last time she had been in anything meaningful. Had she ever been? Motherless, fatherless, and an only child, the truth was Catherine Connor was a loner, a driven perfectionist who lived for her job. At work she was reserved, holding herself at arm's length from her team. She was their boss, not their friend, and everyone who worked for her respected that, imagining that outside the office she led an exciting and glamorous life, full of 'mover and shaker' dinner parties and VIP invites.

Little did they know that, away from the work dinners in Michelin restaurants, most evenings Catherine was curled up on the sofa by herself with a plate of beans on toast and a bottle of Jacob's Creek Sauvignon Blanc. Even her apartment, a fabulously expensive penthouse south-London apartment overlooking the River Thames, set Catherine apart, sitting high above the London skyline, with its floor-to-ceiling views of Battersea Power Station.

Even though Catherine could come across as aloof, underneath she was funny and warm. Originally from Newcastle (her accent had been refined, along with her wardrobe), Catherine had lived in London for nearly twenty years. Despite this, she didn't have any close friends. Catherine always told herself that was just the way she liked it; she had learned early in life to survive on her own. Friendships meant sharing confidences, and Catherine's past hid a dark secret she was determined to keep hidden.

If it ever got out, it would be the end of her.

Chapter 3

In the pretty Cotswold village of Churchminster, another resident was preparing for a move to London. At Mill House on the edge of the village green, Caro Towey, wife of the gorgeous Benedict, was lugging the last of the luggage into the boot of her 4×4.

Caro's two-year-old son Milo, who had been dozing happily in his car seat, had just woken up and was demanding Pickles, his bedraggled teddy bear. She couldn't for the life of her remember where she'd packed it, and it didn't help that her suitcase, which she had been meaning to replace for ages, had finally given up the ghost as she'd heaved it over the front doorstep. Caro's control-panel knickers, and various other bits of underwear, had flown everywhere.

Caro had quickly shoved them into Waitrose carrier bags and was just depositing the last few in the car when her grandmother appeared.

'Darling!' For the warm summer day, Clementine had traded in her usual uniform of Hunter wellies and waxed jacket for a well-cut cotton blouse and tweed skirt. 'I know we've said goodbye already, but I just had to come and see you off.' Her stiff upper lip gave an uncharacteristic wobble. 'I'm being such a sentimental old fool, but I'm going to miss you all dreadfully!'

Caro hugged the upright, grey-haired woman fiercely. 'We'll miss you, too, Granny Clem. Don't worry, I'll come home lots, and you must come and visit us. London's not that far away. And now Benedict has set your hotmail account up, we can email every day!'

Clementine resolutely wiped a tear away. 'That's if I can get into the blasted thing. I keep forgetting the password.'

Caro smiled at her. 'It's "Errol Flynn", remember? We picked it so there was no chance of you forgetting it.' Errol Flynn was Clementine's irascible black Labrador, who spent most of his time making noxious smells and snuffling for imaginary rabbits in hedgerows. 'I've written it on the calendar in your study.'

Clementine surveyed her eldest granddaughter, one eyebrow arched in amusement. 'I've never seen you so organized!'

'I don't feel it,' Caro sighed. 'Benedict keeps saying how much I'm going to love being in London again, but I'm not so sure. I can't help feeling city life just isn't me any more.'

When the subject of relocating temporarily to Benedict's London house had come up three months earlier, Caro had not been enthusiastic. She had just got the house how she wanted, and Milo was happily settled in nursery. Caro and Benedict had married in a candlelit ceremony at St Bartholomew's church the previous Christmas, and she had been revelling in her newfound domestic bliss ever since. She loved being a full-time mum to Milo, walks in the Meadows with her grandmother, and cosy lunches at the Jolly Boot with her dear friend Angie Fox-Titt. Life was happy, fulfilling and uncomplicated. The thought of moving back to London, with its traffic jams, pollution and hectic pace – not to mention the remote chance of running into her bastard of an ex-husband, Sebastian – did not appeal to Caro one bit.

But she'd watched as Benedict had slowly got more exhausted. Five years ago, before they'd met, Benedict had started his own design agency, The Glass Ceiling, located off the salubrious Sloane Square in Chelsea. It had doubled in size since, and for the last six months Benedict had endured a hellish commute, putting brutally long hours in at the office and not returning to Churchminster until gone midnight some evenings, only to get up at 6 a.m. and do it all again. Benedict's beautiful blond looks, which made Caro's heart flutter whenever she laid eyes on him, were becoming washed-out, and violet-coloured shadows had settled under his eyes. Caro was increasingly worried about his health, and told him so in the kitchen one Saturday morning.

'Darling, it's not for ever,' he'd said wearily, wrapping his strong arms around her. 'Once this new partner is on board and we can recruit more staff, things will be a lot easier.'

'That won't be for another year or so, you've said that yourself,' Caro had replied. 'I'm worried you're going to keel over from a heart attack by then! Isn't there anything we can do? You can't go on like this.'

Benedict had gone silent for a moment. It was then that he'd put the idea to her of moving to his mews house in Chelsea. 'I've been thinking about it for a while, actually. It would just be while I get the business under control. There's a fantastic Montessori nursery down the road I'm sure we can get Milo into. The head-mistress is married to one of my clients.' He'd looked into her eyes. 'I know we're happy here, darling, but it would only be for a year at the most.'

Completely taken aback by the suggestion, Caro had been lost for words, but by then Benedict had been in full flow.

'We can spend some proper time together again as a family! And as husband and wife – I can't remember the last time I took you out for a romantic dinner. Isn't that what newly-weds are meant to do, after all?' He'd leaned down and kissed her at this point, and Caro had felt herself weaken as she'd breathed in the familiar woody aftershave. After a moment Benedict had pulled away gently. 'You can catch up with all your old friends. You keep saying you miss female company since your sisters went away.'

'I've got Angie,' Caro had interjected. 'Benedict, I really don't know about this . . .'

'You'll still have Angie. She and Fred can come and stay whenever they want. Besides, it's not even as though we're moving into a street full of strangers. Stephen and Klaus will be over the moon to have us as neighbours.' He'd smiled wryly. 'I'm sure Stephen would be delighted to babysit Milo now and again.'

They'd both laughed at this. Stephen was a flamboyant furniture-maker who lived in Montague Mews with his long-term partner Klaus. The couple's idea of a good evening involved a claret-imbibing dinner party with their colourful literary friends – and not watching *Bob the Builder* for the umpteenth time with a sticky-fingered, pyjama-clad Milo. The two men had a weekend cottage in Churchminster, and had been the ones to introduce Benedict to the village – where he'd met Caro – in the first place.

Caro's face had turned serious again. 'What about Granny Clem? With Camilla and Calypso not there, and Mummy and Daddy thousands of miles away, I'd feel like I was abandoning her.' Caro's two younger sisters were both abroad: Camilla was backpacking with her boyfriend; and the baby of the family, Calypso, had just landed an exciting new job in New York. Meanwhile their parents Johnnie and Tink had emigrated to Barbados several years earlier.

Benedict had brushed a stray eyelash off her cheek. 'Your grandmother is a tough old stick, she'll be fine.' He'd grinned. 'Besides, she was the one who suggested it in the first place.'

Caro had looked into her husband's handsome, tired face at this point and known she couldn't say no. Benedict had been so uncomplaining, and was working so hard to provide for their family. Despite his manic schedule, he still remembered to send her beautiful bouquets of flowers – and rang from the office every evening to say goodnight to Milo. *Stop being so bloody selfish*, she told herself. Most people would jump at the opportunity Benedict was offering. After all, twelve months living in a beautiful little mews in London wasn't exactly going to be a nightmare.

Was it?

Not long after she waved goodbye to Granny Clem, Caro's resolve severely weakened. As she'd driven out under radiant blue skies, Churchminster had never looked so lush and pretty. It was all very well Benedict saying she could catch up with her old friends, but most of them had moved out to various parts of the countryside too, for a better quality of life. The remaining few sounded so materialistic and self-absorbed whenever Caro spoke to them – 'Hugo isn't getting his usual bonus this year, God knows how the two of us are going to exist on five hundred thou!' – she wasn't sure if she wanted to see them at all. Where once she had felt excited about London and forging her own career, now Caro just felt daunted. Admittedly, it had helped a lot that Harriet had just moved there. Even though she was Camilla's best friend, Caro had been cheered by the thought of having a familiar face round the corner. But then again, thought Caro gloomily, Harriet was at work all day and probably out chatting up dashing men all night. She wasn't going to want to hang out at home with her and Milo.

Caro's trepidation was made worse by the fact that she didn't have much idea what the new house was like. Benedict had taken her to see Montague Mews late one evening after a night out at the theatre. The house was being rented out at the time to a rich American financier, so they had just pulled up at the gates at the end. Caro had been feeling rather giddy after too much wine at dinner, and now only had a vague recollection of peering out through the car window into a narrow, dimly lit, cobbled street. The idea of living in a little terraced mews was romantic, but Caro had heard some friends moan about how claustrophobic they were. Used to the wide-open spaces of Churchminster, she wasn't sure she would like being hemmed in.

The house was fully furnished, but Caro was taking a few things of their own to make it feel like home. The American financier had moved out two weeks ago, and Caro had wanted to spend a few days there cleaning, moving their stuff in and making it nice for Milo. Unfortunately, she had been laid up with a nasty virus, and spent most of that time in bed. Instead, a large van from Clayton's Removal Company had turned up to move the stuff down. Benedict had also got a team of domestic cleaners in, while Caro had lain in bed feeling redundant and helpless. Now Benedict, and her new house and life, was waiting for her expectantly.

Two hours later, she was stuck in her own private hell. She'd forgotten how dreadful London traffic was, and they were now sitting in a gridlocked line of cars, vans and motorbikes. Distracted by Milo shouting he'd done a poo in his shorts, she had missed the junction she wanted. When she finally got back on the Fulham Palace Road, which led to Chelsea, she'd been undercut, sworn at, and even had a 'Get out, gas guzzlers!' leaflet stuck under her windscreen wipers by an indignant group of campaigners at Hammersmith roundabout.

Caro's hands-free phone rang. She glanced at the screen. Benedict. Forcing herself to sound upbeat – he was always teasing her about her having no sense of direction – she answered the phone.

'Hi!' she said, her voice unnaturally high.

'Are you all right?' he asked. 'You sound strange.'

'I'm fine!' she replied brightly. 'We stopped a few times for Milo to go to the loo, but we shouldn't be long now.'

'Great. Look, darling, I'm afraid I'm held up at the office, and I might not be able to meet you at the house.' Caro's heart sank. 'I've just called Stephen and he's going to let you in. Just press on the buzzer.'

Out of the corner of her eye, she saw Milo was emptying the remainder of his orange carton into one of the Waitrose bags. 'Shit! I mean, fine. That's fine, darling. Don't worry about us.'

'You're lost, aren't you?' asked Benedict. 'You keep saying fine, which usually means everything isn't.'

'Of course not,' lied Caro.

Benedict paused. 'OK, well, give me a call if you need to. I've briefed the emergency services, and Central London is on red alert for your arrival.'

'Very funny,' said Caro, reaching around to grab the carton off Milo. 'See you later.'

By now it was four in the afternoon, but London was still melting under the unrelenting heat. Sweat trickled down Caro's back, making her linen shirt stick unpleasantly to the seat. She glanced at herself in the rear-view mirror. A red, shiny face with shoulder-length wavy blonde hair plastered to the forehead looked back. Caro's bladder wasn't feeling much better; she knew it had been a mistake having that mocha frappucino at the last service station. Behind her, Milo was looking similarly hot and bothered, with a large orange stain down his top. Caro's chocolate-brown eyes caught his big, blue ones in the rear-view mirror again.

'Not long now, cherub,' she told him as they pulled up at a set of traffic lights. 'Mummy will make you a cold drink, and you can play in your nice new bed-room.'

'Poo!' shouted Milo again. 'I need to go, Mummy!'

'Oh, Milo, you haven't done it again, have you?' said Caro, whipping round. She couldn't tell whether the unpleasant smells wafting from the back seat had got worse, but Milo's hands and face were sticky, and two lurid green trails of snot trailed out from his nose. Where were the Wet Wipes? Reaching across to the passenger seat, she scrabbled around in her handbag.

A horn honked loudly.

Startled, Caro looked up. The lights were just changing from red to amber, and in the dirty white van behind her, a red-faced stocky man was shaking his fist.

'They're not even green yet!' she wailed.

The white van screeched past her, the angry man giving her the V-sign.

Caro's temper finally snapped. 'Arsehole!' she yelled,

sticking her fingers up in return. The man's mouth opened in a silent tirade of abuse as he drove off.

'Arsoll, arsoll, arsoll!' chanted Milo merrily from the back seat.

Caro cringed shamefully. 'Don't say that, darling!' Christ, London driving. She'd only been back two minutes and already she was about to have a coronary. As they crawled along for a further forty minutes, Caro's stress levels rose even more. Car stereos blared from open windows into the thick humid air. An image of the Churchminster village green, postcard-perfect and emerald-fresh, flashed through her mind, and she forced it out again.

After a while, they left behind the grimy thoroughfare, and the surroundings started to take on a more genteel look. Grand houses and delicatessens appeared, along with swanky looking gastropubs with people sitting outside enjoying an after-work drink. Caro barely noticed. Milo had started crying again, and she'd almost run over a man when he walked out in front of her chatting on his mobile.

'*At the next junction, turn left,*' intoned the satnav. The bloody thing had already led her up two dead-end streets and into a private car park. Nonetheless, Caro put her fate in its hands and turned left off the main road. Immediately they were in a long wide road lined with cherry trees in blossom and impressive white houses. Guinevere Road, this sounded familiar . . . Caro crept slowly along, looking for the sign for Montague Mews. A taxi appeared behind her and beeped its horn impatiently.

'Get a move on, luv!' the driver shouted out of the window.

'I am trying,' Caro shouted back. Her raised voice made Milo cry even louder, at exactly the same time the red light on the dashboard started flashing to tell her the engine was overheating. Fighting to hold the tears back, Caro suddenly saw a discreet sign to her left. Montague Mews. She pulled in quickly, forgetting to indicate, and earning herself another outraged honk from the taxi-driver. She drove up to an ornate set of wrought-iron gates and pressed the intercom.

'Stephen? Are you there? It's Caro.'

Seconds passed and there was no reply. Caro felt her heart sink even more. 'I knew this was a terrible idea,' she whispered to herself in despair. 'What have we done?'

Then, as if by magic, the gates to the mews slowly swung open. And suddenly, all was right with the world again.

Chapter 4

Caro was in the prettiest street she had ever seen. A small mews, it had a terrace of five quaint brick houses and a cobbled courtyard in front. Each front door was painted in a vibrant pastel, the candy colours reminding Caro of the seafront at Brighton. The houses were two-storey, with large square windows on the bottom floor and smaller, rounded windows on top. Above each door hung a Dickensian-style street lamp. Caro had seen grander places in her time, but none that were quite as enchanting as Montague Mews.

Along one side of the courtyard was a high brick wall, festooned with passion flowers, clematis and morning glories. Purple, pink and blue flowers nestled between the shiny, clambering green like sparkling jewels. By rights it should have felt claustrophobic, but instead the wall was like a comforting embrace that kept out the rest of the world. A line of mature horse chestnut trees stood on the other side of the wall, their leafy branches dipping down into the courtyard.

Rainbow-bright window boxes and hanging baskets decorated the houses, while one of the middle ones, No. 2, had a huge 'Welcome' banner hanging across the open doorway.

To her delight, Benedict was standing outside. Beside him was Stephen with a bottle of champagne in his hands. Klaus was also there, and a small woman with punky red hair, the colour set off even more by the bright green smock she was wearing.

Caro turned off the engine and opened the car door. As she climbed out, there was a loud POP as the cork flew out of the bottle and sailed over the wall.

'I've never managed to do that before, how wonderful,' chuckled Stephen. 'Hello, my dear!'

Caro laughed. 'What a welcome!'

Benedict strode over and kissed her on the mouth. 'I made it home from the office after all.'

Caro felt like she was in paradise. Blossom lazily floated in the shards of sunlight being thrown down into the courtyard, while all around the air was thick with a heady mix of scents. An exotically coloured butterfly fluttered past before disappearing into the warm summer day.

'I wasn't expecting this,' she gasped. 'It's gorgeous!'

'We don't all live in cardboard boxes under railway arches, you know,' said the red-haired woman, but she was smiling.

Caro blushed. 'Oh, that really wasn't what I meant. I think I was expecting something a bit more, well, urban.'

'I'm Velda,' said the woman, stepping forward and shaking her hand. Up close she had piercing blue eyes and pixie-like features. Caro put her in her early fifties, and noticed a tiny stud glittering in her left nostril. It really suited her.

'It's so nice to meet you,' said Caro.

'I – I mean we – live next door to you. No. 3,' said Velda, cocking her head to the right. 'I also rent No. 5 as my studio.'

'You're an artist?' Caro asked.

'Ceramicist. Pottery is my bread-and-butter money, but my real love is sculpting.' She looked down at her hands, which under the various silver rings were covered in dried clay. 'I'm afraid you're going to have to get used to me walking around looking like I've just crawled out from a swamp,' she laughed. Caro grinned back. There was something kind and earthy – even strangely familiar – about this woman, that made her instantly likeable.

'Champagne time!' announced Stephen, after he had warmly kissed Caro on both cheeks. Klaus followed suit more formally.

'Velcome. Ve are very pleased to have you as neighbours.'

Caro had never seen Klaus smile in all the time he'd been in Churchminster, and he clearly wasn't about to start now. Tall, dark and sparing of words, above the beaky nose and high, Slavic cheekbones his dark eyes were warm and intelligent.

'Thanks, Klaus, it means a lot,' she told him.

'Mummy!'

'Golly, I'd forgotten about you!' Caro turned round but Benedict was already scooping the evil-smelling, orange-squash- and snot-covered Milo out of the car.

Stephen surveyed the little boy with a certain alarm.

'Why don't you, er, see to the little fellow and come over to ours for a celebration drink when you're settled?' he said.

Benedict watched him walk off, then turned to Caro.

'Ready?'

'As I'll ever be!'

Caro walked into her new home, and instantly fell in

love. The living room was light and spacious, with crisp white walls and a polished wooden mahogany floor. A huge open fireplace, with a stunning framed photo of Benedict's sister Amelia on the blackened beam mantelpiece, dominated the room. Caro could instantly imagine cosy winter nights in front of the fire with a large glass of Merlot. In between two comfortable-looking brown leather sofas was a rectangular glass coffee table. An enormous vase of oriental lilies, Caro's favourite flowers, stood in the middle of it.

'I absolutely love it!' she declared. 'And it's so much bigger than you'd expect.'

'I had a bit of work done, knocked through a few walls,' said Benedict. 'It's bloody hard to get planning permission for mews houses, but this place was about to fall down when I bought it. I guess the conservation officers approved of the changes. Let me show you the rest.'

Milo started to wriggle. Putting him down, Benedict led them through to the back of the house. On the wall next to the twisting staircase was a row of blackened iron hooks. Benedict pointed them out. 'That's where the stable boys hung the bridles when horses were kept here.'

A narrow corridor opened up to another room on the right. It was the dining room, housing a fashionably battered-looking wooden table that would easily sit eight. The room didn't have any windows, but a glass brick partition had been built between it and the living room, so light still filtered through.

At the back of the house was a gleaming white, square kitchen with dark brown walnut worktops, a light blue Smeg fridge and an Aga. The room was big enough to hold a small round breakfast table, which had a bowl of succulent fruit placed on it.

The kitchen door was an original stable door, still with the bolts and iron hinges. Benedict pushed it open to reveal a long, narrow decked area outside. Brightly coloured plant pots were grouped in one corner, while in the other was a small garden table and two chairs. Sturdy wooden fencing enclosed them on either side, and at the end was another high brick wall. The chimneys of a large building were visible the other side.

'Montague Mews was originally the stable block for the house over the wall,' Benedict explained. 'It was owned by a rich philanthropist, who turned it into a nursing home for injured soldiers coming back from the Crimean War. Now it's a private hospital. You can get a good view of it from our bedroom window.'

Milo's bedroom was at the front of the house, looking down into the courtyard. The little boy was heavily into anything with wheels at the moment, and it had been decorated with blue racing-car wallpaper, with a big mural of a red racing car zooming along a country lane on one wall. There was even a plastic red Ferrari bed, complete with steering wheel. A box containing the rest of his toys stood in another corner. Milo gave a squeak of delight and, after changing his shorts and cleaning him up, Caro plonked him down.

'Vroom vroom!'

Caro turned to Benedict. 'He's going to be in seventh heaven. What do you say, Milo?'

'Thank you Benny-dict!' came the muffled reply from somewhere under the Ferrari.

Caro noticed a fleck of red paint in Benedict's hair.

'How on earth did you find the time to do it?'

He grinned. 'Oh, I rather enjoyed myself.'

'Boys will be boys,' Caro teased him.

Leaving Milo playing, they went to look at the rest of

the house. Next door there was a small, cosy bedroom, a good-sized family bathroom decorated in crisp blues and whites, and at the back of the house, the master bedroom. It held a king-sized bed dressed with crisp white linen, along with two elegant off-white wardrobes and a beautiful antique dressing table. A fluffy white rug softened the dark wooden floor. A small window faced the back of the property. Caro walked up to get a proper look. The close proximity of the hospital took her completely by surprise. Just over the other side of the brick wall, Sister Beatrice Private Hospital was a huge, forbidding nineteenth-century building with black-framed windows and spiky turrets. Caro could see directly into the room opposite, which had orange curtains drawn across the windows.

Benedict followed her over. 'I think that's one of the consultancy rooms, I once had a rather unfortunate view of a patient who appeared to be having some kind of rectal examination.' He shuddered. 'The downside about mews living is that one is extremely overlooked. But hopefully the positives will make up for it.'

Caro turned round and flung her arms around his broad shoulders. 'I love it! You've gone to such an effort.'

'Thank you,' Benedict murmured in her ear. 'I know it's a big deal for you to do this.' They stayed there for a moment, their bodies pressed together. Benedict's hands travelled down to rest on Caro's bottom.

'I can't wait to see what you think of the bed.'

His hands moved inside the waistband of her shorts and knickers so they were resting on warm flesh. Strong fingers gently kneaded her buttocks, and his mouth found hers, tongue slipping inside. Caro responded back, a warmth growing between her legs that had nothing to do with the heat of the day.

'I'm all sweaty,' she tried to say. Benedict pulled her in closer.

'I don't care.'

Caro didn't put up a fight. As her soft contours melted into his strong, hard body she could feel his erection. She smiled blissfully. Benedict had the nicest cock she had ever seen.

'Mmm . . .'

A shout interrupted the moment.

'Mummy! Where are you?'

They pulled away and looked at each other. Caro smiled ruefully. 'Oh well, it was good while it lasted.'

Benedict's gaze didn't waver. 'We haven't even started yet. I've got plans for you in that bed later.'

Fifteen minutes later she, Velda and Stephen were in Stephen and Klaus's back garden, toasting each other with deliciously chilled glasses of Moët. He and Klaus had squeezed a wooden swing seat into the tiny area, which all three were sitting on. By now it was six in the evening and long shadows were creeping down the walls. The burnt orange light cast a glow over the exotic plants and stepping-stones that had been designed to look like a Japanese botanical garden.

Caro took a sip of champagne. 'It's so peaceful. I can hardly tell we're in the city.'

'These walls do keep out the noise,' agreed Stephen, stretching out an elegant ankle. Today he was dressed in immaculate white linen trousers and a lemon cotton shirt, an ever-present striped cravat knotted jauntily around his neck. In his mid-sixties, Stephen had the soft pink cheeks and bright-blue eyes of a fresh-faced schoolboy. He was pure old school, educated at Eton and Cambridge. That was followed by twenty-six years in the art trade before finding his true vocation designing bespoke, sought-after furniture. It was through this he had met Klaus, who was two decades his junior and the estranged son of a German aristocrat. Stephen was as effusive as Klaus was impassive, wore his heart on his sleeve as much as Klaus kept his emotions in check. For seventeen years the pair had been blissfully happy.

'Yes, I think mews living is going to agree with you,' continued Stephen, leaning forward to top up their glasses. Klaus and Benedict were in the study, where the former was showing Benedict photographs from his recent excursion to Rome, while Milo played happily with his racing cars on the floor of the kitchen.

'I suppose it suits a certain kind of person,' said Stephen. 'One does hear these horror stories about picking up the most unexpected sounds from next door on one's baby monitor and such.' His right eyebrow shot up as one of Milo's cars went round a bend loudly. 'I have to say, at Montague Mews we're rather lucky in that respect. We all just get on with our own thing and live in relative peace and quiet. Of course, it helps there are only five houses, but one doesn't ever feel like one is living in the middle of some ghastly soap opera.'

'There is a nice feeling about this place,' remarked Caro.

'A dear friend of mine lives in a mews just off Marylebone High Street,' said Stephen. 'She always says after coming home from a stressful day at the mercy of the London transport system, as soon as she walks through the door, it all melts away. Describes it as being "enveloped by a warm hug". An overly sentimental thought, maybe, but I do understand what she means.'

Caro mused. 'In a funny way, it reminds me of Churchminster.'

Stephen's eyes twinkled. 'I thought you might say that.'

Caro turned to Velda. 'How many are there of you next door?'

'Just myself and my niece, Saffron. She's twenty-four and isn't at home that much, to be honest. Saffron enjoys a rather full social life.' Velda smiled. 'Actually, we have a connection. Saffron is features writer at *Soirée*, where I believe a friend of yours has just started work.'

'Of course! Harriet!' Caro exclaimed. 'It really is a small world. We were all so chuffed for her when she got the job. *Soirée* did a fabulous piece on our village two years ago, when we put on a charity ball and auction.'

'I remember that, it made all the papers,' said Velda. 'Saffron enjoys working there, anyway. Gets to interview all sorts of celebrities, and writes about frightfully interesting people.' She looked wry. 'Unfortunately she does have rather a problem with getting up in the mornings, I think she's had her knuckles rapped for it recently.'

'She sounds a lot like my youngest sister, Calypso,' smiled Caro. 'Who lives in No. 1?'

On her way to Stephen's, she had noticed the first house in the mews actually looked rather plain and un-loved compared to the rest. No flower boxes adorned the windows, while the downstairs ones had large conspicuous locks and heavy-looking shutters drawn across them.

'Aah, that's the mysterious Rowena,' said Stephen. 'Montague Mews's famous enigma.' Velda smiled and nodded her head in agreement.

'She isn't very sociable?' asked Caro.

'More than that,' said Velda. 'I've lived in here for eight years, and in all that time I don't think she's left the house once. I've no idea what she looks like.'

'Really?' asked Caro. 'How extraordinary!'

'Indeed,' agreed Stephen. 'We think she works from

home, some computer whiz or other. A delivery driver with what Klaus said were several very high-tech laptops knocked on our door by accident once. When Klaus and I moved here, oh, it must be getting on for fifteen years ago now, we went round to introduce ourselves but no one answered. We thought the house was empty until we saw the lights on at night, and occasionally the shadow of someone moving around.'

'Gosh, it sounds like something out of an Agatha Christie novel.'

'We know that she's vegetarian, drinks bottles of Evian and has a weakness for McVities chocolate digestives. The Ocado van comes here once every ten days, and I often see the driver unloading the delivery,' said Stephen. 'He leaves a large box on the doorstep, and at some point Rowena must come out to get it. I've never seen her.' He chuckled. 'One rather expects a jeep full of khaki-clad tourists to turn up hoping to catch a rare sighting.'

'I did see an arm once when I was coming out of my house,' said Velda. 'Rowena obviously thought the coast was clear. I tried to say hello but the door was slammed quicker than you could say: "Ahoy there."'

'In most ways she's the perfect neighbour, really,' Stephen remarked. 'Quiet, unobtrusive, pays all her monitories for the mews on time through her solicitor. But one does feel for the poor woman. She's obviously a severe agoraphobic or something, and ekes out every waking moment next door in that self-imposed prison.'

'Maybe she likes it that way,' said Velda. 'You don't need to step outside the front door for anything nowadays, you can get it all online. Sometimes I long to shut myself away with just my clay and kiln and luxuriate in total solitude.'

'That may well be,' said Stephen thoughtfully. 'But I personally think a life without people and experiences and love must be a desperate existence. Don't you agree?'

An image of a Miss Havisham-type character, surrounded by deathly still, dilapidated rooms and dusty Victorian memorabilia flitted into Caro's mind. In spite of the evening warmth, she shivered.

An hour later it was time to put Milo to bed. Caro scooped him up from the kitchen floor, said a heartfelt 'thank you' to Stephen, Velda and Klaus, and left them opening another bottle of champagne and putting the world to rights. As soon as Benedict pushed open the door to No. 2, Caro could hear her mobile ringing. Putting Milo down, she rushed over to her bag at the bottom of the stairs to answer it. Fairoaks, the name of her grandmother's house, was flashing on the screen.

'Caro, it's me.' Clementine hadn't quite grasped the concept of caller ID yet.

'Hello, Granny Clem!' Caro sat down on the bottom step. 'I was just about to call you, actually.'

'Oh, hold on a minute, Errol Flynn has made a ghastly smell. Errol! Out, now! Hang on a minute.'

Caro could hear a door being opened. For a moment she pictured the large but homely kitchen at Fairoaks House, with its worn stone floors and slightly lopsided path leading out into the glorious garden. Her grandmother would be sitting down to have her nightly glass of Dom Perignon soon, Radio 4 on in the background. Caro felt a pang of homesickness.

The sound of footsteps and Clementine picked up the receiver again.

'Sorry about that, I really must take that dog to the vet; he's been emitting the most noxious vapours recently. Anyway, where were we? What is the mews like?'

'Oh, lovely. The house is perfect. We've just been a few doors down, at Stephen and Klaus's, having a welcome drink.'

'Good, good!' Clementine's voice was a little too bright. 'Well, I won't keep you, I just wanted to check you got there in one piece.' Fiercely independent, Clementine was never the type to insist on daily phone calls, but Caro could still detect a frisson of something in her grandmother's voice.

'How about I call you tomorrow for a proper catchup, once I've unpacked?'

'Whenever suits, you know I'll be here. Send my love to Benedict and Milo.'

Caro smiled. 'I will, I love you, Granny Clem.'

'I love you too, darling.'

While Caro gave Milo his evening bath, Benedict busied himself making dinner. It was eight thirty by the time she came downstairs. Delicious smells were wafting from the kitchen.

'I've just thrown together some salmon steaks in tarragon sauce, and some new potatoes,' said Benedict, carrying two plates through to the table outside. He'd lit two tall white candles, and a bottle of Sauvignon Blanc was chilling expectantly in a wine bucket. Caro's mouth watered; the tuna sandwich she'd had for lunch seemed like a lifetime ago.

'So, do you think you'll like it here?' Benedict asked after they had finished the meal and were enjoying the balmy night air in companionable silence.

'Oh, I hope so. Everyone's made me feel so welcome.'

'It's still not Churchminster, though.'

Caro smiled at her husband reassuringly. 'I think it's magical, I really do.'

Benedict's gaze penetrated through the darkening night. 'Haven't we got some unfinished business to attend to?'

Caro felt a lurch of anticipation. 'Why don't you clear the table while I have a shower? I'll clean up properly tomorrow.'

Upstairs, she undressed in the master bedroom's en suite, pausing to stare critically at her reflection in the mirror. All the Standington-Fulthrope women were blessed with good legs, and with her small waist, full breasts and womanly hips Caro had an enviable hourglass figure. Benedict was always telling her she had a beautiful body, but Caro, never blessed with much self-confidence in the first place, had endured eight years of put-downs and sneering remarks from her ex-husband, Sebastian. The damage was taking a long time to repair.

She had barely been in the shower for two minutes before the bathroom door opened and a naked Benedict walked in. As ever, Caro marvelled at the strong, sculpted body that looked like a classic Greek statue. He also had the most enormous erection, his long, wide cock standing to attention like a sergeant major. A sexy smile played on the edge of his lips.

'Thought you might need some help soaping those difficult-to-reach bits.'

He pulled the screen door open and stepped in, water cascading off his wide, muscular shoulders and back. Taking hold of the loofah, he started rubbing it over Caro's breasts, a mock-solemn look on his face.

'Is that better?'

'Stop it,' she smiled, but Benedict was pushing her against the tiled wall and kissing her. It was all Caro

48

could do to stop crying out, as his lips moved down her neck and then to her breasts, softly biting and licking her nipples. His erection was pushing hard against her, now, and Caro parted her legs as Benedict lifted her up and eased himself inside her. Memories of their first sexual encounter against the bedroom wall of Mill House flashed through her mind, heightening the moment. They rocked and ground together, kissing through the waterfall until their breathing began to quicken. Caro could feel the first blissful tickles of her orgasm starting in her toes, as it worked its way up through her body like some glorious unstoppable upsurge . . . Eventually they both came, gasping, their soaking bodies moulded together.

'We seem to have a thing about christening walls. Weren't we meant to be testing out the bed?' asked Caro, when she finally had her breath back.

'Thought we'd save that for tomorrow,' Benedict replied. She could feel his heart hammering against her chest. He held her even tighter.

'Have I told you lately how much I love you?'

Chapter 5

The next day Caro awoke to an empty bed and quiet
house. She glanced at her wristwatch, 7.45 a.m. On the
bedside table was a scribbled note from Benedict.

Early start. Have a good day, see you later. X

Stretching out in the soft bed, Caro felt surprisingly
rested. The thick white muslin curtains were slightly
ajar, and the early morning sun was streaming
through. It was going to be another scorcher. She
pulled the duvet back and swung her legs on to the
floor. Rummaging through one of the many Waitrose
bags piled up in the corner of the room, she found
a pair of clean knickers and a long T-shirt, threw
them on, and padded down the corridor to Milo's
bedroom.

She opened the door. Her son was still asleep, his
cherubic face smiling as if in the middle of a delightful
dream.

'Biscuits,' he murmured happily.

Tiptoeing across to the window, Caro opened the
curtains an inch and looked down into the mews. The
courtyard looked cool and serene, cobbles spread out

like an earthy patchwork carpet. Behind her, half-conscious of the light in the room, Milo was stirring.

'Morning, my darling,' said Caro, turning around. 'Did mummy's favourite boy sleep well?'

After giving Milo his breakfast, Caro had just sat down to a bowl of organic muesli made more interesting with a dollop of Benedict's full-fat Rachel's yogurt, when the doorbell rang.

Caro put her spoon down. Stephen perhaps? One watchful eye on Milo who was watching *CBeebies* in the living room, she went to the front door and opened it. At first, she thought a supermodel had wandered into the mews by accident. Standing on the doorstep was the most extraordinary girl, tall and slim with short tufts of white-blonde hair sticking out artfully all over her head. Her petrol-blue eyes were set off even more by her flawless, milky skin. She was dressed in a yellow vest and a dark blue ra-ra skirt, incongruously printed with dozens of Minnie Mouse faces. On her feet were bright yellow ballet shoes, while a mountain of silver bangles adorned each wrist. Somehow, it worked.

The girl smiled. She had a slight overbite, which somehow only added to her prettiness. As she stuck out her hand, the bangles jangled loudly.

'You must be Caro, I'm Saffron,' she said. 'Sorry I missed you last night, thought I'd come and say hello on my way to work. I'm late, of course.'

The smile widened, and Caro thought how like her sister Calypso Saffron was, with her quirky style and self-confident manner. Intrigued by the interruption, Milo had come over and was now looking up shyly at the pretty newcomer from between Caro's legs.

Saffron bent down and chucked Milo under the chin.

'Hello! You're a gorgeous little thing. What's your name?'

Milo, usually not the most forthcoming with strangers, was dazzled by this exotic-looking creature. A huge smile lit up his face.

'Mi-lo.'

Saffron took his chubby little hand and shook it earnestly. 'I'm very pleased to meet you. I'm Saffron.' Milo's smile became a beam.

'You've got yourself a fan, there,' observed Caro, smiling, too.

Saffron grinned. 'I love kids. Not that I'd be able to look after one, I have enough trouble looking after myself.'

Caro picked up Milo and he continued to stare at Saffron in wonder. 'I hear we've got someone in common: Harriet Fraser. You work together at *Soirée*?'

Saffron's smile broadened. 'Dearest H, she's the office saviour. We've become really good mates, actually. She only lives ten minutes round the corner.'

'I know, it's marvellous,' said Caro. 'You must all come over for dinner soon.'

A mobile went off, the techno trance tune shattering the tranquillity of the courtyard. Saffron dug around in her bag for it.

'Shit,' she said. 'It's work. I'm meant to be at this charity breakfast thing in Sloane Square. Gwyneth's making a speech.'

Caro was seriously impressed. 'Gwyneth Paltrow?'

Saffron nodded as she answered the call. 'Hello? I'm nearly there, Annabel. All right, keep your hair on!' She rolled her eyes at Caro, grinning, and took off across the courtyard, leaving a trail of perfume and glamour in her wake.

*   *   *

Caro's stomach was grumbling. She checked her watch; to her surprise it was nearly lunchtime. The morning had flown by; it was amazing how long it took unravelling your tights and putting them in an underwear drawer. After a rather uninspired look in the fridge, she decided to take Milo out instead. There were bound to be some nice little cafés in the area, and it was a good chance to check out the neighbourhood. As her son was going through an alarming stage of running off, Caro thought it would be safer to keep him in the pushchair. Strapping him in, she wheeled it out. Benedict had given her her own remote control key fob and as Caro pressed it the electronic gates slowly clanked open

Away from the coolness of the mews, the day was surprisingly hot. A gleaming line of BMW estates and Mercedes lined each side of Guinevere Road, like two presidential fleets. Caro paused to get her bearings. It *is* pretty round here, she reflected, admiring the regal porches flanked by stone pillars, and wrought iron railings. A thundering could be heard overhead, and as Caro looked up she could see blue sky streaked with the fading white lines of Heathrow-bound aeroplanes.

A few minutes later, the pair found themselves at a T-junction on to a main road. Red double-decker buses sat bumper to bumper with 4×4s and black taxis. Lean, Lycra-clad bike couriers wove dangerously fast in and out of the traffic, while a man in a pinstriped suit zoomed past on a trendy-looking silver Vespa.

'Taxi!' shouted a male voice.

The cab swung into the kerb next to Caro. She stepped back as someone dived past her. 'Sorry,' said the man, as he pulled open the door and jumped in.

'No problem,' Caro started to say, but the cab was

already pulling off as the lights turned green, leaving her standing in a cloud of exhaust fumes.

A few minutes later, they'd reached a row of shops. Mouth-watering smells floated out of an organic bakery where candy-coloured cakes were piled high, while next door was an upmarket wedding shop with a bejewelled corset magically suspended in the window, surrounded by the biggest vases of pink lilies Caro had ever seen.

Resisting the urge to go in the bakery and buy a box of muffins, Caro spotted a café up the road where people were sitting outside enjoying an alfresco lunch. Even better, there was a free table. Picking up speed on the pushchair, she hurried over.

Several minutes later a chic French waitress came to take their order. Feeling positively cosmopolitan, Caro decided to throw caution to the winds and ordered a glass of wine. Milo was entranced with his picture book about tigers, and he and his mother sat in companionable silence until their lunch arrived.

Afterwards, as spaghetti-full Milo dozed off in his chair, Caro took the opportunity to people-watch. Everyone looked very stylish, but they seemed in such a rush to get somewhere, she thought, as passers-by hurried past with their heads down or talking loudly into their mobile phones. An Amazonian woman, her caramel-blonde hair flying behind her, cycled past on an old-fashioned bicycle with a little boy strapped into a child's seat. Caro's heart jumped: she could have sworn it was Elle Macpherson! She was sure she'd read in *OK!* magazine the supermodel lived round here. Wait until she told her mother, a glossy magazine devotee, about her new star-studded neighbourhood.

Caro smiled as she imagined Tink's reaction, but her excitement was suddenly replaced by a stab of loneliness. How was she ever going to fit in with celebrities and supermodels? At that moment Milo burped contentedly, waking himself up. Caro took the opportunity to catch the waitress's eye and get the bill, and they began to make their way back to Montague Mews.

As she walked back into the courtyard, Caro saw a flash of movement from an upstairs window. The mysterious Rowena! She looked up expectantly, but the barred panes of glass stared blankly back. Caro noticed a security camera high on the house. It seemed to be trained right on her . . . Trying to shake off the uncomfortable thought that she was under surveillance, Caro unlocked her new front door.

Five minutes later, she was cajoling Milo out of his tomato-stained T-shirt when the phone rang.

'What ho, Mrs Towey!'

'Harriet!'

Caro felt ridiculously happy to hear the familiar voice.

'How are you all settling in? I must come round soon to see you all, your new place sounds fabulous.' There was the sound of drilling in the background.

'We'd love that!' said Caro. 'It's so nice you're practically round the corner.' The drilling got louder. 'Goodness, are you on a building site or something?'

'Just about! I'm down at the Natural History Museum doing a recce for the cocktail party. There're men in hard hats everywhere, I think they're adding on a new extension.'

Visions of a fashionably clad, all-in-black Harriet holding a clipboard and issuing orders flashed through Caro's mind. 'Sounds awfully glamorous, are you sure you want to come and hang out with us? You must get invited to exciting parties all the time!'

There was a slight hesitation. 'To be honest, they're not really my thing. I'd much rather come and see you and Milo.'

Caro felt a flash of happiness. 'Well in that case, you must be our first official guest!'

There was the sound of muffled voices in the background.

'Ooh, I'd better shoot,' said Harriet. 'I'll call you soon to make plans!'

Caro put the phone down, feeling London wasn't such an unfriendly place after all.

Chapter 6

Saffron was late for work. Again. She had stayed at Fernando's last night and he'd been in a particularly amorous mood. At 4 a.m., pleading exhaustion, Saffron had put a pillow between them and rolled over to try and get some sleep. It was all right for Fernando, he didn't have to get up in the morning. Apart from a bar job he didn't turn up to very often, her boyfriend spent the majority of his time sunbathing, lolling around watching *The Jeremy Kyle Show*, or honing his six-pack down the gym. Fernando had joined a small-time modelling agency, and claimed he wanted to get into acting school, but the biggest gig he'd got so far was showing off his torso for some dodgy sounding fat-reduction pills, the kind of advert found in the low-rent Sunday supplement magazines. Still, that hadn't crushed his dreams of becoming the next Al Pacino.

'The world isn't ready for Fernando Romero yet, but when I hit the big time – oh boy!' he'd say to Saffron with his usual air of drama. So far she had stopped herself from pointing out that Al Pacino hadn't hit the big time by lying under his duvet wanking all day.

Sometimes, when it was left to her to get the drinks

in again, or she phoned Fernando at lunchtime to discover he hadn't got out of bed yet, Saffron wondered what she was doing with such a waster. Then again, she knew exactly why: she loved pretty boys, and wasn't embarrassed to put sexy looks before scintillating conversation. At this stage in her life, that was all Saffron wanted. Plus the fact he could do things with his tongue she had scarcely thought possible. A memory of last night came back, and her eyes glazed over.

'Saffron? Have you got a minute?' Catherine's voice interrupted her lustful reverie. Saffron flushed guiltily, her boss didn't look very happy. She followed Catherine into her office and shut the door.

Catherine didn't mince her words. 'Saffron, is your alarm clock not working? This is the third time in the last week you've been late.'

Saffron looked contrite and chewed her bottom lip. 'Sorry, Catherine.'

Catherine eyed her over the desk. 'Sorry I won't do it again? Or sorry I seem to have a problem getting up in the morning?'

Saffron blushed, feeling rather stupid. 'It won't happen again, I promise.'

'See that it doesn't.' Catherine surveyed her features writer over the desk, not unkindly. 'Saffron, I believe you've got a lot of potential, but punctuality is important. I need to know I can trust you to get here on time. We're not in sixth form any more.'

Saffron met her eye. 'You can trust me, Catherine.'

'Good,' Catherine nodded in the direction of the door. 'Dismissed.' Lightening the moment, Saffron did a mock-salute, and left the office.

Catherine couldn't help but smile. She liked Saffron

and had high hopes for her, especially now the timekeeping issue had been addressed. Mind you, if she, Catherine, had to come in and work for the features editor Annabel Trowbridge every day, she'd have a problem getting out of bed in the mornings as well. Catherine groaned inwardly as, yet again, she cursed one of her rare errors of judgement in giving Annabel that job.

With her baggy V-neck M&S jumpers, frumpy skirts and long, lank hair, 37-year-old Annabel Trowbridge hadn't changed her wardrobe since her sixth-form days boarding at St Mary's School in Ascot. She had a pale, moon-shaped face, bulbous blue eyes, and a bottom so wide it could knock a coffee cup off a desk from twenty paces.

Despite her unfortunate appearance and even worse personality, Annabel Trowbridge thought she was the best thing since sliced bread. The features editor was singularly unpopular in the office, a fact to which she was oblivious. Barely a day went past without her extolling her own virtues, usually putting someone else down in the process. Saffron had soon got wise to her ways and given her short shrift, but Annabel had only directed her snide comments at someone else, which at the moment seemed to be poor Harriet.

Annabel had come with good credentials from a reputable paper, but Catherine had found out too late that her glowing track record was only due to the fact she had been sleeping with the deputy editor and was threatening to tell his wife. It had only taken a few weeks for Catherine to realize how work-shy her new recruit actually was. Two years on, she was still trying to work out how to get rid of Annabel.

A few minutes later, Catherine went over to the features desk.

'Any news on Savannah Sexton?'

Annabel hastily closed down her Facebook page and reached for her notepad, flashing Catherine an obsequious smile.

'Yah, still chasing them, but I'm very confident,' she gushed. 'I spoke to Savannah's manager this week and she says Savannah's schedule is *manic,* but as she's been so impressed by the way I've dealt with things, and as Savannah is a fan of *Soirée,* she's sure she'll do something with us for the release of *Power Trip.'*

Savannah Sexton was a young English actress who Hollywood had gone mad for. As well as being hugely talented, and about to appear in the most-hyped film of the last five years, Savannah was beautiful, chic and going out with Casey Fulbeck, star quarterback for the world famous Boston Tigers and the new face of Abercrombie & Fitch. Together they were a dream team. Magazines, newspapers, fashion houses, TV and radio stations alike wanted a piece of Savannah Sexton. Getting her on the front cover was just what *Soirée* needed.

Sitting on the other side of the desk, Saffron's cheeks were red with fury. She'd been the one who had put the calls into Savannah's management, and now that evil old bint was taking all the credit! 'Unbelievable,' she hissed under her breath. Annabel looked over and narrowed her eyes at Saffron.

Catherine didn't miss the exchange. 'Well, keep me posted,' she said, shooting a meaningful glance at Saffron. 'No ifs, no buts, I want Savannah Sexton.'

'Morning, my darling!' Catherine turned round to be confronted by the sight of her flamboyant fashion director, Alexander Napier, bounding across the office. In his mid-thirties, Alexander's OTT histrionics belied a marvellous fashion eye, utter dedication and steely organizational skills. He was the son of a feared High Court judge who was often trumpeted in the *Daily Mail* for his unforgiving approach to hooliganism, repeat offenders and under-age drinkers. Quite what Mr Napier Senior made of Alexander, who was today dressed in a Jean Paul Gaultier sailor's top and what appeared to be a padded lime-green G-string over his skin-tight satin trousers, no one knew.

'Nice outfit,' Catherine remarked. Alexander looked down.

'Oh, I'd forgotten I was still wearing them. Aren't they vile? They were sent in today, apparently the new 'wonder pants' for men. Can't say I notice any difference. Besides that colour is enough to put any potential shag interest off.'

Catherine raised an amused eyebrow. 'How did the shoot with Sienna Miller go?'

'Ms Miller was adorable! That woman would look fabulous in a bin bag,' he said, handing her a Polaroid. Catherine nodded in approval. 'These are great, Al,' she said. 'Did you manage to get her in all the outfits?'

'Of course, darling,' exclaimed Alexander. 'By the way, love your suit. Stella McCartney?' Catherine smiled.

She and Alexander were probably the only people on the planet who were allowed to get away with calling each other 'Al' and 'darling'. 'I've just been sent some delicious Christian Louboutins, your size,' he whispered conspiratorially.

'How high are they?' Catherine asked. Alexander looked down at her feet, in their stockings as usual, and sighed dramatically.

'I am going to get you walking in proper shoes if it kills me!'

As Catherine made her way back into her office her

phone started ringing. A gruff, London accent greeted her.

'Catherine?'

'Gail, how are you?'

'Sorry for the short notice, like, but I've had a few more calls from businesses interested in joining up to *Soirée* Sponsors. They're coming in next Wednesday, and would really like to meet you. Anyway you could come down to the office and give 'em the *Soirée* spiel?'

Catherine got her diary out. 'I can come in at eleven, just as long as you don't play your Daniel O'Donnell CD. My ears are still recovering from last time.'

The other woman gave a throaty chuckle. 'Bloody cheek, the man's a sex god!'

Catherine smiled as she put the phone down. In an industry full of egos and back-stabbing, it was so refreshing to work with Gail. Two years after she had become editor, Catherine had been invited on the off-chance to speak at a young persons' youth group in Peckham, south-east London. The area was extremely disadvantaged, but the local community groups were working hard to breathe in new life and opportunities for the teenagers growing up there. Something about their plight had struck a chord with Catherine, and she had agreed to do it.

The woman who called had turned out to be Gail Barker, a formidable but kind-hearted ex-social-worker who ran the youth group in her spare time. She'd confessed afterwards she'd never expected a big-shot editor like Catherine to take her up on the offer – and when a nervous Catherine had first walked into the centre, she'd expected a wall of hostility or bored indifference at the very best. Instead she was surprised at how intelligent, inquisitive and ambitious these young people were. It quickly became apparent they wanted to make something of their lives, and were frustrated at being marginalized in society, just because of the postcode they lived in.

After the talk, in which she had described her job, *Soirée* and working in the magazine industry, a pretty young girl with black hair cascading down her back had approached Catherine to say how much she had enjoyed the talk. Her name was Nikki, and when Catherine had admired a multi-coloured glass bead necklace Nikki had been wearing, she'd proudly revealed she'd made it herself. 'My dream is to study at the London College of Fashion and become a jewellery designer,' she'd told Catherine wistfully. 'But that's all it is, a dream. Mum's on her own and there's four of us at home. I could never afford to go somewhere like that.'

Afterwards, when she'd got back to the office, Catherine hadn't been able to stop thinking about Nikki. She'd had such talent, that for Catherine to see it all thrown away just because Nikki had had a shitty start in life would be a travesty. Catherine had felt she had to do something. She'd called Alexander, then deputy fashion editor, into her office, and explained what she wanted to do. He'd listened, nodded, and whipped through his neon-pink contacts book to give Catherine the names of several people who might have been willing to take Nikki on for work experience. On only the second one, Catherine had struck lucky. Within two weeks a delighted Nikki had been working part-time for a top Bond Street jewellers, who'd offered to pay her travel expenses and a small daily allowance. She might not have got her coveted place at college, but Nikki had finally been given her big break, especially when one of her designs had made it into the shop just a few months later.

Catherine had realized she was on to something. With the magazine's prestige and connections, they were sitting on a potential gold mine! So she had gone to Valour's board and presented the idea of *Soirée* Sponsors, a scheme that placed disadvantaged young people in south-east London in creative work-placements and traineeships with businesses across the country.

Despite her fear they might not approve, the board had been delighted.

'Just the sort of social cause *Soirée* is known for, advertisers will love it,' they'd told her.

A contract had quickly been drawn up, and Valour had agreed to contribute a substantial amount of money to set up an office to run the scheme. Even though she was to be the figurehead for *Soirée* Sponsors, Catherine had still had her own job to do. She'd needed someone organized, hard-working and determined, and had wasted no time approaching Gail.

In the first year of setting up *Soirée* Sponsors Catherine had wondered at times if she had taken too much on. As well as running the magazine and going to all the social functions she had to attend, Catherine had needed to spend hours ringing round trying to get people on board. Fashion designers, hairdressers, photographers, marketing firms, florists, travel companies, beauty PRs, catering firms, model agencies, health and fitness clubs . . . anyone who *Soirée* had ever featured or worked with had been approached to see if they could do something.

After twelve exhausting months, her efforts had started to pay off. As word spread, more industry people had wanted to come on board and give something back. Each week a growing number of young people had joined up to *Soirée* Sponsors, hopeful that for the first time they could make something of their lives. To cope with the increasing workload, Valour had put up the money to recruit a team, who now worked out of a small office in Brixton, south London. Now in its third year, the scheme was thriving. Only a few months ago, it had been named in an influential survey as one of the most up-and-coming charities for disadvantaged people. Now there was talk about taking *Soirée* Sponsors nationwide, an idea that excited and daunted Catherine in equal measure.

In the last six months, as Gail and the rest of the team had taken on more responsibility, Catherine had had the chance to take her foot off the gas. She had found it very hard to do, however, and as well as editing *Soirée* full-time, Catherine still attended lunches, dinners and other functions to raise awareness of the scheme. To Catherine's delight, Gail had rung her last week to proudly inform her that Nikki, now working at the Bond Street store on a properly salaried job, had just been shortlisted for a young designer of the year award. Although she was driven by her day job, Catherine felt more affinity with these tough, bright-spirited young people than with all the Hooray Henries and spoilt trust-fund kids she had encountered since working in glossy magazines. *Soirée* Sponsors had enriched her life far more than any six-figure salary or designer lifestyle ever could. Although she would never admit it to herself, it was the closest thing Catherine had ever had to a family.

Chapter 7

A few days later Saffron plonked herself down on Harriet's desk.

'Do you fancy a drink after work? I haven't got a press launch to go to for the first time in about a gazillion weeks.'

Harriet had told herself she was off the booze for a while. Her mother had come down last week and taken her out for lunch at Claridges, where she had been quick to point out Harriet was looking a little puffier in the face. It was true: after losing nearly two stone travelling Harriet had returned to her old bad habits and was piling it back on rather fast.

'Are you drinking too much wine again, darling? You know how it bloats you.'

Harriet put Frances's disapproving face out of her mind; a slimline gin and tonic wouldn't hurt.

'Oh, go on then, you've twisted my arm,' she said cheerfully.

Half an hour later they were ensconced at a cosy table for two in the George, a pub down the road. As usual it was full of office workers enjoying a drink after work before rushing off to Waterloo or Paddington to get the train home.

'Cheers! Here's to us!' said Saffron. They clinked glasses. 'To us!' Harriet smiled back at her. It was funny, on paper she and Saffron were polar opposites. Eight years older, Harriet was a home bird, while Saffron was out every night at parties. Harriet hadn't got a clue about fashion, relying mainly on Laura Ashley – or the Boden catalogue if she was feeling daring – while Saffron bought her clothes from designer boutiques and trendy vintage shops. Harriet had classics like *Emma* and *Wuthering Heights* on her bookshelves; Saffron's idea of reading was flicking through *POP* magazine and going on Twitter. Yet for some reason, the two gelled, and genuinely enjoyed each other's company. In a way, Saffron reminded Harriet of the younger sister she'd always wanted.

Saffron drank greedily from her glass. 'God, I needed that.'

'Bad day?'

Saffron sighed. 'Can you believe that stupid cow Annabel took all the credit for the progress I've made with Savannah Sexton?'

'Couldn't you say something?' ventured Harriet.

Saffron sighed again. 'She'll just twist it round and make out I'm moaning for no reason. Besides, as she is so bloody fond of reminding me, she's my line manager and anything she says, goes. Anyway, I don't want to waste a second longer talking about old Troutbridge.'

Instead she started telling Harriet about a media party she had been invited to at Downing Street, which soon led on to a highly entertaining story about the time she'd gone out to an all-night rave with the son of a disgraced Tory peer, and ended up trying to break into the Houses of Parliament.

'I've grown out of that sort of thing, now. At least I hope I have!'

Harriet giggled. 'Have you always lived in London?' she asked.

'I moved here about eight years ago to live with my aunt. Before that I lived all over the place.'

'Oh, right,' said Harriet. She didn't know whether to ask about Saffron's family; her parents could have been killed in an awful road accident or something.

She didn't have to. 'My dad's dead,' said Saffron. 'He died in a yachting accident when I was little. He was a really cool guy.'

'I'm really sorry to hear that,' Harriet told her. 'What about your mother?'

Saffron made a derisive noise. 'She might as well be dead. We never really got on: she was always too wrapped up in herself and her stupid life. It got really bad when I was a teenager, so Aunt Velda said I could go and live with her. I've been there ever since.' She finished her drink. 'Velda's been more of a mum to me than she ever was.'

'Have you stayed in contact?' Harriet asked carefully.

This was clearly a difficult subject for Saffron. Her eyes had become flat, and the spark had gone from her voice. She shrugged. 'She came to visit once, and it was such a disaster I told her never to come back again. She phoned a few times after that, but you could tell she was only doing it because she thought she had to.' She gave a sarcastic smile. 'The phone calls stopped, too. I guess I wasn't worth making the effort for.'

'I'm sure that's not true,' Harriet started to say, but Saffron cut her off.

'Honestly H, it's cool. I'm over it now. I haven't got a clue where she is or what she's doing, and I like it that way. Can we talk about something else? This is boring.

Tell me about where you live, instead. Christchurch or something, isn't it?'

'Churchminster. It's a little village in the Cotswolds,' said Harriet.

Saffron finished her drink. 'I've never been out that way.' She laughed. 'I'm not much of a country girl.'

'You might like it,' said Harriet. 'It really is a wonderful place. A lot more goes on in the country than you might think.'

Saffron smiled. 'Muddy wellies and ruddy-faced farmers? Not really my thing.'

Harriet noticed her empty glass. 'I'll get these,' she said and went off to the bar.

By the time she returned, Saffron had company. 'H!' she said. 'I've just bumped into some mates. Trey, Damien, this is Harriet Fraser. We work together at *Soirée*.'

The short, skinny man sitting in Harriet's seat glanced up. Even though he looked about forty, he was dressed like a teenager: in ridiculously baggy jeans with a chain hanging off them, and an oversized T-shirt over his skinny frame. His rat-like eyes cast themselves over Harriet, unimpressed.

'Delighted,' he said in a mockney accent, sounding anything but.

'Trey's a photographer, he's just done a major advertising campaign with Elizabeth Jagger,' said Saffron. 'And Damien works for a record label.'

A younger man in his mid-twenties, with a shaved eyebrow and a trilby hat, raised his hand unenthusiastically. 'Word.'

'I was just telling the guys about this new bar I've discovered in Hoxton,' said Saffron. Harriet had vaguely heard of the place, it was somewhere really trendy like east London. As the three of them sat there talking about bass lines and dry ice, it sounded as exotic and faraway to Harriet as Zanzibar. Seeing as Trey clearly wasn't going to give her seat back, she went off in search of a stool.

Twenty minutes later, Harriet had had enough. Despite Saffron's repeated attempts to draw her into the conversation, Trey and Damien had barely said two words to her. At last the two men got up to go and play on the fruit machine.

'What do you think of Trey? He's just finished with his girlfriend. I think you could be in there!' whispered Saffron loudly.

Harriet tried to be diplomatic. 'He's not really my type. And I definitely don't think I'm his.'

'Who cares about a type! You just need a shag. Trey told me he's looking for a bit of action.'

Harriet thought about her bikini line, which was looking more overgrown than Hampstead Heath after a year's worth of fertilizer.

'Well . . .'

'When did you last have a cock up you?' Saffron demanded.

Harriet looked sheepish. She had lost her virginity late in life to a braying idiot called Horse, and despite a few nights of sweating, sand-filled passion with a Canadian kayaking instructor in Thailand, there had been nothing – or no one – since. Suddenly, an alarming image of herself as an 80-year-old spinster being eaten alive by cats flashed through her mind.

'Do excuse me,' she said and fled to the bathroom. Inside, looking at her reflection, Harriet half-understood why Trey and Damien were being so sniffy. The purple pussy-bow chiffon shirt – which Saffron had persuaded her to buy from a trendy boutique one lunchtime – made her look more like a matronly schoolmistress.

She also had the beginnings of a cold, and her nose and eyes were starting to go a rather unattractive red. After powdering her face fruitlessly, Harriet gave up and went back to the others. The pub was packed by now, and she was just trying to edge past a group of rowdy men in suits when Trey's reedy voice came floating over.

'What you doing with a frump like her, Saffron? Thought you'd have more taste in mates.'

Damien wheezed with laughter, but Saffron sounded affronted. 'Don't be rude! H is cool. She's just not into high fashion or anything.'

Fighting an out-of-character urge to kick Trey in his puny shins, Harriet approached the table. She looked at Saffron.

'Would you mind awfully if I pushed off?'

Saffron looked disappointed. 'Are you sure?'

'I've got an early start in the morning,' Harriet said apologetically. She did have a mountain of things to get through in the office.

Saffron jumped up. 'I'll walk you out.' After a luke-warm farewell, they left Trey and Damien and made their way to the door.

'Trey's a bit of a knob isn't he?' said Saffron. 'I might as well stay for another drink, though, good for contacts and all that.' A black cab drove up and Harriet flagged it down. *I'll get the tube home tomorrow*, she thought guiltily, as she jumped in and waved goodbye to Saffron.

'Fulham, please,' she told the driver. As the car pulled off in the direction of her cosy garden flat with its M&S risotto for one in the fridge, Harriet yawned and felt relief wash over her.

'I'm not cool and I don't care,' she said. The driver turned his head round.

'What's that, luv?' he said.

'Sorry, just thinking aloud.'

Harriet sank back into the seat. She should have been upset by Trey's comments, but oddly, they had just made her more determined. Mr Right was out there somewhere. Hit by a sudden flash of inspiration, Harriet knew exactly how to find him.

Chapter 8

'Why didn't you return my call last night?' Fernando's tone was petulant. Saffron pulled a face. He was turning out rather more possessive than she liked.

'I didn't get in until 1 a.m. and I was so tired I wasn't in the mood to talk. Anyway, I thought you'd be asleep.'

Saffron could hear the huffy silence. 'I didn't mean it like that,' she said. 'Come on, babe, don't give me a hard time.'

Fernando sighed dramatically.

'I've got two tickets for the launch of this really cool bar tonight,' she said. 'There'll be loads of celebrities and modelling agency people there.'

A short silence, Saffron looked at the ceiling, counting the seconds. She knew what the answer would be.

'OK, sexy, you're forgiven,' he said happily, his umbrage forgotten already. 'What time and where?'

Saffron smiled, a mixture of triumph and exasperation. Sometimes, it was like dealing with a difficult toddler.

When Saffron had met the gorgeous Fernando in an underground club in east London, she'd only been single three days. Her last fling, with a professional skateboarder, had ended after he'd gone to live in

California. Saffron hadn't been that bothered, anyway, especially when she'd laid eyes on Fernando's heavenly physique on the dance floor.

When Fernando had found out what she did for a living, he had been just as impressed. He loved going to events with her. Saffron, who had been doing the job long enough to be blasé about it, thought it was funny how much of a groupie Fernando turned into whenever 'a face' entered the room.

Tonight they were going to the launch night of the Ice Palace, a champagne and vodka bar in Belgravia. It was a three-storey converted church, and the decor alone was reported to have cost two million pounds.

It was a Mediterranean-like summer's evening, and London was making the most of it. By the time Saffron had made her way past all the throngs of people drinking outside various pubs, Fernando was there waiting. He had spent the last few weeks either in the gym or sunbathing on his flat roof, and tonight was wearing a tight V-neck T-shirt that showed off his bronzed, rippling credentials. He was attracting looks of studied indifference from all the Chelsea socialites, and, as Saffron walked up to him, was busy smiling at a pair of blonde girls barely covered by indecently short dresses.

'Hey, baby!' he exclaimed in his heavy accent. 'I didn't see you!'

'Clearly,' said Saffron drily. A goofy smile broke out over Fernando's face.

'Are you jealous? Aah, you do love me!'

'Get off,' said Saffron as he pulled her hand up to his mouth and kissed it. 'Let's go in. I'm dying for a drink.'

Inside, the Ice Palace lived up to its promise. The walls were an exotic gold, and huge art deco chandeliers hung down from the ceilings. A waiter came up with a tray of inviting cocktails. Saffron took two and handed one to Fernando.

'Thanks, baby.' His dark eyes stared at her chest lasciviously. 'Your nipples are hard.'

Saffron looked down at her vest top. Fernando was one of the most highly sexed men she had met. She hoped he wasn't going to get all hot and heavy and embarrass her again; she'd only just recovered from him turning up to meet her in one of the most exclusive bars in town and announcing, in a stage whisper loud enough for everyone else to hear, that he'd spent a blissful day on the sofa sniffing a pair of her knickers. She swore he'd done it on purpose: Fernando always loved to be the centre of attention.

An hour later, Saffron had air-kissed her way round half of London when she found Fernando sulking in a corner.

'Where have you been?' he complained. 'You said you'd introduce me to Liz Hurley.' Fernando loved the upper-crust model, he even had an old picture of her in the infamous 'safety pin' dress at the *Four Weddings and a Funeral* premiere stuck on his kitchen wall.

Saffron rolled her eyes. 'I don't think she's here. Besides, I don't even know her.'

Fernando took a moody gulp of his drink. 'I've been standing here by myself for ages.'

'I'm here now,' Saffron looked at her boyfriend. Despite being high maintenance, he really did look fit tonight. She leaned in and kissed him. Fernando's lips were soft and tasted of fruit and mint chewing gum. Saffron felt her stomach do that familiar flip.

'Mmm, that's better,' he breathed when they finally pulled apart.

Maybe it was the warm evening, or the alcohol

pleasantly flowing through Saffron's veins, but she suddenly felt extremely horny.

'Fancy a fuck?'

Fernando grinned. 'Does a bear shit in the goods?'

Fernando's command of colloquial English was sketchy at best. 'I think you mean "woods",' said Saffron, as she led him through the crowds. She'd seen an empty cloakroom on the second floor, earlier, it would be perfect.

Minutes later she was riding him frantically on a pile of pashminas that had been thrown into the room. Saffron's red miniskirt was up round her waist, one leg still in her tiny G-string. Fernando's naked nut-brown torso, muscles rippling under a minuscule layer of fat, arched upwards so he could grind himself further into her.

'Yeah, yeah,' he moaned. 'Give it to me!'

'Keep your voice down,' Saffron whispered. If there were an Olympics for the loudest vocals in bed, Fernando would win gold.

Her inner thighs were slippery with sweat as she moved back and forth. Below Fernando's eyes were shut as he immersed himself in the rhythmic bliss.

'Aaah, AAAH,' he moaned. Behind them, the door suddenly opened. Saffron threw herself on top of Fernando. They both lay still, hardly daring to breathe.

'You hear something?' said a voice. Saffron's heart was beating so loudly she was sure it would give them away.

'Nah,' said another voice. 'Chuck 'em in there, then, we've got no room downstairs.'

Several more cashmere pashminas landed on top of them, and the door shut.

Typically, Fernando wasn't put off his stride for long.

He ran his hands lightly down over her breasts, and caressed her Brazilian with his thumb, before moving round to hold her small smooth buttocks.

'Now *cariño*, where were we?'

Saffron grinned. 'Let me show you.'

Chapter 9

The bell tinkled as the door to Angie's Antiques swung open. It was a quaint, low-roofed building sitting on the Churchminster village green, a stone's throw from the renowned Jolly Boot pub.

Freddie Fox-Titt stepped into the little shop. After the bright sun outside, his eyes took a few seconds to adjust to the gloom. He was a short, portly man with a kind face always ready to break into a smile.

'Are you in there?' he called out to his wife. No answer. Freddie frowned and, walking over to the counter, put down the bunch of wild flowers he'd hand-picked on the way over. Freddie and Angie Fox-Titt lived in the Maltings, a handsome estate a few minutes' walk from the village green.

'Darling?' Tentatively Freddie stepped round a watercolour of a hunting scene on the floor and opened the door to the tiny back room that doubled as an office. A short, curvaceous woman with waves of shoulder-length brown hair sat on a stool, hands wrapped around a steaming mug of tea. She turned in surprise as the door opened, fixing Freddie with a pair of big brown eyes. Freddie's heart did a little jump: after twenty-five years of marriage he still fancied the pants off her.

'Freds!' she exclaimed. 'I was miles away, I didn't hear the door.'

Freddie retrieved the bunch of flowers and gave them to her. 'Just popped in to see if I could take my gorgeous wife out for lunch.'

Angie broke into a smile and leaned up to kiss him. 'Darling, you really are the most romantic man I've ever met.' She sniffed the bouquet. 'These are beautiful.' Her face dropped.

'I could do with some cheering up.'

'Is everything all right?' asked Freddie in concern.

Angie sighed. 'I'm fine really, I'm being silly. I just really miss Archie, the house has been so dreadfully quiet since he left.'

Archie Fox-Titt was Angie and Freddie's only child. Angie had suffered three miscarriages before finally falling pregnant with him, and had nearly died in childbirth. Much to their grief, they found out afterwards she was unable to have any more children. The pair doted on 19-year-old Archie, a good-natured boy who was away up North at agricultural college studying farm management.

She sniffed dolefully. 'I never thought I'd miss his smelly socks and the trails of mess he left all over the house, but I find myself pining after him like a lovesick Labrador. It feels strange only cooking for us and not having to go shopping every two days to replenish the fridge. I don't like not having someone to look after; it's what mothers are meant to do!'

Freddie put his arms round his wife and squeezed her reassuringly. 'I miss Arch, too, darling. But we're going to see him in a few weeks, and then before you know it, he'll be home for Christmas.'

Angie looked cheered. 'You're right.' She tried to

look brave. 'I just miss having a young person around the house.'

Freddie smiled. 'Would a glass of champers make you feel better?'

Angie laughed for the first time. 'I suppose it would go some way.'

Freddie looked pleased: he hated seeing his wife so sad. 'That's decided, then. I thought we'd pop next door to try out Pierre's latest offering. And then, if you fancy, we can go for a long walk afterwards. It's such a beautiful day.'

Business was quiet, and Angie had been putting off doing her tax returns all morning. She couldn't think of a nicer diversion.

Chapter 10

Caro was starting to find her feet in London. Milo was settled in nursery, and she really loved their quirky little cottage. Churchminster would always be *home* home, but there was something special about living in Montague Mews. Even when the sky was overcast or it was raining, the place radiated quaintness and tranquillity. Caro had had her reservations about living so close to other people, but Stephen had been right. You could happily live your own life, but there was always someone to talk to or share an early evening drink with. One night Velda had had them all round for a North African banquet in her Moroccan-inspired purple-and-gold dining room. The food had been delicious, the company even better.

At home, Caro and Benedict had fallen into a contented domestic routine. He still worked long hours, but made sure he was home two nights a week to tuck Milo up in bed. Afterwards, he and Caro would curl up on the sofa and watch television, or chat over a late supper.

On a few occasions they had ventured into central London to the theatre. After the last play they'd seen, Caro and Benedict had joined the throng and walked to Soho, stumbling across an energetic Vietnamese restaurant where the staff spoke no English, and the chef came and cooked from a flaming wok next to their table. The place had been packed, and Caro had enjoyed watching the kaleidoscope of life pouring in as they tucked into their fresh, steaming plates of food. Outside she had persuaded a reluctant Benedict to get a rickshaw – 'This is so cheesy, if anyone I know sees me . . .' – but they'd ended up helpless with laughter, hanging on for dear life as the driver hurtled through the narrow, bustling streets, scattering pedestrians like dominos.

They'd had a rather embarrassing moment a few nights ago, in a dinky little bistro a five-minute cab ride away. They had just sat down when a large shadow fell over them. Caro had looked up to see Minty Scott-Brocket, who Caro had lived next door to in her halls of residence at university. Caro hadn't seen Minty for years, but with her unruly thatch of straw-blonde hair, wide shoulders and sporty wardrobe, Minty hadn't changed a jot.

'Caro! I thought it was you,' she boomed. 'Bloody hell, it must be ten years. Young Farmers' ball in Cirencester, wasn't it?'

Minty's eyes settled on Benedict. His chiselled jaw was freshly shaved, and he was wearing a light blue shirt that set off his eyes perfectly. Her eyes goggled like a randy bullfrog's.

'Hel-lo! I know who you must be!'

'Minty . . .' Caro tried to say. An awful feeling was growing in the pit of her stomach, as her old school chum charged on, oblivious.

'Been working abroad for a while, but I still get all the gossip on the grapevine. Heard Caro had landed herself a catch, but golly!'

Minty goggled at Benedict again, and stuck out a large, man-sized hand.

'Sebastian, isn't it?'

There was a silence. Caro wished for the ground to open and swallow her up.

To her relief, Benedict gave Minty an easy smile and took her hand.

'Benedict, actually. I'm Caro's second husband.'

Instead of going bright red, Minty laughed raucously.

'Uh-oh, old Mints has put her size tens in it once again! To be honest, I'd heard Sebastian was a bit of a wanker, anyway.'

She looked at Caro.

'What was that I heard about shoe lifts? Anyway, Benedict, I'm sure you're much nicer. No offence meant.'

Benedict's lips twitched. 'None taken.'

Minty looked down at Caro, still cringing in her seat. 'Well, bloody great to see you! Must get back, got a fifteen-ounce steak waiting. Ciao!'

Benedict sat down. 'I'm so sorry . . .' Caro started to say again, but he waved his hand dismissively. 'Don't be. I think it's quite funny.'

'Are you just saying that?' she asked anxiously. He gazed at her over the table. 'Of course not, what would you like to drink?'

As Benedict studied the menu, Caro watched him. When Benedict had moved into Churchminster, she had still been very unhappily married to Sebastian. The rivalry between the two men had been instant and intense, even turning physical on one occasion. Caro and Sebastian had thrashed out a maintenance settlement for Milo, but Caro now had very little contact with her ex-husband. She knew he still lived in London, but

83

where – and whether he was in the same banking job – she had no idea. Despite her efforts, Sebastian had showed little interest in seeing his son. Luckily, as Milo had only been one when Sebastian had left, he'd never really asked for him. Besides, Milo had Benedict now. Caro knew he would never try to replace Sebastian as Milo's father, but he loved the little boy as if he were his own flesh and blood.

Caro cast her mind back again. Throughout the divorce proceedings Benedict had been a tower of strength. When Sebastian had cancelled seeing Milo yet again at the last moment, Benedict had absorbed the news silently, and had taken Milo out for the day himself. He never referred to Sebastian, as though he'd washed her ex-husband out of their new existence. In most ways, it was just what Caro needed, and she was eternally grateful for Benedict's undiminished support. But she had to admit, as she studied her beautiful blond husband across the table, that there were depths to him that still lay hidden. Was it just that he thought Sebastian beneath contempt, a waste of time and space, or was there something more to his feelings?

Benedict looked up. For a second, Caro couldn't read his expression. She smiled. 'You look miles away. What are you thinking?'

'Oh nothing, just about my own university days.'

Caro looked eager. 'I'd love to hear some stories. You've never really talked about that time.'

'That's because there's nothing to tell,' said Benedict. He snapped his menu shut decisively and put it down on the table between them.

'Shall we?'

Chapter 11

On the Saturday morning Caro and Benedict took Milo to one of his nursery friend's birthday parties. It was being held at a private children's members club in Belgravia – 'Good Lord,' Benedict said when he heard the extortionate fees. 'Is Milo expected to drive us there in his own Porsche?' Benedict had been cornered by a skinny blonde dripping in jewels as soon as they'd walked in and Caro got stuck talking to a balding banker with halitosis on his third divorce, as hyperactive children called Artemis and Willow ran round throwing organic frozen yogurt over each other's designer outfits.

'Milo's goody bag alone must be worth £100,' said Benedict, peering into it when they finally got home. 'What on earth happened to fairy cakes and kiss chase in the garden? I'm sure I never got a miniature gardening set and Moschino T-shirt when I was three.'

'I'm sure Milo won't mind you borrowing them,' quipped Caro. 'Would you mind keeping him entertained while I check my emails? Mummy says Camilla's sent us all one about her travels and I'm dying to hear what she's been up to.'

But to her surprise, her grandmother's name was at

the top of the inbox. Despite repeated instructions on how to use hotmail, her grandmother had up till then resisted.

'Quite frankly, I don't see the point. I can just pick up the phone and ring you in half the time it takes to lag on to that thing.'

'I think you mean log, Granny Clem,' Caro had told her.

But there it was, Clementine Standington-Fulthrope. Caro smiled. The name looked incongruous sitting there, next to a spam mail for penis enlargement. She clicked on it and opened the email. It was blank.

'Oh!' said Caro. Maybe Clementine hadn't got to grips with it after all. Scanning down the other list of names, she saw another email from Camilla and one from her mother. No reply to the one she had sent her youngest sister last week, but staying in touch wasn't one of Calypso's strongest points. A few lines further down was her grandmother's name again. This time she struck lucky.

To: Caro Towey
From: Clementine Standington-Fulthrope
Subject: Hello!

Darling, are you there? This really is the most ridiculous contraption, I tried to send you one earlier, but then the blasted screen went all funny and I lost all the words. I saw Jack Turner in the shop earlier; he was kind enough to pop over before he opened the Jolly Boot to show me how to use it. So here we are. I must admit, I'm rather at a loss for words. What is one supposed to write? Does no one write letters any more? Oh, I must tell you what Brenda told me when she came over to clean this morning. You'll

never guess who got so drunk at the church barbecue
they had to be carried home in Ted Briggs's wheel
barrow . . .

Some time later Caro had worked her way through all her emails, including one from Benedict's twenty-eight-year-old sister, Amelia, who was working in Moscow and having the time of her life.

Drinking more vodka than is good for me, but at least
it's keeping the cold out. That's my excuse, anyway
– even if it is summer! The men aren't bad either . . .
out on another date tonight with a twenty-six-year-
old billionaire. He's going to show me his palace,
apparently; I'll keep you posted! Love to you all,
A xxx

Caro smiled, and wondered if she should let Benedict read it. He was notoriously protective of his younger sister. She looked at her watch: time to pick up Milo. As she went for a wee in the downstairs loo, she realized her T-shirt had jam smeared across the front from Milo's breakfast. *That would never do*, she thought, running upstairs to change. *I already look like a country bumpkin next to all the yummy mummies at the nursery gates*. They'd have a field day if she turned up looking like Waynetta Slob.

As she got a clean shirt out of the wardrobe, some-thing caught her eye. Caro peered out of the window. The blinds were open in the hospital room opposite, and she could see that Benedict had been right: it was some kind of consulting area. In one corner stood a hospital bed with a curtain rail round it. A man in a dark suit sat behind a desk in front of the window.

A sturdy woman in a dark-blue tunic entered the

room. She shut the door. Her mouth moved silently as she spoke to the man. Caro was about to turn away when, to her absolute astonishment, the nurse stood in front of the desk and began to unbutton her tunic.

Caro stood frozen to the spot as the woman peeled off her clothes to reveal huge, pendulous boobs squashed into a black PVC bra, and matching knickers. She lifted one meaty finger and beckoned to the man. Caro could clearly make out bottle-top glasses, bushy eyebrows and a large hairy mole on her left cheek. The man obediently stood up and went round the desk. He looked at least a foot shorter than the woman, and as skinny as a schoolboy. He stood there limply as she undressed him.

As if in slow motion, Caro watched the woman push him on the bed and climb on top. It was like a hippopotamus mounting a field mouse. Her huge white thighs almost covering his entire body, she started furiously rocking back and forth.

'Oh my God!' Caro came to her senses and yanked the curtains shut. She stood there, not quite believing what she'd just witnessed.

The bedside phone rang, and Caro went to answer it. 'Hello?'

'Darling, is that you? You sound a bit odd.' It was her mother.

Caro sat down on the bed and began to giggle. 'Yes, I'm fine. Oh, my goodness!'

'What are you laughing at?'

'Mummy, you really don't want to know! All I can say is, I've just seen the game "doctors and nurses" taken to a whole new level.'

On Monday evening Harriet decided to go for her first ever run. She'd gone out that lunchtime to Lillywhites, the huge sports shop at Piccadilly Circus, and on the advice of the gum-chewing shop girl, invested in new trainers, an extremely short pair of cycling shorts, and a 'Shock Absorber' sports bra. It certainly did give one a shock, Harriet thought, as she struggled to get it over her head. She could hardly breathe! At least it was all so tightly packed there was no chance of unwanted movement. She gave herself a quick once-over in the mirror and, rather alarmed by the amount of flesh on display, set off.

It had been an overcast day, and the sky was drab shades of black and grey as Harriet headed for the large park several streets down from her flat. After a few uncertain stretches on the path, she set off one way at a leisurely pace. The park was quite busy, as fellow-runners pounded past her and people wandered home from work. Harriet made her way past an ornamental lake with ducks floating lazily on the surface, thrusting their heads under the water intermittently. Things seemed to be going OK so far! Encouraged, Harriet glanced at her watch. She had been running for three minutes and twenty-seven seconds.

Two gorgeous young women approached from the other direction, each in tiny outfits showing off their Paris Hilton-like physiques. Deep in conversation, they glided past like two graceful gazelles on the Serengeti.

After five minutes, Harriet started to struggle. By ten minutes it felt like her lungs were on fire, her legs two dead weights underneath. As she rounded a corner, she could see a group of well-built young men standing around on the grass. One of them was holding a rugby ball. A few turned to stare as Harriet approached. She adopted a determined expression; what was that she'd read in *Zest* magazine about pumping your arms to run faster?

'Check out Paula Radcliffe!' one cheered.

'Did you know your arse is hanging out?' shouted another. The group hooted with laughter.

Flustered, Harriet put on a final sprint to the fading sounds of catcalls. Rounding the corner, she came to a shuddering halt and gingerly felt her behind. To her utter mortification, her shorts had ridden up and her right buttock was hanging out. Face bright red, and not just from the physical exertion, she fled home. From now on, she was wearing tracksuit bottoms.

An hour later, Harriet was sitting in front of the television with a large, straw-gold glass of Chardonnay. Now her face had returned to its normal colour and the bum-flashing episode was fading by the minute, she was feeling rather good about herself. Must be all those endorphins; Harriet vowed to go running twice a week from now on. There was something else she had been meaning to do as well. Reaching over to the coffee table, she turned on her laptop.

A homepage flashed up, dozens of photos of jolly broad-shouldered men cuddling their Labradors, or red-nosed and roaring with laughter with pints of mulled wine and ski slopes in the background. 'Want to meet your Mr Right?' asked the slogan. 'Join Chapline! South-west London's premier online dating agency for like-minded ladies and gents.' Harriet looked into the hunky, carefree, fun-filled faces again. She noticed one man had exactly the same endearing eyes as his Labrador. Taking another courage-giving glug of wine, Harriet clicked on to the application form.

Chapter 12

For the next few weeks, Harriet was too busy to think about love. There was so much to organize for *Soirée*'s autumn cocktail party. Started in 1964 by then editor Penelope Wainright, it was held on the Wednesday of the third week in October. Over the years, the party had become something of an institution on the London social calendar. As well as attracting all the industry movers and shakers – actors and actresses, playwrights, celebrities, politicians, and even the odd royal had graced the illustrious guest list. The venues had always been show-stopping and Catherine had been impressed when Harriet, on only her third day, had managed to book the main hall at the world-famous Natural History Museum.

Even though it was still over two months away, Harriet was dealing daily with caterers, sponsors, drinks companies, florists, sending invites out, meeting with Health and Safety . . . The list was endless, and every day it seemed to get longer. Harriet didn't mind, though, she wanted it to be perfect. Several times Catherine had come back from works drinks around 9 p.m. and still found Harriet poring over her computer. Catherine always made her go home, but not before filling her own bag with work. It was obviously a case of 'do as I say, not as I do' thought Harriet, as she gathered up her belongings one evening. Judging by the tired lines under her eyes, Catherine could do with a few nights off as well. Not that Harriet would dream of telling her that.

Adam Freshwater had returned from his indulgently long summer holiday, and sauntered into Catherine's office one afternoon as she was up to her eyeballs reading pages for the next issue.

'You look a bit peaky,' he remarked, settling down in the chair opposite hers. He cast a smug glance down at his own suntanned arm.

'Thanks,' she said sardonically. 'Nice break?'

'Yah, really great,' he replied. 'Thomasina and I took the little ones to an organic windmill in Umbria, entirely self-sufficient you know. We ate off the garden for the whole three weeks!'

Catherine's eyes glazed over as Adam droned on about the benefits of solar panels, and how to collect rainwater. He was married to a fanatical herbalist who ruled the roost at home and also thought she should be managing her husband's career. Only last month, Adam had tried to make Catherine run an article on how drinking your own wee increased fertility. Unsurprisingly she had put her foot down.

She finally got a word in edgeways. 'I take it you've heard about us losing the Gucci campaign, then?'

Adam frowned. 'Not good, is it? We need the revenue more than ever at the moment. The board won't be pleased, especially as *Tatler* trounced us again last month.'

Catherine exhaled crossly. 'Tell the board to come down here and try running a magazine they won't invest any money in. We've barely had any advertising in the last year, while our rivals have had TV adverts running every bloody five minutes. If Robin Hackford wants a quality product, he has to put the time and money into it.'

'*Sir* Robin Hackford,' corrected Adam sanctimoniously.

Catherine sighed. 'Whatever.'

There was a pause. 'The last two covers haven't been that strong, either,' Adam pointed out.

Catherine pushed her chair back, wearily running her hands through her hair. 'Point taken,' she conceded. 'In our defence, it's been a crap year for cover stars. No one seems to want to do anything any more, or they want to do the big American magazines instead. But we are working on that, I assure you. We've hopefully got Savannah Sexton for our Christmas issue.'

Adam raised an eyebrow. 'Bloody hell, she never says yes to anything. That would be a coup.' He echoed Catherine's own words to her features team. 'Make sure it happens, then. Boy, do we need Savannah Sexton.'

Later that evening Catherine stood in front of the floor-to-ceiling windows in her living room. It had been yet another thunderous evening and the heavy, dank atmosphere seemed to pervade the penthouse apartment, carpeting the normal airiness. The forbidding shape of Battersea Power Station loomed in the distance. Long derelict, the immense redbrick building still had a commanding presence, the four huge white chimneys striking defiantly into the London skyline. Catherine had always found a strange comfort in their sheer vastness and strength.

Tonight, however, something had changed. The building had become an obstruction, the bricks and mortar morphing into something more symbolic. Catherine couldn't see a way through it, just as she was running out of ideas to make *Soirée* the best on the market again. She really had to talk to Adam about the new cover price, as well as a new advertising campaign. Sighing heavily, Catherine turned away from the glass and made her way to the kitchen. It was a long gallery, sleek glossy white worktops set off by a huge black Smeg fridge. Catherine looked around. It was immaculately clean to the point of unused. It struck her, not for the first time, that there were no photographs of loved ones or holiday snaps adorning the fridge, nor delicious smells of a home-cooked dinner hanging in the air. Suddenly, the self-contained oasis Catherine had worked so hard to create felt horribly lonely.

Maybe I should get a cat, she thought, before giving a cynical snort. She couldn't even look after a house-plant.

Half-heartedly she unpacked the bag of groceries she'd picked up from Tesco Metro on the way home. She'd fancied the fresh pasta and pre-bagged garden salad at the time, but now her appetite was waning. All she wanted was one of the chilled bottles of wine nestling in the cooler. Pulling it out, she emptied half of it into her oversized glass. She was relying on wine more and more to take the edge off the day, but Catherine told herself she deserved it. If she were completely honest with herself, alcohol helped to block out the past as much as the present – not that Catherine would admit that in a million years. Taking a resolute swig she wandered back into the living room to unpack her briefcase and get back to work.

AUGUST

Chapter 13

Ashley King shut the door to the flat. It stuck as he pulled it, yet another thing that now needed repairing. It had been unseasonably grey and drizzly for a few days now, the dampness pervading the dimly lit corridor. Pulling his hood up, Ash walked down and through the open door into the stairwell. It smelt of disinfectant, with undertones of lager from the empty cans littered in the corner of the landing. A few flights below, the outside door clanged and the sound of footsteps started up towards him. Ash hoped it wasn't Mr Gregory from next door, he'd already had a go at Ash that week for playing his music too loudly, although in Ash's defence the walls were so thin they might as well not have been there.

But instead of Mr Gregory's flat cap and angry red face, a tall, leggy young woman dressed in a smart black suit and high heels appeared before him. Her hair was swept back off her face, showing off her almond-shaped eyes and perfectly applied red lipstick. In the dank surroundings of Acorn Court, Peckham, Ash thought she looked like some kind of goddess who'd been beamed down from heaven.

For a second they stood there, before the girl's face broke into a wide grin. 'Ash!' she exclaimed. 'Long time no see, how's it going?'

The young man paused on the step, his face creased into puzzlement. Then his eyebrows shot up in surprise.

'Nikki!' he said. 'I didn't recognize you.' Ash blushed, making his spots stand out like little red studs. 'You look really, well, good.'

Nikki smoothed back her hair. 'You saying I was a minger before?' she asked in mock offence. Take away the angry red acne that criss-crossed his cheeks and forehead, and Nikki Jenson and her mum had always said Ashley King could be a dead ringer for Justin Timberlake.

Ash seemed to have some sort of obstruction in his throat. Nikki was suddenly so sophisticated and confident. He made an embarrassed gargling noise. 'No, that's not what I meant . . .' he started.

Nikki laughed. 'Chill your boots, I'm teasing.' Two years older than Ash, she'd always treated the boy she'd grown up next to as another younger brother. And he'd always been easy to wind up.

'You back seeing your mum, then?' asked Ash, recovering slightly.

'Yeah,' Nikki looked at her watch pointedly. 'I'm running late as usual, gotta be back at work soon.'

Despite the hint, Ash seemed to want to talk. 'You still working up west?'

Nikki smiled. 'Yup. I was made permanent a month ago, got myself a nice little pad in Shepherd's Bush.' She laughed. 'It's the size of a postage stamp, but it's my postage stamp. I love it.'

Ash shot her an ironic look. 'Don't miss this place, then?'

Nikki pulled a face. 'Aside from Mum and my sisters? Can't say I do, surprisingly.'

Ash looked down at his trainers. 'Don't blame you,' he muttered.

It had only been Ash and his dad next door for as long as Nikki could remember. Ash's mum had run off to Spain with a builder years ago, and his older sister Beverley had moved out soon after.

'How are things at home?' Nikki asked.

He shrugged. 'Same as, old man's still a full-on piss head.'

Nikki smiled sympathetically. 'You still going round all those antique markets? Remember when we went to one together, and I bought that china pig? You said it was a load of crap, and you were right. I dropped it a few days later, and inside it said it was from Woolies.' She started laughing. 'I was gutted, I thought I'd discovered the Holy bloody Grail!'

Ash's solemn face broke into a smile. 'Yeah, I remember. That was a good day. Not that I've been doing the markets as much these days; I'm doing temp work now.'

Nikki studied him. 'You shouldn't give up on it, Ash, I reckon you've got a real eye for all that stuff.'

He shrugged again. 'How am I going to get into something like that? All the lads round here think I'm weird enough as it is.'

Nikki looked thoughtful. 'I may be able to help, let me have a think.' She glanced at her watch again.

Ash stepped aside. 'You better go and see your ma.'

Nikki started up the stairs before looking back. 'I mean it, Ash, I will see if I can do anything.'

He flashed her a brief, tight smile. 'Thanks, Niks, but don't waste your time. I gave up on all that stuff a long time ago.' Then he opened the door and vanished into the rainy day.

Chapter 14

It was the Friday before the bank holiday and the weather had finally turned for the better. Britain was in the middle of a heat wave. Every day the *Sun* and *Daily Mirror* were full of bikini-clad babes, splashing around in the sea up and down the country from Blackpool to Brighton. London had grown languid under the intense heat. The parks were packed with office workers lingering over an alfresco sandwich, before returning to work with pink noses and shoulders. Content-looking people ambled along the hot pavements, or sat outside cafés enjoying a chilled beer or glass of rosé. No one seemed in a rush to get anywhere, and, for once, the city slowed down to enjoy a slower pace of life.

In the *Soirée* office, the last issue had just been put to bed. The staff were winding down, in preparation for a few precious extra days away from the office. Harriet was telling Saffron her plans for the weekend when Annabel bustled over.

'Saffron, I want you to go and pick up a preview tape of this new TV show Joely Richardson is in. I'm interviewing her on Tuesday, so I need to watch it over the weekend.'

'Where from?' asked Saffron.

Annabel looked belligerent. 'Flame TV.'

Saffron pulled a face. 'It's going to take me hours to get there. Why can't you get it biked over?'

'Because someone needs to go and meet them in person, and I'm too busy!' she said grandly.

'Busy eating your body weight in biscuits,' Saffron said in an undertone to Harriet.

'Excuse me, what was that?' demanded Annabel.

'Nothing, dear,' said Saffron sardonically. Annabel turned to walk off, and went slap bang into the new designer. 28-year-old Tom Fellows looked more like a train-spotter than a designer on one of the most famous magazines in Britain. Tall and clumsy, he had bottle-top glasses, bushy black hair, and long gangly limbs he always seemed to be falling over.

'Watch it, you great clodhopper!' she cried. Tom went bright red.

'Sorry,' he mumbled.

'He didn't do it on purpose!' Saffron exclaimed as Tom shuffled off, eyes on the floor.

'People should watch where they're going,' huffed Annabel. She eyed Harriet sniffily.

'Where are you going this weekend, anyway?'

'Norfolk, actually, to see an old school friend,' Harriet told her. 'I'm rather looking forward to it, we're going on lots of nice walks and—'

'Well, I'm going to Great Winnington Hall. You must have heard of it, yah? My friend Felix's sister Bella's best friend is married to the sixth Earl of Haverly, who lives there. He's got some events company in to put on the most a-may-zing murder mystery dinner party. I'm going as a French maid.'

The art director, a laid-back Paul Weller lookalike, strolled over at that moment. On overhearing Annabel's revelation, his eyebrows shot into his artfully tousled hairline.

'You know, it's very hard to get an invite to Winnington,' Annabel said grandly. 'Only the movers and shakers get a look-in. Everyone I know is green with envy.'

'Sounds lovely,' said Harriet dutifully. Behind her, Saffron rolled her eyes. 'A-may-zing!' she mouthed.

Harriet tried not to giggle. Just then Catherine came out of her office.

'What's this, a mothers' meeting?' She smiled.

Harriet flushed. 'Er, just discussing our bank holiday plans. Are you up to anything?' she added politely.

As usual, Catherine had no plans. 'Just seeing a few friends, keeping it low-key,' she lied. The thought of rambling round her huge penthouse all weekend suddenly made her feel very lonely.

'Does anyone fancy a drink after work?' she blurted out. 'On me, of course.'

Everyone looked shocked, and then a bit embarrassed. Catherine instantly regretted it.

'I've got plans with the missus,' said the art director apologetically, while everyone else muttered their excuses about getting away before the Friday-night rush.

'No problem,' replied Catherine brightly. 'Just thought I'd mention it.' She turned and went back into her office, cringing to herself. No one fraternized with the boss, especially on a bank holiday weekend. They had probably seen right through her for the sad case she really was.

Chapter 15

The next morning, Caro and Benedict had planned to leave Montague Mews at 11 a.m. for Churchminster. Clementine had organized a drinks party in the garden at Fairoaks.

'We may as well make the most of the weather, darling, my gloriosas are looking splendid.'

Caro threw the last bag in and pulled the boot shut. The mews was unusually quiet today: Benedict had had to go into work unexpectedly for a few hours, and was due back soon. Stephen and Klaus were staying at a friend's castle in Tuscany and Velda had gone to an art fair in Pembrokeshire. Only Rowena's house was the same, still and silent behind the brick facade.

Caro's mobile rang.

'It's me.'

'Is everything OK?'

Her husband sounded preoccupied. 'Not really. We've had a major cock-up with some designs due in next week, and the client's not happy. We're really up against it. I'm really sorry, but I'm going to have to stay up to make sure we meet the deadline.'

Caro's heart sank. 'Oh, Granny Clem was so looking

forward to seeing you. And you really do need a few days off. I was looking forward to spoiling you.'

'I know, me too. Unfortunately, there's nothing I can do about it. I'm sorry, darling, really I am.'

Despite her disappointment, Caro understood he had no option. 'Of course. Look, I'll ring you when I get back. Love you.'

'Love you, too, beautiful.'

It was half past two when Caro finally pulled off the junction on the M4 for Churchminster. Not normally good on long car journeys, Milo had been happily playing with Rory the racing car in his back seat.

'You know where we're going, darling, don't you?' Caro said, smiling at him in the rear-view mirror. She knew how he must be feeling. Since they'd broken free of the hellish jams out of London, excitement had been mounting inside her. They were going home!

Half an hour later, Caro felt like she was entering a different world. The twisty country lanes unfurled in front of them, lined by tall, flourishing hedgerows and the familiar honey-coloured stone walls. Every now and again they would break to reveal vast, Van-Gogh-yellow fields of oil-seed rape, and endless, brilliant-blue skies. Caro opened the sunroof, and warmth flooded in. She looked around her, savouring the view. Every field was so ripe, every plant and tree so lush. The countryside had never looked more alive or beautiful. She felt her spirits soaring.

A signpost appeared on the horizon.

Bedlington 1 mile. Churchminster 3 miles.

Caro turned left at the crossroads. Compared to the smooth tarmac of London, the roads felt more precarious than ever. A large pothole suddenly appeared on the road in front of them and Caro had to swerve right to avoid her tyres being mangled.

As she approached the town of Bedlington, the roads evened out. It was the farmers' market day and the place was bustling. She slowed down as she drove past the large square filled with stalls, where people milled around trying everything from locally reared partridges to shiny, fat green olives. Caro passed the tiny police station on her left and followed the Bedlington Road out of town. Before long, she'd reached the outskirts of Churchminster and her heart gladdened.

In front, the twisting spire of St Bartholomew's church rose up from the horizon like a welcome beacon. As Caro shifted down into third gear to negotiate the winding road, a house appeared on her left. Incongruous as always in the postcard-perfect surroundings, Byron Heights was a nineteenth-century Gothic extravaganza, complete with turrets and jutting towers. The owner, pop sensation Devon Cornwall, was away at the moment on a world tour, much to the disappointment of Clementine's housekeeper, Brenda Briggs, who still hadn't got over the fact that her idol had moved into the village.

Twisty Gables, the gorgeous rambling house Caro had grown up in, appeared a little further on. Mauve-blue flowers caressed the outside walls, almost covering several of the windows. Four ponies were grazing in the fields flanking the house, and Caro noticed the current owners, Lucinda and Nico Reinard, had built an outdoor riding school. She had heard through Clementine that Lucinda had just been made the new district commissioner of the Bedlington Valley Pony Club.

Opposite two gateposts signalled the entrance to the

Maltings. Caro grinned as she passed. Angie! Although they had phoned each other regularly since Caro went to London, she'd missed their lively, fun-filled catch-ups. Her spirits rose even higher when she pulled up at the village green. Across the shimmering mirage of grass, looking more inviting than ever, was Mill House.

Caro couldn't wait to get home, but knew she'd better see her grandmother first. News travelled fast in Churchminster, and Brenda, who lived in one of the cottages on the Bedlington Road, had probably seen her drive past and been straight on the phone to Clementine.

Her grandmother's house was on the opposite side of the green to Mill House, down a little lane fringed by bramble bushes. Brenda was clearly on razor-sharp form today. As Caro drove up the driveway to the large, imposing house, the front door was already opening. A rather portly black Labrador shot out, followed by Clementine in a floppy canvas sun hat.

'Darling!' she said. 'I've just got off the phone to Brenda. How was your journey? Oh, Errol Flynn, do stop barking!'

In the back seat Milo was wriggling. 'Sweeties!' he shouted happily.

Clementine's mouth twitched. 'I see city life hasn't diminished Milo's appetite.'

Opening the car door, Caro got out and threw her arms round her grandmother. 'Oh, Granny Clem, I can't tell you how good it is to be home!'

At six o'clock the village was still bathed in the warmth of the day. Armed with a G and T, Caro was walking with Milo through Clementine's extensive gardens, pointing out all the different flowers. Milo, however, was more interested in finding worms, and so far three were curled in the palm of his hand like forlorn strands of spaghetti.

'Snakies!' he shouted, trying to tip them in Caro's glass.

Caro tried to look disapproving and failed. 'You little bugger!'

Milo ran off, his hand held aloft with the wriggling pink bodies. Caro watched her son in fond exasperation; he was going through an awfully naughty stage at the moment.

'No, darling! Don't put that thing in your mouth! Oh Christ.'

'Having trouble?' a familiar voice chuckled. Caro turned round to see Angie Fox-Titt. She looked fantastically healthy, new sun-kissed streaks running through her hair.

'I can't believe you've got that colour from sitting in the garden!' Caro exclaimed. 'You look fantastic!'

Angie inspected a tanned arm. 'I look grossly fat. Freds has just been on a trip to France with the boys, and he brought back mountains of cheese and wine. I seem to have single-handedly worked my way through most of it. I could barely do up my shorts this morning!'

Caro laughed. 'Don't be so silly.'

'No Benedict?'

'He's having to work this weekend, some drama with one of his clients.'

Angie smiled sympathetically. 'We'll just have to keep you amused ourselves. Freddie is dying to see you.'

On cue, Freddie came bouncing towards them, waving a bottle.

'Caro! Your grandmother said I'd find you out

here. Thought you might be in need of some refreshment.'

A few minutes later, the garden gate swung open and a rather mismatched couple walked in. He was tall, dark and languid-looking, a spotted neckerchief tied casually round his neck, and a crumpled linen shirt undone one button too low. She was blonde, broad-shouldered, and looked just like she'd stepped straight off the pages of *Horse and Hound*, with a horseshoe-patterned neck scarf and matching white shirt with the collar turned up.

'Oh look, it's the Reinards,' said Angie, adding in a mischievous undertone, 'Lucinda's looking *very* district commissioner!'

'*Bonsoir*,' murmured Nico, kissing them all on both cheeks, including a rather taken-aback Freddie. Lucinda sent her husband off to get a corkscrew from the kitchen, then moved straight in on Caro.

'Have you thought about getting Milo a pony when you move back?' She flashed a gap-toothed smile and Caro thought fleetingly how horse-like her teeth were.

Lucinda continued. 'You can always take out one of ours this weekend. Pippin is just standing in the paddock doing bugger all. He'd love the exercise.'

Caro scrabbled around for an excuse. 'I don't think we'll have time, Lucinda, but thank you anyway. Besides, Milo is more into racing cars than anything with four legs at the moment.'

'Well, don't leave it too long!' she trilled. 'Bedlington Valley PC is in dire need of some more youngsters. I'm counting on you!'

Caro was saved by Brenda Briggs, who had appeared brandishing a tray of what looked like little burnt CDs. 'Miss Caro?' she asked. 'Broccoli and Stilton mini-quiche? Made 'em myself this morning.'

Caro looked down at the shrivelled offerings and picked up the least blackened one. If Brenda's house-keeping skills were bad, her cooking was even worse.

'They look lovely, Brenda.' She winced as her teeth encountered rock-hard pastry.

''Ere, did you hear about Babs Sax getting trollied at the church barbie?' Brenda asked. Babs Sax was Churchminster's rather flighty resident artist. 'Drunk as a skunk she was, couldn't even walk in a straight line to her house. Lucky my Ted nipped home and got his wheelbarrow . . .'

A few hours later, Caro was helping her grandmother clear up the last of the glasses in the living room. Milo was fast asleep face down on the sofa, the ever-faithful Pickles squashed underneath him.

'Poor little chap, it's way past his bedtime,' said Caro.

Outside the night air was mild. An owl hooted overhead as Caro carried a sleeping Milo to her car. Clementine followed with her granddaughter's over-sized bag.

'What are your plans tomorrow?' she asked.

'Nothing huge, I was going to meet Angie for lunch at the Jolly Boot. She says Pierre's created his best menu yet.'

'Would you like me to look after Milo?'

'Ooh, that would be great, Granny Clem! Only if you're sure . . .' said Caro.

Clementine smiled. 'Of course! You know I love spending time with my great-grandson.'

'Just keep him away from any worms,' warned Caro, laughing. She wound the window down and started the car. 'See you tomorrow.'

It was a clear starry night and the village green

stood bathed in luminous light. Caro drove past her sister Camilla's cottage with its darkened windows. It felt funny being back in Churchminster without her. By contrast, several doors down the Jolly Boot pub was ablaze with lights, as locals made the most of landlord Jack Turner's lax attitude to calling time.

Following the road round to the left, Caro pulled up outside the impressive three-storey building that had once been the Old Mill. It had been converted into two houses, one of which belonged to Caro, Milo and now Benedict. The other, which Benedict had previously lived in and still owned, was about to go on the market.

Caro cut the engine and looked up at her house. The climbing plants and creepers stretching attractively across the front reminded her for an instant of Montague Mews. She turned around to her son, who was still flat out in the back seat.

'Come on, cherub, let's get you inside.'

Chapter 16

Caro woke up with a start. Where was she? It took a while to adjust, as her eyes took in the low beams, cream walls and rose-patterned curtains. A flush of happiness surged through her: she was home! Sleepily her hands moved over the empty side of the bed before she remembered with a stab of disappointment Benedict wasn't with her. She hoped he'd got some sleep; he'd sounded shattered when they'd spoken late last night.

Swinging her legs out of bed, Caro went to the windows and flung back the curtains. It was another beautiful day. Below, the green was spread out before her like a sparking emerald sea. Caro leaned out of the open window to breathe in the morning air. The scent of freshly cut grass wafted up enticingly. It was not a day to be indoors. Heart light, she pulled on a dressing gown and went to get Milo ready for his day with Granny Clem.

A dusty-looking Angie looked up from behind the counter as Caro pushed open the door of Angie's Antiques.

'Just having a clear-out, won't be a minute!'

'Do you want some help?' asked Caro, putting her bag on the floor beside the counter.

'You are an angel, but I wouldn't inflict this on my worst enemy! I've been here since 8 a.m., and so far I've found three mouldy Tracker bars, a peregrine falcon minus his perch, and a pass to No. 1 court at Wimbledon from 1987. I think I've just about earned myself a break.'

Fifteen minutes later they were sitting in the beer garden of the Jolly Boot. Brightly coloured hanging baskets hung from hooks, while heavy cream canvas umbrellas shaded the wooden tables. As a treat, Angie had ordered a bottle of Bollinger vintage 2003. 'Oh, sod it, I had a good sale in the shop yesterday,' she declared.

Glasses filled, they clinked them together.

'Lovely to see you, darling.'

Caro took a sip of the ice-cold liquid and sighed in contentment.

'Tell me about Archie, is he having fun at college?'

Angie smiled wistfully. 'The last time we spoke he was about to go out to some toga party. And before that I seem to recall it was a Hawaiian-themed ball. His social life sounds fantastic, although I do hope he's getting some work done as well, the fees aren't cheap.'

'You miss him, don't you?'

Angie's lip wobbled momentarily. 'Dreadfully! I'm being such an old bore about it, but I really do feel bereft. Freds has told me I've got to stop calling him every day.' Angie put on a gruff voice. 'Not good for a young chap's street cred.'

'Maybe you should start fostering,' joked Caro.

'Ha, I doubt any sane young person would want to come and stay in our madhouse.' Angie took a glug of champagne. 'Anyway, I'm dying to know all about Montague Mews.'

'It's a dream,' admitted Caro. 'And I must tell you about the enigma living at No. 1.'

'Gosh, how intriguing!' said Angie, when she'd heard about Rowena. 'One must wonder what on earth happened to her, to live a life like that.'

'I'm thinking of inviting her round for dinner,' Caro admitted. 'Stephen says hell will freeze over before she comes, but you never know.'

She refilled their glasses. 'Now then, you must fill me in on all the village gossip. Granny Clem does give a rather sanitized view of things.'

A little light-headed, the pair made their way out of the pub some time later. 'What are you up to now?' Angie asked.

'I must walk and pick Milo up. He's going through the terrible twos stage at the moment, and I'd better get him before he smashes up Granny Clem's beloved Wedgwood collection.'

Angie rolled her eyes. 'Sons!'

'Wonderful day, isn't it?' a well-bred voice called out.

They both looked up. Lady Frances Fraser, wife of Sir Ambrose and mother of Harriet Fraser, was making her way towards them atop a huge brown horse. The horse was at least seventeen hands, with a gleaming coat and handsome, well-shaped head. Lady Frances Fraser was a slender and elegant woman, and anyone else would have looked lost and out of place on such an enormous beast. Somehow, her mount suited her perfectly.

'He's beautiful!' said Caro, as horse and rider made their way off the edge of the green and clip-clopped over to them.

'He's called Harry, he's been with us a few weeks,' said Frances. 'Thoroughbred cross, I got him from an eventing yard in Yorkshire. He's only five, so he's still a bit green, but his schooling is coming on marvellously. Good boy, stand still.' She ran her gloved hand along the animal's neck as he pawed the ground impatiently. Frances looked at Caro. 'You're back for the weekend? Harriet mentioned it on the phone the other night. We rather hoped she'd come back to Clanfield, but she's gone to visit friends in Norfolk.'

'I hear she's doing a marvellous job at *Soirée*,' Caro told her. The slight look of disappointment on Frances's face was swiftly replaced by one of pride.

'Yes, isn't she? I've never heard Harriet so excited about something before. She's in the middle of organizing *Soirée*'s autumn cocktail party.'

'Gosh, I went to one of those in the eighties!' exclaimed Angie. 'It was a riot. I ended up losing my shoes – God only knows where – and we all got drunk as skunks on these deadly cocktails they kept bringing round. We ended up gatecrashing this club in Knightsbridge, where we were swiftly thrown out for trying to limbo dance under a feather boa. Oh, and because one of our party thought it would be a good idea to dance naked.' She chuckled at the memory, and a faraway look came into her eyes. 'Those were the days. I seem to remember an extremely lascivious cross-dressing dwarf turning up at one point . . .'

'I'm sure things are different now,' said Caro hurriedly, noticing Frances's look of alarm.

'Mmm, yes,' said Angie absently. 'No one wears feather boas these days.'

*　　　*　　　*

That evening Caro invited Granny Clem over to Mill House for dinner. She had suggested picking up a takeaway from the Chinese in Bedlington, but received such a look of horror from Clementine that she ended up serving a fresh pasta dish, cheating ever so slightly with a jar of Loyd Grossman sauce.

The two women had dinner outside on the decked patio. Despite the fading light, the garden was bursting with colour and vigour. In Caro's absence Clementine had insisted on looking after it, and Caro thought it had never looked better.

'I wish I was as good as you at gardening, Granny Clem.'

'You could always give it a try,' Clementine pointed out.

'I did, remember? I pulled up five hundred pounds' worth of flowers in one afternoon,' Caro said wryly. 'Sebastian went mad. I can't say I blame him, although in my defence I had just had Milo and was so sleep-deprived I could barely string a sentence together, let alone distinguish between a narcissus and a nettle.'

'Have you heard from Sebastian?' asked Clementine. 'I suppose now you're in London he can't fob you off with ridiculous excuses to not see Milo.' Caro bit her lip and Clementine immediately looked guilt-stricken. 'How rude of me darling, I do apologize.'

Caro refilled her grandmother's glass with a dash of dry sherry. 'It's fine. You're right, of course. The last thing I want is any more confrontations with Sebastian, but I had hoped he'd take Milo out more. He's still paying monthly maintenance, but that's about it.' She sighed and took a sip of wine. 'I really picked one there, didn't I? I just feel for poor Milo, having a father who's not interested in him.'

'He's got Benedict,' her grandmother told her. 'And

115

so have you. That's what matters. Sebastian is the one who will lose out in the end.'

It was eleven o'clock before Caro bid Clementine goodnight at the front door.

'Are you sure I can't walk you home?'

'Don't be ridiculous,' Clementine said, pulling on her stout walking shoes. 'I may be ancient and decrepit, but I haven't lost the ability to put one foot in front of the other.'

Caro smiled. 'That's not what I meant.' She kissed her grandmother gently on the cheek. 'Do you think you'll come and visit us at Montague Mews? There's plenty of room.'

'I think I'm getting a bit too old for gallivanting up to London.'

Clementine shifted slightly, and the porch light fell on her face. For the first time, Caro thought she detected a hint of vulnerability.

'Well, the offer's always there. I could come and pick you up.'

'That's very kind,' Clementine replied. 'Let's see a little further down the line, shall we?'

Somehow Caro knew she never would.

Through the whirling sandstorm, he appeared like a vision. Hair tousled, eyes piercing, he strode forward and took Gabrielle in his arms. As he pressed his parched, full lips down on hers, Gabrielle managed to murmur, 'Oh Salvadore! You came back for me . . .'

Caro sighed and snapped the book shut. Valentina Black's latest novel was her best yet. Famous for her wildly romantic novels set in exotic locations round the world, the notoriously reclusive Ms Black was rumoured to live in tax exile in Switzerland. Regularly topping the bestseller lists, she had been one of Caro's favourite writers for years.

Caro lay back on the pillows and stared at the ceiling. It was nearly midnight, but she felt restless. After her grandmother had left, Caro had phoned her mother in Barbados for a catch-up. They'd been in fits of laughter, as Tink regaled Caro with the latest episode from Camilla and Jed's travels. They were now staying with a shaman on an organic farm just outside Mexico City, making musical instruments out of vegetables. As usual, Tink had been in full dramatic flow.

'Camilla sounds fine, but I'm a bit worried they've inadvertently joined a cult or something. Heavens, they could both be kidnapped and held to ransom for the GNP of Paraguay!' Caro had heard a muffled voice in the background.

'What was that?'

'Your father says I've been watching too many of those trashy detective dramas again. But one never knows!' Tink's fertile imagination was well-known in the family, and many an entertaining but completely exaggerated story had tumbled breathlessly from her lips. Caro had giggled. 'He does have a point, Mummy.'

Caro sat up and strained her ears. She was sure she'd heard a soft knock on the front door, but who could it be at this hour? Throwing on Benedict's too-big dressing gown, she pulled her hair back into a ponytail and went downstairs.

'Hello?' she called out. Keeping the safety chain on, she cautiously opened the door a crack. To her surprised delight, Benedict was standing on the step,

117

an overnight bag in one hand and a bunch of flowers in the other.

'What are you doing here?' Caro cried happily. She opened the door and flung her arms around her husband.

'We got through it quicker than expected,' Benedict said as he nuzzled her neck. 'I was going to drive down first thing tomorrow, but I couldn't wait to see you. Sorry about getting you up, I forgot my keys.'

'Do you fancy a nightcap?' asked Caro, leading him into the hallway. Benedict put the bag and flowers down and slipped his hands inside the dressing gown.

'I fancy you,' he said gravely. He shot her a look and opened the door to the downstairs loo.

'Ssh, we'll wake Milo!' she whispered, half-laughing.

'Not in here, we won't. Come and sit on my lap, I promise to behave myself.'

Like the imaginary Gabrielle, Caro found herself helpless to resist. Benedict deftly kicked the door shut with one foot. For once, he didn't keep his word.

Next morning the family enjoyed a breakfast in the garden. Benedict had brought fresh bread and orange juice, so they ate the spongy loaf with Clementine's homemade blackberry jam, and fluffy scrambled eggs that Caro knocked up on the Aga.

'Have you had any interest in the house?' she asked, inclining her head next door. Benedict paused, a mouthful of egg on his fork. 'It's only been on a week, but the estate agents are very confident about selling it for full price, even in this market. They seem to think it will appeal to families in London, looking to leave the rat race.'

'I hope they're better than the last neighbour,' Caro

said mischievously. 'He was a right pain in the backside, gave me no end of problems.'

'Funny, that. I heard the poor fellow was driven to distraction,' said Benedict.

Caro laughed. 'What do you fancy doing today?'

Benedict stretched. 'Something within walking distance.'

'Why don't you stay out here and keep Milo entertained while I have a shower, then we can go for a walk down to the Meadows? We can pop in and see Granny Clem on the way back.'

They ended up staying for lunch at Fairoaks in the end and, after a pleasurable few hours in the conservatory, the three made their way back towards Mill House.

They had just passed the village shop when the door to the house next door flew open. A tall, skinny woman with long, flame-red hair rushed out. She was carrying a large, lurid canvas under one arm and didn't seem to notice Caro and Benedict until she nearly ran straight into them.

'Oh!' the woman exclaimed. Her bright red lipstick clashed horribly with her floaty orange dress, and along with the hair the whole ensemble resembled an out-of-control bonfire. After a few seconds, recognition dawned and she flashed an overly large smile.

'Caro! Darling! I didn't recognize you for a moment. I've been up all night finishing this, and I'm almost *blind* with tiredness. Hello, Benedict,' she added, fluttering her eyelashes.

He smiled back. 'Babs.'

Babs Sax glanced reluctantly down at Milo, as if not liking what she found there. 'Er, hello young man.' Milo stared up at her and stuck his finger up one nostril.

'Is that your latest painting?' asked Caro. She looked

at the canvas clutched under the other woman's arm.

'It is, indeed,' said Babs Sax grandly. 'It's called *Lilibet Meets Her Nemesis*. I was inspired by the Queen's battle over the last few decades to stop the tarnishing of the monarchy. You know, the dawn of celebrity, commercialization, the effect of global warming on the sacred royal sanctums.'

Benedict's right eyebrow rose almost imperceptibly as he and Caro stared at the hideous mess of colours. Caro thought she could detect a flash of orange, was that meant to be Prince Harry?

'It's very original, Babs,' she said tactfully.

The artist gave a self-satisfied smile. 'Isn't it? I have to say, it's my best work yet.' She looked at them, a little patronizingly. 'Look at you all, playing happy families!' Milo smiled toothily at her and Babs took an inadvertent step back. 'I haven't seen you around, have you been on holiday?'

'We've moved to London for a while,' Caro told her.

Another flash of recognition. 'Of course, it completely slipped my mind. I've been on such a spiritually creative journey lately, the world has passed me by!'

'Yes, we're in Chelsea,' said Caro. 'Benedict's got a wonderful house there.'

'Oh?' Babs replied, gazing towards her rusty old red MG, parked next to the garden fence. The conversation not focused on her any more, she suddenly seemed keen to be off. 'Whereabouts?'

'Montague Mews,' said Caro. 'Stephen and Klaus have a house two doors away. Maybe you've heard them talking about it?'

Just then a loud beep sounded and they all jumped. Lucinda Reinard had pulled up in her new Volvo estate; the back seat crammed with saddles, picnic baskets and jodhpur-clad children.

'Lovely day for it!' she called through the open window. 'We're off to the Bedlington gymkhana!' With that she screeched off in a cloud of dust, a single sweet wrapper floating in her wake.

'I must dash,' Babs said shrilly. 'I have a very urgent appointment.'

They watched her clamber into the MG and pull off rather erratically. Benedict turned to Caro. 'A least I know what to buy you for Christmas now. You seemed utterly enthralled by *Lilibet Meets Her Nemesis.*'

'You bloody dare,' she laughed.

SEPTEMBER

Chapter 17

Two weeks later, at Montague Mews, Saffron was woken by an insistent prodding in her lower back. She had just been in the middle of a very nice dream in which she and Johnny Depp had won the final of *Strictly Come Dancing* with a particularly sizzling rumba. Moments later, she felt Fernando's hands creep round and squeeze her breasts, as if he was standing in the fruit and veg section at Sainsbury's appraising a particularly ripe pair of avocados.

'You woke me up,' she said sleepily. 'I was just about to shag Johnny Depp.'

Fernando sat bolt upright and leant over her. He sounded outraged.

'You were *what*?'

Saffron sat up in exasperation and looked at him. 'It's only a dream, Fernando!'

This didn't placate him. 'It makes me sick! That greasy Yank, I'll knock his clock off. The thought of his slimy hands all over your body . . .'

Saffron gave a laugh of disbelief. Fernando was the most competitive man on earth when it came to sexual prowess, but even this was a new one. 'It was a *dream* for God's sake! It doesn't mean Johnny and I are going to run off together.' *I wish*, she thought wryly.

Her protest was quickly silenced as Fernando dived on top of her, and started what he had to finish.

Downstairs in the kitchen Velda raised her eyes to the ceiling and sighed at the thumping, before turning up the *Today* programme on Radio 4. John Humphreys would be scandalized.

Six miles across London, Ashley King sat on his bed and pulled his trainers on. Taking his coat off the back of the door, he made his way down the narrow hallway to the living room. A scene of utter carnage greeted him. His dad was passed out as usual, fully clothed on the sofa, empty beer cans and vodka bottles scattered around him. The coffee table had been knocked over, and the untouched plate of dinner Ash had made his father last night was strewn across the carpet.

A muscle in Ash's cheek flickered as he looked down at his father. He walked over and hauled the prostrate figure upright.

'Dad, get up.'

His father's bleary eyes opened. 'What?' he mumbled confusedly. 'Where am I?'

Ash blanched: the older man's breath stank of stale booze and unhappiness. 'Dad, get up. Now. You passed out on the sofa again.' He sighed. 'Come on, I don't need this shit.'

His father stood up unsteadily, face still slack and eyes drunken. Ash went to grab his arm, but was pushed away.

'Get off me,' his father growled. 'I'm not a fucking invalid.' He turned and banged into the doorframe, before shuffling off in the direction of his bedroom.

Ash shook his head and went to get a cloth and bowl

of water to clean up the mess on the carpet. It was going to make him late for work again.

They'd been almost happy once, the King family. Ash, his dad Phil, mum Linda, and Ash's older sister Bev. True, there hadn't been much money, and the tenth-storey flat on the housing estate in Peckham was small and poky, but Phil's job as a gas fitter had kept the family in clean clothes and put food in their mouths. Ash had always been closest to his Granddad Bert on his mum's side, who had lived in sheltered accommodation around the corner. It had been Bert who had got Ash interested in antiques, when he'd given him an old silver pocket watch for his tenth birthday, inscribed with the words, *'To Fred, for all eternity, with heartfelt love, Elsie.'* It had been a gift from Bert's mum to his dad, before he went off and got killed in the First World War. The watch had fascinated Ash: it hadn't just been the craftsmanship, but the sense of a moment in time, captured like that, for ever. The rest of his family couldn't understand it. 'What do you want with that old bit of junk?' his mum had laughed, ruffling his hair. But Ash's love for antiques had been ignited, and every weekend Bert would take him round fairs, car boot sales and to Portobello Market. Other lads Ash's age spent their free time eyeing up girls on the high street or hanging round the back of the community centre drinking, and couldn't understand why he'd want to spend his time in musty-smelling shops filled with old people. Ash didn't care. His greatest thrill had been when he had spent two months' pocket money on a porcelain bowl he found at a car boot sale. His mum had gone mental – until it had transpired it was a very nice eighteenth-century piece, which Ash had sold on to a dealer for £80.

127

'You've got a talent for this, young man,' the dealer had told him. Ash had been hooked, and it had become his dream that, one day, he'd run his own antiques shop, his own little treasure trove of lost heirlooms and memories. For his twelfth birthday Granddad Bert had taken Ash to Tate Britain. For a little boy who had grown up in a fume-smoked urban sprawl, the colours of Turner and Samuel Prout's cornfields and water mills had been an intoxicating experience.

'I'm gonna own one of these one day, Gramps,' he had declared afterwards.

Bert had been the only one who didn't mock him. 'I'm sure you will, son, good on you.'

But then it had all gone wrong. Shortly after Ash's thirteenth birthday, his granddad had keeled over on his way to bingo and died of a heart attack. Two months later his mum, Linda, who had been spending more and more time going out by herself, had announced she was in love with a man she'd met down the pub and was going to start a new life abroad, away from all the dreariness. Ash's dad, always a drinker, had really hit the bottle after that. It had been left to a bewildered Ash and his sister Bev to try and deal with the hurt of being abandoned by first one and then the other parent.

Bev had left soon after that, and now lived in domestic bliss in Kent. She wouldn't come back to the flat, not with the state their dad was in these days, while Ash felt guilty at the thought of leaving his dad – he couldn't visit his sister in case he did something stupid. Signed off work for depression years ago, his dad did little apart from go back and forth to the off-licence these days.

Ash grimaced as he scraped up the remains of congealed mashed potato from the living room carpet. His life was shit and he could see no way of it ever improving.

Chapter 18

If Ash's day had started badly, it was nothing in comparison to how Catherine's was heading. She'd just had the latest monthly figures from the sales team, and they had suffered their biggest drop since she'd started working at *Soirée* five years ago. Catherine ran her hands through her hair. She had been so sure the last issue, with a rock-star's-daughter-turned-supermodel feature, was going to be a winner. *Fuck!* thought Catherine. There was no getting away from it now. They were up proverbial shit creek without even a glimpse of a paddle.

Ten minutes later, another email popped up, this time from Adam. He didn't mince his words.

Assume you've seen the latest figures. Sir Robin isn't happy. Board want to see you tomorrow 10 a.m. sharp. It doesn't matter what else you've got on, cancel it.

The meeting would be held at Martyr House, Valour's plush Bond Street office. This was where the board of directors made company decisions: amongst other things, whether to launch and close magazines. As well as several senior management figures from within Valour, there were other non-executive directors who, in their time, had each been regarded as the most influential figures in their industries. Even though most of them were retired, these five men – and one woman – were still tremendously powerful, and held a tight rein over the magazine titles at Valour.

These facts kept running through Catherine's head as she made her way to Martyr House in a black cab the following morning. She'd barely slept a wink and her stomach was twisted into a sick knot. It was all she could do to keep down the black coffee she'd had for breakfast that morning.

'The board need to discuss a plan of action with you,' was all Adam could – or would – say. He'd arranged to meet her in there. How typical, Catherine thought, to abandon her to her fate and retreat to the safest corner.

Adam's appointment as *Soirée*'s publisher eighteen months earlier had come as a surprise to everyone. He'd only had limited experience, of editing marginally successful lifestyle magazines, and that was now becoming a liability. It was increasingly evident that Adam was out of his depth, and no one seemed to know what to do with him. The common consensus amongst the ranks at Valour was that if his father hadn't been shooting friends with a director who had recently retired from the board, Adam wouldn't have got the job in the first place.

For a moment Catherine thought yearningly of her old boss Sue Fletchley-Ross. A firm but fair woman, she had worked exceptionally well with Catherine. She had shared Catherine's vision and given her free rein editorially, as well as offering a reliable sounding board for Catherine's ideas. Sue would have known what to do now, thought Catherine, but she could hardly call her old boss up at the ranch on Australia's Gold Coast where she'd emigrated with her family.

Catherine gave herself a mental shake as the cab pulled up outside the grand Victorian building. She was on her own. Pulling out a hand mirror, she surveyed her immaculate make-up and expensive black power suit. Her reflection, a woman in control, unafraid and single-minded, looked back coolly. Satisfied, she returned the mirror to her handbag. She might be a churning mass of emotions inside, but Catherine Connor was sure as hell not going to let the board see that.

Unfortunately, as she walked in she tripped over the new Jimmy Choo stilettos Alexander had forced her to buy, only just stopping herself from crashing into the reception desk. The snooty-looking girl behind it stifled a nasty giggle. Catherine flushed red and flashed a sarcastic smile. She'd known it would be a mistake to wear them.

'Catherine Connor to see the Valour board at ten o'clock,' she said, trying to regain her composure. The receptionist surveyed her icily and picked up the phone. 'Catherine Connor to see you, Sir Robin,' she said. She listened for a moment and put the phone down.

'Take a seat. I will call you when they're ready.'

Five minutes later, the girl gave Catherine a sharp nod. 'The board will see you now. Seventh floor, first right out of the lifts.'

Feeling the receptionist's eyes on her, Catherine walked determinedly over to the lift, letting it take her up. Catherine counted: one, two, three, four ... Christ, it was claustrophobic in here! After what seemed like an age, the doors slid open. She stepped out onto the thick carpet and glanced up and down the wide, high-ceilinged corridors. There was not a soul to be seen. Turning right she came to stand outside a large, dark-panelled wooden door. She took a deep breath, lifted her hand and knocked twice.

The sound echoed down the corridor. 'Come in,' ordered a crisp male voice from inside.

It was a large, square room, with a long mahogany table in the middle. Ten people were sitting round it. Amongst the dour-faced older men in suits, Catherine saw the familiar faces of Valour's chief executive and group finance director. The chief executive looked strained, while the group finance director gave Catherine a sympathetic smile. Catherine glanced at the po-faced woman sitting next to him; she had to be Fiona MacDonald-Scott, Valour's only female director. Catherine tried smiling at her but was met by a look that could kill grizzly bears. So much for sisterhood. She didn't even bother to acknowledge Adam, who was shrinking in his seat and fiddling nervously with his pen. An older, well-preserved man with a high forehead and neatly brushed-back silver hair stood up.

'Miss Connor, thank you for coming to see us,' he said. 'I don't believe we've met. I'm Sir Robin Hackford. Take a seat.' It was an order, not a welcoming gesture.

'I am sure you know why you're here today,' said Sir Robin. 'As Adam has relayed to you, *Soirée*'s latest sales figures are a real concern for us. It is the tenth consecutive drop in a row. If this carries on, the magazine will become one of the biggest loss-making titles at Valour Publishing.' He surveyed Catherine over his half-moon spectacles, waiting for her reaction.

Catherine tried to keep her cool. 'We're still selling 200,000 a month, that's more than some magazines.'

'And a lot less than others,' Sir Robin shot back. 'In

132

this current time, we have to set the bar high. Research has come back showing that consumers are starting to lose faith in the magazine.'

'You've been doing research groups? Why wasn't I told about it?' Catherine was shocked, not to mention angry. Feedback from the public played an imperative role in improving magazines, and Catherine had always been very involved in the research groups.

Until now.

'We didn't feel it prudent to tell you,' he said.

'What?' Catherine exclaimed, but Sir Robin held an imperious hand up. With the other, he started flicking disdainfully through the latest issue lying in front of him.

'This magazine doesn't seem to know what it is. Interviews with people no one has heard of . . .'

People you've never heard of, you old fart, Catherine fumed inwardly.

'. . . pages of fashion no one would wear. And as for the "vegan living special"!' Sir Robin's eyebrows shot up in disgust.

Down the table, Adam shuffled down in his chair. That bloody wife of his! Much to Catherine's exasperation, Adam had been pushing the alternative living angle for a while now. Catherine had protested violently about the 'vegan living' piece, and told him they'd be an industry laughing stock, but Adam had pulled rank and made her put it in.

'*Soirée* is meant to be about glamour, aspiration, inspiration, interviews with people other magazines would pull their teeth out to get,' Sir Robin continued. 'I – we – are seeing none of that here.'

Catherine's jaw tightened. The point about the vegan living had been fair, but how could a 62-year-old man claim to be an authority on fashion! 'The fact the cover price has been raised doesn't help . . .' she started to say, but Sir Robin cut her off.

'Enough. We need to think about facts and figures. We have been monitoring *Soirée*'s performance carefully for twelve months now. The fact is this magazine is not performing.'

The chief executive sighed unhappily. Catherine opened her mouth, but found she couldn't say anything. Sir Robin fixed Catherine with an unblinking gaze.

'Miss Connor, we are setting you a challenge.'

'What kind of challenge?' Catherine was immediately suspicious.

He smiled like a wolf appraising its prey. 'We are giving you six months to add 100,000 readers to your sales.' He looked round at the others, pleased with himself. 'I have come up with a name myself for your challenge.' Sir Robin paused dramatically. '"Project 300"!'

Catherine looked at him disbelievingly. 'Project what?'

Further down the table, the chief executive picked at his fingernails unhappily.

Sir Robin continued looking smug. 'We feel that if you have something tangible to work towards, it will produce better results. Mr Freshwater will be coming down to give your team a talk on the campaign tomorrow.'

Catherine looked around the table but was met by a wall of granite faces. She couldn't quite believe what she was hearing. Six months. Six months to save the magazine, in possibly the most difficult climate the industry had ever faced.

'You can't expect us to add 100,000 to sales in six months,' she said, trying to stay calm. 'It's virtually impossible. We need at least double the time to achieve anything close to that.'

But Sir Robin carried on as if she hadn't spoken. 'You have until March of next year to turn this magazine's fortunes around.'

Catherine made herself force out the words. 'And if we don't?'

Sir Robin's cold eyes appraised her. 'Then we will have no alternative but to close the title.'

The room was silent. A lump sprang into Catherine's throat, trying to fight its way upward. Keep your composure, she willed herself . . .

'And what about *Soirée* Sponsors?'

Sir Robin's eyes didn't waver. 'That will have to go as well. It's proving to be a far greater drain on resources than expected.'

Catherine couldn't bear it any longer. 'But we're doing such good work!' she cried. Several eyebrows shot up round the table but she was beyond caring. 'You talk about *Soirée* losing its way, but what is *Soirée* Sponsors then? "Glamour with a conscience" – that's been the magazine's heartbeat since the very start! It's all right for you lot sitting up here in your ivory tower. What about all those kids out there with bugger all in life?'

The group finance director cleared his throat uncomfortably. When Sir Robin spoke again, his tone was like steel.

'You may labour under a romantic notion that you're single-handedly clearing up Britain's streets, but I live in the real world, where two things matter,' he said.

'Now hang on a minute,' said the chief executive, alarmed at the sudden air of hostility in the room, but Sir Robin shot him down with a death stare.

'Profit and loss.' He enunciated the two words perfectly. 'That's what counts, Miss Connor.'

'We need to invest in *Soirée* for it to make money,' she replied angrily. 'What about *Soirée* online? We were promised a website to work alongside the magazine months ago and it's not happened. And I was only saying to Adam last week we desperately need another TV campaign to raise our profile.' She looked at him, hands stretched out in a plea. 'We need to build up the brand, not destroy it!'

Sir Robin ignored her. 'In these unstable times, we have to invest money where the market is strongest. *Soirée* is losing Valour Publishing money. If it carries on, the magazine and all ventures associated with it will be closed. It's that simple.'

Chapter 19

Gail looked up from her pot of strawberry Muller Light. 'Jesus, girl, you look like you've seen a ghost!'

Catherine stood in the doorway of the small, bustling *Soirée* Sponsors office. 'Can I have a quick word?'

It was now midday, but she hadn't been able to face going back to the magazine yet. Adam had rung her mobile every ten minutes since she'd walked out of the meeting, but she hadn't picked up his calls. As far as she was concerned, he'd been as much use as a chocolate teapot.

As usual there was an air of organized chaos in the room. Amongst the pot plants, blaring radio and piles of paperwork, several young people were busily working at their desks. A few looked up and grinned at Catherine in recognition.

Gail steered Catherine into a little room off the main one, and shut the door behind them. It was a common room of sorts: there were two squashy beanbags in one corner and a tiny kitchen area with a sink filled with unwashed mugs in the other. A small table stood there, coffee rings and a trail of sugar granules marking the surface. Gail gestured to one of the chairs and Catherine sat down, Gail's large bulk filling the other.

Cork notice-boards with dozens of photographs pinned to them adorned the walls. Faces of *Soirée* Sponsors participants, past and present, beamed out. Catherine noticed one in particular.

'Isn't that Reece Lawrence?' Reece had been one of the first to join up with *Soirée* Sponsors. He'd been brought in by his despairing mother as a sullen, angry seventeen-year-old, but had showed a real talent for taking pictures with a battered old camera he'd picked up on eBay. A photographer involved with the scheme had subsequently taken on Reece as his assistant.

'He's doing great,' said Gail proudly. 'Being worked like a dog, but loving it. His mum dropped in last week. Says Reece wants to set up on his own in a few years' time!'

Catherine looked at the picture of Reece, his cheeky freckled face grinning as he held a camera aloft. 'Good for him.'

Just as quickly the morning's events came flooding back, and her face dropped again.

Gail looked concerned. 'What's going on, Catherine?'

Without sparing any painful detail, Catherine relayed the boardroom meeting to Gail. Including the fact that Sir Robin had put a stop to any new sponsors joining the scheme, as that meant taking on more staff Valour weren't prepared to pay for.

Gail sat still in shock. '"Project 300"? What a load of old rot! What's this Sir Robin bloke on?'

'They'll probably make us all wear compulsory slogan T-shirts as well,' said Catherine gloomily. 'I hate it when management get these stupid ideas.'

'Well, I'm not bloody wearing one,' Gail declared. Her face became more shaken. 'They can't close us down! Don't they *care* about what we're doing here?'

Catherine suddenly felt drained. 'All they care about is profit. I know, it's hard for me to understand as well, but at the end of the day, this is business, Gail.' She sighed. 'Bloody Sir Robin bloody Hackford! What does he know about what the modern woman wants? He'd be better off in charge of *Saga* magazine.'

Despite it all, Gail let out a wheezy laugh. Catherine smiled back. 'I'm being really unprofessional. I shouldn't be saying this . . .'

Gail leaned across and squeezed her arm. 'That's what I'm here for.'

The unexpected gesture made Catherine well up.

'Hey, come on, don't get upset!' Gail jumped up and got her a box of tissues.

'I'm being pathetic,' sniffed Catherine.

'Crap. Even hot-shot editors are allowed to have feelings sometimes. You've got a lot on your plate, Catherine.'

Catherine swallowed. 'I know. It's just . . . well, you said it yourself. We're doing such good things here. Sometimes I think *Soirée* Sponsors has become more important than the magazine.'

Gail squeezed her arm again. 'Come on, don't throw in the towel yet. Let's give those buggers what for. I have faith in you, Catherine. You're a fighter.'

'I don't feel like one at the moment.'

Gail folded her arms across her enormous chest, her spirit back. 'You're not going to take this sitting down, Catherine, I won't let you. You're bloody good at your job, and Valour are lucky to have you. And don't let a bunch of ponces in posh suits tell you otherwise!'

Catherine managed a small smile.

'That's better!' declared Gail. 'You want me to come down and give 'em a piece of my mind?'

A vision of Gail charging into the boardroom to

challenge Sir Robin flashed into Catherine's mind, and she laughed out loud for the first time in weeks. The release felt good. Smiling, Catherine leant down to retrieve her handbag.

'One more thing before you scoot off,' said Gail. 'I wanted to run something past you quickly. I had a call from Nikki Jenson earlier . . .'

It was shortly after 1.30 p.m. when Catherine got back to the *Soirée* office. As it was lunchtime, most of the team were out, probably making the most of the September sunshine. Harriet was at her desk, and she caught Catherine as she strode into her office.

'Catherine?' she called out. 'The *Press Gazette* has called three times today. They want to know if you have any comment on the latest sales figures.'

Catherine paused. 'Can you email me their name and number? I'll call them back.'

'Also, Adam has called a few times for you.'

Catherine looked distinctly unimpressed. 'That can wait,' she said, and disappeared into her office, closing the door behind her.

Harriet bit her lip. There was something going on. Catherine had told Harriet she was going over to Martyr House this morning. And each time he'd called, Adam had sounded increasingly stressed. As if on cue, Harriet's desk phone rang.

'It's Adam. Is Catherine back yet?'

'I'll see if she's free,' said Harriet, and put him on hold.

She dialled Catherine's line. 'It's Adam Freshwater again.'

'Tell him to take a running jump, preferably off a very high building.'

Harriet took Adam off hold. 'Catherine is in a meeting

at the moment,' she said. 'She'll call you back as soon as she can.'

Adam tutted. 'Get her to call me on my mobile.'

Inside her office, Catherine knew she should take Adam's calls, but she was so annoyed at him for not standing up for her. She was dreading his 'Project 300' speech. She also knew she was unfairly directing all of her anger and frustrations at him, and he had probably been given a rollicking by the board himself earlier . . .

Catherine rested her chin on her hands and stared hopelessly out of the window. *Am I getting too old for all this?* The phone interrupted her thoughts.

'Cath-a-rine!' cried a voice. Catherine rolled her eyes. Isabella. How the hell did Isabella have her direct line? Before she had a chance to find out, Isabella cut to the quick.

'I hear your meeting didn't go very well today.'

Catherine sat up. 'How do you know that?'

Isabella laughed lightly, delighted at her consternation. 'Oh, news travels fast in this industry, my dear! Of course, it does help when one is so well-connected. But don't expect me to reveal my sources!' She chuckled again.

'Have you rung up to gloat, Isabella?' Catherine asked sharply. 'Because I'm really not in the mood for it.' She heard an intake of breath.

'Of course not, darling! This is just one editor offering commiserations to another. Really, I feel terribly for you.' Catherine had never heard anyone sound so gleeful. 'Of course, it doesn't help that Sir Robin Hackford has wanted to shut down *Soirée* ever since he joined Valour.'

Catherine's stomach dropped. 'What are you talking about?'

141

Isabella laughed again. 'Oh, darling, you must know. Everyone knows! Sir Robin has made no secret of the fact he thinks *Soirée* had its day long ago. Apparently he's determined to plough the money back into new media ventures. That's the problem with hiring these financial types: they haven't got a creative bone in their body! Who would imagine, the chairman of Valour not liking magazines!'

'Sir Robin Hackford doesn't have the monopoly on *Soirée*'s future,' Catherine pointed out acidly. 'That's what we have a board of directors for.'

'Quite! And other board members – I believe your chief executive and group finance director were among them – resisted his opinions for quite some time. But Sir Robin's predictions seem to be coming true. They can't argue with those disastrous sales figures!'

Catherine resisted the urge to ask which of Valour's directors Isabella was sleeping with.

'Goodbye, Isabella,' she said, and put the phone down. Fuming, she clicked on to her emails. She needed to let off some steam, and her friend *Teen Style*'s Fiona MacKenzie, was always a good outlet.

Hi Fi. I'm about as popular as Bin Laden round here. Got hauled before the board and given a bollocking about our sales figures. What do they expect if they raise the cover price through the roof? Bloody dinosaurs, they wouldn't know a good magazine if it came and bit them on their haemorrhoids! Anyway, just wanted to have a rant, feel better now. How are you?
C x

She quickly typed Fiona's name in and pressed send. A moment later, a horrible thought occurred. Catherine checked her sent items and her stomach dropped. She had sent the email to Valour's director, Fiona MacDonald-Scott instead.

Catherine groaned and put her face in her hands.

Chapter 20

Adam came into the office the next morning to deliver his speech. But before he started, Catherine had a few words of her own she wanted to say to her team.

If Isabella had rung purely to heap more misery on her, she would have been furious to have learned that it had actually had the opposite effect. Spurred into action by her nemesis's foul gloating, Catherine had stayed up half the night formulating a game plan to revitalize the magazine. When she finally turned in at 4 a.m., her newfound resolve had momentarily faltered. She had a hell of a task in front of her. Not only to save *Soirée* and the jobs of her staff, but the hopes and dreams of all the young people on *Soirée* Sponsors. Catherine had forced the thought out of her mind again, and tried to find sanctuary in sleep. The enormity had been almost too much to think about.

'Can we all gather round?' she called across the floor. 'I've got an important announcement to make.' She waited until everyone was standing around her.

'Uh-oh, Catherine's put her heels on,' murmured Saffron to Harriet. 'She always does that when she has bad news.'

Catherine looked at the expectant, nervous faces. 'I

am sure most of you are aware that *Soirée*'s sales have been falling for a while now. Not dramatically, I hasten to add, and in the current climate I can assure you we aren't alone. However, Valour's board have shown concern that *Soirée* isn't performing as well as they would like it to.' She smiled tightly. 'Therefore, they have devised a plan called "Project 300", which Adam will explain to you in a minute.'

You're on your own with this one, buddy, she thought. She had just seen the contents of the box he had brought in with him. A disconcerted hum started amongst the staff, and she held up her hand to quieten it.

'I'm aware that – quite understandably – some of you are worried about what this means for *Soirée*.'

'Are there going to be job cuts?' someone asked nervously.

Catherine crossed her fingers behind her back and tried to stand tall, no mean feat in a pair of circulation-killing Kurt Geigers. 'No, I can't imagine that is going to happen. I'm confident we can meet the target that has been set for us.'

Adam glanced questioningly over, but Catherine ignored him. There was no way she was letting her team carry the burden of closure with her for six months, whether he liked it or not. 'We do need to be realistic and understand that things are changing. *Soirée* is still the best magazine on the market, but we've got to up our game, become even better. We *all* need to dig deep, myself included.' She paused. 'So I'm making some changes. I know it's not ideal, but I've got a few last-minute updates for the next month's issue. I'll need you all to work late for the rest of the week to help me implement them.'

Across the room, the chief sub-editor, who was in charge of production and making sure the magazine

145

got out on time, went green. 'But it's meant to be at the printers by now!' he protested.

Catherine looked solemn. 'I'm asking a lot, I know, but we need an extension on this issue. It will be the first and last time, and I know it's cutting it fine.'

She continued. 'From next Monday, for two weeks, I will be taking half the art team to an office down the corridor to work on a redesign.'

At this the chief sub let out a strangulated cry; with Christmas looming they were coming up to their busiest time of year! Catherine ignored him. 'My belief is that *Soirée* needs something radical to keep it looking fresh and new.'

The art director nodded his head enthusiastically. 'I've got some great ideas I've been dying to try out.'

Catherine nodded. 'We are still going to cover green issues, but we are going to drop the eco-living standpoint we've been taking. It's too niche, too preachy and our readers are intelligent and well-informed enough to make their own choices on how they want to live.'

Draped over Harriet's desk in a frilled shirt and tailored knee-length shorts, Alexander cheered. 'Hear bloody hear! I thought we were going to turn into *Crusty Weekly* at one point. All that hemp wallpaper and "build your own urban compost toilet". Urgh!' There were titters around the office, and Adam went rather pink, but Catherine made no attempt to reprimand her fashion director.

'I'll be speaking to each department individually. We've got an amazing team here, but I need you to put in 110 per cent from now on. With *Soirée* Sponsors going from strength to strength, let's make the *Soirée* brand as good as we can. Are you all with me?'

The team, galvanized by the speech, nodded

enthusiastically. Catherine looked pleased by what she saw. 'Excellent.' Her smile became slightly frozen. 'Now I'll hand you over to Adam, who'll explain the nuts and bolts of the "Project 300".'

Soirée's publisher blinked nervously. Public speaking wasn't his forte. He stepped forward.

'Yes, right!' Adam's Adam's apple bobbed furiously. 'Um . . .'

There was an excruciating silence, before he took a resolute swallow.

'This just isn't good enough!' he said loudly.

Catherine groaned inwardly, he'd obviously had a pep talk from Sir Robin to go in heavy-handed.

Adam started striding up and down in front of them, looking more like he was searching unsuccessfully for his car in a multi-storey car park than an inspirational leader rousing his troops.

'Valour's about winning!' he declared. 'And what are we? Losers!'

Everyone looked at Catherine. Her mouth had dropped open, but by now Adam was in full flow.

'Valour doesn't do losers! We're in it to win it. And that's why the "Project 300", a brilliant idea devised by Sir Robin Hackford himself – has been put into practice. At the moment *Soirée* is selling 200,000 copies a month.'

At this the team looked slightly relieved. That sounded all right, didn't it? Adam noticed their glances and pounced. 'You think that's good enough? It's not. Our rivals are selling tens of thousands more a month!'

Probably because they haven't got a bunch of muppets in charge and an extortionate cover price. Catherine fumed inwardly.

Adam ploughed on. 'We want to be at the top of our

147

game again, where Valour Publishing belongs! So,' he puffed up self-importantly, 'you have all been set the challenge to increase *Soirée*'s sales by 100,000 to reach that "Project 300" mark. And there's no time to waste, because you've got six months to do it!'

'Six months?' someone echoed.

'Yup,' said Adam confidently.

'That's March,' another voice said weakly.

'Uh-huh! Of course I expect you to have it all sewn up by then.'

Mouths gaped, and once again everyone turned to look at Catherine. Her jaw was set like granite. Adam stopped striding and put his hands on his hips, crotch pointing out rather offensively.

'OK?' he said. 'Are we clear on that?' His voice rose louder and he raised his fist in the air, Rocky-style. 'What are we, winners or losers? Let's hear it for "Project 300"!' He punched the air. 'Yeah!'

The only sound was the distant hum of a photocopier. Catherine quickly stepped in.

'I think we all understand the concept, Adam,' she said, trying to keep her voice as neutral as possible.

Adam blinked again, back to his normal ineffective-ness. 'Oh, of course,' he stuttered. 'There is one more thing.' He looked at Saffron, who was standing near the large cardboard box he'd brought in. 'If you could bring that over here . . .'

After a moment's hesitation Saffron bent down to pick it up, but Tom Fellows beat her to it. 'I've got it,' he mumbled.

Everyone looked down curiously as Adam pulled the flaps open.

'To kick-start the "Project 300" campaign, Valour Publishing is generously donating a branded mouse mat and mug for each and every one of you. Please replace your old ones with these, it is compulsory to use them.'

He bent down and triumphantly pulled out a garish black mug with the slogan *'Project 300'* emblazoned across it in bright yellow letters. 'From now on, whenever you step into the building, you'll be living, breathing and working the "Project 300"! This is to ensure maximum success.' Adam thrust the mug aloft, like some kind of abhorrent Father Christmas. 'Are there any questions?' he asked.

This time, Catherine didn't dare look at any of her team.

'Thank you, Adam. I'll make sure everyone gets their new equipment. And thanks everyone, you can all get back to work now.'

People started shuffling back to their desks, talking incredulously in low voices. Catherine knew how they felt. She went back into her office, heart heavy. Adam followed. 'That went well, didn't it?' he said hopefully.

Catherine went round the other side of her desk. 'Depends what you term "well".' She looked over at him. 'I don't appreciate you calling my team "losers", Adam.'

He flushed. 'Maybe that was a bit much. Thomasina bought me this American self-help book on how to motivate one's workforce. It was rather extreme.'

Catherine raised an eyebrow. 'I think they got the message.' What a bloody farce! As if Sir Robin thought spending £50 on a load of tacky Valour merchandise was going to help them achieve the ridiculous target he'd set. Catherine gritted her teeth, they'd be a laughing stock when this got out.

'Was there anything else?' she asked abruptly. Suddenly she wanted Adam out of her office, and as far away from her as possible.

'Er, no. Just keep me up to date with progress, and, of course, I'll be reporting back to Sir Robin with the monthly sales figures.'

No offer of any help or ideas from him, then, she noted. Not that she was surprised: Adam had the creative vision of a concrete bollard. 'As you can imagine, I've got a lot to get on with,' she said.

Adam smoothed down his tie. 'Of course, I'll leave you to it. Well, good luck.'

Catherine shut the door firmly behind him, not even caring that she'd dismissed her own boss. *We'll need more than luck, mate,* she thought grimly as she kicked off her heels and prepared to get stuck into the October issue. *You're asking me to perform a bloody miracle.*

OCTOBER

Chapter 21

As the dying embers of summer moved into autumn, Montague Mews was aglow with new colours. Branches from the horse chestnut trees drooped into the courtyard, their green leaves slowly turning a burnished copper. As they fell, they covered the cobbles, transforming the ground into a flame-coloured carpet. Returning home from shopping late one Wednesday afternoon, the sun was slowly creeping down the century-old brick walls, Caro thought it looked like a golden pocket of loveliness.

That weekend Benedict was away on a work trip, so Caro decided to invite Harriet and Velda round for dinner on Saturday.

Velda popped in the day before to ask if Saffron could come as well. 'Of course,' Caro said. 'I only didn't invite her because I thought she'd have better things to do.'

Velda smiled. 'I know, I couldn't believe it when she asked; I don't think Saffron has stayed in on a Saturday night since she started living with me. The poor girl is a bit run-down at the moment, and needs a few quiet nights in. They're working dreadfully hard at work.'

'I know, Harriet was telling me about this "Project 300" campaign. Seems they're asking a lot.' Caro changed the subject. 'I know it's a long shot, but I was thinking of asking Rowena. Do you think there's any chance she might come? Maybe I'm being an interfering old busybody, but every time I walk past, I think of her locked away in that house . . .'

Velda looked dubious. 'I salute you for doing the good-neighbour thing, but come hell or high water, I don't think you'll get Rowena out.'

Later on that evening, Caro decided to try her chances. Cajoling a grumbling Milo away from his *Lazytown* DVD – 'We're just going for a little walk next door, darling' – Caro took his hand and opened the front door. Helping her son across the cobbles, Caro approached Rowena's house. The only sign that anyone lived there was visible between the thick velvet curtains drawn across one of the upstairs windows. A tiny chink of light. Downstairs, the windows were covered with heavy wooden shutters. The place looked like a fortress.

Feeling rather self-conscious, Caro knocked on the door. 'Hello?' she called. 'Rowena? It's your neighbour at No. 2, Caro. We haven't had the pleasure of meeting yet.'

Silence. Caro felt like an idiot. Milo started to strain on her hand. 'I'm cold, Mummy!' he complained. Caro realized he wasn't wearing a jacket, and was seized by guilt. Velda was right, she told herself. Rowena wants to be left alone. Caro was just turning away when she heard a creak, as if someone was coming down the stairs.

'Hello?' she called again. Nothing. Tentatively she lifted up the letterbox. She could just make out a long, dark hallway and the first couple of stairs. It looked like some washing had been left lying on the bottom step. 'Sorry to disturb you,' she called again. 'I was wondering if you wanted to come to dinner at ours tomorrow.'

More silence. No one was there. 'Mummy!' Milo said even louder. Caro let go of the letterbox and allowed him to start tugging her back to their nice warm house. *Christ, I just shouted through that poor woman's letterbox!* she thought, suddenly appalled. Was she turning into Lucinda Reinard? It was only when she'd got back into No. 2 and closed the door safely behind them that she realized what the pile of washing had been. A pair of baggy trouser-clad legs.

Rowena had been listening all along.

It had been a month since Catherine's rousing speech to the team. Despite her trepidation, the 'Project 300' had started well. Not down to any help from everyone's new branded merchandise, however. Alexander was pointedly using his mouse mat to wipe his feet on every time he came into the office.

Although time had been against them, Catherine's patch-up job on the October issue had actually turned out rather well. Early indications showed they had added on an extra 10,000 sales, which was all good and well, considering. The real coup, however, was the redesign. It had been a real success, and everyone – including Adam – thought the November issue, due to hit the shelves in a few weeks, looked fantastic. It hadn't been without sacrifice: Catherine had worked late every night all month, obsessing over each headline, picture and word, making sure it was all perfect.

They'd had one blow – despite Saffron's (and not Annabel's) best efforts, they still hadn't managed to get Savannah Sexton, and it looked very unlikely they would secure her for the all-important Christmas issue. Catherine had taken the news grim-faced and retreated to her office.

Meanwhile Harriet had quickly realized her boss was a workaholic. In the whole five months she'd worked there, she didn't think she'd heard Catherine talk once about an evening out with friends. Despite the expensive outfits her boss was looking tired and drawn. Catherine had told them all they wouldn't be losing their jobs, but it didn't stop the staff talking. Was the 'Project 300' just a stupid gimmick? If they didn't reach the 300,000 would Valour really close *Soirée* down? Harriet felt dreadfully upset at the thought of losing her job. She was lucky enough to have a life to go back to in Churchminster, but it was more than that. *Soirée* had given her the sense of self-fulfilment she had been searching for all her life.

It was Saturday morning and Harriet was flopped on the sofa in her pyjamas watching an old rerun of *Grand Designs*. Kevin McCloud was awfully dashing, why couldn't she find someone like him? To her delight Camilla had woken her up, unexpectedly calling from a train in Guatemala. They'd chatted excitedly for fifteen minutes, before Camilla said they were going through a tunnel and the phone went dead. Afterwards, Harriet was just thinking how nice it would be to be in Camilla's sweet little cottage having a good old chinwag when her mobile rang again.

'Bills?' she sat up hopefully, using Camilla's nickname.

'No, darling, it's me,' Lady Frances said. 'Were you expecting Bills?'

'I'd just spoken to her, actually. We got cut off. She

156

and Jed are on a train somewhere in the wilds of Guatemala.'

'Good heavens, how ghastly!' Lady Frances Fraser didn't entirely approve of Camilla's rough and ready adventure. 'How are you, anyway? I'm concerned you're working too hard. Ambrose said you looked rather pale when he came up to see you for lunch last week. I do worry all that pollution is playing havoc with your complexion.'

Harriet laughed. 'I'm fine, Mummy! I'm rushed off my feet with the cocktail party, but I'm really enjoying it.'

'Cook sends her love. She wants to know when you're coming home, so she can feed you up. Her words, I hasten to add, not mine. You know I'm trying to get her to introduce a slightly more healthy menu, but so far she's proving rather resistant to change.'

'You know Cook,' said Harriet fondly.

'Indeed I do,' said her mother drily. 'I'm fighting a losing battle to get your father's cholesterol levels down. Of course, it doesn't help that Ambrose still insists on having his Thursday night steak and kidney pudding. Honestly, sometimes I think those two are conspiring against me . . .'

Thirty minutes later Harriet had received a full round-up of events in Churchminster, including Lucinda Reinard's request to hold next year's Bedlington Valley Pony Club camp in the grounds of Clanfield Hall.

'We haven't said yes, but I don't see a problem if they're tucked away in one of the back fields,' her mother had said. 'Your father's not so keen, though, he's grumbling about noise levels and litter.' She'd laughed lightly. 'But really, what can go wrong? For some strange reason Ambrose is convinced it will turn into the Cotswolds' answer to Glastonbury!'

*   *   *

After her lazy start, Harriet had had rather a productive day. She'd cleaned the entire flat from top to bottom, and then gone through her wardrobe, filling three large black bin-liners with old clothes to give to charity. Harriet had been astounded at the amount of unwanted stuff she'd accumulated – how could one person have so many sweaters from Fat Face?

Afterwards, she'd felt so pooped she'd fancied nothing more than sinking back on the sofa with a cup of tea and the *Home and Away* omnibus. But instead she'd made herself go for a run. With her long hours at work and the nights drawing in, Harriet's running had fallen rather by the wayside, and she was determined to get back into it and zap her wobbly bits.

Unfortunately, on this occasion the strap on her sports bra snapped just as she passed a group of people doing a military keep-fit lesson, and they fell about laughing as she tried to carry on, surreptitiously holding up one bouncing boob with her hand. When she got home, Harriet went online to see what Pilates classes were on in the area instead.

It had just turned 8 p.m. by the time Harriet made the short walk from hers over to Caro's. The sky above Guinevere Road was charcoal black, Boeing 747s outbound from Heathrow roaring high away in the distance.

Harriet reached the archway to Montague Mews and buzzed the intercom.

'Hello?' she called. A few seconds passed.

'It's open!' crackled Caro's disembodied voice, and the iron gate slowly swung wide. Harriet walked into the courtyard, where old-fashioned lanterns were aglow over each front door. It reminded her of a scene from a Dickens novel.

Caro was waiting in the doorway, arms open.

'Come in from the cold.'

'Oh, it looks enchanting!' exclaimed Harriet.

Caro did have a knack for making a room look good: white church candles dotted the coffee table and mantelpiece, casting a warm, comforting hue. A rich cinnamon smell floated across the room from a scented oil bowl, while a fire roared away merrily in the hearth. Velda and Saffron were sitting around it, huge goblets of red wine in their hands.

'Benedict's gone out for the night, left us girls to it,' explained Caro as she helped Harriet out of her coat.

'Hey, H!' Saffron put her glass down and went over to kiss her. 'God, you're freezing!'

'It's jolly cold out there. Hello, Velda,' said Harriet. She handed Caro a bottle of wine.

'What can I get you? Red or white?' Caro asked.

'Ooh, I think I'll go for red tonight.'

'Coming right up.' A minute later, she reappeared with red wine and a tray laden with olives and bowls of crisps, dips and cashew nuts.

Saffron dived in. 'Lush, Kettle Chips. Don't let me eat all of these, I'll never have enough room for dinner.'

She paused, a handful of crisps halfway to her mouth.

'Is that burning I can smell?'

'Oh bollocks, the mini-tartlets!' Caro cried, and rushed off into the kitchen.

By ten o'clock the wine and conversation were flowing. After an ominous start, Caro had regained control of the cooking, and her smoked salmon roulade and Nigel Slater chicken dish had actually turned out rather well. Pleasantly replete, they decided to take a breather before dessert, and Velda started telling Caro and Harriet all about Yousef, her Moroccan husband, who lived in an artist's commune in the Atlas Mountains.

'I didn't even know you were married!' Caro exclaimed, as she got up to refill everyone's glass.

Velda smiled. 'I guess it's not what you'd call a conventional set-up, but it suits us. We have our own lives and get together as much as we can. In fact, I'm going out there for Christmas.'

'How long have you been married?' asked Harriet.

'Married for fifteen years, been together for twenty,' Saffron interrupted. 'Yousef is wicked, he's done some really cool paintings for my bedroom. Velda took me out quite a few times to Morocco when I was younger. The markets in Marrakech are something else.'

'How exotic!' exclaimed Harriet.

Velda laughed. 'I don't know about that.'

'How's your chap, Saffron? Are things going well?' said Caro.

Saffron screwed up her face.

'She's fed up with him having no money,' Velda told them, smiling. 'I think he's rather a poppet.'

'Only because he butters you up so much when he comes round!' Saffron turned to the other two. 'Last night I came home from work to find them sitting in front of the fire, Fernando hand-feeding Aunt Velda oysters!'

Velda looked a bit embarrassed. 'I did tell him I was happy with beans on toast, but Fernando is *so* persuasive,' she sighed.

Caro smiled and changed the subject. 'I hear work's rather fraught at the moment.'

'Tell me about it,' said Saffron. 'The redesign looks

fab, but there's still a weird atmosphere in the office. I think people are worried about what's going to happen. Another magazine closed last week, you know.'

'That doesn't sound good,' said Caro. 'Do you think you'll be all right?'

Saffron shrugged. 'Who knows? It doesn't help that Catherine is walking around with a permanent case of PMT. I seriously think she's having some kind of mid-life crisis.'

'You're her PA, Hats, what's she like to work for?' asked Caro.

Harriet paused, her wine glass halfway to her mouth. 'She does work one jolly hard, but I admire her. She's done awfully well for herself.'

Saffron refilled their glasses. 'Don't you think there's something strange about her?'

'Strange?' asked Velda.

Saffron furrowed her brow. 'No, that's not the right word.' She cast about for the correct one. 'I don't know, *hidden*. Like she's keeping something back.'

Harriet thought about her boss: the long hours she worked, and the trendy flat she never seemed to want to go back to. Recently she was sure she'd smelt stale alcohol on Catherine's breath.

'Oh, I don't know,' she said loyally. 'Maybe she thinks it's unprofessional to let her guard down. Catherine must be under awful pressure, what with the magazine and *Soirée* Sponsors.'

'From what I hear, *Soirée* Sponsors is going great guns, though,' Velda remarked. 'There was a very interesting piece on it in the *Observer* last weekend. They're thinking about expanding all over the country, aren't they?'

'I think that's the aim,' said Harriet. 'Although I haven't a clue how Catherine could take on any more. She's stretched from pillar to post as it is.'

Saffron reached across for the bottle again. 'More wine, anyone?'

'I'm fine,' said Caro. She never felt much like drinking when she was hosting a dinner party. She got up to get pudding, a delicious lemon tart she'd bought from the organic bakery down the road. She'd tried to make her own, but it had sunk in the middle like a cowpat and ended up in the bin.

As they tucked in, the conversation got round to Stephen and Klaus.

'It's wonderful having them as neighbours,' said Caro. She laughed, 'I've never seen Stephen without his cravat on, not even when he's taking the rubbish out. He makes me feel like a dreadful scruff in comparison.'

Harriet giggled. 'How's your grandmother? Mummy tells me she's taken Reverend Bellows under her wing.'

'Poor man,' said Caro. 'I think Granny Clem got fed up with him "dithering" as she called it, over church affairs, and has taken over. According to Angie, the Harvest Festival was run out of Fairoaks like a military operation. Reverend Bellows hardly got a look in. I do hope he doesn't get scared off – and realizes Granny Clem means well.'

Someone's phone beeped. 'Oh, that's mine,' said Harriet apologetically. 'I meant to put it on vibrate.'

Saffron looked at her watch. 'I bet that's a bootie call!' She surveyed Harriet wickedly. 'Have you got yourself a bloke?'

'No, of course not!' Harriet protested. She paused. 'Not yet, anyway.'

Caro sat up. 'Ooh, do tell, H! Is there someone on the scene?'

Harriet went pink. 'Well, not quite . . .' and told them about joining Chapline.

Saffron pulled a face. 'You've joined a dating agency? That's really sad!'

Velda swiftly reprimanded her. 'Don't be so rude, Saffron.'

Saffron looked at Harriet. 'Sorry, H. I just didn't think you'd be mad enough to do anything like that.' She grinned, waving her wine glass at Harriet. 'Have you been stalked by any weirdos?'

'There are some strange men out there, I must admit. I'd been emailing one chap, and then he told me he only ate orange foods, had been one of Jesus's disciples in a former life, and had spent the weekend building the Sistine Chapel out of matchsticks. I don't want to sound judgemental, but I was a bit put off.'

'I'm not surprised!' laughed Caro. 'Have you met any nice ones?'

Harriet nodded. 'There is one, called Thomas. He's sent me a picture of himself. He's awfully good looking. Runs his own headhunter's company. He writes children's poems in his spare time, and sent me a few. They were quite good, actually. I thought that was very sweet.'

'Fit, loaded and sensitive,' said Saffron. Her eyes were starting to glaze over. 'Any more like him? Maybe you can set me up.'

Harriet blushed again. 'I'll ask him, if you like. We're meeting up next week.'

Saffron whooped. 'You are so going to get it! Like a rat up a drainpipe!' She hiccupped loudly. 'Fuck, when was the last time you had sex? It must have grown over down there.'

'Caro, would you take that glass of wine off her?' asked Velda.

Chapter 22

Catherine had spent most of the weekend at the office. Ever since all hope of getting Savannah Sexton for the Christmas cover had been extinguished, Catherine had been driving herself – and the team – even harder. The features team had managed to secure a popular British actress for the issue instead, but she lacked the chutzpah of Savannah, and Catherine was determined to make every page of the magazine work twice as hard instead.

The *Soirée* cocktail party was only two days away, and couldn't have come at a better time. Everyone needed a break. In the office, there was rising excitement about what everyone would be wearing. Alexander was planning a grand unveiling on the night. Saffron had bleached her hair almost white, and was going to wear a minidress from Miu Miu dressed up with vintage diamanté jewellery from Portobello Market. After the pussy-bow-shirt debacle, Harriet had played safe and picked a plain, well-cut dress from Jigsaw.

On the day of the party, Harriet arrived at work early. Despite her magnificent organization, there was still a mountain of last-minute things to do. Tom Fellows was already there, poring over his computer screen. He blushed beetroot red behind his bottle-tops when she called out hello. As she sat down and switched on her own computer Harriet wondered if he was going to the party. Tom was such a shrinking violet that she imagined it would be his worst nightmare.

An hour later she was checking the guest list for the final time when the door swung open and Catherine walked in. She headed straight for her office without acknowledging Harriet. Harriet wondered nervously if she had forgotten to do something.

'Morning, Catherine!'

Her boss stopped. 'Sorry, I was miles away. Have you been in long?'

Catherine's head was pounding unpleasantly from the bottle and a half of wine she'd had last night. She hadn't meant to drink so much, but had passed out on the sofa, awaking dry mouthed and disorientated at 3 a.m. She was now filled with self-disgust and a sinking disbelief that she'd let herself get like this on one of the most important days of the year. Did she have any paracetamol left in her desk drawer?

'Not really, just making sure all the VIPs are on the guest list,' Harriet said brightly. Catherine looked exhausted, she thought. Her skin was grey and dull and there were dark circles ringing her eyes.

'Are the *Soirée* Sponsors team on there?' Catherine had made it a priority to invite them. As well as giving them the chance to meet the *Soirée* editorial team and other types, it was a kind of informal 'thank you' for all their hard work throughout the year.

'All except Gail. She phoned me yesterday to say she couldn't make it.'

Catherine smiled. 'That doesn't surprise me. Gail's

always said she doesn't do "la-di-dah". Her words, not mine.' She frowned. 'I hope that building work's finished by now, we can't have our guests getting covered in cement dust.'

'I've been assured by Ken – he's the foreman – and the Natural History's site manager, that it will all be finished this morning.'

Catherine looked concerned. 'God, I hope so. That's cutting it a bit fine.'

Harriet looked downcast. 'It's overrun by two weeks. I had no idea they'd still be there.'

Catherine noticed her PA's expression. 'Hey, it's not your fault. You've done a really great job.'

Harriet looked happier. 'Let's hope it goes smoothly tonight!'

Catherine smiled. 'I am sure it will.' She paused as she opened her office door. 'Would you mind popping out to Boots and getting me some painkillers? I've got a really bad headache coming on, must be a migraine or something.'

Ten minutes later, Harriet was back, along with a steaming hot cappuccino for Catherine.

'You star,' said Catherine. As she reached for her purse, she knocked a pile of papers off her already crowded desk.

'Bollocks!' Catherine cursed, but Harriet had already scooped them up and deposited them back on the desk.

Catherine thanked her. 'It's all my *Soirée* Sponsors stuff. We've been asked to open a new centre in Manchester.'

'That's fantastic news!' Harriet said, but Catherine didn't seem to share her enthusiasm.

'Hmm, well, we've got a lot of things to think about at this end, first.' She paused. 'That reminds me . . .

I don't suppose you know anyone who works in the antiques world, do you?'

A name immediately came into Harriet's mind.

'I do actually, Angie Fox-Titt. She owns an antiques shop in the village I come from.'

Catherine looked mildly surprised. 'Churchminster, isn't it?'

Harriet was rather flattered her boss had remembered.

'Only I'm trying to get this young lad on a placement somewhere, and we're not having much luck so far.'

'Why don't I ask Angie?' offered Harriet. 'You never know.'

'Mrs Fox-Titt would have to join up to the scheme and go through all the usual vetting procedures.' Catherine shot Harriet an apologetic look. 'It's quite a commitment.'

Harriet smiled. 'No harm in trying. In actual fact, my mother is going out riding with Angie tomorrow. I'll get her to mention it then.'

By 4 p.m., work had stopped for the day. Even Catherine had downed tools and gone out for a two-hour pampering session. Music blared out much louder than normal from the stereo, while champagne was handed out in plastic cups from the water cooler to get the party atmosphere going. Mindful she had to keep her wits about her, Harriet topped hers up with tons of orange juice to make a very weak Bucks Fizz.

The beauty team had booked a manicurist to come in, and the woman had set up an impromptu salon in the small room at the back of the office that acted as a fashion cupboard. It was in here, amongst the racks of clothes and piles of shoes that Harriet and Saffron sat, Saffron blowing on her freshly applied bright-orange varnish, and sipping from her plastic cup while the manicurist started to paint Harriet's nails in a pretty coral colour.

'What time are you going down there?' asked Saffron.

'Around 6 p.m. Catherine wants to have a last-minute recce to make sure everything's in place,' said Harriet, watching the manicurist painstakingly apply the varnish to her nails. She wished she could put on polish properly herself: she either ended up smudging it or painting it halfway down to her knuckles. A jolt of nerves flashed through her stomach. 'God, I hope there're no last-minute disasters!'

Saffron opened her mouth to offer reassurance but something caught her eye. Her face froze in astonishment.

'Look out there!' she mouthed to Harriet.

Harriet turned her head to be confronted by the sight of Annabel in a lime-green evening dress that looked like it had been plucked straight out of the eighties. It had a floor-length puffball skirt and flouncy sleeves, and Annabel had coordinated it with a black Alice band and satin evening gloves. As she turned round to model it to a slack-jawed chief sub, they saw there was a huge bow attached to the back of the dress, stretching across her ample bottom. Annabel spotted them staring and bustled across.

'What are you doing in here?' she asked, gooseberry eyes suspicious.

'What does it look like?' asked Saffron. Annabel looked down at Harriet's nails.

'That colour does nothing for your skin tone,' she said patronizingly. 'You should have gone for a French manicure like me.'

'Are you planning on taking those lovely gloves off,

then?' asked Saffron innocently. 'What a shame, they really make your outfit.'

Annabel looked at her, not sure if she was being made fun of. Her ego took over. 'Yah, I look great, don't I? Should do, this bloody thing cost me a fortune.'

There was a sudden commotion outside. Saffron leapt up and ran out, and Annabel cast one more disparaging look at Harriet's nails before following her. Harriet could hear raised voices, one high-pitched hysterical one in particular. After a few moments, Saffron came back in. She had the most peculiar expression on her face.

'What on earth's the matter?' said Harriet, in alarm.

'Alexander has had a slight mishap,' replied Saffron. A giggle erupted and she clapped a hand over her mouth.

'What's happened? Is he OK?' said Harriet. Just then the fashion director flew into the room, hotly pursued by the picture editor who was brandishing a wet paper hand-towel. Alexander stopped and threw his hands in the air.

'Look at me!'

Harriet had never seen anything like it. Alexander was bright orange. Every inch of his flesh glowed radio-actively, while more fake tan congealed unattractively around his eyebrows and hairline.

The picture editor was a mum of three who was experienced in such matters. She dabbed at his face. 'It'll come off if I give it a good scrub . . .'

'I look like a fucking Oompa-Loompa,' shrieked Alexander. He caught sight of himself in the full-length mirror on the wall. 'Those bitches at *Grace* will have a field day!'

'I'm sure it'll wash off,' offered Harriet, but Alexander was beyond consolation.

'Six weeks I've worked on my outfit for tonight! Six weeks! And now it's all ruined! This is a fucking disaster.'

Always one to gain delight from another's misfortunes, Annabel had edged her way in. At this last comment, she adopted her most worthy expression. 'I think you'll find babies starving in Africa is a real disaster, Alexander,' she said condescendingly. This was met with a look that could have felled grown men, and reluctantly Annabel backed out of the room.

Alexander had had enough. His face twisted into a tragicomic mask of outraged despair. 'All of you, out, OUT! I want to be alone.'

'He went to try out this new spray-on fake tan,' whispered the picture editor as they were bundled out, manicurist and all, from the cupboard. 'I think it went a bit wrong.'

There was another plaintive wail from inside. 'Maybe not the best time to ask if Jodie Marsh is his new style icon,' said Saffron, her mouth twitching.

Harriet tried not to laugh. 'Oh, poor Alexander!'

Chapter 23

The party was starting at 7 p.m. By 6.23 p.m. Catherine's taxi was pulling up outside the Natural History Museum. She climbed out and stopped for a moment to savour the vast building with its majestic turrets, stone gargoyles and huge arched windows, all lit up by industrial-sized spotlights. High up on the roof was a flagpole, a crisp Union Jack swaying proudly in the night breeze. Catherine walked towards the entrance gate, where a bored-looking man in a black suit stood sentry. His eyes lit up at the sight of Catherine and he gave her an obvious once-over. Ignoring him, she opened her black clutch bag to produce the glossy laminated ticket everyone in the industry had been falling over themselves to get.

'Party doesn't start yet, darlin',' the man leered.

Catherine smiled. 'I know, it's my party.'

The doorman's face fell and he quickly adopted a more businesslike expression. 'Oh, I'm sorry, ma'am. Name?' He looked down at his clipboard.

'Catherine Connor,' she said, and swept past him.

Just inside the door was a girl dressed in head-to-toe black wearing a small headpiece. Catherine repeated her name, and after confiding breathlessly that *Soirée* was her favourite magazine, the girl waved her through.

'Let me know if you need anything,' she called as Catherine walked into the central hall. It wasn't the first time Catherine had been to the museum, yet it still left her speechless. It was such a commanding place, with its sweeping ornate balcony running both sides of the room. At the far end was a grandiose staircase, overlooked by three beautiful stained-glass windows, while the high domed ceiling was covered with intricate drawings of flora and fauna. The whole thing would have reminded Catherine of a cross between a cathedral and a Victorian railway station, if it hadn't been for the huge black skeleton of a plant-eating Diplodocus dinosaur, its massive frame dwarfing the entire room.

On either side of the room were alcoves that had been transformed into different bars for the evening. One was a neon-lit cocktail bar with a large black cauldron as its centrepiece, bubbling with some kind of alcoholic concoction. *Cute*, Catherine thought. The party had cost a fortune, yet Catherine wasn't surprised Sir Robin had let it go ahead. Heaven forbid that any of his business rivals think Valour was in any kind of *trouble*.

Already the place was alive with activity. Cocktail waitresses dressed as burlesque dancers sashayed past, while handsome barmen busied themselves with last-minute preparations. At the champagne bar, a pyramid made up of hundreds of glasses was being painstakingly assembled, soon to be filled with bottles of cascading golden liquid. In the middle of all this, studying her clipboard intently, was Harriet.

As if suddenly aware of Catherine's presence, she looked up and rushed over. 'Hullo, Catherine, I was hoping you'd be here!'

172

Harriet was looking slightly pale. Her nerves were starting to take over, and she'd had to phone home to Clanfield Hall to get a pep talk from her mother.

'Darling, you'll be fine,' Frances had told her. 'This is what the Frasers do well. Have you had your hair straightened?'

'Yes, Mummy,' Harriet had replied dutifully.

'What about those control knickers I bought you for Easter, instead of the Green & Black's egg you wanted?'

'Present and correct!'

Harriet had heard her mother sigh with satisfaction. 'One word of advice, Harriet, do stay off the champagne – in fact any alcohol – until at least an hour before the end. It's most unbecoming for the hostess to be rolling around drunk.'

Harriet hadn't been able to face telling her mother, once again, that she wasn't actually hosting the party, nor that she'd abandoned her good intentions and had just gulped down a large glass of house white at the bar to calm her nerves.

In fact, she thought she might need another now. Catherine's keen eyes were scanning the room, as usual missing nothing.

'The orchestra have got to set up on the staircase,' Harriet said hurriedly. 'At least they're here, which is more than I can say for the harpist: poor woman is stuck in traffic. And of course, the waiters and wait-resses aren't in position . . .'

Catherine's face broke into a huge smile. 'It looks bloody fantastic! I think it's going to be our best party yet.'

'Oh, thank you!' Harriet felt weak with relief: she had so wanted Catherine to be pleased. 'At least the builders have gone. I was having nightmares about guests getting bumped off by bits of falling scaffolding!'

Catherine smiled. 'Well I didn't see any bodies on the way in, so I think we'll be all right.' She looked around. 'I'm just going to the cloakroom. Is there anything you need me to do?'

'I think we're fine, thank you.' Harriet paused, wondering if she was about to step over the line. 'I have to say, Catherine, you look jolly good! That dress fits you like a glove.'

Catherine looked down at her outfit and laughed. 'It's so bloody tight I won't be able to eat one canapé, but it's nice of you to say so.'

Looking in the bathroom mirror a few minutes later, Catherine conceded she was looking good. That afternoon's facial and body exfoliation had left her skin taut and glowing. Her hair was freshly cut and shiny, while her full lips, which were normally covered by a slick of clear lip-gloss, had been painted a bright, luscious red. She had kept the rest of her make-up to a bare minimum: several coats of carefully applied black mascara which brought out the blue of her eyes, and a subtle pink cream blusher. Square-cut diamond earrings from De Beers jewellers on Bond Street sparkled next to her face, softening her strong bone structure. They had been Catherine's Christmas present to herself two years ago.

Her eyes moved downwards, on to the black knee-length Chanel dress that Alexander had called in for her. Beautifully tailored, it was strapless with a ruffle detail around the bust. Harriet was right, it fitted her like a second skin. Before she'd retired to the sofa with a bucket-sized glass of wine last night, Catherine had practised for ages walking in her new Marc Jacobs heels. Apart from the odd wobble, she seemed OK. *Please, God, don't let me go arse over tit tonight*, she thought, cursing choosing a profession which required vertigo-

174

inducing shoes. It would have been much easier to be a farmer or something.

Catherine stared at her reflection again. Her outward appearance was a complete contrast to how she felt inside. She had expected nerves about the party, but it still wasn't enough to drown out the gnawing anxiety that seemed to be part and parcel of her these days. She sighed. To the outside world, she had it all. So why did she feel so empty?

It was ten to seven. The cloakroom attendants were in position, while the sound of the orchestra tuning up floated across the room. Security men with walkie-talkies strode purposefully about, while waitresses stood around the bar chatting and waiting for their trays of cocktails to be made. Catherine was just on her way to introduce herself to the museum's events manager when a voice stopped her stone dead.

'Cathy? Is that really you?'

Catherine froze. She knew that voice. It was deeper than she remembered, but the familiar intonation was still there, underneath the soft Geordie lilt. My God, she hadn't heard it in nearly twenty years . . .

'It is you, isn't it? I'd recognize that walk anywhere.'

Slowly Catherine turned around. Her jaw slackened and fell open. Standing there was her past, in all of his six-foot-four glory. More muscular than when she'd last seen him, the thick dark hair, strong jaw and arresting green eyes were still the same. His once-perfect nose was now slightly bent and battle-scarred, but the imperfection only enhanced his ruggedness. There was the beginning of a six o'clock shadow on his chin. In contrast to the dinner jackets around him, he was dressed in a paint-splattered T-shirt and jeans, a pair of well-worn Timberland boots on his feet. Somehow, he still looked at ease in the opulent surroundings. As he shifted slightly, Catherine saw a glimpse of a powerful, tanned thigh through a rip in his jeans.

Catherine took an involuntary step backwards.

'John? John Milton? What are you doing here?' She knew her tone wasn't friendly.

Despite this, John Milton gave an easy grin. 'I'm working.' He waved an apologetic hand over his garb, 'Hence the outfit.'

'You're a painter?' Catherine asked stupidly.

John smiled again. 'No, I'm in the building industry. We've had a big contract down here, and I've been doing a few last-minute jobs.'

'Oh,' said Catherine. She felt at a loss for words. Despite standing nearly six feet in her heels John Milton towered over her.

'You're clearly not in a manual labour job,' he said drily, appraising her dress. Somehow his gaze wasn't sleazy like the bouncer's had been.

'I edit a magazine. We're hosting a party here to-night.' Out of the corner of her eye, Catherine could see some of her team arriving, along with a few other faces she knew. A few were looking over at her with interest. Shit!

'Which one?' John asked.

'*Soirée*,' Catherine said. She was feeling more un-nerved by the second.

John shook his head. 'Never heard of it, I'm afraid.' Catherine's eyes darted back to the entrance. 'Look, I'm obviously keeping you . . .'

She jerked her head back. 'I've got to go and meet the VIP guests.' She started to edge away. John studied her, a hint of amusement in his eyes.

'Don't let me stop you.' He held out his hand as a friendly farewell. Catherine hesitated and took it. A jolt of electricity seemed to pass between them. Catherine snatched her hand back awkwardly.

'Anyway, John, it was good to see you.'

He looked at her steadily. 'It's been good to see you, too, Cathy.'

Her stomach dropped again, she hadn't been called that in two decades. 'It's Catherine, actually,' she told him coldly, looking over one of his broad shoulders. 'I really must go.'

John stepped back. 'Of course, have a good night,' he paused, 'Catherine.'

'Ooh, who was that hunk?' asked *Teen Style*'s editor Fiona MacKenzie when Catherine ran into her a few moments later. 'He's a dead ringer for Clive Owen!'

'What? Oh, just someone I used to know,' said Catherine casually, even though her heart was hammering.

Fiona raised one expertly plucked eyebrow.

'Maybe you should get to know him again, darl. Is he single?'

'I have no idea, and I'm not interested,' Catherine said abruptly. A look of surprise crossed Fiona's face, and Catherine tried to lighten the moment with a smile. 'Sorry, Fi, I've just got a million and one things to think about tonight. Would you excuse me? I need a quick drink of water.'

As she gripped the bar for support, Catherine's heart was pounding. It felt as though the rug had literally been pulled out from underneath her. John Milton! What was he doing here? The mere mention of a name she had thought was dead and buried – Cathy – had brought it all rushing back. Taking a deep breath, she tried desperately to keep a jumble of confused, unwelcome memories from crowding into her mind.

They'd first met at school when they were eleven years old and had been thrown together in a science lesson. She was the withdrawn, lanky one who always seemed to be tripping over in netball practice and spent every break and lunchtime by herself. He was the handsome, confident, popular rugby captain worshipped by pupils and teachers alike. But despite their differences, they'd clicked. They'd been friends at first, until the tentative blossoming of romance: a snatched kiss at the rec, illicit embraces in John's bedroom while his parents were out. Then, when they were sixteen, and Catherine's world had already been torn apart for ever, they'd slept together.

Not long after that, something had shifted between them and they had grown apart, and it was only a few months later that Catherine had left Newcastle for the bright lights of London and a stellar career in journalism. From then on, she had had little time or inclination to think about John Milton. Catherine had honestly thought she'd never lay eyes on him again. He knew things about her that had to stay dead and buried.

'A large vodka tonic,' she told the barman. She needed something to calm her down. The chemistry she'd felt when they had shaken hands had both terrified and excited her. John Milton was part of a life that no longer existed. He knew who she was – no, who she had *been*. If anyone ever found that out, Catherine would be ruined. It was that simple.

A light hand on her shoulder raised Catherine from her anguish.

'Someone's got a lot on their mind,' said a smooth, chocolatey voice.

Catherine turned round to see the upright figure of Tolstoy Peake. They kissed on both cheeks.

'You look as gorgeous as ever,' he said. 'Chanel, isn't it?'

'Right as always,' she smiled. 'I've never known a straight man who was so into his labels.'

Tolstoy smiled back, flashing perfect white teeth. In fact, everything about him was immaculate. Descended from Italian aristocracy, forty-four-year-old Tolstoy Peake was very much the dashing man about town. Health editor of an upmarket men's magazine called *Finesse*, Tolstoy's body was a temple. He was teetotal, ran ten miles daily and had a better manicure than Catherine's. Olive-skinned and dark-haired, Tolstoy had a certain charm, and was often seen in the pages of *Hello!* escorting some Russian beauty or another to a glamorous do. Catherine always thought he was a little too clean-cut and anally retentive for her taste.

'Ready for your ball, darling?' he asked, summoning the waiter over with a little hand gesture. 'Evian please. Make sure the glass is clean.'

Catherine looked around. 'Just about, apart from some minor drama with the harpist, apparently.'

Tolstoy's dark eyes sparkled. 'Attention to detail; you've always had it, Catherine. In your parties, your magazine . . .' his eyes looked over her again, '. . . and your outfits.'

'Enough with the compliments!' she laughed. In the background Harriet caught her eye surreptitiously and waved her checklist.

Catherine touched Tolstoy's arm. 'Anyway, will you excuse me? I've just got to check with my PA about something.'

He stepped aside. 'Of course. We must do dinner soon.'

'Fabulous,' said Catherine, and hurried off, all

thoughts of John Milton mercifully forgotten for the moment.

Two hours later, the party was in full swing. Fashionable, well-dressed people were crammed wall-to-wall, waving champagne glasses about as they air-kissed furiously. Amongst the sea of faces were several A-list actresses, a few cool London pop stars, and a big-name Italian designer who had especially flown in from Milan for the occasion.

Once she knew that everyone had turned up, and they weren't going to run out of champagne, cocktails or canapés, Harriet started to relax. She had pulled it off!

'Great party, H,' said Saffron. They were standing by the bar with a cocktail each, observing the melee.

Harriet let out a sigh of relief. 'Phew, am I pleased! No one told me organizing parties was such hard work.'

Suddenly Alexander descended on them like a vision. His silk pantaloons were tucked into black leather riding-boots and his flowing white shirt was unbuttoned virtually to the waist. Even in the dimmed lighting, Harriet could see he had almost returned to his normal colour.

'Tan corrector. The beauty girls dug it out for me,' he whispered. 'Fuck, darlings, I thought I'd have to go into hiding!'

Harriet laughed. 'Well, we're really pleased you've made it.'

Tom Fellows from the art desk had joined them. His hair was its usual tangle of dark curls, but he'd traded his standard shapeless T-shirt and jeans in for a garish seventies-style shirt with matching kipper tie and unflattering tight trousers. They made his feet, encased in policeman-style black shoes, look like German

U-boats. With a pang, Harriet realized Tom had tried to copy the art director's smart, cool ensemble – and failed miserably.

'Good party,' he muttered, looking at the floor.

Saffron looked at Harriet, raising her eyebrows slightly. She debated whether to ask Tom if he wanted to join them for a drink. What if someone she knew saw him with her? Luckily, she was saved from her dilemma.

'I'm just going to look at the insect section,' Tom mumbled, and shuffled off.

'Goodness, he's a funny one!' exclaimed Alexander.

Over the other side of the room Catherine had been talking to Valour's chief executive, who'd told her he loved the redesign and to 'hang in there'. Her pleasure had been short-lived, as she'd then got stuck in a long, intense conversation with the MD of one of the companies that had joined *Soirée* Sponsors. He had just spent the last fifteen minutes interrogating her about the future of *Soirée*, and Catherine was starting to tire of constantly being on the defensive.

Alexander walked past. 'Al!' she exclaimed brightly. 'Do excuse me,' she said to the MD. 'I've got some extremely important business to discuss with my fashion director.'

She dragged Alexander over to the bar. 'Bloody hell, I thought my ear was going to fall off, he was bending it so much.'

'Have you seen, Isabella Montgomery's here! And Vanessa Cunningham, her frightful old crone of a fashion editor. I swear she hasn't eaten for the last century.' They looked over to where an anorexically thin woman was standing, black hair pulled back from her gaunt face. She saw Alexander, muttered something to the person next to her, and then waved at him.

'Darling! You look radiant!'

'You too! We must do lunch!'

'What the fuck is Isabella doing here?' asked Catherine. But before Alexander could answer, a tiny figure in a long, tight red dress had materialized beside them.

'Cath-a-rine!' cried Isabella, standing on tiptoes to air-kiss her. 'How nice to see you!' She looked Catherine up and down. 'Chanel, isn't it? Last season?'

Alexander smiled sweetly. 'I'll leave you ladies to it,' he said and floated off.

You little shit. You'll pay for that, thought Catherine.

'Wonderful turnout!' Isabella cried. Her blue eyes widened. 'Of course, you must be awfully upset that Helen Mirren and Kate Moss couldn't make it. But then again *Soirée* doesn't quite have the cachet to pull in the really big names, I suppose.'

Catherine gritted her teeth. 'They're both out of the country at the moment,' she told her.

'If you say so!' Isabella said gaily.

Catherine couldn't work out what she was doing here, Isabella certainly hadn't been on the guest list. The other woman seemed to read her mind.

'I'm Teddy Barsmann's plus one,' she breathed. 'Ted and I go way back, he's simply a poppet.' Teddy Barsmann was an extremely rich American financier who owned, amongst other properties around the world, a twenty-million-pound townhouse in Belgravia. He was also seventy-eight, four times divorced, and Isabella's latest lover.

Isabella tilted her head on one side and looked at Catherine.

'How *are* you?' she said, trying to sound sympathetic, and failing miserably.

'Great, thanks for asking,' Catherine told her, looking

round for an escape. The familiar irritation Isabella brought out was starting to creep over her like poison ivy.

'One does have to keep up appearances, I agree,' Isabella said. 'For the sake of the team, and all that. Of course, if I'd decided to take the job editing *Soirée* in the first place, it wouldn't be in this mess now.'

She knew she shouldn't rise to the bait, but Catherine couldn't help it. 'I think we both know that's a lie, Isabella,' she snapped. 'I don't know if you've turned up tonight purely to crow over *Soirée*'s sales figures, but you're wasting your time. We're doing fine. Now, if you don't mind? I've got other people to talk to.'

The mask of benevolence dropped momentarily from Isabella's face.

'You *really* don't want to cross me, Catherine.' Her voice was low and quiet, like a hiss. 'You may think you're something special just because you've got *Soirée*, but I wouldn't be so pleased with myself, I really wouldn't.'

Catherine's annoyance was quickly turning into anger.

'Isabella, why don't you get a life? Then you wouldn't have to spend so much time being interested in mine.'

Isabella narrowed her eyes. 'Don't test me, Catherine. I make it my business to know about other people's lives.' She smiled nastily. 'I've found it's come in rather handy when I need things to go to my advantage.'

Catherine didn't bother hiding her distaste. 'You really are a piece of work, aren't you?'

Isabella's smile widened. 'I must say, darling, you're being awfully defensive. Have you got some skeletons in *your* closet you don't want me to find out about?'

Catherine couldn't help stiffening, and Isabella

noticed. 'Oh, I've hit a nerve there, haven't I? Who would have thought it? Miss Goody Two Shoes has a dark past!'

Somehow Catherine managed to keep her composure as she looked down at her rival.

'Isabella, why don't you do us both a favour and fuck off?'

With that, she walked off, one ankle turning over just ever so slightly.

Chapter 24

The party was a huge success. The next day, pictures of the celebrities and high-profile socialites who'd attended were splashed all over the London newspapers. Catherine had also been in talks with one of the national papers, who wanted to run yet another two-page article on *Soirée* Sponsors; and as she sat in her office the next morning, she was delighted to see it had gone in. After her confrontation with Isabella, the night had, thankfully, gone in a more positive direction. She had even persuaded several more influential industry people to sign up to *Soirée* Sponsors.

Harriet, meanwhile, was the heroine of the office. She had been quite overcome when Catherine had presented her with a huge bouquet of flowers at the end of the night.

She was just about to turn her computer off when Saffron bounded across.

'I completely forgot, haven't you got a date this week?'

Harriet blushed. 'Tomorrow, actually. I'm meeting him at eight o'clock in a pub on the Fulham Road.' The Fulham Road was one of the most famous streets in south-west London, and its pubs heaved with a curious mixture of antipodean backpackers and Sloaney men and women every evening.

'Tarquin, wasn't it?'

'Thomas.'

Saffron looked at Harriet's computer screen. 'Let's see a picture. He's got an online profile, right?'

Harriet nodded and pulled up the Chapline website. Moments later, a picture of a blond, heavily tanned man with swept-back hair appeared.

'What do you think?' Harriet asked hopefully.

With his toothy smile and suggestive wink, he reminded Saffron of Lord Flashheart out of *Blackadder Goes Forth*, but she wasn't going to tell Harriet that.

'What does his profile say?'

Harriet clicked on another icon and the details came up.

Name: Thomas Ford-Bugle
Age: 34
Sex: Yes please!!
Lives: Fulham, of course!
Occupation: MD of my own hugely successful
    headhunting agency.
Interests: Game birds (of the human variety – only
    joking, ladies!!), rugby, drinking games, rugby . . . er
Ideal woman: Someone with a good sense of humour
    and an even better pair of hooters!! Ha ha ha
    ha!!!!!!!!!!!!

'He's not like that once you get talking,' Harriet said hurriedly when she saw Saffron's face. 'I told him in one of my emails my dream was to go and help build school classrooms in Uganda, and he replied saying he'd just spent six months in Peru building a village, complete with running water, for a local tribe facing extinction!' She looked at the photo again. 'I suppose that's why he's got such a good tan.'

Saffron looked at Thomas Ford-Bugle's pampered, self-indulgent face and thought his tan was more likely to have come from a booze-filled jaunt to some *castello* in Tuscany with his toff friends than any benevolent urge to save the planet, but again she didn't say anything. She only hoped Harriet's good nature wasn't about to be taken advantage of.

'Oh darling, I'm not sure.'

In Churchminster, Freddie leaned back against the Aga, a glass of Merlot in his hand. It had suddenly turned very chilly, and the huge fireplace that dominated one wall of the kitchen glowed orange, casting out delicious warmth. Angie got up from the table and went to throw another log on it.

'It would only be for a few months, Freds, and I do need a spare pair of hands in the shop. You're always saying I should get someone else in.'

Freddie still looked dubious. 'Where's this fellow going to live?'

Angie stoked the fire, her back to him. 'I thought he could stay in the granny annexe.'

Freddie sounded rather shocked. 'You want him to stay *here*? We can't let a complete stranger into the house! And from what you tell me, he comes from quite a troubled background. I've only just got over Archie's MC Hammer phase.' A few years ago their son Archie had dropped out of college to smoke drugs, and begun talking like a Harlem rapper. It had caused his parents no end of trouble.

Angie came back and sat at the table. 'Freds, not all young people are like that. Besides, Archie's fine now.'

Freddie grumbled something about his eardrums and loud music.

'He won't be in the main house, so we won't hear any music he wants to play,' soothed Angie. 'Come on, Freds, this scheme sounds like such a good idea, and one does like to give something back. Won't you even think about it?'

Freddie sighed. 'All right. But don't get all carried away and start planning things.' He stopped. 'What's this young chap's name again?'

Angie tried to hide her grin; she knew the battle was nearly won.

'It's Ashley. Ashley King.'

NOVEMBER

Chapter 25

Saffron's head was aching. She'd had a shit day: her interview with an American pop star at a suite in the Ritz had been delayed for three hours. When she'd finally got in there, the singer's control-freak press officer had insisted on sitting in on the interview and butting in every ten seconds, telling Saffron she couldn't ask that question or that question. Saffron had only just stopped herself grabbing the PR by her skinny arm and manhandling her out. To make matters worse, Annabel had called in sick for the third day running, but then changed her Facebook status to say she was looking forward to her date with a man called Barnabus that evening. Saffron didn't know if Annabel was just plain stupid, or simply couldn't resist the chance to show off the fact someone actually found her attractive. Saffron was seriously considering putting in a complaint to Catherine, but her boss seemed so preoccupied and stressed at the moment, she didn't know how well it would be received.

It was 9 p.m. by the time she got home to Montague Mews. Velda was out seeing a play with friends, and the house was dark as she let herself in. Dumping her bag at the bottom of the stairs Saffron wearily tramped through to the living room. As she switched on the light by the door and light flooded the place, she screamed. Lying expectantly on the sofa opposite was Fernando, wearing nothing but a huge smile.

'Hey, baby!'

Saffron clutched her heart and collapsed in the chair opposite. 'Fucking hell, Fernando! You nearly gave me a heart attack. What are you doing here?'

His smile dropped slightly. 'I thought you'd be pleased to see me.'

Saffron's breathing started to return to normal. She picked up Velda's latest copy of the *Spectator* and threw it at him.

'For God's sake, sit on this. I don't think Aunt Velda will want to know you've been lounging on her sofa with your meat and two veg out.'

Fernando sat up, looking rather hurt. 'What's this? I thought it would be a sexy surprise for you. Don't you fancy me any more?'

Saffron looked across the room. The rippling muscles that had once been so irresistible now seemed insignificant. All Saffron could think was how silly he looked.

'It's not that,' she sighed. With one bound, Fernando was across the room and crouching beside her.

'What is it, then?' He sounded panicked.

Saffron thought fleetingly of his squalid flat, with skid-marks down the toilet and stale milk in the fridge. Fernando had been spending more and more time at Montague Mews, eating Velda out of house and home. The few times Saffron had tried talking to him about getting a proper job, he had changed the subject. He was on to a good thing here, and knew it. Suddenly, Saffron couldn't stand his freeloading a moment longer.

'Look, babe, it's been great and everything, but I don't think this is working.'

He looked shocked. 'Of course it's working! Come on, baby, we have fun, don't we?' His tone was almost wheedling.

'Life's not just about having fun, Fernando!' Saffron cried, rather surprised at herself. 'Don't you want a career or anything? To earn your own money?'

'Ah! So this is what it's about!' he said sulkily. 'You don't love me any more because I'm not rich enough for you.'

'That's ridiculous!' she shot back. 'I've been paying for everything since we've started going out. You don't have to be rich, Fernando, but it would be nice if you put your hand in your pocket now and again.'

'It takes time!' he said huffily. 'Once I get into acting school, I just know someone is gonna give me my big break. One day, baby, I'll be richer than you can ever imagine . . .'

Saffron had heard it all before. She had a career and life to get on with.

'Fernando, there's no easy way of saying this. It's over.'

He gave a scandalized gasp. 'You're *dumping* me?'

'I'm afraid so.'

He jumped up angrily, grabbing a cushion to preserve his modesty. 'Let me tell you, no one dumps Fernando Romero!'

Saffron stood up. 'I'm afraid they just did.'

His handsome, vain face tightened. 'You think you're such a hot pot, but you'll never get anyone better than me.'

Saffron didn't rise. 'I'll leave you to get dressed.' She went to touch his arm, but he pulled it away as if he'd been scalded.

'Don't touch me!'

'Fine,' Saffron sighed. 'Don't forget to leave your key on the coffee table on your way out.' She left the room and went up to her bedroom.

A few minutes later the whole house reverberated as Fernando slammed the front door angrily. Saffron closed her eyes, but found she felt only relief, not sadness. She didn't care how sexy he had been, she was never going near such a waster again.

'Darling, it's me.'

'Hullo, Granny Clem!' Caro put Milo down and watched, exasperated, as he scampered out of the kitchen. For the last ten minutes she had been trying to get him to eat his bowl of spaghetti hoops, but they seemed to have ended up everywhere but his mouth.

'You sound a bit harassed.'

Caro flopped back down at the breakfast table. 'Just giving Milo his lunch. It's not proving a great success, I'm afraid.'

'Let him go without.' A steely note entered her grandmother's voice. 'That's what I used to do when your father tried to play up. He soon came around. Anyway, I wanted to make sure you're all still attending Bonfire Night . . .' The village was putting on a fireworks display that Saturday in a field at the back of Clementine's house.

'Yup, still coming!' Caro had already told her grandmother this about ten times.

'Excellent. Ted Briggs is in charge of the fireworks display, and Jack and Beryl are putting on a marvellous spread out of the pub kitchen.'

'What time does it start, again?'

'It says on the ticket I sent you. Six o'clock. Sharp.'

Caro smiled to herself. Her grandmother's

organization of village events was meticulous. Her father Johnnie had often joked that Clementine was wasted on Churchminster and should be out commanding the British army.

'See you there, Granny Clem. We won't be late, I promise.'

In the *Soirée* office, Catherine was responding to a pile of emails she'd been putting off when Harriet called through.

'I've got John Milton on the line.'

Catherine's heart leapt up into her mouth. What was he doing calling?

'Thanks, Harriet, can you put him through?'

There was silence for a few seconds. 'Hello?' said Catherine cautiously.

'It's John.' His mere presence at the end of the line seemed to fill the very room.

'John. Hello! What can I do for you?' Her voice was unnaturally high.

'How did the party go?' By contrast he sounded relaxed and confident.

'Good,' Catherine said. She knew she sounded curt, but couldn't help it.

'I'm sure you're really busy, so I won't keep you.'

Catherine interrupted. 'I am, actually.'

'Good for you.' Was that a soft chuckle at the other end? John continued. 'If you're available, I was wondering if I could take you out for dinner next week.'

'Well . . . er,' she stuttered. She hadn't been expecting this.

John didn't say anything, which added to her discomfort.

'The thing is, I'm really snowed under at the moment.'

'Then the least I can do is take you out. You must need a night off.'

Catherine felt she was being backed into a corner.

'I'm seeing someone!' she blurted.

When John answered, he sounded amused.

'I didn't assume that you weren't.'

Catherine cringed at herself. Why was she acting like such an idiot?

'Look, John . . . it's nice of you to ask, but I'm afraid I can't.'

'Take my number, anyway,' he said lightly. 'If you do change your mind about meeting up with an old friend, give me a shout.'

After a second's agonizing, Catherine grabbed her pen and took it down. After she had practically hung up on him, so desperate had she been to get off the phone, Catherine put her face in her hands and groaned. What a neurotic fool he must have thought her! As much as she tried to wish he hadn't called, Catherine could feel a churning in her stomach that wasn't entirely unpleasant.

'You're not going, end of story,' she said to herself, out loud. Screwing up the Post-it note the number was written on, she leant down to throw it in the bin, but something stopped her.

'Oh, for fuck's sake!'

Opening her drawer, Catherine threw the crumpled piece of paper in the furthest corner before slamming it shut again.

Chapter 26

Caro was unloading the dishwasher when the doorbell sounded. 'I'll get it,' Benedict called from the next room. He was working from home. Caro heard footsteps across the wooden floor, and the front door open. There was silence for a few seconds, then Benedict's voice rang out, loud with shock.

'My God, what are you doing here?'

Caro stopped what she was doing.

'Benedict, is everything all right?'

There was a pause. 'Yes, it's fine. Caro, come out. Amelia is here!'

Caro's eyebrows shot up. 'Oh my goodness! What a lovely surprise! Amelia, you should have told me you were coming . . .' As she walked into the living room her words trailed off. Now she could understand why Benedict had sounded so strange.

Twenty-eight-year-old Amelia Towey stood next to her brother. Or at least, a shadow of the tall, vivacious girl Amelia used to be. Her face was pale and wan, her sparkling eyes dulled. Her hair, normally a glossy brown mane, hung drab and lank around her shoulders. As Caro stepped forward and hugged her sister-in-law, she could feel beneath the long, cashmere cardigan just how thin she'd become.

Amelia gave a small smile. 'Sorry to turn up out of the blue like this. I've quit my job and decided to come back to the UK for a bit.'

Caro glanced at Benedict, concerned, then back at Amelia. 'I'm sorry to hear that, it sounded like you were having such fun out there.'

Amelia shrugged. 'I can always get another PA job. Besides, Russia wasn't all it's cracked up to be.' She seemed to be avoiding their eyes.

Caro wasn't quite sure what to say. 'Well, it's lovely to see you, anyway.' She noticed Amelia's suitcase by the door. 'Er, is this a flying visit?'

'Actually, I was wondering if I could stay for a while.'

Caro looked at Benedict. 'Here?'

Amelia flushed slightly. 'Yes, but don't worry if it's not convenient. I know it's very short notice . . .'

'We'd love to have you!' Caro said happily. Amelia smiled for the first time, looking a little like her old self again.

'If you're sure? I'll pay rent and housekeeping.'

'Don't be ridiculous,' said Benedict. 'Our home is your home, you know that.'

'That's settled, then!' declared Caro. 'Benedict, if you get Amelia's suitcase, I'll show her to her room. It really is a darling place, I think you'll like staying here.'

Caro and Benedict were due to be having dinner with Stephen and Klaus that evening. They offered to cancel, but Amelia would hear nothing of it, assuring them that she was fine, and just needed an early night.

'She looks terrible, I'm really worried about her,' said Benedict. They were standing in the kitchen, talking in low voices. 'Do you think she's ill or something?'

'She could just be run down,' said Caro. 'It does sound like she's been burning the candle at both ends for quite a while now.'

'I don't know . . . there's something different about her,' he said. Caro tried to reassure him.

'Darling, I am sure Amelia just needs a bit of rest and relaxation. I'll make sure I feed her up.'

Benedict's expression turned less serious. Caro's cooking skills were a subject of much mirth in the family. 'Christ, I don't know about that. We want to build my sister up, not kill her off.' He sidestepped deftly as Caro went to hit his arm.

'I've found out some rather fascinating things about our very own Rowena,' announced Stephen as he poured everyone another glass of excellent peppery red wine.

'Ooh! Is she harbouring a dark secret?' Caro asked.

'More like harbouring half of London!' Stephen said. 'I met this delightful chap at an antiques fair last week. Eighty-two and still as fit as a fiddle.' He sighed dramatically. 'One can only hope to be in half as good shape when one gets to his age . . .'

Klaus's dark eyes twinkled under their heavy brows.

'Anyway,' Stephen carried on, 'this chap is a water-colour dealer, an exceptionally good one as it happens. Many years ago Rowena's father was one of his main clients. He was an Elgin, you know.'

'Didn't they used to own half of Chelsea?' asked Benedict. 'I read something about it.'

'And the rest!' said Stephen. 'At one time, they were so rich they made the Windsors look like street urchins.'

'Did this dealer ever meet Rowena?' asked Caro.

'Once or twice. Rumour has it her father was very protective and didn't like her going out,' said Stephen.

He studied his wine glass. 'Apparently she was rather a beauty in her day. All the young bucks were queuing up, but Rowena wasn't allowed to see any of them.'

'What about her mother?' Caro was fascinated.

'Died in childbirth. From what this chap tells me, there were no brothers or sisters either. And then Pa Elgin departed this mortal coil, leaving Rowena . . .'

'All alone,' Caro finished. 'Oh, poor woman!'

Stephen arched one eyebrow. 'Hardly the adjective one would use. It seems our dear neighbour is sitting on a veritable goldmine!'

'You're not going on some kind of humanitarian mission to rescue Rowena, are you?' Benedict asked Caro later, as they were getting ready for bed.

'I wouldn't dream of it,' said Caro, pulling her night-shirt over her head. 'I just feel sorry for her. When I look around at you and Milo and Granny Clem and Mummy and Daddy . . . I just know how much nicer life is when there are people you love in it. Rowena's got no one!'

Benedict came over and kissed the tip of her nose. 'And that's one of the reasons I love you, because you care about people. But I think you should leave Rowena to her own devices; she's survived perfectly well until now.'

Caro sighed. 'You're right, I've got to stop poking my nose in.' She went to pull the curtains shut. Despite the late hour, the consultancy room opposite was ablaze with fluorescent light.

'Those poor doctors work hellish hours,' Caro started to say, when a weedy figure appeared in the middle of the room. She blinked. Work had clearly finished a long time ago. The same man she'd seen before was standing there, head bowed, wearing nothing but a black leather pouch and a studded dog collar. Caro's mouth dropped open as a hulking figure emerged from the side of the room. She was holding some kind of long, black whip . . .

'What on earth's the matter?' asked Benedict in confusion, as his wife let out a squeak and ran into the bathroom.

Chapter 27

For once, Harriet had decided not to go back to
Churchminster and she and Saffron were attending
the fireworks display in nearby Battersea Park
instead. Harriet felt a bit bad about not going home,
but Christmas was just round the corner. She missed
her parents dreadfully, but when she'd phoned her
mother earlier that week and heard a huge commotion
in the background as Ambrose had tripped over one
of the dogs and gone flying, whisky and all, she had
decided that London was a lot more peaceful for the
time being.

Caro had asked Amelia if she wanted to go to
Churchminster with them, but she'd turned the invite
down. The three of them were now standing in the
kitchen. Even though it was nearly midday Amelia
was still in her silk pyjamas and looked like she had no
intention of changing.

'Are you sure we can't tempt you? Beryl Turner's
harvest pie really is quite something,' Caro said.

Amelia looked apologetic. 'Thanks, but I think I'll
still pass.' A flash of disappointment crossed Benedict's
face. Amelia noticed and smiled at him. 'You two go,'
she urged. 'I've still got to unpack.'

'Well, if you're sure . . .' Benedict replied.

'Sure I'm sure. Go have fun!'

Benedict walked over and kissed his sister on the cheek. 'I think everyone's away this weekend, so you'll have the mews to yourself.'

Caro thought she saw Amelia stiffen. 'This place has got a burglar alarm, hasn't it?' Amelia asked.

'And security lights, and ten-foot walls, and an impossibly difficult entry system,' Benedict said. 'No one's getting in here unless you want them to.'

A full moon shone down on Churchminster as Caro, Benedict and Milo left Mill House later on. It was a clear fresh night, millions of stars glittering in the velvet sky above. As they made their way across the green towards Fairoaks, the front door of one of the neighbouring cottages opened and two figures shuffled out. It was the elderly Merryweather sisters, two spinsters who had lived in the village for as long as Caro could remember.

'Evening, Dora, hello, Eunice!' Caro called.

'Caroline, dear!' they chorused. 'How nice to see you!'

'Here, let me take that,' Caro said, walking over to relieve Eunice of her large straw basket.

'Thank you, dear,' said Eunice. 'Oh, there's Benedict! And Master Milo!'

Milo blew a big raspberry at her.

'Please excuse Milo's manners,' said Benedict drily. 'Eunice, Dora, how are you both?'

The sisters looked up at him and swooned. 'Very well, thank you for asking.'

Dora turned to Caro. 'You've got a handsome one there!'

'Flattery will get you everywhere, ladies,' said

Benedict, as he offered them both an arm. 'Shall we?'

Twenty minutes later the party had only got as far as the other side of the green. Dora and Eunice tottered along, holding on to Benedict and pointing out every bit of vegetation.

'Look at those blackberries, Dor!'

'They're a bit late in the season, Eunice! I should have put them in that cake.'

'What have you got in the basket? It's very heavy,' said Caro. She was walking ahead hand in hand with Milo, and even he was starting to strain ahead.

'Just our supper, dear!' Eunice called out.

Caro turned around. 'There's going to be food there, you needn't have done that.'

'Yes, but we know what we like, you see,' said Dora. 'All this hot and spicy stuff plays havoc with our stomachs. We've got more than enough, you're welcome to have some.'

Caro lifted the tartan rug covering the top of the basket. They must have been preparing it for days, she thought, as she saw the pork pies, sticky buns and cucumber sandwiches with the crusts cut off. Eunice pointed at a tartan-patterned flask wedged in one corner.

'Have some, dear. It'll warm you up.'

'Oh, thank you, but I had a coffee before I left the house,' Caro said. Eunice and Dora looked at each other and giggled. 'It's a bit stronger than that!'

Caro pulled the top off and sniffed. Her eyes started watering. 'Is that whisky?'

'Bell's finest!' Dora said. 'We like a little winter warmer.'

'There must be a whole bottle in here!' Caro spluttered.

Dora's eyes twinkled. 'Two, actually. We always save a bit for the journey home.'

Caro suddenly had a vision of finding two pairs of Nora Batty legs sticking out of the ditch later. Benedict's eyes met hers through the dark, and she bit her lip to stop bursting into laughter.

'There you are!' Clementine exclaimed, when Caro and Milo eventually walked in the front door. The large house was teeming with people, and several burly men Caro didn't recognize were tramping through the house carrying boxes of what looked like fireworks.

'We ran into Dora and Eunice . . .' Caro said apologetically, as the ambling trio appeared at the end of the garden path. A loud crash sounded from the back garden.

'Oh, do try to be careful!' called Clementine. She turned back to Caro. 'Ted Briggs has enlisted the help of his building friends for the fireworks display. Frightfully nice chaps, but one fears they are a little heavy handed.' Another even louder crash reverberated through the house. Clementine winced.

'I'm sure you've got it all under control,' Caro said as she made her way into the kitchen.

'Evening, troops!'

Angie looked up, her face red and shiny from the heat of the oven. 'Darling!' She rushed over and the two women hugged warmly. Angie stepped back and looked at Caro. 'There's something different about you. Have you had your hair done?'

'No, I was actually just thinking in the car that I ought to get it cut. It's riddled with split ends.'

'Nonsense, you're glowing,' Angie laughed. 'I thought all that pollution was meant to play havoc with one's complexion.'

'I didn't look that great this morning – when I had

205

Milo's Rice Krispies in my hair,' smiled Caro. She turned to the busty, dark-haired woman, who was deftly transferring the contents of a cooking pot into a large serving bowl.

'Hullo, Beryl!'

The landlady of the Jolly Boot looked up and flashed her big smile. 'Hello, Caro! Got the family down with you?'

As ever, Beryl was dressed up to the nines in high heels, a black knee-length skirt, and a tight-fitting satin blouse. Her nails were red and long, and huge diamanté earrings swung from her ears. In her mid-forties, anyone else would have been in danger of looking like mutton dressed as lamb, but somehow Beryl carried it off. Jack and Beryl had run the pub for years, and had a formidable but fair reputation. Their teenage daughter Stacey, who took after her mother in the chest department, worked behind the bar.

Benedict walked into the kitchen carrying another box of fireworks. 'I've put him to work already,' cried Clementine, efficiently shepherding Milo in behind. 'Do come and look at the bonfire, darling. Ted and the others have done a marvellous job.'

'OK, if you're sure I can't help . . .' Caro said.

'Go,' Angie replied. 'We're nearly done.'

Caro and Milo followed Clementine out of the kitchen door and down the long stone path. The way had been lit by dozens of tall garden candles, flames flickering in the gentle breeze. Over the hedge at the bottom, Caro could see an orange glow, spreading upwards into the darkness. As they got closer, the spit and crackle of the bonfire could be heard over the hedgerow.

'Fire! Fire!' shouted Milo.

'Good Lord, I hope we haven't produced the family's

first pyromaniac,' said Clementine, as she opened the small gate. 'Well, here we are.'

They were in the large field that backed on to Fairoaks, and in the far right corner a huge bonfire was starting to take on life, the orange flames twisting and growing. At the top was the stuffed figure of Guy Fawkes, dressed in an old jacket and trousers, a cream cowboy hat on its head. A few men were standing back, admiring their handiwork, and Caro recognized the short, portly figure of Freddie Fox-Titt.

'Evening, all!' He walked over. 'What do you think? I'm rather pleased with our efforts!'

'You've done a marvellous job,' Caro said. She looked down at Milo, whose little eyes were goggling at the spectacle.

'It's nice for young ones,' Freddie replied, eyes shining. He had a smudge of something black on his cheek.

'Liar,' Caro told him, smiling.

Everyone really had pulled the stops out. As well as the pièce de résistance, which was burning away merrily, there were several long trestle tables piled high with tureens of fragrant chilli con carne, sausage casseroles, harvest pies, and bowls of steaming hot jacket potatoes. People were lining up to help themselves, muffled up in jackets, scarves and hats. In the far corner Caro could see dozens of rockets stuck in the earth, ready to be lit and shot into oblivion.

They had a good turnout too: there had to be at least two hundred people there. As well as all the villagers, Caro spotted a few faces she knew from Bedlington and the surrounding villages. Even Sir Ambrose and Lady Fraser had come, both looking immaculate in matching tweeds. They were standing rather stiffly on the edge of the crowd, Ambrose looking grumpier than ever. Frances spotted them and gave a relieved wave.

'I say! Caro!'

Freddie left to fetch something from the house, and the little group made their way over.

'Bonfire looks marvellous!' Frances congratulated Clementine.

'Yes, doesn't it?' she agreed. 'Fred and the boys have done a splendid job.'

'Wish I'd known about it, there's a load of old fencing I could have got rid of,' grumbled Ambrose. 'Blasted stuff is lying about the estate, clogging everything up.'

Frances rolled her eyes. 'Ambrose, do go home if you want.'

'What's that?' he growled.

'Go home! You clearly don't want to be here.'

'Don't be so bloody stupid. I'm not leaving you to walk home by yourself.'

'I don't mind walking,' Frances started to say, but he waved her off impatiently.

'I'm staying, and that's final!'

'He wants to watch the fireworks, even though he says they're just for children,' Frances told the others.

Ambrose stared grumpily into the distance and pretended not to hear.

Frances looked over at Angie. 'Has Freddie come round to the *Soirée* Sponsors idea?'

Angie grinned. 'We had a setback the other day, when Freds found one of those Rizla papers from Archie's unfortunate phase down the back of the sofa and nearly changed his mind, but I think we're nearly there.'

Frances looks confused. 'What's a *Rizla*?' She made it sound like a score from a classic Italian opera.

Angie hesitated. 'Well, er, it's what young people use

to . . .' She stopped. 'Oh, forget it, darling, you don't need to know.'

Caro realized she needed the loo, and, leaving Milo in Angie's capable hands, wandered back to the house. On her way, she bumped into Clementine coming down the path.

'Everyone seems to be having a good time, Granny Clem!'

Her grandmother smiled. 'I was worried the higher ticket prices would put people off, but we've completely sold out. Mind you, it is for a good cause.'

'Which charity is it this year?' asked Caro. Clementine was an ardent fund-raiser. Over the years the village's efforts had helped many causes, from starving Third World countries to the World Wildlife Fund and a local bird sanctuary.

'Frances Fraser gave me the idea, actually. Have you heard of *Soirée* Sponsors?'

'Of course, that's the magazine Harriet works for!' exclaimed Caro. 'You know the Fox-Titts are thinking of getting involved? Angie might be getting a young chap from London to help in her shop.'

'Indeed,' said Clementine. 'Frances has been talking about the scheme for months; she's been very impressed with the way they run things. Coming from a charity connoisseur like Frances Fraser, that's high praise indeed. So I decided to find out more, and Harriet put me in touch with a very able woman called Gail. She sent me an information pack, and I must say I've been thoroughly impressed with the whole organization.'

'Good on you, Granny Clem,' said Caro fondly.

'It's a worthwhile cause to donate to,' the older woman replied briskly. 'We may live in the country, darling, but it doesn't mean we all drift around in an idyllic rural bubble!'

Just then Ted Briggs's voice boomed out over the megaphone, 'Right then, everyone, the fireworks display is about to start! Stand back behind the safety ropes!' A frisson of anticipation ran through the crowd. Above their heads Caro could see Milo, hoisted high on Benedict's shoulders and wriggling with excitement. She went over to stand between them and the Fox-Titts. Freddie had a tray of plastic wine glasses filled with Jack Turner's Bonfire Punch. He offered one to Caro, but she turned it down.

'No thanks, Freddie, I don't really feel like it.'

Benedict raised an eyebrow. 'Are you ill? I've never seen your mother turn down a drink before,' he added in a mischievous voice to Milo. Caro pulled a face at her husband, but she had been feeling a bit peaky recently. There was a spate of illnesses at Milo's nursery at the moment; she hoped she wasn't coming down with something.

Freddie took a sip of his drink. 'Bloody hell, this stuff is strong,' he spluttered. 'What's in it?'

Angie laughed. 'Knowing Jack, everything!'

Someone behind them shouted. 'Look, the guy's caught fire!' The flames had finally worked up to claim their victim.

'Hold on a sec, that hat looks familiar!' exclaimed Angie. She turned to Freddie indignantly. 'Freds, how could you? I only bought that for your last birthday.'

Freddie's face burned the colour of the bonfire. 'Sorry, old thing,' he blustered. 'We needed a hat and well, that one's just a bit too much. Made one feel like bloody J. R. Ewing.'

Luckily Freddie was saved from further reproach by a loud WHOOSH as the first rocket went up and exploded in a ball of light and colour above them. The crowd oohed and aahed, and Milo's eyes nearly popped out on stalks. For the next ten minutes they were treated to a visual extravaganza as Catherine Wheels, whizz-bangs and squealers went up one after the other.

Afterwards, as the last streak of colour faded from the sky, everyone stood around chatting or made their way back to the buffet tables.

Caro started to feel very odd. It was as if the firework display was continuing in her head, as bright lights danced past her eyes, and pins and needles pricked at the back of her lids. The ground suddenly became wobbly under her feet. She tried to clutch on to Angie.

'Caro? Are you OK?' she heard her say. Then Angie's voice and everything else was rushing away as Caro's knees buckled. Just before she went into a dead faint, she was vaguely aware of a strong pair of arms catching her.

Caro felt something cool and wet being pressed against her forehead. She opened her eyes and looked up into Benedict's anxious face. He was tenderly wiping her with a flannel.

'Thank God you've come round, I was so worried,' he said. Clementine and Angie were standing behind, looking equally concerned.

'I've called the doctor,' Clementine said. 'He should be here any minute.'

They were in the large, wood-panelled dining room at Fairoaks. Caro struggled to sit up on the chaise longue, but Benedict gently pushed her down again. 'Stay there, darling,' he said, his voice soft but firm.

'I'm fine!' she protested. 'I just felt a bit woozy. Really, I don't need a doctor.'

'Sweetheart, you went down like a sack of potatoes!' said Angie. 'Thank heavens Freds was there to catch you.'

The front door bell clanged.

'That's Doctor Bond,' said Clementine, as she went to answer it.

Caro looked at Benedict and Angie. 'Really, I'm fine!'

A few moments later Clementine re-entered the room with a tall, silver-haired man wearing an immaculate navy-blue suit. Dr Bond ran his private practice from a very plush surgery in Cheltenham, and had been the Standington-Fulthrope family doctor for years.

'Hello, Caro, got yourself in a spot of bother?' he said, kneeling down beside her. He laid his hand against her face and then held her wrist to get a pulse. He glanced up at Clementine and Angie. 'Would you mind leaving us?'

'Of course,' said Angie, and both retreated, leaving Caro and Benedict with the doctor.

Caro repeated herself. 'I'm OK, honestly, I just had a bit of a funny turn.'

Doctor Bond got out his thermometer. 'You look all right to me, but let's make sure.' He stuck it in her mouth for a minute and then looked at the reading.

'Temperature's OK. Pulse is a bit slow, but that's to be expected under the circumstances. Everything else seems to be in order. Is this the first time this has happened?'

Caro looked sheepish. 'Actually, no. I have been feeling a bit faint recently, but I just put it down to tiredness.'

Benedict looked worried. 'Darling, you never said . . .' Caro squeezed his hand apologetically.

Doctor Bond studied her. 'How about your periods? Are they regular?'

Caro thought for a moment. 'I am rather late, but my periods are always irregular. I mean, I'm not on the pill at the moment . . . it took so long to conceive with Milo I haven't really been thinking about it . . .' she trailed off and looked at Benedict. His face was beginning to show both shock and elation. 'Oh my God!' she gasped. 'Do you think . . .'

Doctor Bond snapped his black medical bag shut. 'I think you need to do a pregnancy test as soon as possible. Then ring up my secretary and book yourself in for an appointment.'

To their astonishment and delight, Caro was twelve weeks pregnant.

'I still can't believe it!' she exclaimed as she and Benedict left Doctor Bond's surgery on Monday. 'But then again, I haven't had morning sickness like I did with Milo. I have put on a bit of weight round my tummy, but I just thought I'd been eating too much.'

'I hadn't noticed,' said Benedict gallantly.

'I know it sounds strange,' Caro said thoughtfully, 'but I do feel pregnant now. Somehow it's different from when I was carrying Milo. Of course, I was overjoyed then, but I did feel anxious and worried the whole way through. And there was Sebastian . . .' she trailed off. 'Maybe, deep down, I knew I was pregnant but I didn't want to admit it to myself. Maybe I was scared I'd equate it with a time when I was miserable. Not about having Milo, of course,' she added quickly. 'It was just, you know . . .' She paused. 'But it's not like that this time, not at all. Now I just feel excited and full of hope. Oh, Benedict, we're having a baby!'

He stopped and pulled her in close, cradling her face in his hands.

'You and Milo are the best thing that has ever happened to me,' he whispered. 'I promise to be the best father I can to our baby. I love you, Caro. I love our baby. I love you all more than anything in the world.'

Her eyes filled up, and the pair embraced passionately. A car drove past and beeped.

'Get in there, my son!' shouted a male voice.

'Bugger off,' murmured Benedict, as he started kissing Caro again.

Chapter 28

Everyone was over the moon at their news. 'I knew you looked different!' shrieked Angie. Caro's mother, Tink, burst into floods of tears when she phoned, and lost the power of speech, so Caro's father had to take over the call.

Both Caro's sisters called too: Calypso from her mobile in what sounded like a very loud nightclub. 'Like, that is so fucking cool!' Camilla managed to make contact on a very crackly line from an ashram in Peru before the phone went dead.

Doctor Bond had advised rest for Caro, so Benedict called into work and they stayed on at Mill House for a few days longer.

When they eventually got back to Montague Mews on the Wednesday, a garish-coloured 'Congratulations' banner was hanging across their front door. Stephen popped round shortly after to own up.

'Sorry it's so ghastly, but I didn't find out about the good news till this afternoon, and the corner shop was the only place I passed on the way home.' He shuddered. 'I wanted to get you a card as well, but everything they offered seemed to involve ample-chested women dressed as French maids, or gorillas riding a tricycle.'

Amelia was waiting when they walked in, with champagne and flowers. 'That is such great news! Congratulations, guys.'

'Thanks, little sis,' replied Benedict, kissing her on the cheek, just as Milo gave a wail and threw Pickles on the floor. 'Uh-oh, it's someone's bedtime,' said Benedict. He leant down and scooped the little boy up.

'Thanks, darling, I'll be up in a minute,' said Caro, and flopped down on the leather sofa. Amelia sat down in the chair opposite. 'Those flowers are beautiful! You shouldn't have,' Caro said.

Amelia smiled. 'It was the least I could do. Besides, I'm looking forward to becoming an aunt for a second time.'

'Did you manage to find everything you needed?' Caro asked.

Amelia nodded. 'Yup, I just chilled out. Watched television, sent a few emails, that sort of thing.'

'Are you going to catch up with your London friends?'

Amelia shrugged evasively. 'At some point. I just feel like keeping a low profile at the moment, you know? Sometimes it's nice just to hide away.'

'To get away from it all,' said Caro, thinking she had never known Amelia to shun the company of others.

Amelia nodded vigorously, as if Caro's words some- how validated everything. 'Exactly!' The landline rang, making Amelia jump. Caro glanced curiously at her as she went to answer it.

'Hello? Hello?' she said. There was no one there. Shaking her head, Caro put the phone down. 'Must be a wrong number.'

Milo started crying upstairs, and as Caro went to placate her son, she failed to notice the sudden change in Amelia. Every drop of blood had drained from her face as she sat there, as still as one of Velda's sculptures.

The *Soirée* team were in the final throes of the Christmas issue, due on magazine stands at the start of December. Three down, three to go. Optimism was cautiously high, and everyone agreed this latest issue was even better than the last. Adam emailed Catherine the mid-month audit of how the on-sale November issue was selling – and it was up by at least 20,000 copies. A great start, but as Catherine told herself, it was very early days yet. Even if circulation did continue to rise, would it be enough to save them? The young British actress they'd chosen as their cover star for the December issue was talented, opinionated and the right side of cool. Definitely *Soirée* material – but she still wasn't Savannah Sexton.

'Just keep on plugging away,' Catherine urged Annabel and Saffron. The former had looked singularly unimpressed at the suggestion, and Catherine had felt a surge of irritation, both at herself and her features editor. How had she let such a lazy, unmotivated woman on to her team? Afterwards, she had taken Annabel into her office and given her short shrift.

'You may think it's a waste of time still going after Savannah Sexton, but I don't,' she'd told her. 'So I'd appreciate it if you showed a little more willingness and enthusiasm.' *Like Saffron, the person you are meant to manage and inspire*, she'd wanted to add, but she'd held her tongue.

'Yes, Catherine,' Annabel had replied sulkily, before returning to her desk to get back on Facebook.

Catherine knew she was being snappy, but she couldn't help it. As much as she tried to push it to the back of her mind, her encounter with John Milton had turned her existence upside down. Just the sound of his name had provoked a sort of chemical reaction in her. She was unnerved by just how attracted she had been to him in that brief encounter, but she knew any further contact would be deadly. Catherine couldn't even contemplate her past being dredged up again. There was far too much at stake.

But then again, she couldn't blame everything on John Milton. Catherine wasn't a fool. Even before he had materialized in her life again, she had known she was fighting off memories that refused to be banished, usually by way of a bottle of Sauvignon Blanc or two. She'd always been able to manage it all before, but now it was as if a fast-forward button had been pressed and she was on the slippery slope to God knows what. For Catherine, who had been tightly in control for all of her adult life, it was a terrifying sensation. It was like she had suddenly become a stranger to herself. But then again, who was she, really? Although she knew she shouldn't let Isabella's threat bother her, Catherine had been shaken to the core by it. What if Isabella did actually start digging around for her secrets? Several times, Catherine had woken from the same nightmare, soaking wet with perspiration.

For Christ's sake, you're pathetic, she found herself thinking one evening, as she stood looking out across the London skyline, glass of wine in one hand. *How have you let yourself get like this?* The glass suddenly slipped out of her hand and smashed on the wooden floor.

'Shit!' cursed Catherine. Swaying slightly, she went to get a tea towel from the kitchen.

The next day, slightly fuzzy-headed, Catherine was editing a six-page special on *Soirée* Sponsors to go in the Christmas issue. She had decided it was perfect timing. The charity had just been put up for another award, and media interest was at an all-time high. As well as photographing some of the scheme's success stories in a glamorous, *Vanity Fair*-type photo shoot, Gail had also agreed to a photograph and interview about her work.

'As long as you don't put me in a poncy dress,' she'd told Catherine. Catherine had laughed out loud. 'As if we'd dare!'

There was a knock at the door. 'Come in,' called Catherine.

Harriet peered round at her. 'There's a John Milton to see you.'

Catherine's face turned ashen. 'Here, now?'

'Er, yes,' Harriet replied. 'Reception called. Shall I send him up?'

Catherine deliberated wildly for a second, and then decided the private confines of her office would be far better for a meeting with John Milton than anywhere near the two gossipy Valour receptionists.

'Yes, do that,' she told Harriet. 'Can you meet him by the lift and bring him through?'

Catherine quickly opened her drawer and got out a small hand mirror. She looked OK, a bit tired, but she quickly ran a brush through her hair and applied a coat of lip-gloss. Immediately annoyed at herself for making the effort, Catherine shoved the mirror back in the drawer. Her stomach had shrunk into a ball of nerves.

A minute later, there was another knock. 'John Milton,' Harriet announced.

Catherine got up to welcome him, but not before noticing every female in the office was staring at this tall, dark, handsome stranger. Across the room Alexander raised an impressed eyebrow at her. Catherine ignored him as she shut the door.

She stood awkwardly, not quite knowing what to do.

'Please, take a seat,' she told him.

John folded his long body comfortably into the chair opposite Catherine's. He looked like a different person from the one she'd encountered the night of the *Soirée* party. The paint-splattered jeans had been replaced by smart navy ones, and he was wearing a well-cut double-breasted wool coat. It looked like Armani, thought Catherine, as she went round to her side of the desk. Why did that surprise her?

'Sorry about turning up like this, I hope it's not a problem.' Charisma and self-assurance radiated off him.

'I was just doing a bit of work,' she said stiffly.

John smiled. 'Well, quite. This is your office.' There was that slightly playful tone again . . . 'Anyway, I'll cut to the chase,' he continued. 'I know you're very busy, but I'd still like to take you for dinner. How about tomorrow?'

Catherine felt a stab of relief. 'I have a work function.' At least that wasn't a lie: she was hosting a dinner at an exclusive members' club for existing businesses involved with *Soirée* Sponsors.

'Thursday?'

She scrabbled desperately for an excuse. 'It's just very short notice . . .'

John Milton stood up decisively. 'I'll take that as a yes, then. Do you know Duvall's?'

'Yes, it's meant to be excellent,' she replied in astonishment. Duvall's was a very expensive French restaurant just off Piccadilly. It had only opened recently, but the chef was something of a legend, and already it was nigh on impossible to get a table.

John grinned down at her. 'I can get us a table for eight thirty. Shall we meet in the bar for a drink before?' This time, Catherine had no excuses.

A moment after John had left, Alexander bounded in. 'Ooh! Wasn't he that divine fellow from the party?'

'I don't know what you're talking about,' Catherine said, shuffling a pile of papers on her desk.

'Rubbish! He's that Clive Owen look-alike I saw you talking to! Did he come in to ask you out?'

'No!' It came out as a shout, and Alexander looked rather taken aback.

'Sorry, darling, I didn't mean anything by it.'

Catherine tried to compose herself. 'Haven't you got any work to do?'

Chapter 29

Catherine was on edge. Her meeting – she refused to think of it as a date – with John was in thirty-one minutes. Everyone had left for the day, and the office was empty as she stood in front of the fashion cupboard's full-length mirror. Deciding what to wear had been tricky. She hadn't wanted to go over the top and give him the wrong impression. After much more deliberation than she'd originally intended, Catherine had chosen her new black Joseph trousers, mid-height Kurt Geiger heels, and a silk jersey vest from Calvin Klein. A delicate wristwatch, stud earrings and an Anya Hindmarch clutch bag provided the only accessories. She gave herself a final once-over and, satisfied, gathered up her things to leave the office.

She still wasn't sure why she was going. After all, it wasn't as if she could start a relationship with John Milton. Getting close to someone messed you up and made you vulnerable, two emotions she had no intention of ever feeling again. As she got out of the cab outside the restaurant, Catherine was tempted for a moment to jump back in and drive away. *It's not too late to change your mind*, she thought, but by then the doorman had pulled open the door to welcome her in.

She found herself in a small, intimate bar with dark panelled walls and a low ceiling. It reminded Catherine of a gentlemen's drinking club, the masculinity softened by the exquisite watercolours hanging on the wall and the huge vase of white lilies on the desk at reception. In the far corner, a small, neat man in a dinner jacket played elegantly on a grand piano. Almost immediately a waiter appeared from nowhere and helped her out of her belted cashmere Burberry trench coat. John was already out of his seat, taking long strides towards her.

'You look great,' he told her. The waiter bowed politely and melted away. Putting his hand on her bare arm, John guided her back to the table. Catherine found her heart leaping at his touch. She forced herself to look at him. He was freshly shaved, and his hair looked as if it had been cut since she last saw him. He was wearing a well-cut dark-grey suit with a black shirt underneath. They both looked like Gucci. As he went to pull her chair out, Catherine noticed he was wearing a Tag watch they had featured in a fashion shoot a few months ago. She recalled it had cost over three thousand pounds. Builders were obviously doing pretty well for themselves these days, she thought, at the same time registering that he wasn't wearing a wedding ring.

A glass of beer stood barely touched on the table. 'What can I get you?' he asked.

Catherine studied the wine list and made her choice. Another waiter materialized to take the order.

John took a sip of his drink. 'How's work?'

'God, don't ask,' Catherine said. She changed the subject. 'How's yours?'

John shrugged. 'Busy. We've just taken on this new contract. We're working all hours, getting as much as we can done before the bad weather sets in.'

'Oh,' Catherine said. She hoped he didn't expect her to hold a conversation about spirit levels.

Another silence, but John didn't seem bothered by it. Catherine looked desperately around for her drink. To her relief, the waiter was making his way over, a glass of white wine held aloft on his tray. He set it down on the table and Catherine immediately took a sip, the familiar silky liquid travelling down her throat and spreading through her like a comfort blanket.

She looked at her watch. It was nearly eight thirty. 'Shall we go through?'

John stood up. 'After you.' He kept a respectful distance behind, but Catherine still imagined she could feel the heat from his body.

The lights in the restaurant were turned down low, casting a soft glow on the starched white tablecloths. Diners sat close together deep in conversation, occasionally laughing in low voices. The food looked delectable. John Milton certainly knew his restaurants, thought Catherine. She found herself again surprised at his choice, but then, what had she been expecting? A meal for two at Burger King?

'I recommend the scallops to start,' he said as the waiter pulled out their chairs.

'So you've been here before?' she asked.

He grinned. 'More than I should in the time it's been open. Good food is my weakness.'

Without looking at the list, John ordered a bottle of wine from the waiter. Catherine realized she hadn't had lunch, and the alcohol was heading straight to her head. Once they had ordered their food she tried to be more conversational.

'So you're a builder?'

'Yes and no,' he said. 'I actually own a construction

company, and am more involved with the management side of things. I just help out when the guys need an extra hand. To be honest, I really enjoy getting stuck in. Makes me realize why I got into the business in the first place.'

'What's the name of your company?' Catherine said out of politeness. It wouldn't mean anything: her and John Milton's worlds were poles apart.

'Castlegate,' he replied. 'I don't know if you've heard of it.'

Catherine couldn't hide her surprise. 'Actually, I read something about it in the *Financial Times*. Haven't you been brought in to take over building the Olympic Village?'

The deal had made the national news a few days running. Castlegate was one of the biggest, most respected construction firms in the South East. Their appointment to the beleaguered site on the outskirts of the capital had brought sighs of relief all round.

'We're not doing the whole project, but yes. Signed the contract a fortnight ago.'

'Slightly bigger job than the Natural History Museum,' she said.

John chuckled. 'Just a bit. I prefer working on the older buildings, though. London's got some of the most beautiful architecture in the world.'

Their starters arrived, but Catherine wasn't hungry. Sitting so close to John was making her stomach twist into knots. It wasn't just his physical size: there was a strength about him that just radiated out. In a room where they were surrounded by fat, red-faced bankers, John Milton oozed raw, rugged manliness. Judging by the eyes that kept flickering in his direction, the other female diners had noticed as well.

'How did you get that scar?' Catherine asked, looking at his eyebrow. John raised his hand and touched it briefly.

'Rugby. That's where the broken nose came from as well. Luckily I seem to have escaped the cauliflower ears.'

'You always loved your rugby,' she smiled. It was the first time she had referred to their past. If John was surprised or pleased, he didn't show it.

'Lived, breathed and ate it. I had trials for Newcastle when I was nineteen, but a right ankle smashed in four places put paid to any dreams of playing professionally.'

Catherine found herself glancing at his shoulders and arms, large and muscular under the fabric of his shirt.

'You look like you still work out,' she said, then cringed madly. That sounded like the worst kind of chat-up line!

John Milton surveyed her across the table. There was a definite hint of amusement in his eyes. Catherine looked away and feigned interest in a painting on the wall.

'Aren't you hungry?' he asked. Catherine stared down at her plate, which had barely been touched. 'I had a late lunch,' she lied.

The waiter came to clear their plates. 'How long have you been in London?' John asked when they were alone again.

'Twenty years, give or take a month or two. God, that makes me feel old.'

'Do you miss Newcastle?'

Catherine stiffened. 'No,' she said shortly. 'Leaving was the best thing I ever did.' To her relief John steered the conversation back to safer waters.

'I still go back. To see my mum. She's retired now, I don't know if you remember she was a teacher?'

Catherine didn't know why she said it, she was so desperate to put distance between herself and the place. 'Shouldn't that be yer *mam,*' she asked mockingly.

John Milton gazed at her steadily. 'I'm not ashamed of where I come from.'

Shame burned through her. At that moment their main courses arrived.

'Can we order another bottle of the same?' she asked the waiter desperately.

For a few moments, they ate their food in silence. Catherine's sea bass was wonderfully moist and light, but she could barely swallow it.

'Look, sorry about that comment,' she said awkwardly. 'I shouldn't have said it.'

John shook his head. 'Don't worry.'

The meal carried on, and Catherine began to relax. Despite her earlier reservations, she was finding John easy to talk to. He asked intelligent questions about her job, and seemed genuinely interested in *Soirée* Sponsors. Catherine was also becoming conscious of a charge running through the air. *Is it just me or does he feel it too?* she wondered uncertainly. John had been nothing but the perfect gentleman. Emboldened by the alcohol flowing through her veins, she strayed into new territory.

'Are you married?'

He put down his knife and fork. 'I had a long-term relationship that finished eighteen months ago. I've pretty much been on my own ever since.'

Catherine wryly thought someone as attractive as John Milton could never be short of female company.

'What happened?'

John shrugged. 'The same old story: we just wanted

different things. Ariana loved the high life, and wasn't too impressed when I came home covered in muck after a day on site. Whereas I didn't want to spend every evening drinking champagne and hearing who'd got what in the latest high-profile divorce. I wish her well, though; I hear she's married to an American financier now. Got an apartment on Fifth Avenue and a two-hundred-foot yacht, amongst other things.' He chuckled. 'Ariana had an admirable talent for always getting what she wanted.'

As he leant forward to fill their water glasses, his knee brushed hers. Catherine's stomach clenched.

'How about you? You said you were involved with someone?' he asked, placing the bottle back on the table.

Catherine had forgotten about that. 'Oh, it's nothing serious,' she said evasively. 'I'm so busy with work, you know how it is . . .'

The waiter came over to ask if they wanted to see the dessert menu. Catherine declined, so John asked for the bill. When it came she tried to put her card down, but John got there first.

'Please, my treat.'

As they stood up, Catherine realized how much wine she'd consumed. They'd had two bottles with dinner and she must have drunk most of it. Concentrating on her step, she made her way out of the restaurant towards the cloakroom. Her heels suddenly felt like they were eight feet high.

Outside, it was bitterly cold. Buses filled with night-shift workers and people on their way home from an evening out rumbled past. A rowdy group of twenty-something men and women, all dressed in suits and on the tail-end of their work drinks staggered by, trying to find a late-night bar.

Catherine looked at her watch; to her surprise it was nearly half past eleven. Suddenly, she lost her footing and stumbled backwards.

John took her arm. 'Are you OK?'

'Bloody shoes,' she muttered.

A black cab approached and John flagged it down. 'Where are you going?'

Catherine told him her address.

'I live that way. Why don't we share a cab back? We'll drop you off first.'

The car pulled up and they got in. John issued directions to the cabbie, and sat back as they started towards Battersea. Even through her cloud of drunkenness, Catherine was still aware of the sexual energy that surged around them.

A few minutes from home the driver took a sharp turn. The sudden movement caused Catherine to slide along the seat into John.

'Sorry about that!' the cabbie called back cheerily.

Catherine barely heard him. It was as if everything had suddenly come into focus. Her body was pressed against John's, and she was acutely aware of every muscle and hard contour. Catherine felt a throb of long-dormant desire. She savoured the moment, drawing in the warm scent of his aftershave.

As the car pulled up to her apartment block, she didn't move.

'Would you like to come in?' Embarrassingly, she found herself tripping up on the words. She'd drunk too much again.

John turned to face her. He was so close Catherine could feel his breath on her cheek. He was going to say yes . . .

'I've got a really early start in the morning,' he murmured.

Catherine burned with the shame of rejection. What had she been thinking? She leant across and tugged at the door handle.

'Of course, goodnight,' she said hurriedly, and got out. John started to say something, but Catherine interrupted.

'Thanks again for dinner.'

She pushed the door shut. Not pausing to look back, she fled inside the building, past the bemused concierge and into the lift. As the doors slid shut, Catherine leant against the wall. She was breathing heavily.

'Well, that was cool,' she said out loud. 'Shit, shit, shit!' She didn't know whether she was more furious at her lack of self-control or the fact that, in that moment, she'd wanted him so badly.

Going out with John Milton had been a horrendous mistake. It was one she had no intention of repeating.

Chapter 30

Two weeks later Caro had her first scan at the private wing of the Chelsea and Westminster Hospital. To her and Benedict's elation and relief, everything was fine.

Benedict put a protective arm round his wife as they made their way out.

'I'm pregnant, not terminally ill,' she told him fondly. He had started treating her like a piece of china, and it was all she could do to stop him employing a full-time housekeeper.

He gave a rueful smile. 'I'm being overprotective, aren't I? It's just that you and this baby are so important . . . I'd never forgive myself if anything happened.'

'Nothing is going to happen, darling.' She squeezed his hand. 'People get pregnant every day.'

'But not with my baby,' he pointed out.

She laughed. 'I should bloody hope not!'

That evening Benedict had a client dinner to attend. Velda had asked Caro over to hers for a simple supper, extending the invite to Amelia, who'd declined.

'Benedict's rather worried about her,' Caro confessed to Velda as they sat in her cosy dining room eating a delicious lamb tagine. 'She looks so thin and pale, and she's barely left the house since she came to stay. You'd never know it to look at her normally, but Amelia suffers terribly from depression. She's told Benedict she's having another bout, and he's awfully upset as he feels he should be able to do something.' Caro sighed. 'It's hardly a surprise the poor girl gets like this, considering what the family has been through.'

'They lost their parents in a car crash, didn't they?' asked Velda. 'How desperately sad.'

Caro nodded. 'Amelia was only young at the time, and it fell to Benedict and his twin brother Harry to look after her. It was a dreadful time for all of them.'

'I didn't know Benedict had a brother!' said Velda. Caro's face changed.

'He's dead as well, now: bacterial meningitis.'

Velda looked shocked. 'Oh, how awful!'

'It really was, especially as he and Benedict had fallen out at the time.' Caro hoped Velda wouldn't press it any further. It really was awkward to explain that the reason they weren't talking was because Harry had run off with Benedict's first wife, Caitlin. It was an area of Benedict's life he still found it difficult to talk about, even with Caro.

Velda, as perceptive as ever, murmured her sympathies and moved the conversation on, telling Caro about her plans for Christmas. She was flying out to Morocco for two weeks to see Yousef.

'Sounds super,' said Caro. 'I hear the climate is glorious this time of year. What's Saffron going to do?'

'Actually, she'll be in your neck of the woods. Harriet's invited her back to stay in Churchminster.'

'At Clanfield Hall? How marvellous!' exclaimed Caro. She laughed. 'I hope Harriet pre-warns her about Sir Ambrose. He's not a bad sort, but he can be rather temperamental at times.'

'I think she's more worried about what clothes to take,' smiled Velda.

'Are her and Fernando still off?'

'Yes, I have to say I was rather sceptical when she said she was swearing off men. But there's been no one since. She's been really focused on her job.'

'Good on her,' said Caro.

'Quite. I wouldn't be surprised if she was made editor of something one day, she's certainly got the talent. More tagine?'

Caro looked at her stomach, which was now sporting a little bump. 'Yes, please. I won't use the eating-for-two line, though. I'm just greedy.'

She watched as Velda spooned more of the casserole from the terracotta pot on to their plates.

'I really don't want to pry,' she said when Velda sat down again. 'But I just wondered about Saffron's parents. Isn't she seeing her mother for Christmas?'

Velda paused. 'Unfortunately, I can't ever see that happening.' She smiled wryly. 'We've got a few family dramas of our own. Did you know about Saffron's father?'

'Harriet did mention it to me,' Caro admitted.

Velda put her fork down. 'That was Harry Walden, the famous yachtsman? I don't know if you've heard of him.'

'The name rings a bell . . .'

'It's probably a bit before your time,' Velda smiled. 'Harry was the superstar of his day in the sailing world. Won dozens of major races. Of course, he loved the glamour of that set. All those parties, women throwing themselves at him . . . He met my sister – Saffron's mother – at Cowes, when she was down there painting. Belle fell completely head over heels in love. She fell pregnant with Saffron after a year, but by then Harry's eye was already wandering. He left them both when Saffron was six months old.'

'Poor girl,' said Caro, putting her fork down.

Velda nodded. 'Saffron was the casualty in the whole sorry mess. I'm afraid Belle has never been good with the reality of day-to-day life, and after Harry left she went to pieces. Could barely look after herself, let alone a daughter. Saffron was packed off to boarding school at age five, and went home to her mother in the holidays, but it wasn't easy. In a funny way, I think each blamed the other for Harry leaving. Saffron idolized him, you see, wouldn't hear a word said against him. When he died in the sailing accident, you can imagine how traumatized she was.'

'When did she come and live with you?'

'Just after her thirteenth birthday,' replied Velda. 'By then things had broken down so irrevocably between her and her mother, there was no other choice. At first it was a culture shock, as much for myself as for Saffron, but we got on with it. Now, I couldn't imagine her not being a part of my life.' A sadness entered Velda's eyes that Caro hadn't seen before. 'Do you know what's the worst thing of all? Belle has missed out on seeing such a spirited, funny, talented – infuriating at times – girl growing up. I know what joy Saffron has brought to my life. How can my sister not feel that void?'

'Are you still in contact with her?'

'The odd phone call or card. It's difficult. She's not a bad person, but I can't condone what she did. Besides, I dread to think what would happen if Saffron knew we'd met up. She'd feel dreadfully betrayed.'

'It must be hard for you, though. No matter what she's done, she's still your sister,' Caro pointed out.

Velda looked away. 'Sometimes in life you have to make difficult choices.'

'Do you think they'll ever be reunited?' asked Caro.

Velda was quiet for a moment. 'I would love nothing more. But in my heart of hearts I think irreversible damage has been done.' She paused. 'Caro, I would love to share something with you. To be honest, it has been playing on my mind ever since you moved here, and now I just don't know what to do.'

'Is it something I've done?' Caro asked in alarm.

'Gosh no! I love having you here. Sorry, I didn't put that very well.' Velda sighed. 'Oh, I don't know if it's fair to burden you with it.'

'Hey, we're friends. You can tell me anything.'

Velda smiled, her green eyes crinkling up at the corners. 'I know. You've become a good friend to me, Caro. In fact, maybe it's better at this stage I don't drag you into it. But I might need your support in the future.' Her face looked serious again. 'You see, I am allowing something to happen that could have dreadful repercussions.'

'I'm always here for you,' Caro told her, wondering what on earth Velda had done. Whatever it was, it didn't sound good.

Chapter 31

Harriet was in the middle of Catherine's expenses form when a new email popped up in her inbox. She looked at the name in surprise: Thomas Ford-Bugle. Harriet felt a rather unpleasant lurch in her stomach. Saffron's prediction had unfortunately come true: her date had been a disaster.

There was no denying that Thomas, with his superhero physique and pale blond hair, swept proudly back over his head, had been good-looking. But he'd also turned out to be a total nightmare. After mysteriously turning up with a green-and-white striped golfing umbrella, even though it was a hot and sunny evening, Thomas had taken Harriet to an Italian round the corner, where he had ordered for both of them without even asking, and then proceeded to talk about himself non-stop for three hours. When Harriet had tried to escape outside afterwards, pleading a headache, Thomas had leapt on her and stuck his tongue in her mouth, like an eel that'd been kept in a tank of liquid Viagra. Harriet had managed to push him off and jump in a cab. She hadn't heard from him since. Heart slightly in mouth, Harriet clicked on the email.

Hi sexy! Been away in Belize scuba-diving, thought you might like to see my tan!

With a feeling of foreboding, Harriet opened the accompanying attachment. There stood Thomas, legs astride and hands on hips, completely naked. Even worse, he had the most enormous erection.

Someone cleared their throat behind her. Harriet jumped guiltily and swivelled round. To her mortification, it was Adam Freshwater, his eyes fixed, limpet-like, on her computer screen.

'Oh!' she squeaked.

Adam looked rather unsettled. 'Where's Catherine?'

'She's in a meeting with marketing,' Harriet stuttered.

'OK, I was just passing through. Can you tell her to give me a call?' Adam lowered his voice. 'Look, Helen . . .'

'It's Harriet,' she said apologetically.

'Oh. Right. Well, look, Harriet. I don't really think you should be looking at that sort of thing in work time. The company has a very strict policy about using pornographic sites.' Adam eyed her sternly. 'I'll ignore it this time, but don't let it happen again.'

As he walked off, Harriet, overwhelmed by shame, buried her face in her keyboard.

Catherine returned from her meeting twenty minutes later. 'Are you feeling all right?' she asked her PA, who was still as white as a sheet.

'Never been better,' replied Harriet faintly, and passed on Adam's message.

Catherine thanked her and went into her office. For once, work wasn't at the forefront of her mind. It had been four days since she'd gone out with John Milton, and she'd been mercilessly beating herself up ever since. He hadn't tried to make contact with her, but then again why would he? She'd got drunk and made an ill-advised pass at him, which had been rebuffed. Christ knows what he thought of her.

It's best this way, Catherine consoled herself. *You know you can't start anything with him.* But deep down, she was gutted he hadn't called.

Her phone rang, startling her. Adam. It felt like he was calling her every five minutes at the moment, he must have realized his job was as much on the line as the rest of them.

'Hi, Adam, what can I do for you?' she asked wearily.

A chuckle sounded at the other end, followed by the now familiar deep voice. 'Sorry to disappoint, it's John.'

Catherine sat bolt upright in her seat. John! 'Hi!' she said, trying to sound nonchalant. 'How are you?'

'I'm great. Thanks for a nice evening last week.'

Well, that's a lie, she thought. He'd obviously called out of some misplaced sense of duty.

'I'd really like to see you again.'

Catherine was so surprised, she didn't respond.

'Are you still there?'

'I'm here,' she told him.

'What do you think?'

Catherine wanted to say no so badly, but found that she couldn't.

'My treat this time. How are you fixed for Friday?'

It was 10 p.m. and Catherine had spent an hour luxuriating in a long hot bath, trying not to think about John Milton. Eventually, when the water had turned cool and her skin wrinkly Catherine reluctantly climbed out and dried herself off. What she really fancied now was a nice nightcap. She went to put on her silk kimono, but it wasn't in its normal place on the back of the bedroom door. After looking around everywhere for it, she remembered she had spilt coffee on it at breakfast, and for some reason had thought it would be a good idea to hang it on the balcony to dry.

'Bollocks,' cursed Catherine. She'd meant to get it in before she'd left for work; it had probably been ravaged by the November temperatures and ruined by now. Still naked – no one was going to see her thirty floors up – she darted across the living room and opened the door on to the decked balcony that ran the full length of the room. The kimono was hanging on the back of the wooden sunlounger she kept out there. Catherine walked over and picked it up, but just then a huge gust of wind came from nowhere and blew the garment out of her hands and straight over the balcony.

'Shit!' shouted Catherine, as she watched the kimono float away like an exotic butterfly across the grey skyline. That thing had cost her a fortune from Liberty's. Sighing, she turned back to the door.

Except that it had swung shut behind her, and was securely locked.

'Fuck! Oh shitting bollocks, open!' wailed Catherine, but it was to no avail. After five minutes of frantic pushing and pulling, the door remained firmly stuck.

In desperation, she looked around. She was butt naked, hundreds of feet up in the air, and it was freezing cold. Her mobile was lying tantalizingly on the coffee table just a few feet away through the glass window. She couldn't even ring for help. What was she going to do?

Looking round the balcony, something caught her eye. As she squinted in the gloom, she saw a Hermès towel lying behind a pot plant in the corner. She'd forgotten it was there, left over from sunbathing in the summer. Catherine retrieved it and shook it, grimacing as a dead spider fell out. Then she wrapped the damp material round her and tried to think rationally.

She was stuck on her balcony with no way of getting back in. So, she had to come up with another strategy, and that meant climbing over her neighbours' balcony and praying they were in. The neighbours were a haughty looking couple called the Edgar-Phillipses. They were in their late sixties and the concierge had told Catherine he was a retired army brigadier who spent most of his time at his private members' club in Pall Mall. Catherine had only exchanged pleasantries in the corridor with them, but even so, they had definitely struck her as a pair who would not be impressed by her sudden arrival, semi-naked, in their living room. Still, needs must, and – steeling herself – Catherine moved forward. The two balconies were only a foot apart, but one false move and she would fall to her death. Heart hammering, she climbed up on the sunlounger and slowly swung one leg over into next-door's balcony.

'Don't look down, don't look down,' she repeated to herself like a mantra. She looked down. 'Oh Christ!' she moaned, feeling sick with terror. The pavement seemed like an eternity away, and a little group of people had gathered to watch, clutching each other and pointing upwards.

The wind howled past, and she almost lost her balance. She screamed, and, with one last effort, hurled herself forward. She was aware of a loud ripping noise as the towel got entangled with the sunlounger and was pulled off her.

Catherine tumbled to the floor in a heap, gasping and sweating. She'd made it! As she lay there shivering, the realization dawned that she was not alone. She blinked into the light streaming out from the other side of the glass door, where four people now stood open-mouthed. Two were the Edgar-Phillipses, he in a navy blazer and war medals, she in an old-fashioned evening dress. The third person was a tall, thin lady with a disapproving look on her face. The fourth person . . . Catherine had to look once, twice, a third time at the fourth person to see if this really was happening to her.

There, in a smart black evening jacket, curling his lips, was Sir Robin Hackford.

After what seemed a lifetime, the men looked away. In a futile attempt to preserve her modesty Catherine scrambled behind the nearest thing to hand, which was a miniature wheelbarrow filled with stone ornaments and flowers. The two women carried on staring in horrified fascination, as if Catherine was some kind of foreign species they had just captured in a net.

'I've locked myself out!' she shouted helplessly. The women looked at each other and said something. Mrs Edgar-Phillips disappeared. A minute later, she returned with a hideous nylon floral dress. The door opened a fraction, and the dress was held out.

'Here,' she said imperiously. 'Come in when you've made yourself decent.'

Thirty seconds later, Catherine was inside but beginning to think the balcony was a better place. She had obviously interrupted a dinner party: silver cutlery and a candelabra stood on the table, while the port had just been brought out.

'So the door locked behind you, Miss Connor, and all your clothes just fell off?' asked Sir Robin coldly. He sounded entirely unconvinced.

'No, I was naked already,' she said. All four of them

looked at each other. 'I'd just got out of the bath,' Catherine offered lamely. 'Bloody door, I've been meaning to get it fixed for ages now.' *God*, she thought, toes curling up inwardly in horror, *get me out of here!*

'Robin, how do you know this woman?' asked Sir Robin's wife frostily.

He looked at Catherine with distaste. 'Ms Connor edits *Soirée*.'

Lady Hackford's eyes swivelled back to Catherine. 'Oh, it's *you*.' By the way her mouth set in a thin line, it was clear Catherine's name wasn't mentioned in glowing terms in the Hackford household.

Mr Edgar-Phillips was looking distinctly put out. 'Is there anyone we can call for you?' he asked reluctantly.

Catherine sprang up from the hard leather chaise longue where she had been sitting.

'No, really. You've been very kind, but I'll go down to the concierge. He can call a locksmith.'

'If you say so,' replied his wife. She looked down pointedly at the dress Catherine was wearing. 'I'd like it dry-cleaned as soon as possible, please, and I only use Buttons of Belgravia.'

Catherine gritted her teeth. 'Of course.' She looked round the room with as much grace as she could muster. 'Sorry to interrupt your evening.'

Sir Robin was the only one who answered. 'Make sure you shut the door properly on the way out.'

Catherine ended up slamming it by mistake. *That'll make them jump in their china teacups*, she thought, with a small amount of satisfaction. She was still reeling. Of all the people in the world, she had to end up living next door to Sir Robin Hackford's snotty friends. Just thinking about Valour's chairman seeing her sprawled out naked in front of him sent Catherine spinning with horror. She groaned out loud; it was sure to give him more ammunition against her.

Catherine's spirits plummeted even more when she saw her reflection in the lift. She couldn't be seen in public like this! She looked like a cross between Margaret Thatcher and Aunt Sally. Frantically, she tucked the huge frilly collars in and hitched up the dress a few inches. A plastic flower pulled out of the arrangement in reception added a makeshift corsage. As Catherine headed for the concierge, to her mortification Hermione Baker was walking straight towards her. Hermione was a highly respected fashion journalist who lived several floors down from Catherine.

Catherine tried to hide behind a potted plant, but it was too late. 'Darling!' Hermione cried, her eyes sweeping over Catherine's outfit.

'Love the dress. Retro is all the rage again!' With that, she disappeared out of the front door in a haze of overpowering perfume.

Catherine staggered over to the bemused concierge.

'Can you call me a locksmith, please?' she asked weakly.

Chapter 32

The whole sorry saga was thankfully a fading memory by the time Catherine sat opposite John Milton in a starkly lit Japanese restaurant that Friday. She'd deliberately chosen it for the austere, unforgiving surroundings. She needed to keep in control tonight, for her sake more than anything. She also wondered if the snob in her was testing John to see how he would behave in these surroundings, but he was perfectly at ease with his chopsticks. In fact, John seemed at home wherever he was.

'More sushi?' she asked.

He shook his head. 'I always forget how filling it is.'

Catherine smiled. 'Funny, I had you down as more of a steak and kidney pie man.' Despite her intentions, she found herself once again disarmed by John. He was so easy-going, it was impossible not to get on with him, no matter how prickly she tried to be.

He eyed her. 'What? Because I work on a building site and come from Oop North?' he asked drily.

Catherine flushed. 'No, that wasn't what I meant.'

'I'm teasing you,' he told her.

I don't know what to make of him, Catherine thought.

John hadn't brought up their background again, but she could feel it there, like a big black albatross. She wondered what he was really thinking.

Luckily the rest of the meal passed without her putting her foot in it. As they left the restaurant in Covent Garden, Catherine looked up. Above the orange glow of city life, London was nestled under a velvet-blue starry sky. Catherine breathed the night air in. For once, her head felt wonderfully clear.

John offered his arm. 'Shall we?'

After a moment's hesitation, Catherine took it. Even through the soft material of his jacket, she could feel how rock-hard his biceps was. They started to walk down past the tube station into the bustling Covent Garden piazza. The smoky windows of pubs were filled with people laughing and vying for attention at the bar, while a large crowd had formed to watch a man, painted entirely white and wearing a Grecian drape, standing as still as a statue.

John and Catherine made their way down across the still-busy Strand and towards Embankment tube station. They crossed over the road to walk along the path beside the Thames, the magnificent Houses of Parliament lit up in front of them. Couples passed, giggling and stopping to kiss each other, inhibitions stripped away by a few drinks at dinner.

Catherine was regretting wearing her Jimmy Choos. She could feel blisters growing with every step she took.

'Are you all right?' John asked.

She winced. 'New shoes.' Why did she never learn to wear them in round the house first?

'Come on, we'll get a cab.' They walked for a few more minutes, Catherine holding on to John's arm and hobbling like a little old lady. Not quite the image she wanted to project. Eventually they hailed a cab and Catherine sank back down on the seat in relief.

'I had a good time tonight,' he told her as the cab sped along. Despite herself, Catherine smiled.

'Me, too.'

A few minutes later, they had pulled up outside her apartment block. Catherine was determined not to repeat what had happened the last time they had been here.

'Well, I'd better be going, then!' she said brightly.

'Here, let me.' Before she knew it John was at her side of the cab, opening the door. He took her hand and helped her out. They stood there in silence, before Catherine broke it.

'Well, thanks again,' she said. John didn't say anything, but looked down at her, his green eyes intense.

Catherine dropped her gaze, but his hand found her chin and gently pushed it up towards him. As she looked into his eyes, she felt an odd mix of familiarity and fear.

'Goodnight, Catherine,' he murmured, and leant down to kiss her. His lips were soft and warm, and in that moment, nothing else existed.

After what seemed like a lifetime, Catherine made herself pull away. Her heart was pounding so much, it was almost painful in her chest. 'Goodnight, John,' she said quickly. As she got to the front door of her apartment block, Catherine made herself turn around. John was still standing by the open door of the cab, watching her. He waved his hand briefly and dropped it again.

Chapter 33

'Darling, it's me. How did it go?'

Caro sat down on the bed. She was just about to start taking her make-up off. Milo was sound asleep in bed, while downstairs Benedict was engrossed in a documentary about a North Pole explorer.

'Fine, Mummy,' she said, putting the phone under her chin so she could unscrew her Clarins cleanser. She'd had a prenatal appointment for blood tests that morning.

'Are you sure?' her mother asked anxiously.

Caro smiled. 'They were just checking for iron levels and things like that. It's all perfectly routine, just like when I was pregnant last time.'

'I don't mean to sound like such an old worrywart. I just wish I was there with you, instead of thousands of miles away!'

'It's not long now,' Caro reminded her. Tink and Johnnie always came back to Churchminster for Christmas. Usually they stayed a month, but this time they were visiting friends in America on the way over, and weren't due to arrive in the Cotswolds until 23 December.

Camilla was still away travelling, but to everyone's

delight, Calypso had managed to get a week off work and was flying back from New York with her parents. They were all going to stay with Caro and Benedict at Mill House, and descend en masse on Clementine for Christmas dinner.

Caro and Tink were discussing the arrangements when there was a loud groan from outside. Caro looked round in alarm. Was someone trying to break in?

Another noise. This time it was more like a cat being strangled.

Her mother stopped talking. 'What on earth was that?'

Caro heard the distinct sound of flesh being slapped.

'Is someone fighting? One of those girl gangs? Oh, darling, I knew you shouldn't have moved to London!' exclaimed Tink.

'Ssh, Mummy,' said Caro, edging over to the window. A nasty realization was dawning. Sure enough, as she looked out tentatively, she became certain the racket was coming from the doctor's room opposite. They might have closed the curtains this time, but not the window.

Slap! The sound pierced the air like a bullet. Another loud groan of ecstasy erupted.

Caro let out a groan of her own. She didn't even want to think about what was going on.

'Shut your bloody window!' she half-yelled. 'I can hear everything!'

A concerned babble erupted from the phone. 'No, Mummy, I wasn't talking to you,' Caro said hurriedly.

Amelia's depression finally seemed to be subsiding. She had firmly rejected Benedict's offer to make an appointment with the doctor: 'He'll just put me back on those awful tablets, and you know how they zonk me out,' she told him. 'I'm feeling a million times better, anyway.'

Benedict hadn't been convinced, but slowly but surely, Amelia was returning to her old self. Instead of spending hours shut away in her bedroom, she would play with Milo downstairs, and delight in one of her favourite pastimes: teasing her brother. She and Caro got rather too into *Loose Women* for their own good, and Amelia even ventured out of the mews a few times to take Milo for a walk, or go for a coffee with her sister-in-law at the little Italian deli round the corner. She still wasn't completely the Amelia they all knew and loved, but the sparkle was returning to her eyes.

It was a filthy winter's evening. Wind howled through the huge trees overlooking Montague Mews, their branches bending and groaning back and forth. In the murky atmosphere high above, sinister rumbles of thunder grew ever closer.

Inside No. 2 Montague Mews, however, the house was warm and cosy. Mouth-watering smells filled the kitchen as the three adults sat at the kitchen table enjoying a convivial supper Amelia had conjured up.

'Mmm, you can stay more often,' said Caro, as she forked up a mouthful.

Amelia laughed. 'Oh, cooking a delicious shepherd's pie is one of my many talents.'

'It's the only thing you can cook,' Benedict reminded her.

Amelia looked mock-hurt. 'Excuse me. What about that Thai chicken curry I made for your birthday?'

He winced. 'My eyes are still watering.'

She stuck her tongue out at him. 'Don't be so ungrateful.' She turned to whisper to Caro. 'I put in a whole packet of chillies by mistake.'

Caro laughed. 'We've all been there!'

'Actually, not all of us have.' Benedict cast a dry look at his wife and sister. 'Why is it that none of the women in my life can cook, and I can? I'm sure it's meant to be the other way round.'

'Chauvinist,' said Caro, her eyes twinkling.

He twinkled back. 'Realist.'

Amelia looked mischievous. 'Anyway, why do either of us need to be Nigella Lawson in the kitchen, when we've got our very own Gordon Ramsay?'

'Hear, hear!' said Caro.

Benedict rolled his eyes and poured his sister more wine, before filling his own glass.

'How's work, darling? You haven't been working so late the last week. That must be a good sign?' Caro asked.

'Fingers crossed,' he replied. 'We finally seem to be making some headway. If it carries on, I can start working from home more.'

'My brother, the star businessman,' teased Amelia.

'I don't know about that.' Benedict looked at his sister. 'You know, there's always a job for you there. God knows The Glass Ceiling could do with a good PA; the last temp we had nearly set fire to the whole place when she left her hair straighteners on one evening.'

Suddenly, there was a loud thunderclap. It sounded like it was right outside in the mews. Caro and Amelia jumped.

'I hate thunder!' Amelia shuddered. 'When I was little, I always imagined it was an army of evil goblins on their way to kidnap someone. Thunderclaps were their drums making a war cry.'

'You always did have an overactive imagination,' Benedict stood up. 'Well, there's no goblins or evil here, I can assure you.'

As Amelia got up to help clear the table, a shadow caught Caro's eye from the living room. She frowned. *Was that Milo?* He'd got into the rather naughty habit of appearing downstairs, tousle-haired and angelic-faced when he was supposed to have gone to sleep hours ago. Leaving the other two, she went to check.

At first glance everything seemed normal: the room didn't contain any errant small children, and the lights were still turned down low. Caro went to the foot of the staircase and listened for any telltale footsteps upstairs. Nothing. She'd obviously imagined it.

'Pud's up!' Amelia called.

'Coming!' answered Caro, her mouth watering. Amelia had made a delicious treacle tart; her other culinary talent, Caro could hear her reminding Benedict. A slight breeze crossed the room from the living room window, and Caro went to close the curtains.

Outside, the mews was cast in darkness. As she stood there, momentarily lost in thought about whether to have ice cream or custard, a figure materialized in the window. Caro could only stare at the horns, blood-red eyes and spike-filled mouth, before the horror hit her.

She was looking into the face of the devil.

She screamed loudly and the apparition vanished. Caro backed away from the window and fell over the arm of the sofa. Benedict rushed out, pulling her up.

'Jesus Christ! Caro!'

'T-t-t-he . . . Someone at the window,' Caro was shaking so much she could hardly get the words out.

'Here? Who?' Benedict strode over to the window. 'I can't see anyone . . .' He started to unlock the front door.

'Benedict, no!' This time it was Amelia, her voice shrill and stretched. Benedict stared at her.

'It could be someone casing the joint.'

There was a loud banging on the door. Amelia screamed again, making Caro's heart fly into her mouth.

'Hello? Is everyone all right?' boomed a deep voice.

Klaus! Caro breathed a sigh of relief as Benedict finished unfastening the door and let him in. A gust of cold air blew in the room, making them all shiver.

Klaus was looking at them uncertainly. 'Ve heard this terrible noise . . .'

'It was me, I just had rather a fright,' Caro apologized. Now that the room was full of people, she was feeling rather foolish.

'Caro thought she saw someone looking in,' Benedict told him.

'Hang on, I *did* see someone!' she protested.

'Vot did they look like?' asked Klaus.

Caro shrugged helplessly. 'They were wearing some kind of horrible devil mask.' She paused. 'It was probably just some kids messing around.'

Klaus frowned. 'How did they get into the mews?'

Stephen and Saffron appeared in the doorway at the same time. They made the most incongruous pairing: she was in an indecently short baby-doll nightdress, lurid green paste all over her face, while he was wearing a mustard cravat, and what looked like a maroon smoking jacket, his initials beautifully monogrammed on the breast pocket.

'Darlings, are you all right? I thought you were all being murdered!'

'We're fine,' Caro told him.

'Thank heavens! I thought my episode of *Poirot* was coming to life.' Pulling a silk paisley handkerchief out of his pocket, Stephen dabbed it against his forehead.

Saffron let out a sigh of relief. 'Fuck, I didn't know

what was going on! Aunt Velda's out, I was shitting myself.'

Stephen turned to look at her, and Caro thought he was going to reprimand Saffron for her language. Instead his eyes widened.

'My dear! I don't want to appear rude, but you seem to have some kind of algae growing all over your face.'

Caro couldn't help but smile at his astonished expression.

Saffron gingerly touched her chin. 'Face mask. I was in the middle of a pampering session.' She looked at Caro. 'Anyway, if you're OK, I'm out of here. This was meant to come off ten minutes ago.'

Caro turned to Stephen. 'Awfully sorry to interrupt your programme.'

He flapped his handkerchief. 'It was a repeat, anyway.'

Benedict and Klaus returned from investigating the mews.

'The gate's open, but there's no sign of forced entry, so one of us must have forgotten to shut it,' Benedict reported.

'It may have been the Ocado man, he was here earlier at Rowena's,' mused Stephen. 'Their drivers are normally so good, though.'

'Do you think ve should call the police?' said Klaus.

Benedict shrugged. 'Whoever it was is long gone. It probably was just kids. They saw the gate open, and decided to come in and scare a few residents.'

'Well, they certainly succeeded!' said Caro. 'Little horrors.'

The four said goodnight and retreated into the warmth of their houses.

Benedict double-locked the door and drew Caro to

him. 'If they come back, I'll give them what for,' he said grimly. 'You could have gone into early labour!'

'I don't really think so, darling,' she laughed. 'It just gave me a fright.'

'Hmmm,' said Benedict. He looked at her. 'Where's Amelia?'

In the melee, Caro had completely forgotten about her. 'I don't know. Amelia?' she called into the kitchen. There was no answer. 'I'll go and see if she's OK, poor girl sounded terrified.'

'I'll go and put the kettle on,' said Benedict. 'I think we could all do with a warm drink.'

As Caro climbed the stairs, she became aware of a low moaning, as if the wind was still whistling through the house. She reached the top and realized it was the sound of someone crying. And it was coming from Amelia's room.

'Amelia?' Caro knocked softly on the door. The noise stopped.

'Sweetpea, are you OK?' she said. There was no answer.

DECEMBER

Chapter 34

Catherine turned the new Christmas issue around in her hands. She had to admit, it did look amazing. Along with a huge fifty-page fashion party supplement Alexander and his team had put together, it was packed with innovative photo shoots and exclusive interviews. Even better, she had somehow persuaded the marketing department to give away a free black clutch bag on the cover. Anya Hindmarch had designed it exclusively for them, and the little sequinned satin number was far superior to the usual tat given away with magazines. The Christmas issue always sold well and Catherine had a good feeling about this one.

With overseas sales added on, *Soirée* had put an extra 23,000 copies on their November issue in the end, taking them up to 233,000. Things seemed to be on course but it had been strangely quiet from Sir Robin Hackford's end. Catherine was sure this wasn't in his game plan: the more she thought about it, the more she was convinced that he wanted to shut the magazine down so he could pursue his own money-making interests. There had been rumours about a new, multi-million-pound business brand being launched by

Valour, which was far more in keeping with Sir Robin's background. Catherine felt sick at the unfairness of this.

Catherine had taken the decision early on that she wouldn't tell her team the exact sales figures every month, in case they got either complacent or despondent, depending on how well they'd done. They still had a long way to go, even though she was hoping to add even more on the Christmas issue, which traditionally had the highest sales of the year, even without the Anya Hindmarch trump card.

As she stroked the gold-embossed cover absent-mindedly, her phone started ringing.

'It's me.'

'Who?' Catherine replied, even though she knew perfectly well.

'Was our date that unmemorable?'

She smiled down the phone. 'It wasn't a date, as far as I remember.'

John laughed. 'Are you free for lunch? I'm in the area.'

Catherine felt thrown. 'I don't know . . .' She never took lunch, especially with someone as devilishly attractive as John Milton.

'Come on, I'm sure they can spare you for a couple of hours.'

Catherine looked through her window into the office, where everyone sat working industriously. They'd had a few good days . . .

'All right. But I really can't be long.'

Caro was beginning to regret driving into central London to do all her Christmas shopping. Every year she seemed to leave it to the last minute, and end up flapping around in a mad panic on Christmas Eve, buying just anything. Last year Benedict had got a pair of flashing Rudolph underpants that he, unsurprisingly, hadn't worn once. Caro was determined not to let the same thing happen again this year, especially with the credit crunch.

Unfortunately, it seemed half of London had decided to get their Christmas shopping done early. As she stop-started her way along the choked streets Caro was seriously kicking herself for not doing it all online. She needed to get to Fenwicks, where in heaven was she going to park? In desperation, she pulled off down a slightly quieter street, lined with grand houses. As Caro passed one with scaffolding criss-crossing it, she noticed a tall, elegant woman standing outside, gazing up. Her smart suit seemed at odds with the scruffiness of the building. Caro noticed the woman was wearing a sky-scraping pair of Gucci heels that had been in Vogue that month. She felt a pang of envy: the woman was probably one of those amazing super-mums who managed to combine six children with a stylish wardrobe and a million-pound salary. Caro glanced down at her own battered old ankle boots from Hobbs. Was that a blob of ketchup on the toe? Her own life would never be that together. Changing gear into second she edged forward, looking for an elusive parking space.

John had told Catherine to meet him at an address five minutes round the corner, but when Catherine got there she was puzzled. It was a derelict house being renovated! A few men in hard hats high up on the scaffolding wolf-whistled at her.

'Nice pins, darlin'!' Catherine looked up and shot them a sardonic glance. She hadn't realized her skirt was quite so short. She looked up and down the street, wondering what to do. Just then John emerged from the open door of the house, dressed down in jeans and a khaki jacket, a hard hat on his head. He looked so gorgeously masculine that Catherine's heart did an involuntary jump.

'Sorry if I confused you, but I thought you might like to see the house we're working on.' He leant forward and kissed her on the cheek. This time, Catherine's stomach dropped. Dammit, she wasn't supposed to be feeling like this!

John handed her a hat.

'You want me to wear that?' she asked.

He shot her a cheeky look. 'It's a special one that won't mess up your hair.'

'Ha ha,' retorted Catherine. She went to follow him in, but couldn't move her right foot. Then she looked down and realized one of her new Gucci heels had got stuck in a crack in the pavement. She tried to pull it out, nothing happened. Embarrassment flowed into her cheeks, and she gave one final yank before the heel finally came out. Nearly toppling over, Catherine had to grab on to a parking meter to right herself.

John turned around on the doorstep, one eyebrow arched quizzically.

'Everything all right?'

'Fine,' Catherine gasped. 'Just having a problem with my shoe.'

John's lips curved into a smile. 'I've never met a woman who looked so good in high heels, yet was so bad at walking in them.'

'You're funny today,' said Catherine acerbically, secretly delighted at the backhanded compliment.

Inside, the house was in complete disarray, but Catherine could see it had once been quite something. Sweeping corridors and high ceilings gave it a feel of long-forgotten grandeur. Original cornices ran the length of the ceilings, while the floor was patterned with beautiful black and white mosaic tiles. A magnificent mahogany staircase stretched up and up.

'It was owned by a Lord Fairfax in the mid-nineteenth century,' John told her. 'He was a notorious figure on the London social scene. His wife left him due to his excessive philandering, and Lord Fairfax bought this place to carry on his carousing. He hosted some of the wildest parties of that era, mostly involving upper-class gentlemen like himself and East End prostitutes. London society was scandalized at the time, and soon Fairfax had drunk himself into an early grave. Syphilis would have finished him off otherwise.'

'Sounds like a nice guy.'

John grinned. 'But he did have great taste in houses. Come here, I want to show you something.'

Carefully, she followed him up the stairs, acutely aware of the noise her heels were making on the polished wood. Builders stuck their heads out of different rooms as she passed, looking appreciatively at her legs. Catherine ignored them. They had climbed four storeys and she was getting out of breath when John stopped.

'Here's the attic room. Not a bad view.'

Catherine was mesmerized. She could see all the way across London out of the tiny window, from the Gherkin in the City to the Millennium Wheel on the south side of the Thames. They were so high up it was completely quiet, the only noise coming from straggly pigeons swooping past looking for somewhere to land.

'It's stunning! Like looking at a completely different city.'

'Lord Fairfax thought so, too, until one of his guests

took a tumble out of the window after a particularly big session. The papers made a huge thing of it, speculating that Lord Fairfax had actually pushed his guest out to his death. Our titled friend sold this place shortly afterwards.'

Instinctively Catherine took a step back away from the window, straight on to John's foot.

'Sorry!' she exclaimed, but he didn't move.

'One of the benefits of hob-nailed boots,' he said. 'You never know on a building site when some gorgeous woman is going to grind her stiletto heel into your foot.'

Catherine giggled. John studied her. 'You look like a girl I used to know.'

Catherine stopped laughing abruptly. 'She disappeared a long time ago.' There was an uncomfortable silence.

'Shall we go and get some lunch?' John asked.

Harriet cradled her cappuccino between her hands. London had woken up to freezing fog hanging over the rooftops, and temperatures hadn't improved as the day went on.

Saffron finished her lunch and eyed Harriet's half-eaten chicken and avocado salad. 'Aren't you eating that? Do you mind if I have some?'

'Of course, help yourself,' said Harriet. Her clothes had been feeling even tighter recently, and she'd vowed to eat healthily in the run-up to Christmas. As the dark, cold evenings had drawn in, she'd decided to take up swimming, too. She'd only made it to the health club near her flat twice, and had spent more time in the Jacuzzi than the pool, but it was a start. Harriet watched enviously as Saffron applied more full-fat salad dressing and tucked in.

'Catherine seems very cheery at the moment,' Saffron said after a few mouthfuls. 'I had a meeting with her this morning and she was positively beaming. Let me tell you, Catherine Connor isn't the kind of woman who "beams" very often.'

'I know!' said Harriet. 'She went out on an awfully long lunch yesterday. I can't remember her ever doing that before.'

Saffron looked hopeful. 'Maybe that means things are improving, if she's taking her foot off the brake a bit.'

Harriet took a sip of her coffee. 'Are you worried about your job?'

Saffron shrugged. 'A bit, I suppose. I mean, I haven't got a family to support like some people in the office. Maybe I'm being naïve – there's all this doom and gloom but people seem to forget Catherine *is* shit-hot at her job. I do have faith in her.'

'It must be hard for her, though. All that responsibility and no one to talk to.'

Saffron shrugged. 'They say an editor's job is a lonely one.'

She wasn't aware just how lonely it could get.

Chapter 35

The festive season had descended upon London. Flashing decorations stretched high above the towering streets, while each pub and restaurant sported big, fat, overdressed Christmas trees. Slade's 'I Wish It Could Be Christmas' blasted from every shop, and pretty girls dressed in red minidresses with a white fur trim hovered by the entrances of department stores, enticing shoppers in with a smile and a mince pie.

Montague Mews was looking magical. The residents had decorated the iron gates with fairy lights, while Christmas wreaths adorned the doors and candle arches twinkled in the windows. All except Rowena's; her house remained as dark and still as ever.

At No. 2, Caro, Benedict and Milo had spent all afternoon decorating the tree. There had been one sticky moment when Milo, desperate to hang a bauble on one of the higher branches, had pulled it down and ended up with the whole tree on top of him, but luckily they hadn't been far into decorating at that stage. Once Caro had pulled the last of the pine needles out of his hair and jumper, the little boy had been raring to get going again.

By contrast, Amelia had completely retreated inside

herself once more. Benedict had tried talking to her, but she'd almost completely shut down, answering his questions with monosyllabic answers.

'It's not healthy for her to be shut away in that room,' he'd said to Caro. 'No job, no social life, watching television for twelve hours a day.'

There had been no more frightening faces at the window, although Benedict had invested in new locks. Caro didn't want to mention it to Benedict, but she wondered if the intruder had been linked to Amelia. Several times, Caro had heard urgent whispering inside Amelia's room, as if she was pleading with someone on the phone. She had assumed it was boyfriend issues at first, but now she wasn't so sure.

She tried to broach it one evening, when she took Amelia up a bowl of homemade soup for dinner.

'Amelia, I don't know how to put this,' she said hesitantly. Amelia looked up from where she was lying on her bed.

'I mean, I don't want to pry or anything,' Caro continued. 'But, well, are you in any kind of trouble?'

Amelia sat up and hugged her knees. 'What do you mean?' Her tone was defensive.

'Because if you are, if there's anything we can do to help . . .' Caro stopped, not really knowing what else to say. Amelia stared at her, and just for a moment, Caro thought she saw her plead with her eyes. 'Honestly, darling, if there's anything you want to talk about . . .'

Amelia cut her off. 'I'm fine, Caro. Really.' She forced a smile. 'Thanks for the soup. It smells delicious.'

After her Oxford Street nightmare, where all she'd got was a parking ticket, a congestion-charge penalty and a stress-induced headache, Caro decided it was far cheaper and more pleasant to travel by bus to the nearby King's Road for her Christmas shopping. Once famous for being part of the 'Swinging Sixties' social scene, it now boasted a variety of boutiques, high street stores, wine bars and restaurants – all packed with ultra-tanned Euro Sloanes.

A biting wind was blowing as Caro stepped down from the bus. Hordes of red-nosed shoppers streamed past, laden down with beautifully wrapped parcels and designer carrier bags. Heaving her handbag over her arm, Caro started towards Peter Jones department store. She had seen a set of silver napkin holders on their website that would be perfect for her grandmother.

This time her trip was a lot more successful, and two hours later Caro had got nearly all her presents. All that was left was a visit to the Crabtree & Evelyn store for her mother's favourite rose water hand cream. Benedict's present, a pair of cufflinks from a jeweller's off Piccadilly, was already wrapped in its box at the back of Caro's knicker drawer.

'Watch it!' said a male voice crossly as someone banged into her. 'Bloody people, why don't you watch where you're going?'

'Oh, I'm frightfully sorry—' Caro began to say, even though it had been the man's fault. Then her jaw dropped.

'What are you doing here?' she gasped.

Her ex-husband looked equally surprised for a moment, before his cold blue eyes focused. Sebastian was dressed in a loud pinstriped suit with a pink tie. His blond bouffant hair looked freshly streaked, and Caro noticed he'd put on a few pounds around his jawline. It looked like all those boozy client lunches were catching up with him.

Sebastian looked down his nose. 'I live here, what's

your excuse, darling? Annual country bumpkins' coach trip to London?'

Caro resisted the urge to stamp on his foot. Thank God she was wearing a big coat and you couldn't see her bump. She didn't want Sebastian knowing anything about her life with Benedict.

'You know we're in London, my solicitor informed yours. Why haven't you been in contact with Milo?' she asked, trying to keep down the familiar flame of anger Sebastian always ignited when it came to their son.

Sebastian actually looked a bit shamefaced. 'Yah, sorry about that. I've been frightfully busy at work recently. How is the little fellow?'

'He would appreciate a Christmas present from you, at the very least,' Caro said. Her voice rose. 'You've got responsibilities, Sebastian, you could at least pretend you care!'

Several shoppers turned to look at them. Sebastian pulled Caro to the side of the pavement by her elbow. 'Come on, darling, don't go all Jerry Springer on me and start rowing in public,' he said patronizingly. 'It's frightfully vulgar.'

A homeless man was sitting near them, his back against a shop window. He looked up hopefully. 'Spare a little change, guv?'

Caro looked at him apologetically before turning back to Sebastian. 'I just want you to be a proper father to your son,' she said angrily. 'Is that really so hard?'

Sebastian blew on his nails and polished them against his lapel. 'I pay maintenance, don't I?'

'You can't buy his love!' Caro retorted. 'Benedict has been more of a father to Milo than you ever have.'

At the mention of Benedict's name Sebastian looked furious. 'I was wondering when that twat's name was going to come up! Towey must be feeling very pleased with himself after stealing my wife off me.'

'No one stole me, I was divorcing you anyway,' she pointed out.

'Whatever,' said Sebastian. A funny look crossed his face, one that Caro hadn't seen before. He almost looked vulnerable.

'What, so you're happy? I bet he hasn't got a bigger cock than me.'

Caro sighed. 'Is that what this is about?'

Sebastian flashed his white teeth at her nastily.

'Don't flatter yourself, darling. I've got more birds hanging off my arm than a Balmoral gamekeeper.'

Caro picked up her shopping bags. 'I give up on you,' she said wearily. 'You're never going to change. I just feel sorry for poor Milo.'

Sebastian narrowed his eyes. 'I feel sorry for the poor little sod, having to put up with that fucking codpiece Towey. Anyway, if you'll excuse me, I've got a few million-pound deals to make.'

He turned round. The homeless man looked up at him again. Sebastian curled his lip and made a great show of digging in his pocket. He pulled out a big handful of one- and two-pound coins, and flung them at the man. One coin hit the poor fellow above the eye, and he winced.

'Help yourself, old chap, I hate carrying all that fucking shrapnel around, anyway,' Sebastian drawled as he strode off.

Horrified, Caro rushed over to the man and crouched down. 'Are you all right?' she cried. 'I really must apologize for his behaviour.'

The man touched his head gingerly. 'No wonder you divorced him. What a wanker. Still, there must be thirty quid here.' Moments later they both had a prize view as Sebastian went slap bang into a passer-by, spilling her Starbucks coffee all down himself.

The homeless man held up some of the coins and grinned. 'You want some of these back for your dry-cleaning bill, mate?'

Sebastian shot a furious look at them. 'Go and get fucked,' he snarled, stomping off, a halo of blond malevolence amongst the happy Christmas shoppers.

Chapter 36

Catherine felt strange. No, it wasn't that, she felt *happy*. No matter how much she'd tried to resist letting John into her life, he had changed things. She had started to look forward to his phone calls and text messages, their meandering walks through nearby Green Park when Catherine could get away at lunchtime.

Catherine could still feel that kiss on her lips if she tried hard enough. There had been no real physical contact since, aside from John putting a protective arm on hers as they crossed a road, or a hand on her back as he guided her through a door. But this was still enough to make Catherine tingle, and she found herself aching for his touch, imagining his strong hands running all over her body . . .

Then she would come back to earth with a bump again. The subject of her past had still been studiously avoided by both of them, but Catherine could feel it hanging over her like an ugly cloud, seeping into everything. There was no future for her and John. How could there be when she couldn't let him in? *I'll break it off tomorrow*, she found herself saying more than once, *I'll make up an excuse*.

She still hadn't quite brought herself to do it.

That Friday Catherine had arranged to meet John at Somerset House, an eighteenth-century art museum on the Strand that was famous with Londoners for its seasonal ice-skating rink. Catherine could easily have done another few hours of work, but she made herself switch off the computer.

'Off out?' asked Harriet. She was one of the few people left in the office.

'Yes, I'm going ice-skating,' Catherine told her. 'Don't work too late!'

'I won't, goodnight,' Harriet called after her, smiling. This new chap must really be something.

'Nice bobbles.'

'Thanks.' Catherine grinned at John as he admired her knitted Chloé scarf.

The rink looked magical, its white surface glittering under the overhead lights. Skaters of varying speeds laughed as they went round in circles. A young man in a bright red hat sped past going backwards. He did a graceful figure of eight to applause from the impressed onlookers. As they queued up to get their skates Catherine started to feel slightly self-conscious.

'I think I'm too old for this.'

'Nonsense,' John replied. He was wearing a thick olive-green jumper that matched his eyes, and Catherine noticed he was getting admiring glances from a few women in the line.

They swapped their footwear for a retro pair of skates and made their way clumsily towards the rink, tripping over the uneven rubber surface. John gestured, 'After you.' Catherine stepped out tentatively. She hadn't been ice-skating for years. What if she fell flat on her arse?

Luckily her fears were unfounded. She wobbled

precariously for the first few seconds, but somehow kept her balance.

'Bravo!' shouted John. Catherine turned round to watch him. As soon as John put one skate on the ice, his legs went from underneath him like Bambi. Flying up into the air, he crash-landed flat on his back.

'Oh God, are you OK?' Catherine called, slowly making her way over to where he was trying to stand up.

'I thought I'd be good at this,' he said wryly.

For the next hour, Catherine couldn't remember the last time she had laughed so much. She got the hang of it quite quickly, but for all his manly prowess, John was the worst skater she had ever seen. Every time he let go of the barrier, he fell over. Tears of merriment coursed down her cheeks as she helped him up time and time again. His jumper and trousers were completely sodden with ice.

'I will master this,' he said through gritted teeth as he pushed off again. 'Oh shit!' His arms started flailing like a windmill besieged by a force-nine gale. 'Watch out!' The skaters gave him a wide berth as he disappeared into the middle of them. Ten seconds later, John's legs flew up in the air again and he landed spectacularly on his bottom.

Catherine couldn't breathe for laughing. She skated over, to where John was still lying on his back, looking at the stars.

'Thought I'd stay down here, it's safer.' As Catherine offered her arm to give him a hand up, he pulled her down on top of him.

'John, what are you doing!' she gasped.

'I feel a bit faint. You might have to give me mouth-to-mouth.' Before she knew it, he had pulled her lips down on to his.

'Get a room, you two!' someone yelled good-naturedly. They stopped and looked at each other, smiling. Catherine's cheeks were burning pink from embarrassment and pleasure.

They decided to retire before John did himself some permanent damage. As they walked back down the Strand afterwards, Catherine's spirits were so high, she was practically skipping. She was having real, proper fun.

At first, he said it so quietly she didn't hear.

'Sorry, what was that?' she smiled, turning to him.

'You left without saying goodbye.'

The simplicity of his words startled her into silence.

John carried on looking ahead as he walked. 'I understand the reasons you went, but it was still a shock.'

'We'd grown apart,' was all she could say, but John Milton shook his head.

'It was just a blip. We were just kids. Sleeping together for the first time probably threw us.'

'Yes, we were just kids,' she reminded him. 'It was a long time ago.'

'We had something, though, didn't we?' He stopped walking and turned to her. 'There was always something different about you, Catherine.'

'Didn't I know it,' she said bitterly.

John smiled tenderly. 'I meant that in a good way. In a funny sense, I felt like the odd one out, too. Rugby captain, good marks, the popular one everyone wanted to be mates with. But underneath, I never felt like one of them. Do you know what I mean?'

'Oh, yes,' she said softly.

He lifted a hand and traced the outline of her face. Every fibre of her skin tingled.

'Why didn't you leave a forwarding address, a phone number, anything? You just vanished.'

Catherine sighed. 'I didn't leave any forwarding details because I didn't know where I was going. Besides, it was better that way. It wasn't easy being a figure of hate.' She smiled grimly. '"Rot in hell" I think was one of the nicer comments I got.'

John shook his head but didn't say anything. They were down a quieter side street now, away from the main thoroughfare. Catherine took a step backwards, away from him.

'No. Please, John, I can't do this.'

He moved towards her. 'I know how difficult things must have been for you . . .'

Catherine interrupted, her voice suddenly choked with tears. 'You have no idea what it was like! I was *fifteen years old!*'

A couple walking past turned round at her raised voice. Catherine dropped her head, furiously blinking back the tears. 'Look, I don't know what you want from me, but I can't give it to you. You're part of what I was, and I can't go back. Do you know what it's taken to get this far?'

The tears coursed down her face, blinding her. 'Sorry,' Catherine whispered and walked away quickly. She had to get away from him.

She heard John shout after her, but it was just a blur. Oblivious to the looks people were giving her, Catherine started to run, down the road and through the crowds of late-night shoppers and revellers, just wanting to put as much space between her and John as she could.

Suddenly she tripped and fell to her knees. A sharp pain went through her right leg, making her wince. Catherine quickly pulled herself up, hoping no one had noticed. Hobbling over to the side of the road, she propped herself against a shop wall.

Why is this happening to me? she moaned inwardly. Trying to steady herself, Catherine opened her bag and started scrabbling around for a tissue. She needed to calm down, and dry her eyes before she drew any more attention to herself.

The black cab pulled up without Catherine realizing it. The door flung open and John Milton jumped out. He looked frantic with worry.

'Catherine, for God's sake . . .'

'Just leave me alone,' she said, suddenly embarrassed by her behaviour. 'I mean it, John, I'm no good for you. I'm damaged goods.'

His strong jaw tensed, eyes full of a million questions.

'Let me be the judge of that.' He held out his hand. 'Please, Catherine. We need to talk. Can't we go back to mine and sort this out once and for all?'

'There's nothing to sort out!' she told him with more anger than she actually felt.

'OK,' he sighed. 'But at least let me help you, you're in no state to walk.'

Catherine looked down, and was shocked to see blood seeping through a hole in her tights. She must have cut her knee.

John held out his arm. After what seemed an age, Catherine took it. Slowly they walked over to the car, where the impatient cabbie was waiting. He'd seen it all before, it was just another young lovers' tiff.

John gave the man his address, and the cab set off for south London. Catherine sat as far away from John as she could, as if she would literally scald herself if she touched him.

'How's the leg?' he asked.

'Fine,' Catherine replied through gritted teeth. It was really starting to sting.

*   *   *

They didn't talk again until the car pulled up outside a row of stunning three-storey houses on Clapham Common. John paid the driver and went to help Catherine out, but she pushed him away.

'I can manage.'

John looked hurt for a moment, and Catherine hated herself even more. Why was she such a bitch to him?

Trying not to hobble, Catherine followed him up the path. Even in the dark, she could see how beautiful the house was, with its impressive frontage and original sash windows. John unlocked the door and, standing aside, ushered her in.

Inside was not the bare, modern bachelor pad she had been expecting, but the stunning interior of an elegant country home. The wide floorboards were painted dark brown, a beautifully woven rug running the length of the corridor. The walls were simple white, with evocative gilt-framed pictures of eighteenth-century hunting scenes. A huge grandfather clock stood to the right, like a sentry. On cue, the hands moved to midnight, and it started chiming.

'The first-aid kit is in the kitchen,' John said, walking down the corridor. Catherine followed him and found herself in a large square room with marble worktops and duck-egg-blue cupboards.

'This is all very refined,' she said quietly. John pulled out a chair from the table in the corner and she sank down gratefully.

He glanced at her. 'You sound surprised, were you expecting my underpants to be drying on the hot-plate?'

Catherine managed a smile. 'Not quite that bad, but I am impressed.'

John put a clean flannel under the tap, then came and sat opposite her. 'Here, let me.' Catherine winced again as he tried to clean the wound.

He looked up at her. 'Don't take this the wrong way, but you may have to take your tights off. I can't get at it properly.'

Catherine raised an eyebrow. 'That's one I haven't heard before.'

John grinned. 'It's purely professional, I'm only concerned for your welfare.'

Catherine hesitated for a moment, and then stood up. 'I'm actually wearing suspenders,' she said, self-consciously.

John's grin got even wider. 'Even easier to take off. I mean, for you,' he added, noticing her unimpressed expression.

Catherine couldn't help herself. 'Had a lot of practice, have you?'

John laughed softly and averted his eyes as she slowly took them off. There was silence apart from the ticking of the clock on the wall. Catherine surreptitiously stowed the stockings in her handbag and sat back down again.

John took her knee between his hands and inspected it. Luckily the cut wasn't very deep. He dabbed at it gently.

'There's no dirt in there; I think you'll live. I'll put a bit of Savlon on, just in case.'

'Ow, ow, ow,' protested Catherine as he smoothed the antiseptic cream on.

John looked up, amused. 'Come on, you're a big girl now.'

'Still bloody hurts,' she said through gritted teeth.

John got a plaster out of the first-aid kit and, using both hands, carefully put it over the cut.

'There, that's better.'

His hands didn't move from her leg, and Catherine felt her stomach do a slow somersault.

'I am so undeniably attracted to you, Catherine,' John said, his voice husky. 'I always have been.' Very gently, his fingers started to stroke her bare skin.

Catherine tried to make light of it, even though her heart was racing furiously. 'Hey, you're only human.'

He looked up at her, a slight smile playing on his lips. 'I'm starting to believe you are, too.'

'Appearances can be deceptive,' Catherine started to say, but suddenly John was up, pulling her into his strong arms.

'Tell me you want me as much as I want you.'

'I want you,' gasped Catherine, and then his lips were on hers, soft yet firm, his tongue insistent and probing, wanting to taste every part of her. Catherine found herself responding back, more and more passionately, until her hands were raking through his hair with desire. With one swift movement John had her in his arms and was striding out of the room towards the mahogany staircase.

'It's time for bed,' he said, kissing her all the way upstairs. The next time Catherine opened her eyes they were in a large, stylishly furnished bedroom. Arms firm and solid, John gently lowered her feet to the ground. Catherine felt as if she was in a trance, every part of her body alive with lust and anticipation. As she and John kissed his hands ran through her hair and down her body. She savoured the taut outline of his back and buttocks.

John started undoing the buttons on her black chiffon blouse. Underneath, Catherine was wearing a plunging lacy bra, her cleavage deep and succulent. John groaned with appreciation. His hands moved around to find the zip of her skirt. One tug, and it was off, and Catherine stood before him, still in her suspender belt. She'd always preferred suspenders over tights, and, judging by the look in his eyes, so did John Milton.

Slowly, John undid her bra and ran a hand down between her breasts, placing it over Catherine's heart. He looked into her eyes, intense and passionate. 'You are so incredibly beautiful.'

Almost picking her up, he pushed her backwards towards the bed. Catherine's feet hardly touched the floor. She was totally in his power.

John's breathing was heavy now. 'I promised myself I'd be a gentleman with you, Catherine,' he murmured. 'But you turn me on so much, I can't help myself.'

He stood back, and without taking his eyes off her, undid his shirt and threw it on the floor. Through the half-light, she could see how magnificent his physique was. Wide, capable shoulders and solid, muscular arms that could only have been achieved by years of sheer physical labour. Catherine moved to unbutton his trousers, but he pushed her down.

'I want to please you first.'

Kissing her neck, he savoured her perfume, before his tongue moved down and he circled and licked her erect nipples. Involuntarily, Catherine arched her back with pleasure as John continued his inexorably pleasant journey southwards. His lips brushed across her flat stomach, before she felt his tongue run tantalizingly along the top of her knicker line. Catherine lifted her hips to help him, as John pulled her La Perla G-string down the length of her long legs, before moving slowly up, kissing every inch of her calves and inner thighs. Catherine moaned in anticipation as finally, he moved in – between her legs.

John's tongue pleasured and teased her until she was brought to the brink. Her hands ran through his thick, dark hair, pushing his face into her.

She could wait no longer.

'I want you inside me,' she whispered.

He kicked off his trousers and Hugo Boss pants. Against the half-light filtering into the room, Catherine could see the silhouette of his huge erection. He reached into the bedside drawer and brought out a condom. She opened her legs and waited. As he lowered himself down and gently eased into her, Catherine felt a surge of elation.

'Oh my God,' she whispered.

They started to move, slowly at first, each enjoying the feel and touch of the other. Gradually, they moved faster and faster until John was driving himself into her urgently. Catherine gasped with pleasure, and wrapped her legs around his back. John pulled her up effortlessly on to his lap. They were so close now, her breasts pressed against his chest, arms wrapped around each other, kissing furiously. Catherine could feel herself close to orgasm as he drove himself back and forward inside her.

Her breathing quickened. 'Oh John . . .' she cried out. The climax exploded inside her, waves of pleasure pulsating through her body like an aftershock. John came seconds later, holding her so tightly she could hardly breathe.

At that precise moment, Catherine had never felt so close to anyone. Gripped by an unassailable wave of emotion, she burst into tears. John held her even closer.

'It's all right,' he said, stroking her hair. 'I've found you now. I'm here.'

*　　　*　　　*

It was early morning when she opened her eyes. They lay as they had fallen asleep, John on his back and Catherine cradled in his arms. For a moment she stayed there, feeling the throb of his heart.

What had happened last night? She had been so carried away in the throes of passion. John Milton had taken her to places she'd never thought possible – and places she'd never wanted to visit again. He'd made her feel vulnerable, and that was not a word Catherine could allow in her vocabulary. The intense emotions she'd experienced now felt confusing and alien – frightening, even. Poor Catherine Connor, who'd had to build a protective armour from a young age, was ill-equipped to deal with them. So she did the only thing she knew.

She got up and quietly dressed, before leaving him again.

Catherine stood under a steaming hot shower, as if it would eradicate all traces of what had just happened. Afterwards she made herself a coffee and went to lie down on her sofa. She stared unseeing at the television screen, but then her eyelids grew heavy and sleep rescued her.

The sound of her mobile ringing woke her some time later. 'Private number' was flashing up on the screen. Catherine leant forward and picked it up from the coffee table. No one called her, especially at weekends, unless it was work.

'Hello,' she said groggily. The wall clock opposite said 2 p.m. She'd been asleep for hours.

'Was my snoring that bad?'

Catherine jerked upright. Her heart was pounding, but she forced herself to speak.

'I'm sorry about earlier, I just had things to do,' she said, aware of the chill in her voice.

John paused. 'Are you OK?'

'I'm fine!' she snapped.

'Look, if now is a bad time . . .'

'Yes, it is. In fact, it's always going to be a bad time. John, nothing has changed. I told you, I'm damaged goods. It can never work.'

He didn't say anything.

'Did you hear me?' she asked.

'Yes,' he replied quietly. 'Catherine, last night was . . .' He paused. 'You felt something, too, I know you did.'

Catherine felt sick. 'Don't tell me what I feel,' she said furiously. 'You don't know anything about me.'

'I know enough,' he said simply. 'Enough that I want to be with you.'

Catherine felt like it wasn't her voice speaking. 'Look, John, it was a bit of fun, but that's all.'

'Do you really mean that?'

Catherine's nerves broke. 'Yes, I do! And I'd appreciate it if you didn't call me again. It was a one-off. That's it. That's all.'

With that she hung up.

Then the tears really started.

Chapter 37

The whirl of Christmas drinks parties was well under way at *Soirée*. Barely a morning went by without hungover staff members gulping down huge bottles of Evian water at their desks, or sending round sheepish emails asking if anyone had any Nurofen. To her mortification, Saffron had thrown up in the toilets two mornings running.

Harriet was elbow-deep in a pile of invoices when Annabel appeared at her desk. 'I'm on my way out to an extremely important brunch with Keira Knightley's agent. If Catherine needs me, I'll be on my mobile.' She stopped and looked closely at Harriet's bowed head.

'Oh. My. God!' Annabel paused and looked round, making sure she had everyone's attention.

'Do you know you've got *loads* of white hairs? If I were you, I'd do something about that.'

Harriet burned with embarrassment, but Saffron was over there in a flash.

'Don't be so rude, Annabel!'

Annabel's eyes bulged indignantly. 'Well!' she huffed. 'I was only telling Harriet as a friend.'

'If that's what you're like as a friend, I'd hate to be

your enemy,' retorted Saffron acidly. She looked down at Harriet.

'Don't pay any attention, H, I can't see any.' She glared back at Annabel.

'Why don't you go and tell Keira she's grown a second head, instead?'

Muttering something about lack of respect, Annabel shot an evil look at Saffron and bustled out of the office.

It was nearly midday when Catherine walked into the office from her early breakfast meeting. It had been the last thing she'd needed – like many of her staff Catherine was feeling the effects of too much imbibing. But unlike everyone else, who had racked up their hangovers after one party or another, Catherine had got drunk alone at home. Again. If she actually stopped to think about it – and Catherine didn't – she had been drunk virtually every night for the last week. Every morning as she woke, head throbbing mercilessly and a nasty taste stagnating at the back of her throat, Catherine vowed not to drink again. In the daytime she was fine, but it was the evenings stretching ahead that scared her. It was simple: Catherine didn't want to be alone with her thoughts, so she blotted them out with alcohol. No matter how hard she tried, though, snapshots of her night with John kept coming back. The scent of his aftershave, his hands running over her body, the way he'd made her feel . . .

Even more disconcerting, Catherine was also dreaming about her mother for the first time in years. It all seemed so real, like it had only been yesterday. Annie's sweet smile, and the light, flowery perfume Catherine had loved inhaling when she was swept up in her mother's arms. The way her heels had clacked around the kitchen of their immaculate house while she made Catherine her dinner. Or 'tea' as her mum used to call it. 'Come on Cathy, be a good girl and eat up!'

Once Catherine woke in the middle of the night, her cheeks wet with tears. Although she couldn't remember the dream, she knew it had been about her mother. As she lay there in the darkness, an almost unbearable sense of loss had overwhelmed her.

'See what he's done? You were fine until he came along,' she whispered to herself. Her throat tightened. It was another sign she was better off without him.

It was the editors' annual Christmas dinner. Rivalry and egos were put aside for the evening – at least on the surface – because this was a chance for the great and the good of the publishing industry to rub shoulders and congratulate themselves and each other.

Catherine really hadn't wanted to go. She was exhausted, and the last thing she felt like doing was sitting at a table with Adam Freshwater and the other Valour head honchos making polite small talk. On the plus side, she could go there and hold her head high: they were well on their way to smashing the Christmas target. Not that you'd guess that from Sir Robin's behaviour.

It had transpired he'd sent one of his henchmen down to the *Soirée* Sponsors office. They hadn't counted on coming up against Gail, however, who had given the haughty man in a suit short shrift when he'd asked to look through her financial records and been even curter when he'd told her he would most likely be sending several estate agents around to value the place.

'Snooty little git he was, turning up out of the blue and snooping through our filing cabinets,' Gail had told Catherine. 'When he told me I should be lucky *Soirée* Sponsors was still going, and then pulled the estate-agent gubbins, I sent him off with a flea in his ear!' Gail had paused uncertainly. 'They're just trying to put the frighteners on us, aren't they? They're not really going to sell the office?'

'They probably just wanted to come down and see how everything was going.' Catherine had placated her, but inside she had been angry. How dare 'Hatchet' Hackford do that behind her back?

In fact, Catherine had been close to crying off the evening with a headache, and might have if *Teen Style*'s Fiona MacKenzie hadn't been going. Fiona was a straightforward, no-bullshit person and the closest thing to a friend Catherine had. The two women didn't meet very often, but liked and respected each other, kindred spirits in an industry where style often ruled over substance.

After a three-course dinner, during which she was forced to endure a long conversation about the wonder of spreadsheets with the finance director, Catherine escaped the table and went to find Fiona at the bar. She asked the barman for a large glass of white wine, and drank half of it in one gulp.

'Steady on there, gal, you'll be flat on your back!'

'I need it after the conversation I've just had.'

'Talking shop?' asked Fiona sympathetically.

'That and other things. It just feels so fake. There we all are, sitting round and toasting *Soirée* when we all know we could bloody fold in a few months. It would be the end of *Soirée* Sponsors, too.'

Fiona's eyes widened. 'Are things really that bad?'

Catherine stopped. 'Look, Fi, I shouldn't have said that. I'm just pissed off . . .'

Her friend nodded perceptively. 'It gets to us all.'

Catherine stared at the floor.

'I mean it, Catherine, it's crap for all of us at the moment. You mustn't let yourself get down. *Soirée* is one of the biggest titles out there. When the shit hit the fan it was always going to fly your way first. More to stick to.'

'Nicely put,' said Catherine, allowing herself a smile. 'What if they're right, though? What if *Soirée* has had its day?'

'Somehow, I don't think the whole magazine industry is going to fall like a pack of cards overnight. I know it must be scary carrying the can, but you can do it. You've got bigger balls than any man I know!'

Catherine laughed. 'I *think* that's a compliment, thanks Fi. Another drink?'

'OK,' Fiona said. She watched Catherine signal for the barman again before adding, 'There is something I need to talk to you about . . .'

'That sounds ominous.'

Fiona glanced round. 'It's probably nothing, but I've heard on the grapevine that Isabella's been saying things about you.'

Catherine's stomach dropped. 'Like what?'

'Oh, the usual Isabella stuff. How badly *Soirée*'s doing, how they should get her to do the job . . .'

Catherine rolled her eyes. 'Not that old chestnut.'

Fiona wasn't finished. 'Apparently she's been saying personal stuff about you, as well. Like you can't cope, and the board don't trust you and want you out.'

'I knew she was shagging one of them!' said Catherine furiously. 'That poisonous dwarf, how dare she cast aspersions about me!'

Fiona put a placating hand on her arm. 'I don't want to upset you. In normal circumstances, I wouldn't even have said anything. No one would believe that horse shit anyway, especially when you're so bloody good at your job.'

She paused. 'You do need to watch your back with Isabella, though. Tittle-tattle aside, I've heard she's destroyed people's reputations before. She hates anyone who's got more than she has. Just keep an eye on her.'

Catherine was on the way to the loo when someone touched her arm.

'Would you hold it against me if I said how gorgeous you look tonight?' Tolstoy Peake was looking rather dashing in a beautifully cut dinner jacket. He was also sporting a deep tan, his dark eyes even more alert than usual.

'My God, look at the colour of you!' Catherine laughed. 'Have you been away somewhere?'

'I've just got back from Hawaii, actually, doing another Iron Man race.'

Catherine was impressed, even though it reminded her she had only used her hugely expensive gym membership twice in the last six months. Tolstoy did look well. He was leaner than ever, while his skin had the clearness of someone who had never gone near an additive in their life.

'You make me feel like such a slob.'

Tolstoy looked her up and down. 'Oh, I think you're getting away with it so far, darling. If you ever fancy training with me, though . . .'

Tolstoy had once done two triathlons back-to-back, and then swum the English Channel.

'I'll think I'll pass, if you don't mind,' smiled Catherine. 'Anyway, sorry to love you and leave you, but I must go to the loo.'

Tolstoy bowed and stepped aside. 'Of course. Don't forget about that dinner we're going to have.'

Catherine had only gone a few metres when her

heel caught on something on the carpet, making her stumble. She clutched a nearby table, spilling wine glasses everywhere. Everyone turned round and stared. As she raised her head, Catherine literally wanted to die with embarrassment.

'Oh dear, darling!' Someone was leaning over her. 'You really must watch where you're going.' It was Isabella Montgomery, eye-blinding in a fuchsia-pink dress.

'Did you just trip me up?' shouted Catherine furiously.

Isabella's eyes widened. 'Of course not! Take better care next time. She's probably had too much to drink,' she whispered loudly to the group of guests who had crowded round.

'I've only had two glasses, how dare you!' shouted Catherine. By then Tolstoy Peake was upon her, an arm around her waist. Catherine caught a waft of strong aftershave.

'I say, darling, are you all right?'

Blood boiling, Catherine looked around, but Isabella was nowhere to be seen. Catherine's eyes pricked with rage and humiliation.

'If you don't mind, I'm going to call it an early night,' she told him, and made a sharp exit. Once outside, Catherine tried to compose herself. Her hands were shaking from what had just happened; was Fiona's warning about to come true?

Chapter 38

Ash's head was spinning. He'd never actually thought Nikki would go ahead and do what she'd promised, but now he'd had a call from a woman called Gail Barker from *Soirée* Sponsors, and been asked down to her office for a meeting.

'So what do you think?' Gail asked him. 'I've spoken to Angelica Fox-Titt, and she's more than happy for you to go and do a placement at her shop.'

Ash didn't know what to say. Apart from a school trip to the Brecon Beacons when he was eleven, he'd never been to the countryside. It felt more alien than exciting.

Gail knew it was a lot for him to take in. Nikki had told her all about Ash and his unhappy home life.

'Shall I leave you to think about it?' she asked kindly.

Ash nodded dumbly. The thoughts were coming thick and fast. Could his dad cope without him? Would the temp agency take him back afterwards? And what was he going to do for money?

Gail seemed to read his mind. 'Mrs Fox-Titt has already said she will pay you an hourly rate, and there is separate accommodation at her house that you can use, free of charge.' She looked at her notes. 'The place is called the Maltings.' Gail grinned at Ash. 'Sounds very posh.'

'Dad! Are you here?' Ash called as he let himself into the flat sometime later. There was a sour smell in the hallway; his dad still hadn't taken out the rubbish like Ash'd asked him to. Ash stepped over the bin bags and made his way down the corridor to the living room. No decorations had been put up, there was no Christmas tree in the corner. Ash had always thought that his dad had stopped living the moment his mum had walked out. Now his dad just existed, taking no notice of everyday life. Today he was sitting under a blanket watching a daytime telly quiz show. His greying hair and unshaven, sunken face made Ash suddenly realize how old he was.

'Hi, son,' Mr King said wearily. For once, he had a cup of tea in his hand instead of a can of lager. That would change later, though. 'Can I make you a brew?'

Ash shook his head. 'Don't get up. I've got something to tell you.'

Mr King looked up. 'This sounds a bit serious. You doing a runner and leaving me?' He said it in a jokey manner, but Ash saw the panic in his eyes. Ash sat down on the other end of the sofa.

'I've been offered a new job. Well, kind of, it's a work-placement at this antiques shop. In this place called Churchminster. Starts next month.'

Mr King eyed him. 'What about your job?'

Ash shrugged, 'My contract runs out soon, anyway, I can always get a new one when I come back.'

His dad took a sip of tea. 'Antiques, eh? You've always been interested in them.' His brow furrowed. 'Is this stuff legit? I mean, who's in charge here?'

Ash felt unexpected emotion: his dad never normally cared about that stuff. 'Yeah, Dad, it's through this scheme called *Soirée* Sponsors. They give kids like me the chance to work in really cool places.'

'*Soirée* Sponsors.' Mr King rolled the words around his mouth reflectively. 'How long's it for?'

Ash shrugged casually, trying to hide the guilt building up inside. 'Only a few months. I might even come back early if it's boring.'

Mr King looked round the tiny room, with the broken armchair and cracked window that was held together with gaffer tape. Despite Ash's repeated phone calls the council still hadn't been round to fix it. He turned and studied Ash, his own tired sad eyes on Ash's pale-blue ones.

'I want you to make something of your life, son, and not be stuck here looking after me.'

'Dad . . .' Ash started to say, but the older man stopped him.

'You've got potential, kid, I can see it. Don't make a mess of your life like me. I'll be all right. Just send me the odd postcard.'

The two shared their first smile for what seemed like years.

'Thanks, Dad,' said Ash. He really meant it.

Catherine was parched, another legacy from drinking too much wine last night. She walked out of the office and headed down to reception to get a Diet Coke from the vending machine.

As she turned the corner, she saw a man standing with his back to her at the front desk. Those powerful shoulders looked familiar . . . Catherine felt a sudden jolt of sickness as she realized it was John. Ducking out of sight, she raced back down the corridor and took the stairs two at a time, past a startled person from accounts. She had to get Harriet to stop him coming up . . .

'Tell him I'm not in,' she gasped as she screeched to a halt in front of her desk. Harriet was already on the phone. Had reception beaten her to it? Catherine watched Harriet's face anxiously.

If Harriet was startled by her normally ultra-cool boss arriving wide-eyed and panting, she didn't show it.

'I'm afraid Catherine is in a meeting,' she said. 'No, I don't think she'll be back in the office today.' Harriet listened. 'Jolly good. Will do.'

'I know who it was,' Catherine interrupted, as Harriet opened her mouth to relay the message. She took a deep breath. 'Sorry, it's just that I'm really busy today, and I don't have time to see anyone.'

Harriet smiled cheerfully. 'Don't worry, I'll take any messages.'

Unnerved, Catherine went into her office. What more did she have to do to put the man off? Walking over to the window, she pulled the blinds apart and looked down on to the street. After a few moments, John Milton's dark head appeared. As if aware that Catherine was watching, he looked up. Catherine dropped the blind. Shit! Heart thumping, she sat down behind her desk and tried to get on with some work.

Leave me alone, for God's sake, please, she said to herself. *Don't you know it's better like this?*

Chapter 39

The residents of Montague Mews were busy preparing for the holidays. Stephen and Klaus had already departed for their month-long tour of the Napa Valley vineyards, while a taxi had turned up at the crack of dawn that morning to take Velda to Heathrow. It was mid-afternoon and shadows were already lengthening through the house. Benedict had gone to the shops with Milo, and Caro was making the most of it by having a much-needed lie-down on the sofa. Her energy levels had been flagging recently, and she hadn't been able to chase round as much as normal after her son.

As she stared up at the ceiling, it dawned on her just how much there was to do back in Churchminster. Excluding Camilla, her entire family were descending on Mill House in under a week's time. Caro hadn't stayed in the place since Bonfire Night, and it was probably lying under a foot of dust. Then she had the decorations to put up, beds to make, food to get in . . . oh God, why wasn't she more organized? At least they were going to Granny Clem's for Christmas dinner. Even better, they would be spared Brenda's distinctly unholy cooking, as Caro's father Johnnie was traditionally in charge of the festive feast.

Despite her growing panic about getting everything ready in time, Caro was excited about going home for the holidays. Christmas was one of the few times her close-knit family all got together, and they always had a wonderful time, even if it had taken her three days and as many packets of Nurofen to get over last year's champagne-induced hangover.

She found her thoughts wandering to Rowena, two doors down. What would her Christmas be like? Caro pictured her waking on Christmas morning to a dark, empty house. Who would Rowena toast the day with, or tell off for talking all the way through the Queen's speech? For some reason, Caro found this last thought unbearably sad, and her eyes started filling up with tears.

'What's wrong?' exclaimed Benedict, when he and Milo returned a short while later. Caro looked up from the sofa, eyes swollen and red with tears. Milo ambled over to his mother and laid a little mitten-clad hand on her arm. His sweet gesture made Caro cry even harder.

'I was thinking about Rowena,' she sobbed. 'How alone and unloved she'll be on Christmas Day. She hasn't even got anyone to pull her c-c-cracker with!'

Benedict sat down beside her. 'Do you always get this emotional when you're pregnant?' he asked sympathetically.

'S-s-sometimes!' She let out a snot-filled snort.

'There, there, my darling.' Benedict stroked her wet cheek.

'I'm being p-p-pathetic,' Caro wept. 'For all I know Rowena could be a bloody J-j-jehovah's Witness.'

For the last few years, Valour had put on a Christmas party for the *Soirée* Sponsors team and apprentices. As well as being an informal way to catch up with each other outside the formalities of progress reports and paperwork, it was a good chance for young people who wanted to join to come and find out what it was all about. Not that they could take on anyone else at the moment, as Adam reminded Catherine on a regular basis.

Adam had also told her Valour would not be putting up the usual financial contribution to pay for the party. To be honest, Catherine hadn't been surprised, but it still didn't stop her feeling angry and disappointed. When Gail had phoned to ask if she could go ahead and choose the venue as normal, Catherine hadn't had the heart to tell her. In a spur-of-the-moment decision, she had decided to foot the bill herself. Not that she would ever tell Gail that, but this was too important an occasion to miss.

The party was being held in a leisure centre near the *Soirée* Sponsors office. While it wasn't compulsory for her own team to come and show their support, Catherine felt it was important that they were kept informed about the scheme as much as possible. After all, they were all part of the same brand. So she'd sent round an email, and everyone in the office – apart from the picture editor who had a sick child at home, and Annabel, who apparently had an important commitment – had said they'd come down and help.

Catherine arrived late because of a meeting over-running, and was greeted by a long queue of girls lining up to have their make-up done by the beauty team. Meanwhile Alexander was teaching another giggling group how to walk down the catwalk. 'Work it, own it!' he shouted like a camp drill-instructor, as he sashayed back and forth with them trailing behind him.

The room was decked out with colourful balloons and long strands of tinsel, and a rectangular table with platters of sandwiches, crisps and fizzy drinks stood against the wall on one side. On the other, a couple of teenage boys were intently spinning tunes behind a set of decks. *Soirée* Sponsors posters were stuck on the walls with photos of some of the scheme's success stories. One of the team had set up a stand with leaflets and other literature explaining what the scheme did.

Despite everything, Catherine's heart lifted. This was what it was all about! The room was buzzing with life and energy. Most people would write those here off as hoodies and troublemakers, but there wasn't a hint of menace. More than ever, it made Catherine believe these kids just needed a chance in life.

Gail walked up with two plastic glasses of Coke. She was wearing a tent-like sequinned top and Pat-Butcher-inspired dangly earrings.

'Great bash, Catherine! Maybe that Sir Robin bloke isn't such a baddun' after all.'

Catherine smiled diplomatically and took a fizzy drink. Suddenly one of her ankles gave, and she had to grab on to Gail's arm for support.

'Easy, girl!' Gail looked down at Catherine's vertigo-inducing heels. 'Bloody hell, I'm not surprised you can't stand up in those! I'd need a bloody ladder to get up there in the first place!'

A funny look crossed Catherine's face.

'I was only joking,' Gail said in bemusement.

'Oh, it wasn't that,' said Catherine. 'You just reminded me of something my mum used to say.' The memory had surprised her. When she was little Catherine used to play dressing-up in her mother's wardrobe, and had once come downstairs in a pair of Annie's highest heels. Her mother had laughed affectionately as her daughter, already showing a tendency to be clumsy, had wobbled round the kitchen.

'Heavens, pet, we're going to need a ladder to get you down from those!'

Catherine smiled, reminiscing, before realizing Gail was watching her expectantly. She forced herself back to the present.

'It's all going OK, then?'

'A few idiots tried to gatecrash earlier, off their heads on something. I soon sent 'em on their way.'

Catherine smiled. 'Nothing frightens you, does it?'

Gail looked serious for a second. 'Losing *Soirée* Sponsors bloody does, I can tell you.'

'Hi, Catherine!' Saffron came up, puncturing the moment. She was holding hands with a small thin girl, who didn't look more than seven.

'This is Sasha. She's here with her older brother, who wants to join *Soirée* Sponsors.'

Catherine looked down at the little figure. 'Hello, Sasha, that's a pretty name.'

Sasha smiled shyly. She looked back up at Saffron. 'I love your necklace, it's like a princess would wear.'

Saffron looked down at her star-shaped pendant, then unclipped it and leant down to put it round Sasha's neck.

'It's yours now, Princess Sasha!'

Sasha looked like all her Christmases had come at once.

It was past eleven by the time Saffron got back to the *Soirée* office after the party. She'd left her BlackBerry on her desk and the thought of being without it for even one night had made her feel rather panicky.

To her surprise, Annabel was still at her desk. 'What

are you doing here?' Saffron said in surprise. 'I thought you had some sooper dooper function to go to?'

Annabel's head snapped up, her cheeks flushed.

'What do you think? Working.' Annabel adopted a self-righteous expression. 'Someone's got to hold the fort while you lot swan off and party.'

Saffron had never known Annabel to work late in her life. 'C'mon, what are you really up to?' she asked, walking round the side of the desk.

'Don't be so nosy!' yelled Annabel, immediately closing down whatever she'd had open on the screen.

Saffron couldn't help but laugh. Annabel looked like an outraged bullfrog. 'I don't think Catherine would be very impressed to know you're using your work computer to look for a new job.'

Annabel started to bluster. 'Don't be so ridiculous. Why would I want to do that?' She made a big show of switching her computer off and gathering her things up. 'Anyway, excuse me but I've got a life to get to.'

'Good for you,' Saffron replied acerbically, as she watched Annabel lumber out of the door. She looked over at Catherine's office. The door was shut, but the lights were on. Saffron frowned, they came on automatically when someone walked in, but the only person here had been Annabel. Why had she been snooping around in Catherine's office?

Chapter 40

It was the day of the *Soirée* Christmas lunch. It was always held at a fashionable restaurant, and then, depending on how generous Valour Publishing was feeling, they'd all go on to another bar where a tab would be set up. It had been Harriet's job this year to source the venue, pre-order everyone's menu, and report the budget back to Catherine. Everyone had wondered if they would be asked to dip into their own pockets for the first time, with the credit crunch snapping round their heels, but Valour had proved surprisingly generous. *Guilty conscience before they give us the chop*, thought Catherine, before chastising herself for a lack of Christmas spirit.

She knew, more than anyone, how difficult she had been to work with these last few months. Nevertheless, the team had still given it their all, and she was immensely grateful to them. Catherine was determined to make sure they all enjoyed themselves. Predictably, not much work had been done in the *Soirée* office that morning, as people sat around chatting about their plans for the holiday, or seeing who could think up the wittiest out-of-office reply on their email. For once, Catherine had turned a blind eye. It was 12.30 p.m.

when she summoned them all to the middle of the office.

'As you know, taxis will be turning up shortly to take us to the restaurant, which Harriet, with her usual organizational brilliance, has booked.' Everyone cheered, and Harriet stepped forward to take a mock-bow. Catherine couldn't help but smile; her PA's confidence had soared since she'd joined *Soirée*.

As the clapping died down, she addressed them again. 'I know it's been a tough three months for us all.' A few nods around the room. 'I've asked everyone to go above and beyond the call of duty, but I really think our efforts have paid off. *Soirée* is looking better than ever, and we've hit each of our monthly targets so far.' Catherine grinned. 'We've just passed the 260,000 mark!'

Everyone cheered, including Catherine. She looked round at them.

'I'm not going to pretend we can take our foot off the brake, and I'm going to ask just as much from you going forward into next year. But I feel very proud with what we've achieved, and I want to take this opportunity to thank you for all your hard work. So come on, let's go and have our extremely well-deserved Christmas dinner.'

As they all gathered their coats and bags together and headed downstairs, Tom Fellows remained at his computer, staring at the screen.

'Hey, Tom, do you want to come with us?' called out Saffron. He looked up and blinked behind his bottle-tops.

'I've still got some stuff to do,' he mumbled.

Saffron smiled cheerily. 'Don't be too long, all work and no play!'

Tom's cheeks flamed and he dived back behind his computer screen.

Saffron and Harriet got into the lift with the chief sub. 'We rock, officially,' Saffron declared. 'Let's forget about work for once, and get on it!'

The chief sub, a man who cared more about deadlines than debauchery, shuddered. At last year's Christmas dinner, someone had spiked his orange juice with vodka all the way through lunch. Normally teetotal, he'd ended up climbing on the table to do an impromptu version of 'My Way' using someone's half-eaten baguette as a microphone.

An hour later everyone was in fine spirits. Alexander was on his third Campari and lemonade and keeping the team in stitches with outrageous tales of the fashion industry. As he launched into an anecdote about a world-famous supermodel who had an outlandish sexual foot-fetish, Catherine turned to Harriet.

'Everyone seems to be enjoying themselves.'

Harriet smiled. 'Rather!'

They were seated in their own private area, around a large oval table. On the other side of it, Annabel glowered at Harriet. She'd made no secret of the fact she'd wanted to sit next to Catherine and suck up to her all the way through lunch. Annabel had been furious when she'd patted the empty seat next to her and Catherine had gone to sit in-between Harriet and Alexander instead.

With the wine and conversation flowing it wasn't long before everyone was well on their way to becoming blotto. The picture editor, a single mum of three who hadn't been out for six months, was telling a very rude joke about a Frenchman and a camel, while one of the beauty girls was trying to put red lipstick on the highly alarmed chief sub.

After inhaling her Christmas pudding in about

three gulps, Saffron looked reproachfully down at her stomach and groaned.

'Fuck, I'm stuffed! Why did I wear these high-waisted trousers?'

'More vino, darling?' Alexander asked Catherine. She moved her glass across. 'Just a splash.'

'You having fun?' he asked.

She smiled. 'Yes, it's so good to see everyone letting off some steam. I know I've been the boss from hell the last few months.'

'Nonsense,' said Alexander loyally. 'What are your plans for Christmas, anyway?'

'Oh, I've got a few friends coming to stay,' Catherine said quickly. The actual truth was that she had no one to spend Christmas Day with, but there was no way she was telling Alexander that. She changed the subject.

'You?'

'Going to the family pile in Northampton. Pa has organized a shooting party the minute I get back, so I'd better pack my plus fours. Luckily Prada have done some divine ones for autumn/winter.'

Catherine laughed. 'I wouldn't have had you down as the country sort!'

'Crack shot, actually. Represented England at under twenty-one rifle shooting. Oh, my father would have loved me to be a county gentleman like him and my brother. It didn't quite turn out like that, but luckily I can still hold my own grouse shooting with him. It's the only reason I haven't been cut out of the family will!'

'You'll be telling me you can milk cows, next.'

Alexander looked mortally offended. 'Darling, we have staff for that!' He readjusted one of his huge cuffs. 'I may be straying on to dangerous territory, but has anything happened with that chap of yours?'

'He's not my chap!' Catherine retorted quickly. She

sighed. 'I don't know, Al, it's complicated for reasons I can't go into.'

'If you say so, darling. I just don't want to see you ending up all alone. A woman needs sex, especially when she's got a fabulous pair of pins like yours. It's a waste!'

'Enough,' smiled Catherine. 'Tell me about your love life instead, it's far more interesting.'

Alexander's eyes flashed wickedly. 'Well, I have just started seeing a new man. He's married, but I do always like a challenge.'

'What are you like?' she laughed. 'Anyone I know?'

Alexander mouthed the name at her and Catherine looked shocked. 'He's just renewed his wedding vows in *Hello!*'

'Takes all sorts, darling. And before you write me off as some kind of home wrecker, his wife is enjoying an extremely hot and heavy affair with a Bulgarian weightlifter.'

An hour later, Catherine left them all to it.

'Will you be all right looking after things here?' she asked Harriet.

Harriet nodded. 'Five hundred pounds bar tab, and then people start paying for themselves.' There was a scream of laughter and she looked over at the picture editor, who was now sitting uninvited on Tom Fellows's lap, trying to feed him the grapes off her cheeseboard. Tom sat there stiffly, the red napkin tucked into his T-shirt matching the colour of his face.

Catherine stood up. 'Bye, everyone, have a great Christmas.'

'You too! Bye Catherine!' they all yelled back. 'Love you!' someone drunkenly shouted. With their happy cries ringing in her ears, Catherine headed home. She'd only have one or two more glasses. It was a special occasion after all . . .

Saffron watched Catherine walk out the door and then glanced around wickedly.

'Right, let's get shit-faced!'

As she poured everyone yet more glasses of wine, there was a commotion outside. It sounded like a herd of buffalo were approaching when, suddenly, the front doors burst open. A dozen pink-faced, pink-shirted men piled in. They were braying more loudly than the donkey section at a children's zoo.

Everyone in the restaurant stared. 'Oh, great,' said Saffron. 'Invasion of the Hooray Henries.'

'How unpleasant,' said Alexander. He surveyed the newcomers with distaste. 'I think I was forced to play rugby against one of those oiks at prep school.'

Harriet thought another of the new arrivals looked familiar. She squinted across the room. Then the man waved a large striped golfing umbrella in the air.

'Oh no!' Harriet said.

'What's wrong?' Saffron and Alexander both asked in unison.

Harriet sighed. 'I went out with that chap over there a few months ago.'

'Thomas Twat-Bumford or whatever his name was?' said Saffron.

Harriet nodded miserably. The three of them watched as Thomas pretended to roger one of his friends with the umbrella.

Alexander handed Harriet a large glass of wine. 'You have my deepest sympathies.'

An hour later, the din from Thomas and his friends was so loud everyone was struggling to be heard. Several tables of diners had walked out in disgust, and the party had already drunk the restaurant dry of champagne. Despite being told by the manager to keep the noise down, they had started singing rugby songs. They had just finished a particularly lewd one about sitting on people's faces when the manager rushed over, quivering with fury.

'Gentlemen! If you do not start behaving in a more respectable manner, I will have to ask you to leave!'

'Sorry, old boy!' one of them shouted.

The manager glared at them and stalked off, a bread roll narrowly missing the back of his head.

Over the other side of the room, Harriet's bladder was bursting, but she didn't dare leave her seat in case Thomas saw her. A shadow fell over her, and she looked up. To her surprise, it was Adam Freshwater. In the commotion, no one had seen *Soirée*'s publisher come in.

Adam looked distinctly out of his comfort zone. 'Is Catherine here?'

'No, she left a while ago. I think she had some Christmas shopping to do.'

Adam sat down in the vacant seat. 'Oh. I see. I just popped in on the off-chance, thought it might be nice to see you all . . .' He trailed off.

Harriet felt rather sorry for him. In his oversized shirt and collar, Adam looked about twelve years old. He'd obviously made an effort to come down.

'Would you like a drink?' she asked.

Adam's eyes brightened. 'Yes, I'll have a large glass of whatever you're having.'

Some time later, Harriet realized inviting Adam to sit down had been a mistake. He'd already polished off three large glasses of wine, and was halfway through his fourth. Saffron and Alexander had both got up to talk to other people, and for the last ten minutes Adam

306

had been telling Harriet how unhappily married he was.

'Thomasina just doesn't understand me,' he slurred. 'The sex has all but dried up, as well. All she cares about is whether there's the right amount of spirulina in her breakfast algae.'

'Spiru-what?' asked Harriet in bemusement.

Adam gaped at her. 'S-s-spriru-what! Exactly! You know where I'm coming from. We're obviously kindred spirits.'

His hand found Harriet's thigh and squeezed it.

'You know, if you ever fancy getting together for a drink . . .'

Harriet pushed his hand off. 'Er, thank you, but no,' she said hurriedly.

Adam shrugged drunkenly and turned back to nurse his glass.

In desperation, Harriet looked around for an escape. Instead, she was greeted by the sight of Thomas head-butting a lump of Christmas pudding that had been lobbed at him. As the dessert hit his beautifully-coiffed bulbous head, cake and currants sprayed everywhere. It was the final straw for the manager. Flanked by some beefy looking chefs from the kitchen, he rushed over and ordered the whole party out.

Harriet watched as the last man was ejected through the doors. At least she could escape to the loo now. She turned to make her excuses to Adam, but he had already passed out, face down in the stagnant remains of Catherine's cheese plate.

Chapter 41

The next morning Catherine woke early. She was stiff and cold and realized that, yet again, she had slept fully clothed on the sofa. Wearily, she tried to stand up and knocked over a half-full bottle of wine, which had been left on the floor. Judging by the look of things, it hadn't been the only one. Catherine didn't even bother to pick it up. Instead she headed to the kitchen for a glass of water and two extra-strong Nurofen. Then it was straight to her bedroom and, hopefully, the oblivion of sleep again.

When Catherine opened her eyes a few hours later, she was momentarily disorientated. The curtains were still open and bright winter light mercilessly filled the room, starting her temples throbbing again. She turned over in bed and saw her designer clothes, lying like a heap of rags on the floor.

Catherine groaned and sat up. She looked at her watch. To her surprise it was midday. It was only the second time in her whole life that she'd slept that late. Then again, what did she have to get up for? Work was finished for two weeks.

Gingerly she stood up and walked through to her en suite bathroom. She surveyed herself in the mirror.

Passing out in her make-up was getting to be a bad habit. Catherine pulled at the grey circles under her eyes and noticed a breakout of spots on her chin. She wondered briefly about booking in for a facial.

She leaned over the sink and turned the taps. The ice-cold water on her face made her gasp, but at least she felt more awake. She looked in the mirror again. Alexander's words came back to her as she studied her body. Would it ever be touched or enjoyed again? She forced thoughts of John Milton out of her mind.

Half an hour later, Catherine was feeling better. She'd had a steaming hot shower, and was now standing in the kitchen sipping a strong black coffee. As she looked round the spotless kitchen, she felt strangely at a loss. What should she do? She didn't feel like watching a DVD or reading.

Wrapping her hands around the mug, she padded barefoot into the living room. With its sleek, contemporary lines and brilliant whiteness, this was Catherine's favourite room. Today, however, it felt self-consciously bare. She never normally bothered with Christmas decorations, but her eyes wandered to an empty corner of the room. There was a Christmas tree market five minutes' walk away; maybe a little one would look good over there . . .

'You're going soft in your old age,' Catherine said aloud. She looked at herself in the huge square mirror over the fireplace. 'And talking to yourself. Oh God!'

Catherine thought for a second, before walking back into the kitchen to deposit her mug in the sink. Then she went to get her coat.

The impromptu trip was proving to be a good idea. Catherine was sitting in a warm, bustling coffee shop with a frothy latte and a cranberry muffin. The window seat was an excellent place to watch the world go by, and the streets were full today with people of all ages. Mums and children walked abreast, their arms full of Waitrose bags and long rolls of wrapping paper. Middle-aged men staggered under the weight of boxes of beer, champagne and wine as they loaded up the backs of their Land Cruisers and estate cars. Across the road outside WH Smith, a steel band had struck up the opening bars to 'Good King Wenceslas', and a crowd had gathered around.

Catherine had been to the florist and bought a beautiful Christmas bouquet to go on her mantelpiece. She had also bought some 'winter spice' scented candles to place around the apartment. There was one thing left to do. Draining her cup of coffee, she stood up.

Five minutes later, she arrived at the quaint little church hall. A banner with the words 'Christmas Tree Fayre' was stretched across the entrance. As she walked in, a cheery-faced man in reindeer ears and a money belt called out.

'Whatcha looking for, love? Big one, small one? I got all sizes here!'

His comic expression made Catherine laugh.

'Not sure yet, can I have a look?'

The man waved her through. 'Be my guest.'

Inside, the air was thick with the smell of pine. Various-sized trees stood lined up against the walls, and Catherine walked around trying to decide. The place was packed, and she kept bumping into people.

'How about this one, darling?'

'Looks good to me. Phoebe, Charlie, what do you think?'

A husband and wife were standing to her left, arms wrapped around each other. Two cherub-faced children ran over to look.

'That's our favourite! That one, Daddy.'

'A minute ago they wanted that one over there,' the woman laughed to her husband. She made eye-contact with Catherine and smiled, her face full of happiness.

Catherine smiled back awkwardly. As she looked around, she realized she was the only one there by herself. Suddenly the idea of getting a Christmas tree seemed pathetic. She didn't even have anyone to help her carry it home.

Catherine turned abruptly and headed for the door.

'Don't you want one, love?' the man called out as she rushed past.

'I might come back later,' Catherine muttered. She was a fraud. This was no place for someone like her. Christmas was not for her. She needed to get away from all this goodwill and cheer.

She was barely through her front door when her phone started ringing in the bottom of her handbag. Dumping her other bags, she scrabbled round to find it.

'Hello?'

'You sound out of breath.'

Catherine stood perfectly still in the hallway.

'Why are you calling me?'

'I wanted to wish you a happy Christmas,' said John Milton.

'So now you have.'

'What are your plans? Are you going away any-where?'

'No,' she replied shortly.

'I'm going to Canada. Heli-skiing. A few of us are going, should be good fun.'

'Good for you,' said Catherine. What had made him think she was interested, anyway? 'Look, if you've just rung up to boast . . .'

311

'Of course that's not why I called.' For the first time, John sounded exasperated. 'I just wanted to see how you are.'

'Well, I'm fine,' she replied. 'But if you don't mind . . .'

John gave a weary laugh. 'Don't tell me, you're busy.'

The silence lay heavy between them before John spoke again.

'I miss you, Catherine.'

She felt sick. 'You don't miss me,' she said angrily. 'The Catherine you miss died years ago. I've told you, you don't know me. And you never will.'

When John spoke again, his voice was like a stranger's. 'Goodbye, Catherine, I wish you all the best.'

Then there was a dialling tone in her ear. This time, he'd been the first to hang up. As she pressed her forehead against the wall in the hallway, Catherine reflected how Christmas was over before it had even started.

Chapter 42

Harriet and Saffron had made a surprisingly quick exit out of town. Harriet's Golf, packed with suitcases and bags of presents, was speeding out on the M4 towards the countryside.

'Have you heard from your aunt?' asked Harriet.

'A few times, she's going to a retreat up in the Atlas mountains somewhere. She didn't think there would be phone reception there, so I doubt I'll hear from her until after Christmas.'

Saffron looked out the window. It was a perfect winter's day, ice-cold and clear. The suburbs were giving way to rolling fields and villages now, and high above them mauve clouds hung heavy on the pale horizon. 'Tell me about Churchminster, I haven't really asked you much about it.'

'Well, I'm biased, of course, but I think it's the best place in the world,' Harriet said.

'Can't be that great . . . you left,' said Saffron teasingly.

Harriet grinned. 'I still think of it as home. There's such a variety of characters there, and everyone knows everyone else . . .'

Saffron grimaced. 'That would do my head in,

everyone knowing my business.' She dived into her bag and came up with a packet of Haribo.

'Want one?'

'Oh, go on, then,' said Harriet.

'Have you got any other family staying for Christmas?' Saffron mumbled through a mouthful of pure sugar.

'No, it's just us and Mummy and Daddy. Daddy's sister lives in a castle in Scotland, but she doesn't like the climate down here. Says it's too warm and plays havoc with her digestion. Of course Cook and Mrs Bantry the housekeeper will be there. Oh, and Hawkins. He's our butler.'

Saffron stopped shovelling sweets into her mouth. 'You've got a butler?'

'Er, yes,' Harriet said apologetically. 'He looks a bit stern, but Hawkins is a dear. Been with the family for years.'

Saffron laughed. 'This is going to be some Christmas!'

An hour later, they were negotiating the winding lanes towards Churchminster. A line of bare trees stood on the horizon, their black boughs drooping like marionette puppets. Suddenly a large reddish bird ran out from the hedgerow into the path of their car. Saffron screamed as Harriet swerved to avoid it.

'Blasted pheasants!' she said cheerfully. 'I think they've got a death wish, sometimes.'

Saffron sank back in her seat, heart going like the clappers. She didn't think her nerves could cope with any more incidents like that. They passed a rambling house where several ponies swathed in bright winter rugs methodically chomped at piles of hay in paddocks. Opposite was a five-bar wooden gate, which was propped open. A large square sign stood beside it.

'The Maltings,' Saffron read.

'That's where the Fox-Titts live. Freddie and Angie are a hoot, they're holding a party on Christmas Eve, if you fancy it.' Harriet shifted the car down a gear. 'Have I told you they're taking someone on from *Soirée* Sponsors? He's going to work in Angie's antique shop. Some young chap called Ashley.'

'Wow,' said Saffron. 'It's going to be a bit different for him out here.' A trio of quaint thatched cottages had materialized on their right, each front door adorned with a colourful wreath.

Harriet was giving a running commentary. 'That first one with the wishing well is Bluebell Cottage, Stephen and Klaus's.'

'Ah, the famous weekend retreat!' said Saffron. 'I always wondered where they disappeared to. It's very cute.'

'Isn't it? And Pearl Potts lives next door at Rose Cottage. She keeps an eye on the place when they're away.'

A flashing Santa Claus took pride of place in one of the windows of the end cottage.

'Who lives there?'

'Brenda and Ted Briggs. Brenda runs the village store. If you want any local gossip, she's your woman.'

A few hundred metres down the road, they pulled up at a T-junction.

'Well, this is the heart of Churchminster. What do you think?'

Saffron felt like she had just stepped on to a film set. In front of her was a large village green, with a striped maypole in one corner and a war memorial in the other. A collection of houses, all built in the famous yellow Cotswold stone, stood nestled around it. Dusk was starting to fall and welcoming light shone out from windows, while puffs of grey smoke curled up out of several chimneys. On the other side of the green stood a large, handsome church.

'That's St Bartholomew's. Mummy and Daddy got married there, and it's where I was christened.'

Harriet indicated right and they passed another trio of cottages, slightly larger than the first ones. Saffron had a sudden vision of herself in an apron, pulling a freshly baked cake out of a gleaming Aga range.

'That's Camilla's cottage.' Harriet pulled up outside the last one, which had the number '5' etched into the garden gate. Behind it, the house sat dark and quiet.

'Must be weird not having her around for Christmas,' said Saffron. Harriet had told her at length about her best friend.

Harriet sighed. 'It does feel a bit strange, like I'm missing a body part. Although she and Jed are having a jolly good time, by all accounts.'

Two minutes later they were on another road heading out of the village. Everywhere she looked, Saffron could see swathes of muddy brown fields, the frozen ploughed furrows looking like piles of half-mixed cement. She shuddered slightly; this was most definitely farming country. What if Harriet's parents expected her to get up at the crack of dawn every day to milk the sheep or something?

'Nearly there!' announced Harriet cheerfully. On the left of the road stood a pair of impressive stone pillars. Slowing down, Harriet pulled off and drove in over a cattle grid.

'Bloody hell!' said Saffron. Even through the fading light, she could see the long drive flanked by sweeping grounds. At the top was a magnificent manor house. Built in the finest Cotswold stone, it rose up imperiously out of the landscape with a frontage that seemed to go on for ever.

As they drove forwards, a small cottage appeared out of the gloom.

'That's where I live. I'll bring you back tomorrow for a look,' Harriet said. She desperately wanted to go in, but she knew her mother was expecting them. They were staying at the Hall for the holiday; Gate Cottage's antiquated heating had finally given up the ghost, and needed a whole new system installed.

'I'd much prefer to have our guest in the Hall, anyway,' her mother had told her. 'We can't have you living like a pair of barn animals at the end of the drive.'

As the car approached, Saffron had another chance to take in the sheer size and splendour of the building. Saffron knew Harriet came from a good family, but she'd always been very modest about it. Saffron hadn't been expecting something on this scale. In front of the house the drive widened into a large gravel turning circle. A huge stone fountain stood in the middle of it. Saffron imagined that long ago this had been where carriages would deposit their well-heeled occupants for one grand ball or another.

Harriet pulled to a stop outside the front door, which Saffron noticed was big enough to get an elephant through.

'Now, I must just tell you about Daddy,' she started. 'He's a bit . . .'

But before Harriet could finish, the door opened and two silky grey lurchers came bounding out. A trim, elegant woman appeared behind them on the step. Her blonde hair was styled immaculately, and she was dressed in a cashmere cardigan and expensive wool skirt.

'Darling!' she cried, in a voice that could slice through diamonds.

Struggling to move in her thick quilted jacket, Harriet somehow got her foot caught in the seat belt and fell out of the car. Lady Frances Fraser winced.

'Hello, Mummy!' said Harriet. Saffron watched as the two embraced warmly. Lady Fraser stepped back to look at her daughter.

'Darling, haven't you been using that serum I sent you? Your hair looks dreadfully frizzy.'

Harriet rolled her eyes good-naturedly. 'I didn't have time to blow-dry it this morning.'

Saffron made her way round to the other side of the car. She pulled her coat around her, trying to keep the cold out.

'Mummy, this is my good friend Saffron Walden. Saffron, this is my mother, Frances.'

Saffron wondered briefly if she should curtsy, but decided on a smile instead.

'Hi, Lady Fraser. Thank you so much for inviting me.'

The other woman smiled, revealing well-kept teeth. 'Frances, please.' She stepped forward and delicately kissed Saffron on both cheeks. 'Welcome to Clanfield Hall!'

'Your father's out in the Land Rover. Something about poachers in one of the fields,' said Frances, as she led the two girls through to her private sitting room. 'I don't expect he'll be too long.'

Saffron's eyes were out on stalks. This was like something from *To The Manor Born*! Every room they passed was easily as big as the whole of her aunt's house in Montague Mews. Tapestries and family portraits hung from every wall, while the stone floors were covered with huge, ornately woven rugs. Saffron would put money on them being fabulously expensive family heirlooms.

Despite the wood panelling, dark portraits and a suit of armour at the bottom of the imposing staircase, Clanfield Hall definitely had a woman's touch. Vases of flowers stood in every room, while Frances's sitting room was elegant but comfy with pale-pink striped wallpaper and heavy cream curtains. A large water-colour of the Hall hung over the fireplace, where someone had just lit a fire. Saffron guessed that would not have been Lady Fraser.

'Mrs Bantry just laid the fire,' said Frances. 'Ambrose hasn't put the heating on yet, I'm afraid.' She gestured to an immaculately upholstered sofa.

'Do sit down.'

Saffron sank down, as close to the fire as she could get. The house was freezing.

There was a knock at the door.

'Come in,' Frances called. A tall, trim man in a pristine butler's uniform entered. Saffron couldn't believe it: they really did have a butler!

'Hawkins,' said Frances.

'Lady Fraser?'

'We'd like a pot of tea, please.'

Frances looked at the two girls.

'Was there anything else?'

'Ooh, I wonder if there's any of Cook's homemade shortbread?' asked Harriet eagerly. Her mother looked disapproving, but didn't say anything.

'I believe the requested items are already waiting for you in the kitchen.'

'Good old Cookster! They're world-famous, you know,' she told Saffron.

Hawkins gave a ghost of a smile as he exited the room as noiselessly as he had come in.

A few minutes later, they were seated round the fire drinking sweet, hot tea from bone china mugs. Cook's biscuits had indeed lived up to their reputation. Saffron had just had her fourth, but refrained from dunking them like she normally did.

'Did your Christmas party go well?' Frances asked. Saffron noticed that, even sitting down, she had the elegant, upright poise of a ballerina.

A memory of Thomas head-butting the Christmas pudding swam into Harriet's mind. 'Yes thanks, Mummy.' She changed the subject. 'How are things here?'

'Oh, the usual. Your father's latest thing is driving round bawling out any hapless ramblers that stray on to the estate. I really think he needs to get a new hobby. He's been rather trying to live with since he decided he was too old to carry on shooting.'

'I'm sure that won't last, Daddy lives for his shooting trips in Scotland!'

Saffron, who couldn't even kill a spider if she found it in her room, wasn't sure if she liked the sound of Sir Ambrose Fraser.

Frances noticed her face. 'We must be painting a dreadful picture!' she laughed. 'It's not like that at all. Ambrose is just rather set in his ways and . . .'

A door slammed somewhere in the building, and footsteps headed their way. The closer they got, the more they sounded as if the person who was making them was stamping. Saffron found she was holding her breath. Frances and Harriet looked at each other.

'Oh dear, it doesn't sound like Daddy's in a very good mood,' said Harriet.

Just then the door flew open, bringing with it a cold gust of air and a very muddy black and white dog.

'Ambrose!' Frances exclaimed. 'Get Sailor out. I don't want her jumping all over the furniture.'

'Get, girl! Sailor, OUT.' Tail wagging furiously, the dog scampered away.

Sir Ambrose Fraser stood in the middle of the room, clad in a pair of plus fours and a waxed jacket. Beneath the red face and watery blue eyes were the unmistakable high cheekbones of the aristocracy. He had the look of someone who'd had a lot of outdoor living and even more whisky. He was much older than Frances; Saffron would have put him in his late seventies. He also looked distinctly grumpy.

'Bloody vermin, crawling all over my land!'

Harriet jumped up. 'Daddy!'

Sir Ambrose Fraser's eyes swivelled on to his daughter, as if he hadn't realized she was there.

'What are you doing here? I thought you weren't back until the twenty-second.'

'It is the twenty-second,' Frances told him patiently. 'I reminded you yesterday morning that Harriet was coming.'

'What's that? Well, I can't remember.'

'You probably weren't listening.'

'Humph,' said Ambrose. He turned to Harriet. 'Let's have a look at you, then!'

Harriet ran across and flung her arms around him. 'It's so good to see you!'

'Good grief, girl, you almost knocked me over,' Ambrose said, but his face had softened. Over Harriet's shoulder, he noticed Saffron. 'Who's this?'

Frances rolled her eyes. 'This is Harriet's friend, Saffron Walden. She's staying for Christmas. I did tell you all of this.'

'Saffron Walden? As in the village? Nice little place;

I've hunted with the Cambridgeshire over there a few times.'

Saffron smiled sweetly. 'I'm really not sure. I think my dad named me after a boat.'

Ambrose looked her up and down, taking in the skin-tight jeans, peroxide hair and black pixie boots. 'Are you in one of these God-awful rock groups? I won't have you playing your bloody guitar all hours of the day and night, it'll send the dogs mad.'

'Ambrose!'

'Oh, Daddy.'

His eyes glinted mischievously. 'Settle down, I was only pulling her leg.' He stuck out a hand. 'How do you do?'

Saffron grinned. Despite her earlier reservations, she thought she might rather like Sir Ambrose Fraser.

After a tour of the Hall, including the kitchens and an introduction to the revered Cook, Harriet showed Saffron up to her room. It was huge, with a high ceiling, four-poster bed, and an impressive fireplace. A pair of unseen hands, most probably Hawkins's, had brought up Saffron's bag. A vase of freshly cut winter flowers stood on the dressing table.

'That'll be Mummy,' said Harriet fondly. 'She likes all our guests to have flowers in their rooms.'

Despite the grandeur Saffron shivered. *This place was bloody freezing!*

'It is a bit chilly,' said Harriet apologetically. 'Daddy doesn't like putting on the heating unless it's completely necessary, says it's a waste of money.'

'It's D-d-december,' said Saffron. Her teeth were chattering.

Harriet smiled. 'Never fear, Mummy's persuaded him to put it on tonight. Now, your bathroom is next door, and I'm just down the hall. Shall I come and knock on your door for dinner?'

'Cool,' said Saffron. 'I didn't pack my ball gown,' she added, only half-joking.

'You don't have to dress up,' Harriet laughed. 'Stay as you are, I think Daddy was rather taken with your outfit.'

Dinner was served at eight o'clock precisely in the dining room. Saffron had expected it to be a stuffy affair, but it was rather more informal, with Frances bringing in the plates herself on a silver tray from the kitchen. Saffron noticed hers had more on it than everyone else's; Cook had obviously taken in her slender frame and decided to feed her up. Thankfully, it seemed Ambrose had stuck to his word and the radiators were on, although Saffron was still wearing three vests under her jumper.

'I've sent Cook home early tonight, she looks as if she could do with a rest,' announced Frances.

'Cook has been with us ever since I was little,' Harriet told Saffron. 'She's almost like a grandmother to me.'

Frances took a sip of wine. 'I think that's the only reason she stays on.'

They were sitting round a long, mahogany table. Ambrose eyed Saffron the way a farmer would appraise a bullock at a country fair.

'Where do you come from?'

'I live in London. Chelsea. A place called Montague Mews.'

'Where Caro Towey is living at the moment,' added Harriet. 'It's really very pretty.'

Ambrose looked perplexed. 'Caro who?'

'Caro, Daddy. Camilla's sister.'

'I thought she was called Belmont. Husband works in the City?'

'Sebastian was her first husband. She's remarried to Benedict now, you know him.'

Ambrose harrumphed. 'Woman's had more surnames than Elizabeth Taylor.'

Harriet flushed. 'Hold on, Daddy, that's a bit unfair!'

'Ignore him,' Frances said, shooting her husband a warning look. He was still in a combative mood from his encounter with the poachers earlier.

'How long are you staying for, darling? You do know your father and I are going up to Leicestershire for New Year?'

At the other end of the table Ambrose was looking distinctly unimpressed at the prospect.

'Not sure yet. There are still a few tickets left for the party at the Jolly Boot. I was going to ask Saffron if she'd like to stay for it.'

'I've got plans in London, actually,' said Saffron quickly. A week in the countryside would be enough for her.

'Not to worry, I can always find someone else to go with,' Harriet said.

Ambrose had been chewing his food as he listened to the exchange.

'Your family from London, are they?' he asked Saffron.

'I live with my aunt, Velda. There's just the two of us.'

'What about your father?'

'He died.'

'Oh. Mother?'

Harriet laughed nervously. 'Come on, Daddy, stop giving poor Saffron the third degree!'

Sensing Saffron's discomfort, Frances expertly changed the subject.

'Harriet tells me your aunt is a sculptor, Saffron. I've always thought that must be *fascinating* . . .'

After dinner, the four retreated to a small sitting room off the main hallway to watch *The Vicar of Dibley*. Frances and Ambrose eventually retired to their separate bedrooms while Harriet and Saffron stayed by the fire drinking red wine and chatting.

It was gone midnight by the time Saffron climbed between the cold bed sheets, in pyjamas, hooded jumper and her thickest pair of socks. She had been dreading having to mind her Ps and Qs, but the Frasers had made her feel very welcome. Even though they seemed hard on Harriet sometimes, it was obvious Frances and Ambrose adored their only child.

Saffron couldn't help feeling a pang of envy. Switching off the light, she lay back and let the darkness envelop her.

'I miss you, Daddy,' she whispered.

Chapter 43

Down in the heart of the village, Caro had been preparing for her family's arrival. She'd arrived at Mill House a few days ago to find the electrics had blown, and a sleepy dormouse had somehow got in and made a new home in one of Benedict's Wellingtons. Luckily he'd shaken them out before putting them on for their walk.

Once the electrician had been called and order restored, everyone pulled together to get the house ready for Christmas. Clementine lent Brenda Briggs for the morning to clean the bits Caro's bump couldn't get to, but Caro still had to go round with the Hoover afterwards to get all the fluff and dirt Brenda had mysteriously missed. Caro and Amelia had then gone into Bedlington to do a huge shop at Waitrose, while Benedict put up the decorations.

After lunch Benedict took Milo off to a local farm to pick up an eight-foot Christmas tree to go in the corner of the living room. The little boy was beside himself with excitement at the thought of another tree to decorate.

Caro and Amelia were sitting at the kitchen table with a pot of tea and the remains of a chocolate Yule log between them. Caro had hoped getting away from London would help her sister-in-law; she felt there was something about living there that was upsetting Amelia.

The day before she'd left, she'd found Amelia crying in the kitchen. Amelia had quickly brushed away the tears and said it was the time of the month, but when Caro had gone to use the phone afterwards, she'd found someone had left it off the hook. She'd had a few more silent phone calls herself, recently, and maybe she was being paranoid, but they only seemed to happen when Benedict wasn't there. It was almost as if someone was watching the place.

Amelia warmed her hands on her mug contentedly. 'I didn't quite realize how nice it would feel to get away from it all. London, I mean.' To everyone's relief, there had already been a change in Amelia since they'd got back. Somehow she seemed freer and happier.

Caro decided now was the time to bring her concerns up; at least she and Amelia were talking properly again.

'Darling, there's something I've been meaning to talk to you about.'

'Oh?'

'It's these funny phone calls we've been having.'

Amelia leant back in her chair, arms crossed. The defensive gesture didn't escape Caro's notice. 'What phone calls?'

Caro looked at her uncertainly. 'You know, where I've gone to pick up and there's been no one there. I mean, they could all be wrong numbers, but there've been so many of them recently.'

Across the table Amelia's face had become distinctly wintery.

'Then there was that awful devil mask at the window.

327

I mean, it scared the life out of all of us, but, Amelia, you seemed really terrified by it.'

'So what are you saying?' Amelia's voice was hostile.

Caro gulped, she hated confrontation, especially with someone as dear to her as her sister-in-law.

'I'm just saying, darling, that these things could be coincidence, but they have started since you've come to live with us.'

Amelia was up from her seat like an uncoiled spring. 'You want me to move out? I've imposed on you and Benedict for long enough . . .'

Caro was horrified. 'No, darling, that's not what we want at all!' She searched in vain for the right words. 'Oh Amelia, I want to make sure you're all right, that's all.' Without realizing it, Caro's eyes had filled with tears. She was feeling tired and emotional as it was.

Instantly Amelia was round the table, throwing her arms around her. 'Please don't cry! It's lovely how much you care about me, but I'm fine, honestly.'

'You're sure?' Caro sniffed.

Amelia smiled at her. 'Completely! Now come on, I just want us all to have a good Christmas. No more silly talk of phantom phone calls or faces at windows.' She pulled a mock-horror face, lightening the moment.

Caro couldn't help but laugh. Sod it, she probably *was* just being silly; her pregnancy hormones were in overdrive.

As Amelia went to leave the kitchen, she paused in the doorway. 'You haven't told Benedict, have you? About the phone calls, I mean.'

Caro looked up from clearing the teacups. 'No, I wanted to speak to you first.'

'I wouldn't bother,' Amelia said lightly. 'You know

how he gets, he'll probably get a SWAT team trained on the house and keep us all prisoner.'

'Darling!'

As soon as Caro opened the front door, Tink burst into happy tears. 'You look radiant! Oh, I've missed you!' She threw her arms around her eldest daughter. Errol Flynn, who had come over with Clementine earlier, rushed round their legs barking madly.

Tink rubbed Caro's bump ecstatically. 'You look further along this time. Doesn't she, Johnnie?'

'Probably all the cakes I keep scoffing. You'd think I was eating for eight. Hello, Daddy!'

Johnnie Standington-Fulthrope, as tall and dashing as ever, stood behind his wife on the doorstep.

'Hello, pumpkin!'

The barking intensified.

'Errol Flynn!' they all chorused. 'Do shut up!'

Through the melee, Calypso's voice rang out.

'Can we hurry along the heartfelt reunions please? It's bloody freezing out here.'

As usual, Caro's youngest sister was dressed completely inappropriately for the weather in a neon pink minidress, low-slung belt with silver tassels hanging off it, and a black trilby hat. Her long caramel blonde hair was fashionably tousled, with what looked like pink streaks running through it.

She heaved a huge suitcase over the doorstep and dumped it on the hallway floor.

'I'm surprised we even took off at JFK with that thing,' remarked Johnnie. 'I'm sure I saw the back row being led off to make way for it.'

Caro giggled.

'Oh shut up, Daddy!' said Calypso, grinning.

For the next ten minutes it was utter chaos, as

everyone hugged and kissed each other. While the women sat talking and laughing in the living room, Benedict helped Johnnie with the rest of the suitcases. By the time the new guests were settled in their respective bedrooms and freshened up, it was nearly supper time. They congregated in the living room for a champagne toast.

'Here's to a wonderful Christmas!' said Tink afterwards, raising her glass.

'Hear, hear!'

Benedict had cooked a succulent fish pie stuffed with prawns and cod, and the whole family sat round the dining room table. Tink soon had them all in stitches about their new neighbours in Barbados, who were naturalists.

'Esmé and Gerard, they're a frightfully nice couple in their fifties,' she said. 'Although it is rather disconcerting when one looks out of one's bedroom window to see them playing tennis on the court at the end of their garden.' She giggled. 'I had no idea things could jiggle so much!'

'Your mother has applied for the job of ball-girl to bring in some extra money,' said Johnnie.

Everyone snorted with laughter, but on the other side of the table Clementine looked mildly disapproving.

'Barbados is making you awfully vulgar, darling,' she told her son. Johnnie flashed a contrite grin.

'Sorry, old stick! One's forgetting oneself. Anyway, you must fill us in on all the news. I hear the Bonfire Night raised a heap of money. We'd like to throw some in, too.'

Mollified, Clementine smiled at her son. 'That would be wonderful.'

'How's New York?' Caro asked Calypso.

'Mental. I love it, though.' She looked at Amelia. 'That reminds me, I've got those jeans for you.'

Tink smiled proudly. 'Calypso's boss has been so pleased with all her hard work, she's just been promoted.'

'Clever girl!' and 'Congratulations!' rang out round the table.

'Thanks, guys,' Calypso grinned. 'I'll be working my butt off, but it's all good for the CV. I reckon I'll be out there another year or so, then I want to come back here and set up my own company.'

'You should go into partnership with Harriet,' Caro told her. 'She's doing that sort of thing at *Soirée*.'

Calypso laughed. 'I can't imagine old Hats living it up in the Big Smoke! Good on her.'

'I know! Going down a storm, apparently. I must admit, it's so nice to have her living round the corner.'

Benedict went to fetch another bottle from the kitchen, and Tink turned to Amelia.

'And now you're at the mews! It's like a regular Churchminster convention.'

Amelia smiled. 'Quite!'

'What are your plans, darling? Are you going back to Moscow?'

'I don't think so,' said Amelia carefully. 'I'm just going to see how things go. As long as Caro and Benedict don't mind me staying.'

'Of course not!' said Caro.

'I've heard the clubs in Moscow are awesome,' Calypso said as she helped herself to seconds.

Amelia shrugged. 'They're OK. One seems like all the others after a while.'

'Did you land yourself an oligarch?' asked Calypso. 'I wouldn't mind a Russian sugar daddy.'

'Darling!' Clementine reprimanded her as the rest of the table giggled.

Amelia didn't laugh with them.

'No, I didn't meet anyone special. But enough about me, I want to hear more about New York! I was thinking of coming out to visit you next year, actually.'

'I can't tell you how good it is to be back,' said Tink later that night. Caro and her mother were standing in the spare room that looked out on to the village green. Through the window, lights from other houses shone out against the blackness. 'I just wish Camilla was here as well,' said Tink sadly.

Caro slipped her arm round her mother's waist. 'I'm sure she will be next year.'

'I'm just being silly.' Tink rested her head on her daughter's shoulder and they looked out in the direction of Camilla's cottage. In the reflection in the glass, they could almost have passed for sisters.

'Is Amelia all right?'

Caro turned and looked at her mother. 'What makes you say that?'

'I just thought she seems a bit flat.'

Caro hesitated. 'Benedict thinks her depression is back again. Since she's got back from Moscow, she's barely left the house. I don't think she's seen any of her friends.'

'Most unlike Amelia,' Tink agreed thoughtfully. 'She seemed a bit short when Calypso mentioned the oligarchs earlier. Maybe she's having boyfriend trouble.'

But, Caro thought, if it were something as simple as that, surely Amelia would have told her. Wouldn't she?

Chapter 44

On Christmas Eve, Saffron woke to the sound of chattering birdsong. Even though the dying embers of the fire were still warm in the grate, the cold morning air had started to creep in through the windows. Throwing on a hooded jumper, Saffron went to pull the heavy curtains back. It certainly was quite a view.

The estate lay before her, like a regal patchwork quilt. The rolling lawns, which went on for as far as the eye could see, were cloaked in an ethereal grey mist. Frost sprinkled the tops of the trees and the intricate carvings at the top of the fountain. Once again, Saffron marvelled at how peaceful everything was. At first she'd found the silence, punctuated only by the birds' morning chorus, almost deafening. Accustomed to the traffic and roar of London buses, roads in the country seemed almost empty by comparison. No one seemed in a rush to get anywhere; yesterday she and Harriet had driven to Bedlington to pick up some duck pâté for Frances, and had got stuck behind a huge mud-encrusted tractor on the way back. Their journey had taken almost forty minutes but rather than shake her fist in rage and beep her horn, Harriet had shrugged and trailed the tractor patiently nearly all the way home instead.

Saffron was also getting accustomed to new sounds on their walks around the estate. Instead of the bleep of London taxis or the blare of music from shop windows, Harriet was trying to teach her to recognize the different calls of the birds that inhabited Churchminster. The warbling of robins outside her bedroom window, the wheezing shriek of a barn owl, and the earthy croak of the pheasants who roamed the estate, dashing from one hedgerow to another.

Saffron watched now as the lithe outlines of the two lurchers appeared out of the mist, followed by the figure of Lady Frances, elegant as ever in a full-length brown waxed jacket and a Barbour Bushman hat. She looked so at home in these surroundings, thought Saffron, as she watched Frances call the dogs to heel.

There was a soft knock on the bedroom door.

'I'm up, come in,' Saffron called. Harriet's head popped round. Her hair was a mass of brown frizz, sleep lines tracking down the right side of her face.

'Morning! Did you sleep well?'

'Like a log.'

'Good-oh,' said Harriet. 'Ready for breakfast? Cook always makes cinnamon pancakes on Christmas Eve.'

Saffron laughed. 'At this rate I'm going to go back to London looking like Ten Ton Tessa.'

At Mill House, everyone was up breakfasting round the kitchen table. As usual, Calypso had been the last family member to appear, wearing what looked like a bright-pink romper suit.

'Have you been rifling through Milo's wardrobe?' her father enquired over the top of his *Daily Telegraph*.

'Ha ha. It's a Tangro.'

'A what?'

Calypso rolled her eyes impatiently. 'A Tangro. You

wear it to bed when you've got fake tan on. Stops the sheets from getting dirty.'

'Good Lord, now I've seen it all,' said Johnnie, disappearing behind his paper.

There was a mountain of things to be done. The turkey had to be picked up from the farm down the road, and Clementine had asked someone to come over and put the star on the top of her Christmas tree, as her stepladder had broken. Milo needed to be fed, bathed and entertained, and Caro had to pop to the bakery in Bedlington to pick up some more of their homemade croissants and *pains au chocolat* for breakfast tomorrow. She'd forgotten quite how much her family ate when they got together.

The house was looking wonderful, though. Fresh pine wafted through the downstairs rooms, mingling with the smell of the mince pies Tink was baking in the Aga. A mountain of presents festooned with bows and ribbon was piled high under the Christmas tree. Twice already Milo had been found trying to open those with the most interesting shapes. There had been a sticky moment when he'd ripped open a gift to find a wind-up 'Wanking Santa' toy that one of Calypso's friends had given her as a joke.

'Father Christmas's got a pink fing!' Milo gleefully announced as he ran into the kitchen to show everyone, 'Wanking Santa' in full flow.

'Milo, give that to me!' said Caro, snatching it out of her son's hands. He promptly burst into tears.

'Gimme back Father Christmas!'

'There, there, darling,' said Tink, scooping her grandson up. 'Let's go and see what Pickles is up to.' She raised an eyebrow at Caro and whisked the little boy off to the living room.

'I don't know how I'd feel if I saw that coming down

the chimney,' said Benedict, recovering enough to finish his marmalade on toast.

That evening, Angie and Fred were holding a mulled wine and mince pie party. It was actually more of a Moët, caviar and smoked salmon affair, but the gathering had become something of an institution, attracting many of the Fox-Titts's glamorous, fun friends, as well as most of the village.

Clementine had offered to babysit Milo, as long as they were back in time for her to attend Midnight Mass. At eight o'clock Caro, Benedict, Johnnie, Tink, Calypso and Amelia drove over to the Maltings. Angie greeted them at the front door in a matching red silk hat and apron, fringed with white fur.

'Merry Christmas! Tink, Johnnie – how wonderful to see you.'

'Hullo, darling,' said Johnnie, kissing her on both cheeks. 'You look as gorgeous as ever.'

'You can come more often,' laughed Angie, enveloping Tink in a warm embrace.

The house was already jam-packed with people, talking and toasting each other with tall, fizzing flutes of champagne. Freddie, resplendent in a Father Christmas beard and silver bow tie, deftly moved amongst the crowd with delicious trays of canapés.

While Amelia went off to find the loo, Calypso scanned the living room. Across the sea of faces, she spotted Harriet helping herself to a canapé. Calypso waved her hand. 'Hats! Over here.'

Harriet spotted her and broke into a huge smile. She made her way over, followed by a tall, slim girl with short peroxide-blonde hair. The girl was wearing black hot pants, thick red tights and lethal-looking pointy ankle boots.

'Hello, Calypso!' Harriet hugged her. Calypso smiled at Harriet's friend.

'Your boots are fabulous!'

The girl looked down and smiled. 'Cheers. They're from some vintage bonkers shop off the King's Road. The guy tried to tell me they used to belong to Debbie Harry, but I'm not convinced.'

Calypso laughed and stuck her hand out. 'I'm Calypso Standington-Fulthrope.'

Saffron shook it. 'Saffron Walden. I live next door to your sister in London.'

'Saffron's staying with us for Christmas,' explained Harriet.

'Can I top you up, ladies?' A tall, broad-shouldered young man had appeared, clutching a bottle of champagne. Dressed in an open-necked blue shirt and chinos, he had a handsome, good-natured face.

'Hi, Archie, are you back for the holidays?' asked Calypso.

'Just a few days, actually. I'm off skiing on the twenty-seventh with a couple of the chaps from college.'

'Where are you going?'

'Val d'Isère.'

'Wicked,' said Calypso as Archie filled her glass up.

'Yeah, it should be good. Although by the looks of things, I'd be better off staying here. Pa and I were watching the farming forecast earlier. It looks like we might get snow in Churchminster.'

'I hear you've got a new house guest on the horizon,' said Harriet.

'Yeah, it's a guy from the project your magazine runs, isn't it?' Archie grinned. 'My father is doing his nut about it, keeps going on about hoodies and Broken Britain.'

'Archie, darling, can I borrow you for a sec?' called Angie.

'Uh-oh, she probably wants me to brave the perilously steep steps into the cellar for more bubbles,' Archie chuckled. He smiled at them, eyes briefly resting on Saffron.

'Excuse me, ladies.'

'He's quite cute,' remarked Saffron as Archie strode off towards the kitchen.

'I thought you were off men,' laughed Harriet.

'I am! But I can window-shop. He's quite fit in that Prince Harry kind of way.'

'Hope he hasn't got ginger pubes, though,' said Calypso mischievously, and they all fell about laughing.

By eleven thirty the party was starting to break up. It had been a typically sociable affair and everyone had been in very high spirits. Halfway through the evening, one of Freddie's old rugby friends had done a streak across the front lawn wearing nothing but a bauble from Angie's Christmas tree.

'Can I offer you a lift to Midnight Mass?' Caro asked Harriet and Saffron. As she wasn't drinking, Caro had offered to be designated driver that Christmas. Brenda had kindly offered to baby-sit Milo.

'That would be lovely, can you fit us in?'

Caro looked at her huge Land Cruiser, parked by the front of the house. 'I could fit half of Gloucestershire in that thing!'

Saffron wasn't sure she was dressed appropriately for the occasion, until she looked at Calypso, in her black PVC leggings, her blonde mane wilder than ever. After the bauble streaking, Saffron was quickly learning that Churchminster wasn't a village that was easily shocked.

Caro opened her eyes to darkness. At first she thought she was dreaming. Batman was standing by the bed. *I am dreaming*, she thought sleepily, *it's the middle of the night*. Then Batman clambered up on the bed and starting bouncing on her.

'Mummy! Benny-dict!'

There was a muffled groan beside her. 'It's 6 a.m.'

Milo threw himself on Benedict's prostrate form.

'Wake up!'

Benedict rolled over and looked at Caro.

'Merry Christmas.' He kissed her softly on the lips, before Milo jumped on them, Pickles and all. Caro got a paw shoved up her nose.

'OK, Milo, we're getting up!' She sat up and surveyed her son. Batman aside, Pickles was wearing a matching black eye mask and what seemed to be a mini-Robin outfit.

'Good Lord, I've seen it all now,' said Benedict.

'Aren't they great? I got them from this mad shop in New York that does fancy dress for people and their pets.' Calypso was standing in the kitchen watching Milo hurtle himself around like a superhero.

'Na na na, Batman!'

Caro laughed. 'I can't believe Milo dressed Pickles up, I have enough trouble getting him in his own clothes! Thanks, darling, it's awfully sweet of you.'

The two sisters were in their dressing gowns, drinking tea and sitting at opposite ends of the window seat that looked out on the village green. It was spectacularly pretty: a frost had settled overnight, cloaking everything in an iridescent gleam, and capping the roofs of the houses like the peaks of a mountain range. A watery sun had managed to break through the leaden skies; the rays sparkling against the snowy whiteness. Inches away through the glass pane a spider's web glistened like the finest silk, while a portly red robin suddenly appeared on the windowsill, cocked its head cheekily at them and flew off.

'There's nowhere quite like it, is there?' said Calypso contently. She raised her mug and clinked it with Caro's.

'Happy Christmas, sis.'

There were footsteps on the stairs, and moments later their parents came into the room. Tink was dressed up to the nines in a fabulous wrap dress and black heels, while her husband was looking dapper in sharply pressed chinos and a new striped Turnbull & Asser shirt. He was also wearing a rather incongruous reindeer hat, complete with horns and red nose.

'Look what your mother got me,' he sighed, but it didn't sound like he minded too much.

Tink bounced over, as giddy as a schoolgirl. 'Merry Christmas, my gorgeous girls!'

The pop of a champagne cork sounded in the kitchen. Benedict walked in with a tray of Buck's Fizz and a freshly squeezed orange juice for Caro. 'Breakfast's nearly ready, but I thought we'd have these first,' he announced. He stuck his head back out the door.

'Amelia, are you up yet?'

'I think I heard her in the shower,' Tink told him.

Calypso took a glass from Benedict. 'I'm going to be pissed by midday at this rate,' she said happily.

'Don't get too blotto, you're on vegetable-peeling duty later,' said her father.

She looked unimpressed. 'Isn't that what M&S is for?'

At 11 a.m., they had all attended the Christmas Day service at St Bartholomew's. It had been a wonderfully uplifting service, and virtually the whole village had turned up in their Christmas Day finery. Buoyed up by a glass of sherry from one of his parishioners, the vicar Brian Bellows had only stuttered a handful of times, even if he had dropped a Bible on his foot at one point and mouthed the word, 'Bugger.' Afterwards, Clementine had led everyone off for a bracing walk around the Meadows, while Johnnie had returned to Mill House to put the goose in the oven. It was a bitingly cold day, the kind that got one round the cheeks and ears and refused to let go. Half of Gloucestershire seemed to be out in the countryside, muffled up against the elements to work up an appetite.

It was 4 p.m. by the time they sat down to a table groaning with food. Johnnie had surpassed himself, while Amelia wowed everyone with a homemade Christmas pudding, flickering with blue brandy flames as she carried it into the dining room. Full and happy, they ended the meal with port and delicious great hunks of smelly blue-veined cheese. Finally, it was time to open the presents.

'More champagne, chaps?' asked Johnnie, waving the bottle.

Sitting down on the sofa, Tink groaned. 'Oh, darling, I don't think I could. Why do you have to make such marvellous roast potatoes? I must have had about ten.'

'I've never known you to turn down bubbles, Mummy,' laughed Caro.

'Oh, you're right!' Tink smiled and held out her glass.

Benedict had been put in charge of handing out presents by Clementine. He reached for a soft, square parcel with a sumptuous red velvet bow and looked at the label.

To dearest Mummy, you're the best in the world!
Oodles of love,
Caro
xxx

Everyone watched as Tink peeled open the paper to reveal an exquisitely embroidered silk caftan.

'Darling, it's exquisite!'

'I thought it would be good for all those glamorous pool parties you and Daddy go to.'

'Oh, I shall feel just like Joan Collins,' Tink cried. 'Here, open this one.' She passed Caro a rectangular parcel. Caro unwrapped it to find the latest Valentina Black novel.

'Oh, how marvellous! This has had rave reviews.'

'I had a sneak peek, I hope you don't mind,' admitted Tink.

Johnnie picked up *Love Under the Sun*, its cover was a photo of a glistening male body from the neck down, a red-taloned hand disappearing into its bathing trunks.

'Good Lord, woman, you've given our daughter pornography!' he spluttered.

For the next half an hour, the floor gradually disappeared under a sea of wrapping paper. Benedict loved his cufflinks from Caro, Tink was over the moon with her Jo Malone candle set from Calypso, and Clementine was surprisingly touched by a beautiful set of Smythson's stationery Camilla had bought and wrapped up before going off travelling.

Caro had just received a stunning amber and gold necklace from Benedict, when he left the room. Moments later, he re-entered with a beautiful, antique rocking horse.

'I thought it would look good in the nursery,' he smiled.

'Uh-oh! She's off again!' joked Calypso, as Caro's eyes glistened.

Despite her happiness, there was something gnawing away at Caro. The pile of presents was quickly diminishing, but still there had been nothing from Sebastian for Milo. She'd been sent a few parcels through the post, and had assumed one of those would be for her son, but there had been nothing. Benedict handed the last few gifts out: some Chanel No. 5 for Tink from Clementine, and a rather old-looking bottle of Crabtree & Evelyn bubble bath for Amelia from an aged auntie. Now, the space was empty under the Christmas tree.

Caro looked at Milo, who was gleefully playing with another new racing car from his grandparents.

'Nothing from Sebastian?' Tink asked hesitantly.

Caro bit her lip. Over on the other side of the room, Benedict's face was like stone.

'Your mother told me about your run-in with him,' said Johnnie. Disapproving noises sounded round the room.

Calypso went over and looked under the Christmas tree.

'Hold on, there *is* something.'

She picked up a long, narrow envelope and turned it over. The writing looked vaguely familiar. Caro thought she must have put it under the tree without really registering who it was from.

She opened it and an HMV voucher for £5 fell out.

There was an accompanying card. Caro recognized the girlish scrawl now: it had been written by Sebastian's secretary, Bethany. She read the card out, the spelling mistake painfully obvious.

Dear Millo,
Happy Christmas,
Love Daddy

'For Christ's sake!' said Johnnie. Milo glanced up, surprised at his grandfather's unusually harsh tone.

'What's a three-year-old boy going to do with an HMV voucher?' asked Calypso scornfully.

'It's OK, really,' Caro said hastily. 'At least he sent something . . .' Her words fell away.

As they sat there in an uncomfortable silence, Milo, completely oblivious to the tension above his head, suddenly pointed at the window.

'Look!' he shouted. 'S'gone white!'

For the first Christmas Day in a decade, snow was falling on Churchminster.

Across the village, people were contentedly settling into the embers of the day. At Hollyhocks Cottage, Ted Briggs was fast asleep in front of the telly, a half-eaten mince pie on a plate on his lap. At the Maltings, Angie, Freddie and Archie had just returned from lunch with some old chums in Chipping Campden. And at Twisty Gables a lusty Nico Reinard tried to tempt his wife Lucinda into bed with the Barbarella outfit he'd put in her stocking. At Clanfield Hall, Saffron was still recovering from being served a wood pigeon inside a pheasant inside a partridge, all of which had been shot on the estate just hours earlier.

The clink of champagne glasses rang out across

Churchminster, as everyone raised one toast after another.

'To absent loved ones!'

'Friends and family!'

'Merry, *merry* Christmas!'

Chapter 45

Saffron had thought she would be itching to get back to London, but she was surprised how much she had been enjoying herself. Every day she and Harriet had gone on long walks around the estate, then spent cosy afternoons by the fire drinking tea and watching television or reading. She hadn't felt so rested or healthy for ages.

'Got some colour in your cheeks at last,' Ambrose boomed one evening. They'd had Christmas dinner in the Great Hall, a huge chilly room where they'd needed to shout to hear each other, but, to Saffron's relief, had gone back to using the smaller, cosier dining room since. Even though it was an informal supper of shepherd's pie, Hawkins had still laid out the table beautifully, with bone china plates and polished silverware.

'Have you decided what you're doing for New Year's Eve yet?' Frances asked Harriet.

'Yup, I'm going to the Jolly Boot's party.' Harriet sighed. 'I must admit, it won't be the same without Camilla.'

Saffron cleared her throat. 'Actually, if you don't mind, I think I'll stay and come with you.'

Harriet looked delighted. 'Of course! Haven't you got something to go to in London, though?'

'I can always sell my ticket.' Saffron was meant to be going to a party in Kensington where several big name DJs were playing. Normally this would be a dream night out, but for some reason she didn't fancy returning to the mayhem of the capital yet. Saffron still couldn't believe she was giving up her coveted ticket for some do at the local pub; she'd have to make an excuse to her clubbing mates about getting the flu.

'My dear, stay as long as you want,' Frances said.

'What's that?' barked Ambrose.

'Saffron is staying for New Year's Eve, dear,' Frances repeated. She looked at Harriet. 'Darling, you haven't forgotten your father and I are leaving around lunchtime for Gravely Hall? Hawkins has a few days off, but Cook will be here.'

'We'll be fine, Mummy.'

Ambrose looked across at Saffron, who was wearing a diamanté skull-and-crossbones T-shirt, and metallic purple eyeliner. Her hair was spiked up so she looked like a rather exotic parakeet.

'I wasn't aware it was fancy dress code tonight. Would have dug out my Napoleon Bonaparte costume if I'd known,' he said, adding a 'humph' for good measure.

By the time New Year's Eve arrived, tickets to the Jolly Boot had sold out. With the Hall to themselves, Harriet and Saffron had great fun getting ready, sharing a bottle of champagne in Harriet's bedroom, with Girls Aloud blaring out from her iPod speakers.

'I wonder if there'll be any hotties there tonight,' said Saffron, as she gelled her hair up into tufts. 'Shame that Archie won't be around, I could have had my first farmer!'

Harriet suspected she probably still could: a few of the locals were going to have heart attacks when she walked into the pub in her tight black vest, latex leggings and six-inch heels.

As they couldn't get a taxi, Cook had very kindly offered to give them a lift down to the Boot in her ancient Citroën. The snow had almost gone from the rolling acres of Clanfield Hall as they bumped down the road. The grey clouds that had hung over Churchminster like a blanket for the last week had disappeared, too, and the starry sky sparkled like a million fireflies.

They passed Mill House, which was dark and empty again. Calypso had flown back to New York a few days earlier, while Caro and the rest of the family had gone to stay with family friends in Henley-upon-Thames.

After issuing them with strict instructions to line their stomachs before they started drinking, Cook dropped them off as near to the pub as she could get. Harriet waved the old lady off fondly.

'She does worry, I was too scared to tell her we'd had a bottle of Moët already.'

It looked like the party was already in full swing. The car park was packed, so later arrivals had had to park up on the verge. As the girls walked past, they could hear a strange moaning.

'Oh, I hope it isn't an injured animal,' said Harriet anxiously. They followed the noise. It seemed to be coming from several cars away.

Saffron had visions of a cute little bunny with its guts spilling everywhere. Oh God, she was really squeamish . . .

'Oh!' Harriet exclaimed. In front of them, a steamed-up Volvo estate was rocking from side to side. A huge pair of white buttocks were pressed firmly against the back window.

'Give it to me, Fenella, you naughty little fox!'

'Oh, Rory! Just there, darling. Harder! Faster!'

Saffron clamped her hand over her mouth as she and Harriet hurried on towards the pub. 'Someone couldn't wait,' she giggled.

Jack Turner was standing at the front door, welcoming newcomers in. He was wearing a loud multi-coloured striped waistcoat, his red hair standing on end.

'Evening, Harriet!' he cried cheerfully. 'Come in before you catch your death, you could freeze the tits off an Eskimo out there.'

'Hullo, Jack, this is my friend, Saffron.'

Jack ushered them inside. 'How's that colleague of yours doing? Annabel, isn't it? I hear she's a right pain in the rear end.'

He laughed at Saffron's surprised expression. 'I ran into Lady Fraser yesterday.'

'Mummy does like a gossip,' said Harriet fondly.

A fresh-faced young man in a black waistcoat appeared with a tray of champagne. 'Madam?' he asked Saffron solicitously.

'Cheers.'

The pub was heaving. People stood wall-to-wall, dressed up in their finery. 'You've had a jolly good turn-out,' said Harriet.

Jack looked pleased. 'All right, isn't it? I was a bit worried about selling tickets. The Crown at Bedlington haven't even shifted half of theirs.' He sighed. 'Business is quiet for most of the pubs round here, but for some reason we're doing OK. Touch wood.' He tapped his forehead.

'That's because you're such a wonderful landlord!'

Jack's long face broke into a wide grin. 'Flattery will

get you everywhere! Have some more champagne.' The door opened again and more people piled in. 'No rest for the wicked,' he declared. 'You two girls have a good night.'

For thirty pounds, a ticket bought an unlimited amount of alcohol and a fantastic seafood spread put on by chef Pierre and his team. And this was no ordinary buffet. A long table at the back of the restaurant groaned with lobster, caviar, langoustines and steaming tureens of moules marinières. A queue of people were already loading their plates, and heavenly vapours floated through the pub.

Saffron felt her mouth watering. 'Bloody hell, that smells good. Let's go and put Cook's advice to the test.'

By half past nine, they were having a whale of a time. Angie and Freddie had invited them to sit at their lively table, and for the past ten minutes a friend of theirs had been regaling them with a story about the time he'd accidentally trodden on Princess Anne's hem at a function and pulled her dress halfway down her waist.

As Freddie refilled everyone's glasses from the magnum of Dom Perignon in the middle of the table, Saffron took a slurp and looked across at Harriet.

'Y'know, I would never have expected myself to be spending New Year's Eve here. Not that I mean that in a bad way, it's just so different. I've always thought that all the interesting people lived in London, and people in the country were . . .'

'Bumpkins?' smiled Harriet.

'Yeah! But I was totally wrong. You've got all types here.'

They looked round the room. On the next table sat

Lucinda and Nico Reinard with a group of their friends. Lucinda was dressed in a velvet bodice and matching Alice band, her face flushed with laughter and alcohol.

'Looks like something Annabel would wear,' said Saffron wickedly.

Harriet giggled. 'Lucinda's a good sort, really.'

They watched as Lucinda started to play footsie under the table with a florid-faced man sitting next to her.

'Is everyone in this village at it?' laughed Saffron.

Harriet suddenly noticed a rather cute blond man standing on the other side of the room, wearing a red-and-white-checked gingham shirt. As he scanned the crowd, his eyes rested on Harriet. He raised his champagne glass and smiled.

'He totally fancies you,' said Saffron.

Harriet blushed. 'Don't be silly.'

Jack Turner had started to serve his special New Year's Eve cocktails. Customers were taking one sip and spluttering, their eyes streaming with water. Jack was not known to be stingy when it came to measures.

'Shall we try one?' said Saffron.

Harriet nodded. 'I hope you're ready to have your head blown off!' They excused themselves from the table and made their way to the crowded bar.

'Won't be a minute, girls!' Beryl Turner called out. A young woman appeared beside Beryl, her pretty round face caked in make-up. To say she gave Jordan a run for her money in the cleavage stakes was no exaggeration. She was extremely well-endowed and carefully exaggerating this with a plunging red top and black lacy push-up bra.

'That's Stacey, Jack and Beryl's daughter,' whispered Harriet.

351

A chorus of wolf-whistles rang out down the bar.

'I say! Check out the bouncers on that!' shouted one man in a quilted waistcoat.

Before they knew it, Jack Turner had stopped pulling pints and rushed over to his daughter, throwing a soggy bar towel over the offending cleavage.

Stacey looked furious. 'Dad! What d'ya think you're doing? That's soaking wet!' She tried wriggling away, but Jack had the towel firmly pinned against her shoulders.

'When I told you to change into something more suitable, I didn't bleeding mean that!'

'Daaad! This is so embarrassing. Get off!'

Spinning her around, Jack marched his daughter off. 'Get upstairs and put a polo neck on!'

'A polo neck? Shut up! They're for grandmas!'

'I don't care if you come down in a bloody tablecloth. Go and cover yourself up!'

With a face like thunder, Stacey narrowed her eyes and gave her father the 'evils' before stomping off.

'This place is brilliant!' said Saffron. She squinted at the blackboard behind the bar. 'Can you get me one of Jack's Jumping Flashes if you get served? I'm just going to the loo.'

As Saffron disappeared into the throng, Harriet glanced around the room. The blond man was still there, deep in conversation. As if suddenly aware of her gaze, he glanced up and winked. The man said something to his friend and started to make his way through the crowds.

Oh God, he was coming over! Harriet smoothed down her hair and tried to look nonchalant. But before he could reach her, she was assailed by a strong musky perfume.

'Harriet, darling!' Babs Sax had materialized in

front of her. She was wearing lime-green wide-legged trousers and a billowing patterned blouse, cinched in with a leather belt to show off her minuscule waist. Her hair looked a brighter red than ever, and was flowing loose round her shoulders.

'Er, hello, Babs,' Harriet replied, surreptitiously looking over Babs's shoulder. Blondie was nowhere to be seen. Harriet tried to ignore the stab of disappointment, and smiled at Babs. 'How are you? We haven't seen much of you this Christmas. Have you been away?'

'Yah, I've been in San Francisco painting,' Babs breathed. 'The light there is wonderful this time of year.'

'Sounds lovely,' said Harriet, but Babs's eyes were already darting round the room.

'Are you here with Camilla?' she asked, vaguely.

'No, she's away travelling at the moment. I'm here with a friend from London.'

'How fascinating,' said Babs, sounding like it was anything but. 'You must excuse me, I've just seen an old friend I simply must catch up with.'

'What the fuck are you doing here?'

Harriet whirled round. Saffron was standing before them, her face as white as a sheet. She was staring at Babs with a mixture of shock and undisguised hostility.

'This is Babs Sax . . .' Harriet started, but Saffron cut her off.

'I know who she is.'

Panic flooded Babs's face. She opened her arms. 'Darling, how wonderful to see you!' Her voice was quivering.

Saffron took a step back. 'Get the fuck away from me,' she spat.

353

Harriet was baffled. 'I'm sorry, do you two know each other?'

The two women seemed frozen to the ground, Babs's face beseeching, while Saffron's was a mask of anger.

'Unfortunately, yes.' Saffron's voice was like steel. 'This woman . . .' She could barely get the words out. 'This woman is my mother.'

Harriet couldn't quite believe what she'd heard.

Babs took another tentative step forward. 'Saffron, darling . . .'

'Don't call me that,' said Saffron through clenched teeth. 'Does Aunt Velda know you live here? Have you been plotting behind my back or something?'

'I haven't spoken to my sister for months!' Babs laid one bony hand on Saffron's arm, but she shook it off as if she'd been scalded.

'Don't you dare touch me!' Eyes filling with tears, Saffron fled for the door.

Harriet found her outside several minutes later. Even through the dark, she could see Saffron's face was swollen with tears.

'Saffron, I'm so sorry,' Harriet gasped. 'I had no idea.'

Saffron wiped a hand across her face. 'I should have known she'd turn up one day. She's like a fucking locust.' She sniffed. 'Aunt Velda must have known she was here, why the fuck didn't she say anything?'

'Let's go back to the Hall and talk about things.'

'No,' Saffron's tone was final. 'I don't want to give her another moment's thought.'

A cab pulled up, dropping off some more party-goers. The cabbie stuck his head out of the window. 'Going anywhere, girls?'

'Can you take me to Clanfield Hall?' Saffron asked. The cabbie nodded.

'I'll come back as well,' said Harriet. 'Saffron, I'm worried about you.'

Saffron gave her a strained smile. 'H, I'm fine. I just want to be alone for a bit. Don't let that stupid cow spoil your New Year's Eve as well.'

With that she briefly hugged Harriet and climbed into the cab.

Chapter 46

Harriet needed a stiff drink. Babs Sax was Saffron's mother! What were the chances of her turning up in Churchminster, of all places? Harriet felt dreadful, but then again how could she have known? Saffron had never liked talking about her mother and Velda rarely mentioned her, either. *Had* she known Babs was living in Churchminster? Why on earth hadn't she said something? Harriet's mind was whirling with possibilities, not to mention a large amount of Dom Perignon.

'You look like a lady with things on her mind,' said a deep voice. Harriet turned and her heart jumped: it was the blond man from earlier. She fleetingly thought how red her nose must be after standing outside in the cold.

Blondie was holding two glasses of champagne. 'I'm Rupert Huxley. Delighted to make your acquaintance.'

'Thank you.' Harriet took a flute. 'I'm Harriet Fraser.'

Rupert smiled, his eyes crinkling up at the corners. 'Cheer up! It might never happen.'

Harriet sighed. 'I think it already has. I'm worried about my friend.'

'I'm sure she's fine,' said Rupert smoothly. He raised his glass. The signet ring on his little finger glinted in the overhead lights. 'Cheers!'

'Cheers!' said Harriet, some of her good mood returning.

An hour later Harriet and Rupert were deep in conversation. He really was a most interesting chap. Instead of taking over his father's thousand-acre farm in Worcestershire, Rupert had devised the prototype for a solar-powered lawnmower. He was just waiting to hear from a large engineering company whether they were willing to take it on.

'My theory is that people only mow their grass when it's sunny. So with the rise in oil and fuel prices, what better way to run a vehicle than off the energy from the sun?'

'I wish I could think of something as clever as that,' Harriet told him. 'It's a brilliant idea.'

Rupert looked rather pleased with himself. 'I think so, too.'

A squat man with enormous shoulders came over. 'Another drink, Rupe? It's almost midnight!'

'Please, old chap,' said Rupert. 'This is Harriet . . . Harriet, this is Biff.'

Biff gave Harriet a perfunctory glance. 'Delighted,' he said, and headed for the bar.

'Why's he called Biff?'

'Nutter on the rugger pitch.'

Biff returned with more champagne, and Harriet and Rupert clinked glasses. All the alcohol was suddenly going to Harriet's head. She'd better ease off after this one and besides, she didn't want to be a dribbling mess when she got home in case Saffron needed a shoulder to cry on.

The music stopped. They both looked over to the bar, where Jack Turner had climbed up on to a stool.

'All right everyone! It's nearly New Year. Let's have a countdown. Ten . . .'

'Nine, eight, seven, six,' everyone shouted. 'Five, four, three, two . . .'

'Happy New Year!' The pub erupted as everyone cheered, grown men threw their arms round each other and kissed, and champagne corks flew through the air like missiles.

Rupert gazed at Harriet. 'So, do I get a celebration kiss?'

Harriet blushed. She went to kiss his cheek, but he turned his head and caught her full on the lips.

'I've wanted to do that all night,' he whispered. 'Do you fancy getting out of here?'

This was a bit fast, Harriet thought. 'Well, er . . .'

Rupert smiled. 'Don't worry, I'm not a murderer or anything. Biff will vouch for my credentials.'

Looking at the hulking Biff, Harriet wasn't sure if he was capable of vouching for anything, but the vision of her as an old spinster being eaten alive by cats swam into her mind again. She was thirty-two years old, and had slept with only two men. She needed to start living life a little.

'That sounds good . . . Not that I'm easy or anything,' she added awkwardly.

The crinkles came out again and Harriet decided she had definitely made the right choice. 'You're a lady and I'm the perfect gentleman. Let's start with coffee, shall we?'

'Coffee,' agreed Harriet. As she went to get her coat, someone threw a leftover scallop from the buffet straight down Stacey Turner's still gaping cleavage. A murderous look crossed Jack's face as he scanned the bar for the perpetrator. Harriet decided it was definitely a good time to leave.

Outside, Lucinda Reinard was arguing with a cab driver.

'We didn't book you until 2 a.m.!' she told him. A bottle and a half of Bollinger had made her voice even louder than normal.

'I was told midnight,' said the cabbie stubbornly.

Lucinda rolled her eyes. 'My dear fellow, as if anyone would book a cab for midnight on New Year's Eve!'

Harriet interrupted. 'Lucinda? Why don't I take this one and you can have mine. It's booked for 2 a.m.'

Lucinda looked at Harriet. She was slightly cross-eyed. 'Well, if you don't mind.' She looked over Harriet's shoulder at Rupert and laughed horsily. 'Well, hel-lo handsome! I can see why you want to sneak off early—'

'Happy New Year,' said Harriet hurriedly and climbed into the cab, pulling Rupert in behind her. They watched Lucinda stagger off into the pub.

The cabbie turned round. 'Where to?'

They looked at each other. 'I'm staying with a few chums in the Bedlington, we could always go back there,' said Rupert. 'Might be a jot crowded, though.'

Harriet thought for a moment. 'Come back to mine,' she said.

Rupert cocked his head. 'If you're sure.'

Harriet leaned forward. 'Gate Cottage please, driver. It's just off Clanfield Road.'

A few minutes later they pulled up at the entrance to the hall. Rupert whistled at the sight of Clanfield Hall. 'Nice pile.'

'This is my place, actually. My parents live at the Hall,' said Harriet. She had already decided there was no way she was taking him back to the main house. It would be just her luck if her father had thrown one of his legendary fits and insisted on coming home early.

'So that makes you Lady Harriet?' asked Rupert as he paid the cab driver.

Harriet fumbled for her door key. 'No. It's just my parents who have the title. I think I'd feel a bit silly anyway, being called a "lady".'

Inside the hallway the air was stale and fusty. It was also freezing. 'I haven't been here for a while, the heating hasn't been on,' apologized Harriet. 'Come through and I'll make the coffee.'

As she flicked on the kitchen light, harsh illumination filled the room. Rupert blinked and Harriet noticed his eyes were rather bloodshot. She switched on the kettle. 'Won't be a minute.'

In the downstairs loo, she looked at herself in the mirror. She didn't look that bad actually, the superstrength hair serum Frances had put in her stocking had worked wonders. Confidence buoyed, Harriet applied another coat of lipstick.

The kettle was whistling by the time she got back. Rupert was leaning against the work surface, hands in pockets. 'Everything all right?' he enquired.

'Perfectly, thank you.' Harriet opened one of the cupboards. 'I'm afraid I've only got powdered milk, I haven't had a chance to stock up.'

Before she knew it Rupert had bounded across the room and taken her in his arms. 'I must have you now,' he murmured into her ear.

'Oh!' Harriet hadn't quite been expecting this. His lips found hers, and his tongue moved sloppily into her mouth. Harriet felt rather like she had fallen face first into a washing machine on the rinse cycle.

Rupert's hands found a buttock each and squeezed

hard. The pair moved out into the hallway, snogging furiously, and Harriet felt her bra ping open. Rupert stopped kissing her for a moment and, putting one arm round her shoulders and the other under her leg, tried to pick Harriet up. To her mortification, she stayed firmly on the ground.

'Christ, you must weigh more than Biff!' he exclaimed. 'I've picked him up in a wedgie enough times. Only joking, I like a girl with a bit of meat on her.' He kissed her again and they started shuffling awkwardly up the stairs.

By the time they got into Harriet's bedroom she was topless, having lost her blouse and bra somewhere between the sixth and seventh steps. It was so cold her nipples were sticking out like two thimbles from Cook's prized sewing box. Breathing heavily, Rupert pushed her on to the bed, jumped on top of her and began furiously dry humping. Harriet *really* hadn't been expecting this. She lay underneath with her arms by her sides, feeling rather foolish.

'Wait a minute.' Rupert sat back and pulled his trousers off. He rummaged in one of the pockets and produced a silver packet.

'Are you a horse lover?' he asked huskily.

'Excuse me?' Harriet asked in alarm. Horse was, in fact, the name of the braying oik she had lost her virginity to a couple of years earlier.

'I know you country girls, you like something big and strong between your thighs.' As Rupert pulled her skirt and knickers off with all the romantic flair of someone stripping a bed, Harriet quickly realized he wasn't a foreplay man. After a couple of seconds grunting and pushing, he was inside her, thrusting back and forth.

'Oh yeah, oh yeah!' Rupert groaned.

Harriet felt strangely disassociated, like it was happening to someone else. She hadn't had much experience at this, but she wasn't sure if Rupert was very good at it.

He tweaked one of her nipples and Harriet winced. She half expected him to announce he was trying to tune into Classic FM.

'I can see I'm making you nice and hard. Let's do it doggy.' Before Harriet knew it, Rupert had flipped her over on to all fours. Maybe this position would be better.

As Rupert entered her again, Harriet could feel his balls slapping against her inner thighs. It was kind of tickly. She was concentrating on getting into the rhythm of things when a searing pain shot up her rectum.

'Ow!' she shrieked.

Rupert stopped, his hands on her hips. 'Sorry old girl, I went in the back door by mistake! Are you OK?'

'Fine, thank you,' she said, trying to regain her composure.

A few thrusts later, it was over. 'Rupe's home and dry! Or wet, should I say.' He chuckled indulgently. 'Did you come?'

'Er, of course,' lied Harriet.

Looking smug, Rupert flopped down next to her. A few seconds later, his phone beeped. He sat up and rifled through his clothes.

'Bugger, my fiancée. I thought she wasn't back until tomorrow.'

'Your fiancée?' asked Harriet weakly.

Rupert gave her a fond slap on the bottom. 'Yup, the fragrant Cecilia. I'm making an honest woman of her in May. Can you call me a cab, old bean?'

JANUARY

Chapter 47

Catherine's Christmas Day had been terrible. She'd watched television virtually non-stop, then in the evening made herself a microwave meal and gone to bed early. On Boxing Day, depressed beyond belief at the thought of another twenty-four hours alone, she'd drunk herself into a blur. When she'd woken on the twenty-seventh, dehydrated, exhausted and wretched, she'd decided to drag herself into the office.

John Milton still hadn't called, but then again, she hadn't expected him to. The one occasion her phone had rung, Catherine's heart had been in her mouth. But it hadn't been him. At one particularly low point on New Year's Eve, she had even considered texting him, before putting the phone down again. She couldn't contact him after the things she'd said, he'd probably laugh in her face. Catherine made herself face up to the fact that she would never hear from him again.

The only positive thing that kept her going was the news that the Christmas issue of *Soirée* had flown off the shelves, selling a very respectable 265,000 copies. They were now only 35,000 copies – and three more issues – off the 'Project 300' mark. According to Adam, all they had to do now was keep the momentum going.

Hope was growing by the day and even though it was January, the office felt a happier place than it had been for months. If they carried on at this rate, they'd sail past the 300,000 mark.

Despite this achievement, Catherine still didn't feel happy. So many people's futures were riding on her, and she was now under the most incredible pressure to deliver the goods. If the December issue always sold well, the January one didn't. Adam appeared to think it didn't matter, saying they were on a roll, but Catherine wasn't so sure. She felt tired to her bones, and her once indefatigable energy was becoming harder to draw on. Her dream of getting a Savannah Sexton cover was also quashed. Despite Saffron's best efforts, it hadn't happened. Savannah was taking an extended holiday in the States to see her boyfriend Casey, and wasn't doing any press.

To make matters worse, a supposed exclusive interview with an ex-catwalk model, who had just married the new Italian prime minister, had also ended up in *Grace* magazine. Catherine hated it when they were screwed over, and had angrily told Annabel to get on to the ex-model's management to find out what the hell had happened.

Then, three days after the team returned to work, a national media supplement published an article on *Soirée*'s 'Project 300' campaign, calling it 'over-ambitious and unrealistic'. The same day, a 'wicked whisper' appeared in a column in the *Daily Mercy*, a salacious paper aimed at the middle classes which was nothing more than a jumped-up gossip column.

Which glossy magazine editor is struggling to hold on to her position after repeated fallings-out with big bosses? It won't be a soirée if she gets kicked out!

'Bloody libellous shit!' Catherine shouted angrily to Adam when he came into her office, thrusting the offending item under his nose. She had no doubt who was behind it. Isabella Montgomery was best friends with the columnist, a fifty-something bitter divorcée called Henrietta Lord-Wyatt.

Adam shrugged feebly and said it was best not to draw attention to it, but Catherine wondered if he'd have felt the same way if it had been him they had written about. The fact that he hadn't disagreed with the wicked whisper made her feel even worse.

Saffron had an equally unpleasant start to the year. The day after her run-in with her mother, she and Harriet had driven back to London in virtual silence. Any attempt at conversation by Harriet had been met with short shrift. Saffron knew her friend was worried about her, but she couldn't help it: she wanted to be by herself and away from anyone or anything who was connected with Churchminster. The place had transformed from a garden of Eden to a chamber of horrors in a matter of hours, and her world had been turned upside down. Things would never be the same again.

Burning with anger, Saffron felt so deceived by her aunt that when she got back to Montague Mews later that day she packed up her things and moved in with friends across town. She left a furious note for Velda on the kitchen table, telling her exactly what she thought of her and asking her not to make contact.

The day Velda got back from Morocco she came round to Caro's in a terrible state, eyes red from crying.

'Oh my goodness,' Caro cried when she opened her front door. 'What on earth's the matter? Come in.'

Velda burst into tears again. 'I've done something terrible.'

'Oh, I'm sure it can't be that bad,' said Caro kindly.

Velda wiped a paint-streaked hand across her face, leaving a little trail of something purple. 'You know that thing I said I couldn't talk to you about, the one I had been thinking about since you moved in?' She paused. 'Well, I've always called my sister by her childhood nickname Belle, but you probably know her as Babs Sax.'

Caro was stunned for a few seconds. 'Babs is your *sister*?' The penny dropped. 'But that makes her Saffron's mother!'

Velda tried to smile through her tears. 'Messed up, isn't it? I honestly thought that I would never persuade her and Saffron to meet again, and they would each grow up without a mother or daughter. I always knew Stephen and Klaus had a cottage in Churchminster, of course, but when you moved here as well – well I started to think it was fate. And when Saffron and Harriet became such good friends, and Harriet invited Saffron back for Christmas, I really thought it was a sign.'

Caro handed Velda a tissue and she took it, blowing her nose loudly.

'I agonized over it, you know, whether to tell Saffron her mother had moved to Churchminster. But I knew she would refuse point blank to go.' Velda smiled sadly. 'I just thought that maybe if they bumped into each other, there might be some chance . . . So many years have passed now.' She sniffed. 'I should have known better, what a fool I've been! Saffron's moved out, she

368

won't take my calls, and I've no idea how to get hold of her!'

Caro patted her shoulder. She was still trying to take it all in. She now knew why Velda had looked so familiar to her when they'd first met. Although Babs was taller and thinner than her older sister, they both shared the same colouring and bone-structure. As did Saffron. Saffron had even told Caro she was a natural strawberry blonde.

'Velda, you're not a fool. You've only got Saffron's best interests at heart, and you did what you thought was right.'

'I was wrong, though, wasn't I?' said Velda. 'How could I have misjudged it so badly?'

Caro didn't know quite what to say. 'Give it time, I'm sure Saffron will come round.'

Velda looked at her through reddened eyes. 'And if she doesn't?'

Unfortunately Caro had no answer for that one.

Saffron was deep in thought as she stepped into the lift at lunchtime. She didn't realize Tom was there until he spoke.

'Did you have a good Christmas?'

Saffron looked up. 'I've had better,' she said, a little shortly.

Tom went a mottled red, and Saffron felt a bit of a heel. It wasn't her fault she had the family from hell, after all.

'How was yours?' she asked, trying to sound more friendly.

'All right,' he muttered.

The two lapsed into silence. Saffron looked down at the floor. Christ, he had big feet! Tom was wearing an unfashionable pair of trainers, the laces done up in huge bows. For some reason Saffron found herself wondering if big feet did really mean a big cock . . .

The lift door pinged open. 'See you later,' she said quickly, and made a swift exit.

Chapter 48

Ash stepped uncertainly off the train at Bedlington. He felt like he was in the middle of a *Heartbeat* episode. The station had just one platform and a tiny stationmaster's office, an old-fashioned clock ticking loudly overhead and flower boxes neatly lined up outside.

Ash still wasn't sure if this was a good idea, and the two-hour train journey had only unsettled his thoughts further. He had two months in this place. This Mrs Fox-Titt woman – what kind of name was that? – had sounded dead posh when they'd spoken on the phone. What the hell was he going to have in common with these people? They probably drank tea out of china cups with their little finger stuck up.

'The 10:04 a.m. from London Paddington has now arrived,' a woman's voice called cheerily over the loud-speaker. Ash noticed no one else had got on or off. He was in the middle of the bloody wilderness! Slinging his sports bag over his shoulder, he walked towards the exit.

'Hello there!' someone cried as he walked out of the station. Ash turned to see a short, round-faced man standing by a muddy Range Rover. He was wearing a quilted jacket, and corduroys tucked into equally muddy boots. 'You must be Ashley!' said the man cheerily, striding up, arm outstretched. 'I'm Freddie Fox-Titt.'

Ash shook his hand limply. 'All right,' he mumbled. There was an awkward silence.

'Come on, then!' said Freddie, a little too heartily. 'Let me take your bag and we'll be off home.'

Climbing up into the Range Rover, Ash had to move aside several copies of *Horse and Hound* from the passenger seat. The back seat had a saddle on it, and a blanket covered in dog hair. Ash was a bit scared of animals. His reservations grew even stronger.

'Just chuck them in the back,' said Freddie. 'I've been meaning to have a clear-out for ages.' He looked down at Ash's gleaming white trainers and chuckled. 'Those aren't going to stay clean long!'

Ash looked dismayed: his vintage Nike Air Jordans were his pride and joy. *Take me back to Peckham*, he thought miserably, as the vehicle pulled out of the car park, narrowly missing a tractor coming the other way.

Fifteen minutes later Freddie indicated right. Archie had been mesmerized by the size of the houses they'd passed. He couldn't believe people lived like this.

'Nearly home!' Freddie announced, to Ash's relief. The winding lanes had been making him feel sick. As they bumped over the cattle grid, he could see a large square farmhouse at the end of a drive in front of them. Big green fields surrounded by wooden fences stretched as far as he could see. Ash raised an eyebrow. This gaff had to be worth a few million.

Freddie pulled up outside the house, and Ash could hear the sound of frantic barking from inside. The nausea returned.

Freddie got Ash's bag out of the back and opened the front door, 'After you.'

Accustomed to his poky flat, Ash was once again struck by the size of the place. There seemed to be doorways leading off everywhere, while the ceilings stretched up high. For someone used to living in municipal straightness, the old house seemed to curve and lean in every direction. Every inch of wall space seemed to be filled with paintings: it was like walking into an art gallery.

Suddenly, two large brown dogs appeared from nowhere and threw themselves at Ash. He couldn't help but let out an involuntary scream: they were massive!

'Avon! Barksdale!' Freddie pulled them off. 'Sorry, Ashley, they're just being friendly.' With some difficulty he pushed the yapping creatures into a nearby room and shut the door. Ash wasn't sure if he'd heard the dogs' names right. Freddie second-guessed him.

'Our son Archie named them. Apparently after a character in a TV show – *High Wire*, or something. I must admit, I wasn't sure, but Angie thought "Barksdale" was a rather jolly name for a dog.'

'*The Wire?*' Ash asked, incredulously.

Freddie looked pleased. 'That's the one! Do you know it?'

'Yeah,' Ash muttered. *Shit, man, these people were nut jobs!*

Freddie turned and looked up the stairs hopefully.

'Darling, are you there?'

A muffled voice replied. 'I thought I heard the dogs. I didn't think you'd be back yet!'

Moments later, a middle-aged woman appeared on the top step. Ash thought she looked quite pretty in a mumsy, outdoorsy way. As she made her way down towards them Ash could see some kind of weird white cream smeared along her top lip.

Freddie evidently didn't know what to make of his wife's appearance, either.

'Er, darling,' he said staring at her mouth quizzically. 'This is Ashley King.'

'It's Ash,' he mumbled.

Freddie held his hand behind his ear. 'Didn't quite catch that, sorry.'

Ash blushed. 'It's Ash. Hi, Mrs, er, Mrs . . .' Shit, he'd forgotten her name!

She smiled, 'Angie, please. I like the name "Ash", it's got rather a ring to it.'

Freddie cleared his throat. 'Darling, what's that on your face?'

His wife laughed without embarrassment.

'Sorry, you caught me in the middle of bleaching my moustache! You must think we live in a madhouse,' she added to Ash, noticing his horrified expression.

'Anyway, come through to the kitchen, I'll put the kettle on.' As they walked down the hallway Ash noticed a painting on the wall.

'Is that Thomas Gertin?' he asked without thinking.

Freddie looked bemused, Ash dropped his 't's so he hadn't got a clue what he'd just said. Angie however, looked delighted.

'Yes! Do you know him?'

Ash shrugged, blushing under their gaze.

'Is this Gertin some kind of whizz? I'm afraid art's not my strong point,' said Freddie.

'Darling, he wasn't just any old artist!' Angie said. 'Thomas Gertin was one of the earliest pioneers of using watercolour paint as an art form!'

She sighed regretfully.

'Of course, his life was cut tragically short. Who knows? He could have been one of the greats.'

'What did he die of?' asked Freddie brightly, trying to make an effort.

Ash spoke up. 'Consumption.' He stuttered on the word several times and went deep red. Angie thought momentarily that under the spots he was a very handsome young man. She smiled at him reassuringly.

'So you like English watercolours? I'm thrilled to have a cohort, Freddie says I've clogged up the house with them, but don't you find the expressive qualities of the brushwork just so enchanting?'

Ash didn't answer; he was finding Angie's moustache cream rather distracting.

Freddie noticed and pulled a face. 'Dar-ling!'

Angie looked at him, 'What?'

Freddie made a frantic movement above his top lip.

'Oh, bugger, I'd forgotten about that!' Angie looked apologetic. 'I got so carried away with having Ash here. Won't be two secs.'

She left the kitchen. Freddie and Ash looked awkwardly at each other.

'Here we are then, young Ashley, I mean Ash!' said Freddie. Outside Ash heard a strange screeching noise. It sounded like someone was being murdered.

'What's that?' he asked in alarm.

Freddie smiled, 'Just the peacocks. We've got a pair of them. Beautiful creatures, but they can get a bit nasty if you get them on an off day. I'd keep my distance if I were you.'

Once again Ash wondered what on earth he was doing there.

Chapter 49

Harriet was walking back to the office after lunch when her mobile went. To her surprise, it was Saffron's home number.

'Harriet, it's Velda.'

'Velda! How are you?'

Velda gave a dry laugh. 'I've been better. I suppose you've heard about Saffron moving out?'

'She did mention it,' Harriet admitted. 'Not that she says much to me at the moment. I think she's avoiding me.'

Velda paused. 'I – we – really need your help. Would you be able to come over after work tonight? My sister is here.'

Despite the turmoil within, Montague Mews looked typically enchanting that evening. The candy-coloured doors peeked out of the darkness, while the overhead lamps threw a triangle of light down on to the patchwork of cobbles. An old sports car was parked haphazardly outside No. 3.

Luckily Saffron had been out on a photo shoot all day, otherwise Harriet wouldn't have been able to look her in the eye. She somehow felt she was going behind her friend's back in agreeing to meet Velda. But on the other hand Velda had sounded so worried that Harriet hadn't had the heart to say no.

Velda opened the front door even before Harriet had had a chance to knock. She looked pale and tired, like she hadn't had a good night's sleep in quite a while.

'It really is very good of you to come over,' she told Harriet as she ushered her into the living room. 'Can I get you something to drink?'

'A cup of tea would be lovely,' said Harriet.

Velda nodded. 'Won't be a minute.'

Harriet heard voices and footsteps in the hallway, and moments later Babs Sax stumbled in. It seemed so incongruous to see her here. The artist's tumbling red hair looked wilder than ever, and there was a desperate look in her eyes. She threw herself down on the sofa and burst into tears.

'You've got to help me!' she sobbed. 'I don't know what else to do.'

Harriet felt awful. Babs was normally so full of flounce and flamboyance that it was horribly disconcerting to see her sitting there crying what looked to be genuine, heartfelt tears. Tentatively, she laid a hand on her scrawny shoulder.

'There, there.'

Babs cried even harder. One false eyelash had fallen off and was stuck to her cheek like an intoxicated tarantula. 'You're Saffron's friend, please talk to her! I've left it so long, and now I'm scared it's too late.'

Velda came back into the room carrying a tray. She placed it down, looked at Babs and sighed, producing a tissue from the box on the coffee table. 'Belle got here last night,' Velda said. 'I opened the front door and there she was. She was rather hoping for a reconciliation with

Saffron, but of course she didn't know she'd moved out.'

'It's all my fault!' sobbed Babs. 'If I hadn't been such a terrible mother in the first place, none of this would have happened.'

Velda looked at her sister. 'Belle, how can it have come to this?'

Babs was in a pit of self-loathing. 'He broke my heart, and I never thought I would recover,' she breathed unhappily.

Harriet looked confused. 'Harry Walden, Saffron's father,' explained Velda.

Babs took a big, shuddering breath. 'Saffron is the image of him. Every time I looked at her, it was like my heart was ripped out all over again.'

Velda had had enough of her sister's self-pity. 'She was only a child!' she told her angrily. 'It's not Saffron's fault she looks like her father.'

'I know!' Babs's lower lip quivered. 'But she's like him in so many ways, too. Wilful, headstrong . . . after a while it just got too much. I could tell she blamed me for Harry leaving.' Her voice had risen high, like a child's. 'What was I supposed to do? *He* left *me*!'

Velda handed her sister another tissue. 'Please try and calm down, this is doing you no good at all.'

Babs blew her nose loudly and turned a pair of reddened, beseeching eyes towards Harriet.

'You must talk to her, please! She'll listen to you.'

Velda's voice was calmer, but Harriet detected the hint of a tremor. 'I know we're putting you in a difficult situation, but if there's anything you can do. Anything . . .'

'Leave it with me, I'll have a talk with Saffron,' said Harriet, sounding a lot more confident than she felt.

*   *   *

'What do you think to this hairstyle?' Annabel held up a magazine with a picture of Jennifer Aniston at a red-carpet do, looking ultra-glamorous.

On the other side of the desk Saffron's jaw tightened. She was trying to write up her interview with a major heart-throb, who'd turned out to be a boring git with too much fake tan on. She was having enough trouble trying to make him sound interesting without Annabel's constant interruptions.

'Yah, I might have some highlights put in like that. Actually . . .' Annabel cocked her head and studied the picture, before holding it up next to her pallid moon face. 'Don't you think we look alike? We could pass for sisters. I'd be the younger one, of course.'

Saffron's mouth fell open as she realized the features editor was serious. God, Annabel had some ego! Out of the corner of her eye, she saw Harriet coming over.

'Er, Saffron?' Harriet sounded really nervous. Saffron tried to look nonchalant.

'What?'

'Do you fancy going out for lunch?'

'Sorry, I'm really busy . . .' Saffron started to say, but just then Annabel started waving the picture of Jennifer Aniston at her again, obviously wanting her to agree. She had to get out of there.

'OK, just a quick one.'

They went to what had been their favourite café down the road, and sat at their regular table. For the first ten minutes, conversation was painfully stilted, before Saffron looked at Harriet and sighed.

'I'm sorry, H, I've been a real bitch to you.'

Harriet looked down at her can of Diet Coke.

'You've been through a horrible time, it doesn't matter.'

379

'It does matter. You've been nothing but a good friend to me, and I had such a nice Christmas with you and your parents. I just wasn't expecting to see her. It totally threw me.'

'Where are you staying?'

'Knightsbridge, with an old school friend and her boyfriend. They've got a flat right behind Harrods, but it's one bedroom and bloody tiny. I'm sleeping on the sofa and I have to listen to them shagging all night.'

'You can always stay with me,' Harriet offered.

Saffron smiled. 'Thanks, but it's a bit too close to Montague Mews for my liking. Besides, Tara and Tim are going skiing for a few days tomorrow, so I'll have the place to myself.'

Harriet hesitated. 'Are you going to move back home after that?'

'I don't know where home is any more,' Saffron said flatly.

'Your aunt is desperately worried about you.'

'Has she asked you to talk to me?'

Harriet shrugged helplessly, and Saffron sighed.

'I know in some kind of fucked-up way, she probably thought she was trying to help. I'm just pissed off. Why didn't she tell me? It's like she tricked me.'

'I think she thought Babs and you would be able to make things up. I think it was a last resort.'

Saffron's face was set. 'Well then, she doesn't know me at all. I will never make up with that woman for as long as I live.' She looked away moodily. There was a man buying a sandwich at the counter, and his height and broad shoulders caught her eye. As he turned to leave, Saffron saw to her surprise that it was Tom from the art desk.

Their food arrived. 'Anyway, we haven't spoken

380

about that guy from New Year's Eve,' said Saffron as she tucked in to her potato. 'Did you pull him?'

'Actually, yes,' said Harriet. She blushed.

Saffron stopped eating. 'Did you *shag* him?' Harriet went even redder, and Saffron burst out laughing. 'At bloody last! Was it any good?'

'Not really,' admitted Harriet, too embarrassed to tell Saffron the details. 'Besides, he had a fiancée.'

'No! What a twat! Never mind, at least it got you back in the saddle. You wait, they'll be queuing up from now on.'

Harriet clenched her bum cheeks together and shifted uncomfortably on her seat.

Chapter 50

It was nearing the end of January, and Catherine was about to receive a crushing blow. Normally every month, Laura, the head of sales, would send a 'Project 300' update to Catherine and Adam with the latest figures. Since the redesign, she had hardly been able to contain her glee about the soaring sales, but this month no email had come. Catherine had been in to see her, but Laura had gone bright red and muttered something about a hold-up with the data. Catherine knew she was being fobbed off – and it wasn't long before she found out why.

On the last Wednesday of the month, Catherine received an email from Adam instructing her to attend a meeting that afternoon with him and the head of sales.

'So what's going on? This isn't normal procedure,' she'd asked as soon as they'd sat down. She looked at Laura, a pleasant-faced blonde woman who always wore big colourful scarves pinned in place with a diamanté brooch.

Laura didn't look so happy today, however. 'I'm afraid we have some bad news about January's figures . . .' she started, looking at Adam for backup.

Adam flushed and passed the buck as usual, 'I think it's better coming from you.'

Catherine clenched her jaw, she was having an unpleasant sensation of déjà vu.

Laura looked down at a piece of paper in front of her. 'Of course, we haven't got the final edit yet,' she started, 'but it looks like we've suffered a drop in sales.' She shot Catherine a loaded glance. 'A *big* drop in sales.'

Catherine was perfectly still. 'How much?'

The other woman took a deep breath. 'Well, er, the on-sale issue is looking to sell 235,000. So that's a drop of,' she gulped, '30,000.'

Catherine's jaw fell. 'Thirty thousand? I mean, I know the January issue is always tough, but this is bullshit!' She controlled her voice. 'Are you sure?'

She was met by an unhappy nod. 'Of course, there have been some circulation problems as well, which hasn't helped . . .'

Catherine was on her instantly. 'What do you mean?'

Laura looked uncomfortable. 'We're still investigating, but for some reason 15,000 copies sat in a warehouse on the Norfolk coast and didn't get delivered to the retail outlets. We've had to have them pulped.'

Catherine put her head in her hands and groaned. 'This is a fucking disaster.' After all their hard work they were back down to 235,000 – 65,000 short of their target. They only had the February and March issues left to try and make it up. There was no way they could do it.

'Bloody "Project 300",' Laura muttered, looking as deflated as Catherine felt.

'So do you ladies have any ideas how to get sales back up, then?' asked Adam, hopefully.

*　　*　　*

'Can I make you a Lemsip?' asked Amelia. Caro was curled up under a blanket on the sofa with a heavy cold. She'd had it for three days, and the blasted thing showed no sign of abating.

'Thanks, darling, but I'll probably turn into a citrus fruit if I have another one.'

Amelia smiled sympathetically. 'Let me know if you need anything, I'm just going to go for a bath.' Milo was in bed, and the house was silent for once, except for a 'tap tap' from the next room as Benedict worked on his laptop.

'You still alive?' he called out.

'Just about,' Caro called back. She settled back under the blanket, trying to breathe through her nose. The house felt like a cocoon, drawing in comfortingly around her. Caro huddled further into the blanket, reflecting. It had been quite a few weeks here, what with the awful hoo-ha next door and Babs Sax. There had been no more silent phone calls, thank God, and Amelia seemed much happier again. Maybe it was all just a coincidence, Caro tried to tell herself blurrily. Her eyelids were becoming heavier by the second, she was feeling so tired again . . .

The fire had nearly gone out in the grate when Caro awoke. She looked at her watch: 9.31 p.m. She'd never get to sleep later.

The dining room was empty as she went through to the kitchen; Benedict had to be upstairs. As she blew her nose on a piece of kitchen roll Amelia appeared in the doorway in a dressing gown.

'Fancy a hot chocolate? I was just about to make some,' Caro asked.

'Super.'

'There's a Fortnum & Mason's jar in the cupboard by

the door, if you wouldn't mind getting it. I'm afraid the bump is rather limiting my reach.'

Caro was just pouring the hot water out when a loud smash made her jump. The jar was lying in pieces among a debris of chocolate powder on the floor.

'Are you all right?' Caro gasped.

Amelia was frozen to the spot, a wild look on her face. Caro followed her gaze out of the kitchen window. What was she staring at? Oh Jesus Christ! Out of the darkness, a swarthy figure stepped forward.

The man locked his hooded eyes on to Amelia, then slowly lifted a finger and drew it across his throat. The gesture was chilling. Face stretched with fear, Amelia staggered backwards, gripping the worktop.

'Amelia!' Caro cried. She moved towards her, but Amelia turned and fled down the passage. Caro turned back fearfully, but the man had gone. Summoning up her courage, she crept up to the window and peered out. The garden was empty.

Caro had to get to the bottom of this. She rushed up the stairs. 'Amelia, let me in!' She tried the handle, and slowly, afraid of what she might find, opened the door.

Amelia was standing in the middle of the room, arms wrapped around herself like a frightened child. She was pale with terror.

Caro was by her side in a flash. 'Darling, what's going on? Who was that man?' Her sister-in-law's teeth were chattering so loudly she couldn't speak.

'Amelia!' Caro was seriously frightened now. The phone calls, the face at the window, the intruder . . . Of course they were all linked! Why had she been kidding herself?

'Amelia!' she said again, gripping her arm. 'We can't go on like this. I can't go on like this. I've been giving you the benefit of the doubt, but I've got Benedict and Milo to think about.' She gestured at her stomach. 'I've got *this* one to think about. Darling, if you're in some kind of trouble you have to tell me! I won't have my family put in danger.'

'What's going on?' Benedict materialized in the room with a towel wrapped round his waist. 'I thought I heard shouting.'

'You knew him, didn't you?' prompted Caro gently.

'Knew who?' Benedict demanded. He took in the stricken faces. 'Amelia, what on earth's going on?'

It was all too much. Tears running down her face, Amelia collapsed on her bed.

'I'm sorry, I'm so sorry. I thought I'd be able to deal with it by myself.'

Benedict knelt down beside her, his voice gentle. 'Darling, what is it? Please let me help you.'

Amelia took a deep breath, steeling herself. 'His name is Vladimir Kirillov,' she said in a small voice. 'I met him in a nightclub in Moscow. He told me he owned the place, but that was a lie, along with everything else he said. Vladimir was a dream boyfriend at first. He told me he was a successful businessman, although he never talked about his work. I didn't pry, and besides, when I was with him Vladimir had the ability to make me feel like I was the centre of his universe. He was so generous and so attentive.'

She sniffed. 'Then one of my friends told me she'd heard he was mixed up in some bad stuff, and that I should stay away from him. Of course, I was so in love by then I didn't listen. But Vladimir changed. Maybe he noticed I was more curious about his work. He got more and more possessive, phoning me the whole time to see where I was, turning up at work.'

Amelia smiled bitterly. 'Of course, I was never able

to question him about anything. One night we'd been out, and when we got back Vladimir went mad and accused me of flirting with one of his friends. I hadn't, of course, but I just lost it and accused him of trying to control me.' Amelia hesitated. 'That's when he hit me.'

A muscle flickered in Benedict's cheek. 'The bastard. If I ever get my hands on him . . .'

'Benedict, you mustn't!' Amelia cried. The fear was back in her voice. 'You must never, ever go near him. I finished with him there and then, and he swore he'd come back to haunt me.' Her eyes filled with tears again. 'That's when I found out what he really was.'

'What is he?' asked Caro fearfully.

'Money laundering, blackmail, extortion . . . you name it, he's involved in it. He's even rumoured to have ordered hit men to kill off other "business" rivals.' Amelia shivered. 'And now he's followed me here.'

'Is he blackmailing you?' Benedict asked quietly.

The tears were free-falling now. 'I've been so stupid!' she sobbed. 'There were these pictures of me, before I met Vladimir. I met this guy and when he offered me cocaine I knew it was wrong, but I tried it anyway. There were other people there as well, it was quite a party. Someone had a camera,' she added, ashamed. 'Somehow Vladimir found out about them and started saying if I didn't give him money, he was going to put the pictures all over the internet and I'd never work again, that my life would be ruined.'

She looked in such a state that Caro's heart almost broke. She sat beside her sister-in-law, rubbing her back soothingly. 'Does he know you've got family money?'

Amelia nodded miserably. 'I talked about my life and family when we were happy together, of course I did. Vladimir was always very interested, asking what you did, Benedict, and where we had houses.' She sounded bitter again. 'I always thought he wanted to know all about me because he'd come back here with me one day, but he was obviously just sizing me up.'

'Did you give him any money?' Benedict's voice was so low and quiet, it sent a shiver down Caro's spine.

Amelia nodded her head. 'I thought if I gave him it, he'd go away, but then he started asking for more and more.' She gulped. 'That's when I fled back here; I thought he wouldn't come looking for me. But I was so stupid. Vladimir's got eyes everywhere!'

'How much money have you given him?' asked Benedict.

Amelia avoided his eyes. 'At first it was twenty-five thousand, then it was double that, and now he's demanding a hundred. Whatever I give him, it's never enough.'

Benedict looked completely appalled. 'You've given him seventy-five thousand pounds of your inheritance?'

'That's why I didn't tell you, I knew you'd be upset! I've been so scared. I thought if I kept a low profile, he wouldn't come looking for me.' Amelia smiled tightly. 'I don't think he even needs the money. He's such a sick fuck, he's tormenting me for pleasure.'

'Was he behind that devil mask? The man's a complete psychopath!' gasped Caro. 'You poor thing. I can't bear that you've gone through this by yourself.'

Benedict stood up. 'Have you got his number?'

She shook her head. 'The calls always come from a private number.'

Just then, Amelia's mobile starting ringing on her dressing table.

'Benedict, no!' Amelia cried, but it was too late. He snatched the phone up.

'Vladimir Kirillov?' His voice was like ice. 'This is

Benedict Towey, Amelia's brother. I've had enough of you harassing my family, I suggest we meet once and for all to sort this out. Since you've spent so much time in the area, I assume you know the Horse and Groom pub off Guinevere Road. I'll be there in five minutes.' He hung up.

Caro rushed over to her husband. 'Benedict, please, it's too dangerous! You have no idea what you're getting yourself into, this chap could be mafia for all we know.'

'Please listen to her,' Amelia said quietly.

Their pleas fell on deaf ears. A white-hot rage seemed to have taken over Benedict's face. Every muscle had come alive, his eyes flashed, and his strong jaw was rigid, defining the contours more than ever. Caro thought he had never looked more beautiful or frightening. He stood up. 'I need to go and sort this.' He strode out, Caro following him into their bedroom.

'Please don't go,' she pleaded. 'We should go to the police and let them sort it out. This is dangerous!'

He pulled a sweater over his head. 'And what will they do? They're not going to stand and keep watch over the place until this Kirillov character turns up again. Amelia's at breaking point, Caro, I can't let her go on like this. And I can't risk him coming back here, near you both, and Milo.'

Benedict came over and dropped a kiss on Caro's forehead. 'I love you,' he said. 'Don't worry.' As he left the room, the tang of aftershave trailing in his wake, she collapsed sobbing on the bed.

It was the longest hour of Caro's life. She and Amelia were in the living room anxiously waiting Benedict's return. Caro was pacing the floor like a madwoman. She kept picking up the phone to dial 999 and putting it down again. Horrible scenarios kept running through her mind; she should have said something before! Instinctively Caro cradled her bump. What if something terrible happened, and their unborn child had to grow up without a father? What would she tell Milo? Caro loved her husband so much the thought of never seeing him again filled her with the most desolate grief she had ever known. She moaned softly, barely aware of Amelia trying to comfort her.

Finally, they heard a key turning in the lock, and to her unimaginable relief, Benedict walked in. His face was pale and set, but aside from that he looked unharmed.

'Oh my God, you're safe!' cried Caro, racing across the room.

'What happened?'

Benedict put his arms around her. 'It doesn't matter, it's all over.'

'But are you hurt? Did he threaten you?'

'No darling, please don't upset yourself. Everything's OK. Kirillov is out of our lives – *all* of our lives – for good.' He shot Amelia a meaningful look, and she broke down completely.

'Thank you, thank you,' she sobbed. Benedict opened one of his arms and Amelia snuggled into it, pushing her face into his strong chest. He squeezed her tightly.

'Hey, come on. That's what big brothers are for.'

FEBRUARY

Chapter 51

Saffron groaned and pulled the pillow round her ears. The banging of the headboard next door was getting even louder. If she'd known what shaggers Tara and Tim were, she would never have moved here in the first place. The noise reached a hammering crescendo, there was a single wail, and then it all fell silent. Saffron knew it was a brief respite – they'd be at it again within ten minutes.

Lying awake every night listening to Tara and Tim's carnal habits had made Saffron think, amongst other things, about her own love life. She had never gone without sex for this long before. Saffron thought she'd have been gagging for it by now, but strangely, she wasn't that bothered.

A lanky, naked figure appeared in the living room doorway. 'Are you asleep, Saffron?'

'No such luck,' she sighed.

Tim moved closer. 'I say, Tara and I were wondering. Do you fancy a threesome?' He said it so casually he could have been asking if she wanted one sugar in her tea or two.

Tim had a spotty back and the beginnings of nostril

hair. Saffron rolled her eyes in the darkness. 'No offence, Timbo, but I think I'll pass.'

It was definitely time to move on.

Harriet gazed happily across the table from her date. She couldn't believe how nice and well, *normal*, he was. She'd been seriously thinking of cancelling her subscription to Chapline, especially after the last fellow. A wet-lipped brand-manager from Surrey called Jonty, he had invited her to the cinema to see *Sleepy Hollow*. Harriet had been delighted, she'd always been a Johnny Depp fan, but her excitement soon waned when it turned out they were actually going to see something called *Sleepy's Hollow*, a rather dubious low-budget erotica film about a young sultry blonde who suffered from narcolepsy every time she had sex. Harriet had lasted halfway through the performance before Jonty's wandering hands got too much, and she'd excused herself to go to the loo, never to return.

Samuel, however, seemed different. They'd met at a champagne bar in Knightsbridge. He'd been older than he looked in his photo, but charming and attentive, asking her lots of questions about herself. They were now round the corner in a candlelit tapas place. It was very romantic, Harriet thought, as she watched Samuel expertly fork up a mouthful of marinated squid.

'Tell me more about yourself,' he said, wiping his mouth with a napkin before putting it down in his lap. He reached across to fill Harriet's wine glass again. She found herself thinking he had beautiful table manners; her mother would like him.

'There's not much to tell, really. I work for a magazine called *Soirée*, editor's PA mainly, but I organize their parties and stuff.'

Samuel raised his eyebrow, impressed. 'That's a fantastic magazine. I bet you're awfully good at your job.'

'You know *Soirée*?' asked Harriet, liking him more by the moment.

'Of course. I used to buy it for my . . .' Samuel hesitated for a moment. 'Look, Harriet, I didn't want to tell you earlier, because I like you so much, but technically I'm still married.'

'Oh,' said Harriet, her heart sinking. She had known Samuel was too good to be true.

He leant forward and put his hand over hers. '*Technically* I'm still married,' he repeated. 'Marina and I separated months ago, it's just that the divorce is taking months to go through.'

'Oh?' asked Harriet again, her spirits rising. 'Do you have any, er, children together?'

'No,' replied Samuel. He squeezed her hand meaningfully. 'But I do want them some day, I just haven't met the right woman yet . . .'

Harriet felt a surge of happiness.

Just then, there was a cold gust of air as the front door flew open and a woman stormed in. 'Samuel!' she screeched across the restaurant.

He turned and cringed. 'Oh, God!'

'Do you know her?' Harriet asked in confusion, but the fuming blonde woman was already upon them, car keys in hand.

'I knew I'd find you here!'

Everyone turned to observe the commotion, but the woman didn't seem to care. 'Up to your old tricks again! I can't trust you for five minutes!'

Samuel had transformed into a cowering wreck. The woman turned her furious glare on Harriet.

'In case you're wondering, I'm Samuel's wife.'

'But he told me you were divorcing,' stuttered Harriet.

The woman rolled her eyes. 'That's what he tells all the silly bitches who fall for his crap! I tell you, if he weren't about to get his bonus and put all our kids through university I'd leave him right this moment.' She yanked on his collar. 'Come on, you. Home!'

Samuel stood up like a naughty schoolboy. He didn't even look at Harriet as he was pushed out of the restaurant.

Harriet could feel thirty pairs of eyes on her. She literally wanted to cry with embarrassment. Out of nowhere, a waiter glided up with a large glass of white wine.

'On the house, madam,' he said sympathetically.

Saffron was working late again. Partly because she had loads to do, but mostly because she couldn't bear to go back to Tara's cramped little flat, with its damp washing hanging everywhere and dirty dishes in the sink. No wonder the place was such a mess: Tara and Tim spent most of their time in the bedroom. Saffron had even found an old used condom under one of the sofa cushions last night. She had probably been sleeping on it for weeks. The thought made her feel quite sick.

Britain was in the grip of a cold, dark winter. The black night loomed in through the office window, making the strip lighting inside even harsher. Saffron's skin felt dry and dull from the air conditioning. For a moment, she longed to be in Churchminster, with its fresh air and wide-open country spaces. But she could never go back there. It was another thing that woman had ruined.

Saffron gave herself a mental shake. She wasn't

going to let herself think about that. Tim and Tara were out tonight; at least she'd have the place to herself. They'd been really good about it, but she knew she'd outstayed her welcome. A wave of depression washed over Saffron. She couldn't stay on friends' floors for the rest of her life. *On this salary*, she reflected glumly, *I can't even afford a shoebox in Surbiton.*

The building was deserted as she made her way out. A security guard was at the desk fast asleep, his mouth wide open. So much for Valour's stringent security measures. Saffron stepped on to the street, meeting an icy blast of wind. God, this country was miserable! Maybe she should emigrate . . . she had loads of mates in Australia. Thinking wistfully of barbecues and volleyball games on Bondi Beach, Saffron pulled her coat around her and set off.

A few minutes later she turned off the main street to take the familiar short cut to the tube. It was such a foul evening there weren't many people about, but she could hear footsteps behind her. *You have my sympathies*, Saffron thought. *What are we doing out on a night like this?*

The blow to her face took her completely by surprise. Her knees buckling from shock more than anything, Saffron fell back on the pavement. Her attacker leant down and tried to grab her handbag. He was wearing a dark hat pulled down low over his face.

'Get off me!' she shouted hysterically. As the man lunged again, Saffron brought her fist up and, as hard as she could, punched him in the groin.

It worked. The man let out a shriek of pain. 'Bitch!' His hands clasped over his nether regions, he staggered off into the darkness.

Too shocked to move, Saffron lay still on the ground. She was soaking wet and probably filthy, but at least she still had her bag. 'Calm down,' she gasped to herself, 'you're fine.'

But then the shadow leant over her again.

'Police! Help! Fire!' she screamed.

'Saffron, it's me!'

It was a familiar voice, but she couldn't place it. As she stared, Tom Fellows's features came into focus.

'Are you all right?' he asked concernedly. It had started to rain, and drips were running down his glasses.

Saffron rubbed her cheek where she'd been hit, and winced. 'I'll live.'

Tom awkwardly pulled her up by her arm, and she brushed herself down with shaking hands. She was still breathing heavily. 'What are you *doing* here?'

'I left something at the office.' As if it was the most natural thing in the world Tom gently lifted her chin with his giant hand and peered at her cheek. 'You shouldn't be out by yourself.' Saffron just stared at him, taken aback by the gesture. Blushing, Tom dropped his hand, pushing the bottle-tops back up his nose.

Saffron was starting to feel a bit silly. She'd probably been screaming like a complete freak, but it was just her luck that she had been rescued by Tom, and not some really fit stranger. 'I'm a big girl, don't worry about me,' she declared. 'See ya.' Picking up her bag she sauntered off, leaving Tom standing there uselessly.

Once round the corner, however, Saffron's chutzpah dissolved as her legs went completely. Leaning against the wall, she fumbled around in her bag for her phone. Her hands were shaking so much, it took several attempts to dial the number.

'Aunt Velda?' she sobbed. 'Can you come and get me? Someone's just tried to mug me.'

*   *   *

398

An hour later, Velda's old Beetle pulled up at the entrance to Montague Mews. The boot was full of Saffron's things, hastily retrieved from Tara and Tim's. As Saffron got out of the car outside No. 3, she had never felt so glad to be home.

Velda put the key in the door. 'I was just making a stew when you called, would you like some?'

Saffron stepped in behind her, savouring the rich spicy smell filling the house. 'Yes, please.'

She put her suitcase down, and for a moment they just stood inside the front door, not sure what to say.

'Saffron, I—' started Velda.

Saffron caught her aunt's hand and squeezed it. 'Don't. It's me who should be apologizing. I know you only had my best interests at heart.'

'Your mother is dreadfully upset—'

Saffron interrupted again. 'Can we please just forget about it all? I want to go back to how things were, just you and me.'

Velda seemed to want to say something, but stopped. She put her arms round her niece and hugged her. 'Just you and me. Now go and get those wet clothes off, and I'll get dinner ready.'

As Saffron lugged her bag upstairs, she felt her spirits lift for the first time in weeks. She was home again. Everything was back to normal.

At least, for now.

Chapter 52

Ash had been living at the Maltings for almost a month, ensconced in the little granny annexe that had been converted at one end of the stable block. It was warm and generously furnished, but Ash couldn't get used to all the different noises outside every night. He had grown up to the backdrop of ambulance and police sirens, loud music and people who didn't care about keeping their voices down. Here, there was a whole new cacophony of noise: birds hooting, the wind howling through the eaves, the insistent 'caw caw' of the peacocks. Ash thought the countryside was meant to be quiet! He'd nearly had a heart attack the first night. There had been a fearful screaming right outside his window. When he'd eventually plucked up the courage to peek outside, he'd been confronted with the grisly sight of a huge barn owl dismembering a mouse.

Angie invited him to the 'big house' for dinner every night, but Ash preferred to heat something up in the microwave at his lodgings. It wasn't that he didn't like the Fox-Titts, they'd been nothing but hospitable (aside from not being able to understand what he was saying, sometimes), but Ash had been out of a family environment for so long, he'd forgotten how to act in one. It made him uncomfortable, to say the least. At least they had Sky, and he had his iPod.

The place he had really taken to was Angie's shop. From the moment he had walked into the crowded, low-beamed building and smelt the history in the air, Ash had felt like he had found his own personal heaven. It triggered so many happy memories and thoughts, and whatever job Angie gave him – whether it was cleaning and waxing bits of furniture, or listing new items – Ash threw himself into it. Angie, who had been rather worried about her withdrawn protégé until then, was encouraged by his progress.

That morning Ash was in the shop alone for the first time. Angie was out at a house clearance, seeing if there was anything worth picking up. Although he didn't show it, Ash was really flattered Angie had thought him good enough to look after things. Though he was a bit worried about having to serve a customer. What if someone asked him a question and he couldn't answer it? Angie had said to call her mobile if he had any problems, but it still made him feel anxious.

Mercifully the first hour or so he was undisturbed, and Ash had busied himself with polishing an old mahogany chest Angie had recently brought in. *It really was beautiful*, he thought, as his hands ran over it, savouring every detail, wondering how many owners it had passed through.

Suddenly the doorbell jangled. Ash's heart jumped. He stood up to find a tall, grey-haired woman with a rather severe facial expression. Ash gulped.

'You must be Ashley,' said the woman. She sounded really posh, like the Queen. Ash felt tongue-tied. Unperturbed, the woman stuck out a hand encased in a leather glove. 'I'm Clementine Standington-Fulthrope. I live at Fairoaks. I expect Angie has told you about me.'

Ash had no idea what she was going on about. 'Hi,' he muttered, turning puce under her steely gaze.

'I must admit, I thought I would have seen you about the village by now, but you've obviously been keeping yourself busy.'

Ash shifted on to one leg. 'Yeah.'

'I see.' Clementine wasn't quite sure what to make of this pale, spotty youth with a gold stud in one ear. 'Well, do tell Angie I dropped in. Goodbye, Ashley.'

Ash nearly gave a bow, but stopped just in time. 'Bye, Mrs Stanley – er.'

'Standington-Fulthrope,' said Clementine, and swept out of the shop.

To: Caro Towey
From: Clementine Standington-Fulthrope
Subject: A new face

Darling, are you there? Oh, do pick up. I've had the most interesting morning, I went into Angie's shop to meet this young Ashley fellow she's got working for her. I must admit, I was rather put out we hadn't been introduced before. One does like to keep abreast of all the new faces in the village. Angie warned me he was a little on the shy side, but my goodness! The poor chap couldn't put two words together, and he was wearing one of those rather menacing hooded jumpers I saw on Crimewatch last week. He was dreadfully spotty as well; maybe I should take him out on a good walk to get the fresh air to his complexion. I haven't seen a skin condition Churchminster hasn't cleared up yet. I digress. Angie seems to think this Ashley (isn't that a girl's name?) has potential, so I will wait and see. One can't praise the work Soirée *Sponsors are doing highly enough, after all.*

Has there been any development with the Saffron and Babs Sax situation? I do hope they come together and resolve it soon. That silly woman has been drinking herself into a stupor for weeks.

Anyway, I must dash: Errol Flynn is due his worming tablets. Do hope all is well with you, and that your indigestion is better. Try drinking dried nettle leaves with plenty of hot water.

Lots of love, Granny Clem Xxxx

PS. Look what Freddie taught me to do when he came round last week. :) It's a funny face, in case you were wondering!

Despite the hopeful start, an uneasy gloom had settled over the *Soirée* office. Catherine seemed permanently to have a face of thunder, and most of the staff were keeping out of her way. They had received a terse email from her, saying the January issue hadn't performed as well as expected, and that she needed even more effort from them from now on.

'As if we aren't working hard enough,' grumbled Saffron to Harriet one evening. It was half past five and Catherine had already left the office. Her overworked staff were making the most of it, and packing up for the day.

Harriet sighed. 'I know, that email didn't sound too good, did it?'

Saffron looked round the office; there wasn't a happy face in sight. 'I'm sick of all this doom and gloom!' she declared. She raised her voice. 'Does anyone fancy a drink?'

Sure enough, quite a large group of them descended on the Snooty Fox, a nice little pub down the road. Saffron secured a large table at the back and Alexander slapped his company credit card on the bar to buy a couple of bottles of the house champagne.

'I'll put it through on expenses,' he said conspiratorially.

'Where's Catherine?' someone asked.

'She left early to go down to the *Soirée* Sponsors office,' said Harriet. 'I'm not sure what's going on, but she had a face like a wet weekend in Wales. I hope there's not a problem.'

'Oh, great,' said someone else. 'That's all we need, she's stressed enough as it is.'

'I don't know why she bothers with that stupid scheme anyway, they're a bunch of wasters,' announced Annabel. Despite declaring she had a very exclusive party to go to, she had followed them down the pub for 'one quick drink'.

Saffron looked at her in distaste. 'Shut up, Annabel.'

Annabel bristled. 'How dare you! I could have you disciplined for that.'

'More champagne, anyone?' asked Harriet hastily, as Saffron looked like she was about to wrap Annabel's Alice band around her throat.

Alexander, who had been chatting up the barman, came and plonked himself down. He raised his glass in the air. 'Here's to us!' he announced. 'And to that young man over there, with the buttocks you could crack walnuts in. Oh my!'

Everyone giggled. Alexander could always be depended on to raise their spirits.

An hour later, everyone was feeling pretty merry. The

art director and chief sub had gone to play snooker, and everyone else was playing a game of: 'I have never.'

'I have never been naked in a public place,' said the picture editor.

Everyone except Annabel took a sip from their glass. 'This is *so* childish,' she huffed, clearly annoyed she was the odd one out.

'I have never had it off with a member of the royal family,' said Alexander. He drank heavily from his flute.

'You haven't!' someone cried. 'Alexander!' His eyes flashed wickedly. 'Oh, he was only a very minor member, don't worry!' He paused for effect. 'Although I seem to remember there was nothing minor about his member.' They all howled with laughter.

'You're disgusting,' said Annabel sanctimoniously.

Alexander dismissed her with a flick of his hand. 'Haven't you got a party to go to, darling?'

'Not while there's free champagne here,' muttered Saffron, a little too loudly.

Annabel glared at her. 'Well, I've clearly outstayed my welcome. Excuse me, I've got some grown-ups to go and meet.' She stood up and tried to walk off, but someone had tied the laces together on her frumpy ankle boots, and she managed one step before falling flat on her face.

'I say, Annabel, are you all right?' Harriet asked, trying desperately not to laugh.

Red with fury, she surfaced from under the table. 'That is so immature! I ought to report all of you to human resources.' With some difficulty Annabel yanked her laces apart and stomped out.

A few minutes later, Saffron turned from her conversation with Harriet to see Tom Fellows sitting beside her. He was perched awkwardly on a stool, long legs folded up underneath him like a dead spider.

'Hi,' he muttered. He was wearing a crumpled lumberjack shirt, which was open to reveal a 'Mr Messy' T-shirt underneath. His mane of black curls was wilder than ever, bottle-top glasses steaming up slightly from the heat of the room.

'Tom, I didn't see you there,' said Saffron. 'Are you enjoying yourself?'

Tom looked down at his huge feet. 'It's all right,' he muttered.

'Good stuff!' said Saffron, hoping someone would come along and save her. Tom carried on looking at the floor. Saffron glanced around desperately. 'Anyway, if you don't mind, I've got to go to the loo,' she said eventually. 'All that champagne . . .'

She started to squeeze past him, but Tom suddenly looked up so they were face to face. His bottle-tops seemed thicker than ever. 'Would you like to go out for a drink some time?' he blurted.

Saffron was so shocked she said yes.

It was Valentine's Day. Everywhere Catherine looked she seemed to be confronted by smug girls skipping along the street with huge bouquets of flowers. Restaurants were booked up with 'couples only' meals, and radio stations were playing a marathon of non-stop love songs.

Catherine normally dismissed the day as a load of rubbish. This year, however, it had really got her thinking. She didn't want to admit how much she missed John, but maybe she *had* been too hasty in cutting him out of her life. Maybe her past didn't have to come between them, and he seemed to be the first person who hadn't judged her. But then surely John would become part of her lie . . . and could she really trust him?

Catherine rubbed her eyes. She felt so confused. Relationships had always been a no-go zone, she'd made sure of that. But John had made her feel properly alive for the first time in her life. Catherine could hardly dare consider it . . . but *could* they make a go of things after all? When she considered the prospect, she felt a lurch of both excitement and fear.

She ran her hands through her hair. It had been a trying couple of days. Adam had broken the news that Valour's board needed to cut costs, and could no longer afford to pay all the *Soirée* Sponsors staff salaries. As Gail's super-efficient PA, a twenty-something single mum called Cheryl, had been the most recent joiner, it was her that the axe was falling on. Valour had 'generously' given her a three-month notice period, but it still didn't make breaking the news to Gail or Cheryl any easier. It was as if they had started shutting up shop already.

On top of this, Catherine felt trapped in a relentless grind of deadlines. She had made everyone go hell for leather on the February issue, but mid-month sales indicated it was barely going to make a dent in the huge sales increase expected of her. The enthusiasm everyone had summoned up was starting to wear off, and they were behind on the March issue. Saffron had landed a sought-after aristocratic model for the cover, but even that hadn't lifted spirits. Everyone was tired, demoralized and uncertain about their future.

Catherine didn't feel like going out tonight, but it was the third time Tolstoy had asked and it was difficult to keep saying no. Besides, she thought as she switched off her computer, what had all this hard work achieved?

Nothing. Yet again, she was the last person left in the office, and no doubt everyone else was enjoying a romantic dinner with their other half, or drinks with friends. *I have to get a life*, thought Catherine decisively. *It's not all about magazines and busting a gut to meet pie-in-the-sky targets.*

By total coincidence Tolstoy had booked a table at Duvall's, the restaurant Catherine and John had been to on their first date together. This was another reason Catherine hadn't been so keen on going, and she was momentarily overcome by a set of the wobbles as she walked in. It was as if John's ghost was hanging over the place, and it only highlighted the fact that this time she was meeting a man she didn't care about. She had to phone John, but what if he didn't want to know? She could hardly blame him.

Tolstoy was already at the table as Catherine entered the familiar room. To her discomfort, there was an undeniable air of romance in the air. Pink roses adorned each table, gentle piano music played, and couples sat hands entwined and staring into each other's eyes.

'You look a dream, I'm the envy of every man here,' Tolstoy said as he stood up to kiss her, his lips lingering on both cheeks.

'Thanks,' said Catherine rather self-consciously. She was wearing a low-cut Stella McCartney blouse that showed off a little more than she liked of her cleavage. She noticed Tolstoy's eyes brush over it.

He looked as impeccable as ever, his olive complexion set off perfectly by a midnight-blue suit and crisp white shirt.

'What can I get you to drink?' As usual, Tolstoy had a glass of still mineral water.

'Large glass of house white, please.'

Tolstoy frowned. 'That's more than all your daily recommended units in one glass, you know.'

'Oh well!' said Catherine. 'It hasn't killed me yet. Besides,' she shot him a sardonic glance, 'I really am old enough to know whether I want a glass of wine or not.'

Tolstoy conceded with grace. 'Of course, I'm being rude.' He smiled, a flash of white over the table. 'You're just such a perfect specimen I'd hate to see you damage yourself in any way.'

Bit too late for that, thought Catherine, as the waiter came up and handed them a menu each. After choosing the pea and watercress soup for a starter and asking about the calorific content of the seared tuna steak, Tolstoy leaned back and looked at Catherine.

'I've finally got you out then. I was beginning to think you were playing hard to get.'

'I've been busy,' apologized Catherine.

The Colgate white smile again. 'Oh, don't worry, as you know I like a *physical* challenge.'

He leaned back and cocked his head at Catherine. 'You know, you do remind me of someone. I can't think who, though.' He smiled. 'You weren't some huge child star back in the day, were you?'

Catherine fixed a smile on her face. 'Sorry to disappoint.'

Tolstoy shrugged. 'You have such a familiar face. I'm sure I'll get it at some point. My memory is normally excellent.'

The waiter appeared at Catherine's elbow. 'Bread, madam?'

'No, thank you,' said Tolstoy before she could answer.

She glared at him. 'I was hungry!'

409

'White carbs play havoc with your blood sugar levels,' he replied smoothly.

Catherine took a defiant glug of her wine.

Tolstoy waited for her to put her glass back on the table. 'I've never had you to myself properly before. So, what makes Catherine Connor tick?'

Catherine began to feel like she was on a psychiatrist's couch. It wasn't a nice sensation.

'Would you like to start a family one day?' Tolstoy asked.

'No,' said Catherine shortly. As if she'd tell him anyway.

Tolstoy smiled. 'Sorry, darling, I wasn't trying to get your back up.' His tone was genuine. 'It's hard for women to have it all in this industry, isn't it?'

'I suppose so,' she admitted, eager to move the conversation on from being about her. 'So tell me, have you got any more Iron Man races lined up?'

Half an hour later, Catherine knew more about training techniques and personal bests than she cared to, and Tolstoy had excused himself to go to the gents. Catherine finished her wine just as someone appeared at her elbow.

'Oh, can I have another glass of this please?' she said, thinking it was a waiter.

'Catherine? I didn't expect to see you here.'

She looked up and her stomach dropped to the floor. Standing there, as impossibly handsome as ever, was John Milton. He looked as astonished as she did.

'John! I think I could say the same thing.'

To her relief John smiled, his green eyes as arresting as ever under the midnight black hair. 'You look great, how are you?'

'Couldn't be better,' Catherine lied.

His face fell, but only for a moment. Catherine felt

mean and happy all at the same time. 'How was the heli-skiing?'

John looked surprised. 'You remembered . . . It was great.' He smiled the wry boyish grin that made her stomach go funny. 'I think it may be the start of a rather expensive new pastime.'

'Men and their hobbies,' she teased.

He grinned at her, and Catherine suddenly felt the greyness had been lifted from her world. She took a deep breath.

'Look, John, I've behaved appallingly. I know I don't deserve a second chance, but can I take you out for a drink to talk about things?'

John opened his mouth, but someone else got there first.

'Cath-a-rine!'

To her absolute horror, Isabella Montgomery had materialized next to John like a malevolent genie.

She linked a possessive arm through John's. 'I see you've met my date. I do hope you weren't trying to steal him off me.'

Catherine gaped at John. 'You're with *her*?'

A look of discomfort passed over his face, but before he had a chance to reply Isabella started gushing. 'John and I have become very good friends, haven't we, darling?' She leaned up to wipe a lipstick mark off his cheek. 'Come on, Johnny, our first course has arrived.' Isabella looked down at Catherine. 'Here by yourself again, darling? You're going to end up an old maid at this rate!'

Johnny? Catherine could take no more. 'Enjoy your meal. If you'll excuse me . . .' she said quietly, and jumped up from the table, pushing past them for the ladies.

It took her fifteen minutes to calm down. By the

time Catherine got back to the table, Tolstoy was sitting there with two cold starters in front of him, looking rather put out.

'I thought you'd run off!'

Catherine didn't want to glance up and risk seeing John and her nemesis all over each other. 'Tolstoy, I've suddenly lost my appetite. I'm sorry, but do you mind if we get out of here? I'll pay for dinner.'

He looked at her curiously. 'Are you all right?'

'I'm fine,' she said through clenched teeth. *Of all the people John Milton could end up with!* Her humiliation at asking him for another chance was turning to anger. At least she knew what kind of person he was now, going for someone like Isabella. It still didn't make her feel any better.

If Tolstoy was confused by her change of mood, he recovered quickly. 'Of course, darling, you look quite pale, where would you like to go?'

'Anywhere with a bar.'

Catherine opened her eyes. She felt dreadful. Her tongue was thick and furry, and a drum was banging relentlessly inside her head. She stared up at the ceiling – hang on, that looked different . . . As her eyes frantically swept round the unfamiliar room, the horrified realization struck . . . she was in someone else's bed.

'Morning, darling.'

Pulling the covers right up to her chin, Catherine slowly turned over. Tolstoy Peake was standing by the end of the bed in a minuscule pair of pants. Aside from the fact that he was balancing on one leg, his hands pressed together in front of him as if in prayer, Tolstoy didn't appear to have one hair on his entire body. Catherine wondered with a shudder if he shaved his legs.

'Tree pose,' he said, his eyes fixed on a spot on the wall above the bed. 'I always like to start the day with ninety minutes of yoga.'

Catherine was in shock. She needed to know what she'd done. 'Have we, I mean did we . . .' she gabbled. At least she still had her underwear on, unless Tolstoy had put it back on afterwards. She felt sick.

He turned his head and looked at her, a faint smile playing over his lips.

'Did we have sex, do you mean? I'm afraid not. You were so drunk by the end of the night you could hardly stand up. I thought it best to bring you back here, so I could keep an eye on you.' A faintly lascivious look crossed his face.

Catherine was mortified. 'Tolstoy, I can only apologize. I don't know what came over me.'

He looked smug. 'I do. You're not the first lady who has drunk too much around me because of nerves. I seem to have that effect on women.' Suddenly he threw himself to the floor and started doing vigorous one-armed press-ups.

'I always like to do one hundred press-ups before sex,' he said, barely out of breath. 'It makes me last longer.'

'Before sex?' Catherine gasped.

The one-armed press-ups got even more frantic. 'I hope you can keep up. My PB is three hours, forty-five minutes. Mind you, we did go out for a ten-mile run in the middle of it.'

Chapter 53

Somehow, Catherine made her excuses and left Tolstoy to himself, but not before he had made her swallow a disgusting algae drink to flush away the toxins.

The whole, nightmarish experience was the wake-up call Catherine needed. She had been skirting dangerously close to the edge with her drinking for months, and finding herself in Tolstoy Peake's bed with no memory of how she had got there was the final nail in the coffin. She was furious with herself. Even worse, they had apparently bumped into Fiona MacKenzie, and Catherine hadn't even remembered it.

Fi emailed her not long after she had sat down at her desk, to see if she'd got home OK.

I think Tolstoy Peake thought he was going to get his end away with you last night! Did anything happen?!

Catherine groaned, and quickly replied he'd dropped her off at home. This was one confidence she was never going to share with her friend.

One hour later, her hangover hadn't abated. But worse than that was the gut-wrenching devastation she felt knowing John was dating Isabella. Catherine tried to tell herself she'd had a lucky escape, but it didn't stop the hollow feeling that numbed her insides.

Her desk phone rang. 'Oh God, what now?' she muttered. She really wasn't in the mood for Adam. Wearily, she picked up the receiver. 'Hello?'

'It's me.'

Catherine froze. A fresh wave of nausea swept over her that had nothing to do with the hangover.

'What do you want?'

'To try and explain.'

John sounded as tired as her. *Probably been up shagging that stupid bitch all night,* Catherine thought. Her stomach clenched in misery.

'It didn't look as if it needed any explaining to me,' she said icily. 'Is Duvall's where you take all your conquests? No wonder you're a regular.'

'This isn't fair,' he said. 'And I didn't know you and Isabella knew each other.'

Catherine's paranoia reared its ugly head. 'Were you talking about me? What did you tell her? Look, I really haven't got time for this.' She tried to sound cool, even though her heart was racing so fast it was painful. Unable to help herself, Catherine couldn't stop. 'After all, I don't want to keep you from adding any more notches to your bedpost.'

'Since when do you care who I go out with?' John asked, suddenly angry. 'After all, you've made it perfectly clear *you* don't want me.' He paused. 'I noticed you didn't leave alone, either.'

'Sorry, did I hurt your manly pride? I'm sure Isabella won't mind kissing it better.' She hated the viciousness in her voice, but Catherine was so hurt she wanted him to feel pain, too.

There was a silence. 'I just don't understand you, Catherine,' he said.

Catherine gripped the receiver with white knuckles. 'Oh, but I understand you perfectly now. I just thought you'd have more taste than Isabella Montgomery.'

John sighed heavily. 'I'm sorry things had to turn out like this.'

Not trusting herself to speak any further, Catherine put the phone down.

Caro and Benedict were in bed reading. At six and a half months pregnant, Caro was feeling more whale-like by the day. She sighed loudly, trying to get comfortable for the umpteenth time. She needed the loo again.

Benedict put down his *Literary Review* and turned to her. 'Are you all right?'

'As much as one can be with elephantiasis of the ankles, and boobs like Zeppelins.'

Benedict's gaze swept up and down her body. 'Oh, I don't know, I find you rather sexy in full bloom.'

Caro smiled at her husband. 'I feel anything but sexy, but it's very sweet of you to say I am.'

Benedict kissed her swollen belly, and then lay back on his pillow for a few moments. 'Amelia seems like her old self again. At least we've seen the last of that Kirillov character.'

Despite the warmth of the room, a shiver passed over Caro. 'I still can't believe you rushed out like that to confront him. I was so worried, darling, please don't do anything like it again.'

'And I can't believe you didn't tell me about the phone calls, or the fact he'd been hanging around outside,' chided Benedict. 'I could have sorted it out a lot sooner.'

'It was stupid of me,' Caro admitted. 'If I'm honest, I *knew* deep down something was going on, but I guess I was in denial. Family life is so good at the moment, I didn't want to upset the apple cart and ruin everything.' She sighed. 'Some reasoning.'

'Why didn't she tell me, Caro? We've always been so close.'

Caro snuggled up to her husband. 'I think she got herself in such a hole, she didn't know how to get out of it. She was frightened, and didn't want to drag us into her problems.'

Privately, Amelia had told Caro she hadn't wanted to go to her brother because he'd always got her out of sticky situations before. She had wanted to sort this one out on her own.

Benedict sighed. 'I suppose you're right,' he said. 'Anyway, it's all over now.' He rolled his head round, releasing tension. 'Christ, it's hot in here. I think there's something wrong with the central heating. Do you mind if I open the window?'

'Go ahead.' Caro lay back and closed her eyes.

A few moments later Benedict spoke. 'Darling, come and look at this.'

Caro heaved herself out of bed and padded over. He was standing at the window with the curtain in his hand, his mouth wide open.

Caro looked out, straight into the consultancy room. Both the doctor and nurse were standing by the desk, completely naked. The nurse was holding what looked like a bright orange space hopper with a black dildo attached to it. With some difficulty she heaved herself on to it and started bouncing round the room.

Caro's eyes goggled. She'd seen one of those recently, when Calypso had used her computer at Christmas and left it open on a sex toys website. 'That's a Horny Hopper!' she exclaimed.

Benedict winced as the bouncing got faster. 'How on earth do you *know* that?'

'They do this quite a lot,' she said apologetically. As if on cue, the nurse hopped past the window, boobs slapping around like giant udders, and looked straight up at them. Caro dived back behind the curtain, pulling Benedict with her.

He was in shock. 'Christ, now I've seen it all!'

'I don't remember them making space hoppers like that in my day,' said Caro.

They looked at each other and exploded with laughter.

John Milton, it seemed, had one last fight in him. The next day, a beautiful bouquet of stargazer lilies, peonies and freesias was delivered to Catherine. The message was simple.

> *Please don't think any less of me.*
> *John x*

Catherine stared at the card for a moment and then gave a short bitter laugh. She picked up the bouquet, opened her door and marched into the middle of the office.

'Does anyone want these flowers? They were sent to me by mistake.' She swept back into her office and threw herself into the mountain of work piling up on her desk.

But the card's message kept coming back to her.

> *Don't think any less of me.*
> *John x*

Catherine couldn't believe the gall of the man. She'd wondered at the time why someone like him was single. Now it was obvious. John Milton was a player.

He'd been ready with all those smooth lines and she'd fallen for it, hook, line and sinker.

You had a lucky escape, girl, she told herself.

It had taken a while, but Ash was finally starting to come out of his shell. In the shop he was more animated, constantly asking questions and soaking up everything Angie told him. As well as the antiques side of the business, she had started teaching him accounting, overheads and stocktaking.

Angie was thrilled with his progress, and had been even more astonished when he'd asked if he could start accompanying her, Avon and Barksdale on their walks round the countryside. She had quickly picked up on Ash's fear but it was hard to keep the bouncy border collies away from him – they just wanted to lick everyone to death. Ash had eventually realized the dogs were harmless, and had even taken to patting them tentatively on the head while keeping the rest of his body at a safe distance.

Today they were walking around the trout lake at the back of the Maltings estate. Even though the sun was out it had rained heavily overnight and the ground was wet and muddy underfoot. Angie had lent Ash a pair of Archie's Hunter wellies, and he was now striding on in front, throwing a stick for Avon. Freddie had given him an old flat cap he didn't use any more and Ash had taken to wearing it every day.

'Look at you,' she laughed. 'Quite the country gent.'

Ash grinned and looked down at his mud-splattered wellies. 'My old man would laugh his nut off if he saw me.' Just as quickly his face darkened.

The night before, unable to get Ash on his mobile because of the erratic reception, Mr King had rung the Maltings instead. Unfortunately he had been blind drunk, and Ash had nearly died of mortification when Freddie fetched him into the house to take the call. His father could barely speak, except for a few incoherent sentences about how proud he was of Ash. Luckily, Freddie and Angie had been really nice about it.

'You could always have your father to come and stay, we'd be delighted to put him up,' Angie had offered.

Ash had refused, Angie was only saying it to be kind, and there was no way he was letting his dad come down here and mess things up. It was funny, really, in a short space of time, he, Freddie and Angie had become like a little family. Ash joined them more often for dinner now, proper food with local meat and fresh vegetables, and not the microwave crap he and his dad were used to living on. Afterwards he'd sometimes watch the football with Freddie, a fellow Liverpool supporter, in the games room, where they sat in companionable silence, exchanging the odd remark about the game. Ash couldn't get his head round 'rugger' as Freddie called it, though, and had given up after only one match.

It was a delightful day. Daffodils festooned every grassy bank, while an egg-yolk sun shone down from the sky. Angie, Ash and the dogs had just finished circling the trout lake, Ash in full flow about an eighteenth-century bed-pan he'd sold to a wide-eyed customer from Japan earlier that week. Angie had no problems leaving Ash in charge of the shop now while she popped out to run a few errands, or drove over to Bedlington to pay cheques into the bank.

'The geezer asked me if Queen Victoria had used it! I mean, what?' Ash shook his head and laughed. He liked being with Angie, she was the first person who'd ever really listened to him.

Angie smiled and shot him a sideways glance. 'Are

you enjoying your time in Churchminster? It must have been quite a culture shock.'

'You're telling me,' he admitted. 'But yeah, I like it now.'

Angie looked pleased. 'I was rather worried we'd be too boring for you, what with you being used to London life.'

At that moment, two pheasants ran squawking out of the hedgerow and disappeared across a field. Ash nearly jumped a foot in the air. 'Fuck!' The two dogs took off in hot pursuit.

'Avon! Barksdale!' shouted Angie. 'Heel, boys. I said, HEEL!' Reluctantly the two labradors gave up their chase and starting trotting back, tongues lolling like fat pink ribbons. 'What was I just saying about it being too quiet round here?' she laughed. Ash grinned back. They walked in an easy silence for a few minutes before he spoke.

'What do you think to "Ash's Antiques"?' He'd gone rather red and shy again. 'I know it's quite similar to yours, and stuff, but I thought maybe one day . . .'

Angie smiled at him. 'I think it has quite a ring to it, darling. And I have complete faith that you'll do it one day.'

A warm feeling spread through Ash. Everything seemed to be going his way for once.

MARCH

Chapter 54

The March issue of *Soirée* had gone on sale, the final chance for Catherine and the team to reach that elusive 'Project 300' mark. Everyone in the office agreed it was a corker, but now the magazine's fate – and theirs – was in the lap of the gods and the British consumer.

After January's fiasco, they'd managed to put 20,000 sales back on for the previous month's February issue, bringing their current sales up to 255,000. It was a long way short of their target. Adam was still holding out desperate hope that this month's sales figures would achieve a miracle, but Catherine didn't share his optimism. There was no way they were going to add on 45,000 sales in one month. She could almost hear the sound of Sir Robin's hands rubbing gleefully together over at Martyr House. This was surely what he'd wanted all along. Some mornings, in her darkest moments, Catherine wondered why she even bothered putting on her suit and going to work.

When Catherine thought about the awful news she would have to give her staff one day soon, or about breaking it to Gail that *Soirée* Sponsors was closing down, she felt sick to her stomach. She kept picturing the kids they had helped over the last few years: like

Reece Lawrence, Nikki Jenson and Ashley King, who, from what Harriet had told her, was coming along in leaps and bounds at the antiques shop in Churchminster. They still had so much more to do, but Sir Robin had made it clear he saw the charity as an unnecessary expenditure. Catherine's hatred for him increased; all that man cared about was making money and lining his pockets in the process. She didn't even care about losing her own job any more, although she was sure she'd be given a pay-off and assigned to one of the company's dreaded 'development projects' that never took off.

Catherine had even wondered whether she could try and keep the scheme going herself. But without the money Valour put into it, it would be impossible. Besides, with the reputation they'd built up and contacts they'd secured, *Soirée* Sponsors *was* part of *Soirée*. The two went hand in hand together.

March dragged on, and the atmosphere in the office grew even worse. The art director had accidentally overheard a phone conversation between Catherine and the head of sales about the impossibility of meeting the 'Project 300' and had relayed it back to the rest of the office. Now, it was as if people were just waiting for the axe to fall.

As Catherine sat in her office one morning, trying to work her way through a pile of emails, the door flew open. Catherine looked up crossly; she liked people to knock first.

It was Saffron. She'd had a new haircut that made her look even more elfin-like, and her eyes were shining. 'We've only gone and got her!' she yelled.

Catherine was confused. 'Who?'

Saffron waved a piece of paper in the air. 'Savannah

Sexton! She's just found out Casey has been cheating on her with a cheerleader, and she's dumped him. I've been speaking with her people and they've emailed me to say they want to give *us* the story. They're flying Savannah in for twelve hours to do it!'

Catherine sat bolt upright. She couldn't believe it. 'Bloody hell! When?'

Saffron looked at her watch. 'Savannah and her entourage are due to touch down at Heathrow in six hours and thirty-three minutes exactly.'

Catherine paused. They were well into the third week of March, and the April issue was hitting the magazine stands in less than ten days. They had never shot and interviewed a cover star this late before. She stuck her head out of the door and shouted for the chief sub, who came running.

Quickly, she explained the situation to him. Could they do it? The chief sub looked pained. 'It'll cost us. But if there are *no* cock-ups and we turn it around super quick, then yes.'

Catherine's lethargy vanished. *This* was what she'd got into magazines for! She'd been weighed down by targets, bureaucracy and management politics for too long now. She fleetingly regretted that they hadn't got this break last month, but quickly brushed the thought aside. They had got Savannah Sexton, and at that moment, nothing else mattered.

Two minutes later Catherine Connor gathered the team in the middle of the office.

'We're dropping Alexa Blake from the April cover.'

Alexa Blake was a sought-after aristocrat, and it had been a real coup to get her. But Catherine grinned broadly at the puzzled faces around her. 'Saffron has got us Savannah Sexton!'

427

There was a loud team gasp, and then cries of 'Well done, Saff!' Standing on the edge of the group, Annabel glowered. She had given up trying to get the superstar months ago, and was clearly furious Saffron was now getting all the praise and attention.

Catherine continued. 'Savannah's flying in tonight for our shoot and interview, and is on a plane out of here first thing in the morning. So everyone, listen up.'

She turned to Alexander, dazzling in an Alexander McQueen jumpsuit and brilliant white fedora. 'Al, I want her looking vulnerable but beautiful, so lots of neutral colours and simple fabrics. Same brief goes for hair and make-up.' She looked apologetic. 'I know you normally have weeks to prepare, but you're going to have to pull this off. Same goes for the photographer. We've only got a few hours to get the perfect shot, so they need to nail it. Who were you thinking of getting?'

Her fashion director stopped scribbling furiously in his polka-dot notepad and looked up. 'Tabitha Young. She's normally booked up months ahead, but she'll do this for us. She's a dear friend of mine.'

At the age of twenty-six, Tabitha Young was already a legendary photographer. She was young, hip and had an innate knack of drawing emotion out of her subjects where her contemporaries couldn't. She and Savannah Sexton would be dynamite together. Catherine nodded approvingly. 'Excellent.'

She looked at Saffron and smiled. 'Since you're the one who got Savannah in the first place, I'd like you to interview her.'

Saffron looked shocked, then gave a huge grin.

'But that's my job!' Annabel's fleshy face was purple with indignation. 'I'm the one in charge of cover stories, so I should be the one interviewing her!'

Catherine gave her a hard look. 'If you'd done your job in the first place you would be. But as Saffron put in the hard work, she deserves it.'

Annabel started to bluster, but Catherine was already walking back into her office.

'Saffron, we'll meet in thirty minutes to go through questions,' she called over her shoulder.

Savannah Sexton had been driven straight from the airport in a blacked-out people carrier to a secret location in north London. News of her break-up with Casey had leaked out and a few paparazzi had pounced on her as she came through arrivals. She was sure to be all over the papers tomorrow. Catherine didn't care, it would only add to the hype. Savannah's new film, *Power Trip*, was also out next month, and there was already talk of her getting an Oscar. As a woman, Catherine empathized with Savannah's situation, but as a magazine editor she couldn't believe the God-sent good timing.

Hiding behind a huge pair of Chanel sunglasses, Savannah Sexton had been devastated but dignified for her interview. She wanted to set the record straight before any scurrilous rumours started. Casey had been having an affair with the cheerleader, the youngest daughter of a US senator, for over six months. Savannah had only found out when Casey sent her a bouquet of flowers intended for the cheerleader. After a huge confrontation, Savannah had ended it. Casey was now begging for forgiveness, but Savannah, an independent, clear-minded young woman, was refusing to take him back. The interview was explosive and heart-warming, and Savannah had never looked more stunning.

When Catherine looked at the cover the next day,

she felt a tingle all over her body. It would surely be their best edition yet . . .

She hadn't even thought to inform Adam; so inconsequential was he now, in the daily running of the magazine. The next day she relished the opportunity to quieten him when he came bustling angrily into her office.

'What's all this about dropping our cover?' he asked. 'Have you gone mad?'

Without a word, Catherine held up a print-out of the new cover. Above Savannah's name were the words 'WORLD EXCLUSIVE!' in huge letters.

Adam's mouth fell open and he sank down in a chair. 'Fucking hell!'

'I had exactly the same sentiments,' Catherine said with a grin.

'It's amazing! How did you get it?' Adam's face dropped. 'If only we'd got this last month. It's too late for "Project 300".'

'Yes, I realize that, Adam.'

Strangely, Catherine still felt a sense of euphoria. There had never been such a buzz about a cover, and the chief executive had already been on the phone with his congratulations. Many times in the last twenty-four hours, Catherine had imagined the look on Isabella Montgomery's face when she found out.

The whole experience had reminded her why she'd got into magazines in the first place. They had done their best – and pulled off the exclusive of the year in the process. If *Soirée* was going down, at least they were going to do it in style.

Saffron was flying. She had really liked the film star, and she and Savannah had struck up an immediate rapport, something that her colleagues said came across in her interview. The compliments were pouring in thick and fast, but Annabel hadn't been so charitable.

'I suppose you think you're Miss Star Interviewer now,' she hissed across her desk the next day. 'Well, let me tell you, that won't be happening again.'

'Don't you think Catherine might have a say in that?' Saffron replied sarcastically. She didn't know if she could take much more of Annabel. Ignoring the death stare, she went back to writing up her piece about women in politics.

A new email flashed up on her screen. It was Tom Fellows.

Still up for that drink tonight?

Saffron grimaced. She'd been so busy, she hadn't given Tom another thought since he'd asked her out. She looked over to where he was sitting, staring intently as usual at his computer screen. His glasses had slipped halfway down his nose and he was wearing a sludge-brown cardigan that looked like it had come from his granddad's wardrobe. Saffron was tempted to lie and say something had come up, but that felt mean. She'd go for one drink, and make up an excuse about having to be somewhere.

Tom left the choice of venue up to her, so Saffron deliberately suggested they meet at the Frog and Stoat, a dingy old pub out of the way, so there was no chance of anyone seeing them together. As she made her way there that evening, Saffron again wondered at the wisdom of what she was doing. Surely Tom didn't think there was a chance of them getting it on?

He was already at the bar when Saffron walked in.

He was so tall he had to stoop to avoid banging his head on the low ceiling.

Saffron sighed and walked over. 'Hiya.'

There was something that looked like tomato ketch-up down the front of his T-shirt. 'Hi,' he mumbled.

Saffron found herself staring at his feet again. 'Your laces are undone.'

'Oh, right.' Tom bent down to tie them up, and Saffron ordered a double vodka; she needed it to get through this.

'What size *are* your feet?' she asked.

Tom blushed. 'Thirteen.'

'That's more than double mine!' Saffron put one foot next to his. Her ballet shoe looked microscopic next to his Titanic-sized trainer.

'Well you know what they say about men with big feet,' Tom said. Saffron cringed. He wasn't going to, was he? 'They've got big socks.'

Saffron laughed, more out of relief than anything. 'That's a terrible joke!'

Tom actually grinned, and up close, Saffron noticed for the first time how long his eyelashes were.

'Do you want to sit down?' he asked. The pub was practically deserted as they made their way over to a corner table. They sat in silence.

Saffron looked around. It looked like the place hadn't been decorated since the 1950s. 'This place is a dump.' She downed her vodka, asking herself for the umpteenth time what she was doing there.

Tom got up. 'Let me get you another.'

Saffron watched him lollop over to the bar. One more wouldn't hurt.

He returned with more drinks and sat down awk-wardly. His legs were so long he didn't seem to know what to do with them.

Saffron took a sip of her drink. 'I never said thanks for that night you helped me in the street.'

Tom shrugged. 'It was nothing. Besides, the guy had run off before I got there.'

'He could have come back. It was very nice of you.'

'You seemed upset,' he said. 'I noticed you hadn't been yourself for a few days before that happened. Is everything OK?'

The question took her aback. Saffron looked at him. Under all that hair, he had an honest, even handsome face. Despite his shyness, there was a directness about Tom Fellows she quite liked. Before she could change her mind, Saffron found herself telling him all about her mother.

'Your mum knows she's messed up,' said Tom, an hour later. Saffron had finished her story and they'd been sitting in silence for a few moments.

'That's the understatement of the century,' said Saffron moodily. 'I don't know, everything was so much easier before she turned up. I never thought about her, not that much, anyway. When I first saw her again, I felt so much hatred, you know? But now all that hate is becoming exhausting. I feel like it's eating into me, and I don't like it.'

'My mum's dead,' Tom told her. 'Died of breast cancer seven years ago.'

'I'm sorry,' Saffron told him. She couldn't think what else to say.

'Don't be,' he said simply. 'She was a very unhappy woman all her life: made me, my brother and Dad's life a misery. But even at the end, I still loved her. She was my mother, and no matter how it all turned out, I do believe she brought me into this world with good intentions.' He eyed her through the bottle-tops, eyelashes more appealing by the minute. 'I wouldn't give up on yours just yet, Saffron.'

A while later a bell clanged, the landlord calling time. Saffron looked at her watch. To her surprise it was ten to eleven. They had been in the pub for three hours, and she'd had a really nice time. Although he didn't waste words, she had found Tom surprisingly easy to be around. Saffron had never spoken so openly about her mother, even to Velda.

Outside the pub, Tom reverted to his usual mumbling self. 'So, er, do you want to do this again?'

'Yeah, that'd be cool.' Saffron didn't know how to say goodbye, so gave him an awkward hug. Tom didn't respond for a moment, then stiffly put his arms around her. Saffron was surprised how hard and lean his body was. After a second, she pulled away. 'See you tomorrow, then.' Saffron walked off in the direction of the tube station, her heart beating inappropriately fast.

Tom Fellows hadn't just made her feel like that, had he?

Chapter 55

Angie and Ash had just said goodbye to a happy customer in the shop. They had sold him a very nice seventeenth-century ceramic fingerbowl for £90, and it had been Ash who had picked it out at a local antiques fair the day before, for just £30.

Angie insisted on giving Ash half of the profit. 'I wouldn't have got it without you, darling. You've got a real eye for this!'

Feeling very pleased with himself, Ash tucked the money away. Maybe he'd get his dad a new toaster; theirs had been broken for ages.

Just before lunchtime the phone rang. Angie picked it up. 'Hello, Angie's Antiques! Oh, hello, Freds.' She stopped and listened. 'Oh, I see.' Ash saw her cast an anxious glance over. 'Yes, OK, we're on our way home.' Angie replaced the receiver, hesitating before she said, 'Ash, it's about your father . . .'

Ash felt his stomach drop. 'He hasn't done something stupid, has he?'

Angie picked up her handbag. 'He's at the house. I think we'd better go.'

Ash felt the colour drain from his face. One tiny part of him wished that his dad had just turned up for a friendly visit, but he knew it was too much to hope for.

'He sounds a bit drunk, darling,' Angie said gently.

By the time they'd got back, Freddie had somehow managed to get Mr King upstairs, where he'd passed out on the spare room bed. He reeked of booze, and there was a graze on his head. To Ash's mortification, there was also a dark stain round the crotch of his dad's dirty jeans where he'd wet himself.

The three stood staring down at him.

'He fell over getting out of the cab,' said Freddie apologetically. 'Luckily the driver was able to help me get him inside.'

A cab? All the way from London? There was no way his dad could afford something like that. Ash felt quite shaky at the thought.

'I took care of the fare,' Freddie told him kindly.

'I'll pay you back,' said Ash tightly, but Freddie waved his hand.

'Don't worry about that now. Do you think we should get a doctor?'

They looked down at the comatose figure. The graze looked more superficial than anything serious, Ash had seen him with a lot worse. 'Don't bother, he'll sleep it off,' he said bitterly. 'He always does.'

Angie and Freddie glanced at each other, not sure what to say. 'Well, he's welcome to stay here, like I said,' Angie said, a little too brightly.

Ash shook his head. 'You don't want a stupid old drunk in your house. I'll make sure he's on the next train back to London.'

Before she could answer, Ash turned and ran out, his throat clenched in shame and misery. He needed some fresh air.

Angie said she would get him when his dad woke up, but it was 7 p.m. when she knocked on the granny annexe door. Ash had been getting more agitated by the hour; he knew what his dad could be like when he came round sometimes.

'You don't have to look after him, Angie.'

'Oh, it was no problem,' she assured him. 'I think your father is feeling a bit better now. Come on over, Freddie's going to knock up some supper for us all in the kitchen.'

Ash found his dad sitting at the kitchen table with a mug of coffee. He was freshly showered and shaved for once, and was wearing one of Freddie's old checked shirts and a pair of red jeans. He looked deeply guilty, but Ash wouldn't register it, he couldn't believe his dad had come here and embarrassed him like this.

'All right son?' Mr King's voice was hoarse and croaky, as it often was after a mammoth drinking binge.

Ash stared at him with hostility. 'What do you think?'

'Angie and I will leave you to it,' Freddie said, and they tactfully withdrew.

'I'm sorry, son.'

'What are you doing here?' Ash asked angrily. 'You've made me look a fool in front of Angie and Freddie, you know.'

Mr King stared into his coffee. 'They seem decent. Angie was telling me how well you're doing at the shop.' He looked up, eyes more hopeful. 'I'm proud of you, son.'

'You can't just turn up here, pissed out of your head,' Ash said, his voice hard.

His dad looked unhappy. 'I know I've embarrassed you. I was lonely.'

'Why didn't you just call?' Ash was shouting now. 'I would have come back and seen you! Then you wouldn't have dragged Angie and Freddie into all our shit.' Ash sighed, his anger dissolving as quickly as it started. 'They're good people, Dad.'

'I didn't want to bother you,' his dad said. 'But I am going to get sober this time, I promise.'

Ash laughed mirthlessly. 'If I had a pound coin . . .' He chucked the thirty pounds from earlier on the table. 'This is for your train journey home, I'll call you a taxi.'

'Ashley, son . . .' his dad's voice was pleading.

'Leave it, Dad,' Ashley said, and walked out of the room.

Caro was making her way home from the shops when a large, stout woman stopped her. Something about her was very familiar, and as Caro took in the horn-rimmed glasses and giant mole on her cheek, the shock realization hit her.

It was the nurse from the hospital!

Up close, she wasn't any more attractive. She was wearing a frumpy dress and cardigan, thick tan tights stretched over tree-trunk legs. A passer-by would never imagine in their wildest nightmares that she had been merrily bouncing around on an enormous black dildo just a few days earlier.

'I don't believe we've had the pleasure of being introduced properly,' the nurse said in a deep, husky voice. 'Of course, Aubrey and I enjoy what one would call an adventurous sex life . . .'

Caro blinked away visions of flopping pendulous breasts.

'. . . But it's always good to know we are bringing pleasure to others. Have you been doing it long?'

Caro had no idea what she was going on about. 'I'm sorry?'

They moved aside to let someone pass.

'Voyeurism,' the nurse whispered loudly. 'It certainly has spiced things up for Aubrey and myself. What did you think to the Horny Hopper? We discussed at length whether you'd like it.'

She looked down at Caro's stomach. 'It's nice to see that even pregnancy hasn't stopped you living out your fantasies. How kinky!'

Caro started to stutter. 'Oh no, you've got the wrong end of the stick.'

The nurse winked. 'It's our little secret, don't worry. I'm sorry to say I've got a new job at a different hospital, so we won't be able to entertain you any longer. Never mind, you've been quite the talk of our swinging set! I must be off. Goodbye.'

'G-g-goodbye,' Caro managed as she watched the other woman trudge off. Dear Lord, had that just really happened?

Benedict and Amelia exploded with laughter when she arrived home with her curious tale.

'I had no idea you were into voyeurism, darling,' Benedict said. 'Would you like me to drill a peephole in the bathroom door for you?'

'Oh shut up, it's not funny!'

'I can't get over the Horny Hopper!' said Amelia. 'To think they must have sat around for hours pondering whether it would turn you on or not!'

There was a knock at the door. 'That's probably Stephen, he said he was popping over to borrow some of my fresh thyme,' said Caro, leaving the others giggling away.

She went to the front door and pulled it open. But

she wasn't greeted by the familiar, twinkling eyes of her next-door neighbour.

Instead she found herself staring into the cold eyes of Vladimir Kirillov. And this time, he had brought company.

Caro stared at the men on her doorstep for what seemed like an age before Benedict appeared and instantly stepped in front of her. 'Get back,' he ordered.

The thickset man beside Vladimir seemed to fill the doorway. He had a long black leather jacket on, but Caro could see his neck was covered with tattoos. She prayed to God Milo wouldn't wake up and come downstairs.

In the corner of the lounge Amelia whimpered like a frightened animal.

'What the hell do you want, Kirillov?' Benedict's voice was low and dangerous. 'I paid you off, didn't I?'

Vladimir gave a slow smile that showcased several gold teeth. He threw a cursory look at Amelia, as if displeased by what he saw.

'And you should know, Mr Towey, that eighty thousand pounds isn't enough to keep me in the lifestyle I have been accustomed to.' His black eyes swept round the room. 'You have a very nice place here, Mr Towey.' His cold gaze settled back on Benedict. 'You know, I've been reading up about you. You run a very successful business, congratulations. So I was thinking that, really, you should be more generously disposed to me if you want to keep yourself safe.'

The black eyes shifted downwards, to a glint of metal. Vladimir was holding a large kitchen knife. Caro could hardly breathe with the fear flooding into her lungs.

440

Vladimir's gaze flickered on her, catching sight of her two-carat diamond engagement ring.

'That pretty piece would be a nice start. We can do this pleasantly, or,' Vladimir's snake-like eyes glinted, 'we can do this my way. I assure you the first is the better option.'

No one moved. Caro felt frozen to the spot in fear. Then, with a sudden violence, Vladimir barged his way in, followed closely by his henchman. Benedict stepped back, accidentally knocking a glass lamp off a table by the door. It fell to the ground with a resounding smash.

Vladimir tutted regretfully. 'I would be much more careful with your possessions, Mr Towey, because by the time my associate Yuri and I have finished here, you won't have many left.'

'Is everything all right?' Suddenly Klaus was standing in the doorway, looking at the two strangers warily. 'We heard something.'

Everything happened so quickly. 'They're trying to rob us!' screamed Caro. Vladimir shot a wild glance at his henchman, and the two of them pushed past Klaus, almost knocking him over. Benedict took off in hot pursuit. Caro rushed to the doorway to stop him, but just a few feet away he was already engaged in a fierce hand-to-hand fight with Vladimir.

'Benedict!' she screamed as the Russian swung his weapon in a vicious arc. 'He's got a knife!' Benedict somehow managed to jump back at the last moment, crashing down against the mews wall.

Meanwhile Klaus had thrown himself at the henchman, Yuri. Despite his heavy stature, the Russian was ferociously quick, and Klaus had to work hard to miss the punches raining down on him.

The doors of No. 3 and No. 4 were open now, and

Velda, Saffron and Stephen stood watching the scene in shock. Stephen clutched a hand to his chest, his face as white as his hair.

'I've called the police!' screamed Saffron, waving her mobile in the air. Benedict glanced over at her, and Vladimir took the opportunity to rush at him.

'Benedict!' cried Caro. Her husband did a neat side-step, kicking the knife out of Vladimir's hand instead. It skittered across the cobbles, and Saffron bravely darted out and grabbed it, before running back to the shelter of her hallway.

Without his weapon, Vladimir seemed suddenly unsure what to do. He charged at Benedict, roaring like a wounded bull. As Caro screamed again, Benedict fended him off with a perfectly placed punch to the lower jaw. Vladimir stopped dead and then keeled over, unconscious.

The onlookers' attentions were quickly switched to Klaus and Yuri, who were grappling near the entrance to the mews. The blows were still coming thick and hard; Klaus's opponent seemed unstoppable. But just as the fight showed no signs of abating, Yuri lost his footing and stumbled, and Klaus pounced. Almost in slow motion he brought up one of his long legs and swung it round in an arc to deliver a perfect roundhouse kick at Yuri's head. Yuri looked dazed for a moment and crumpled on to the cobbles.

'Go, Bruce Lee!' shouted Saffron. Klaus turned around and flashed a rare grin. He was breathing heavily. 'Looks like ve have done the police vork for them.'

'Klaus, look out!' shouted Stephen. Yuri had somehow managed to stand, and, to everyone's horror, produced an even bigger knife. Klaus turned, but it was too late. Yuri's hand was raised high. He couldn't miss . . .

Suddenly, a large brown plant pot fell from the sky

and landed squarely on Yuri's head. His eyes rolled back and he fell to his knees, before collapsing face-first on the cobbles. This time he wouldn't be getting up for a while. Open-mouthed, everyone looked up to see where the fortuitous pot had come from. One of Rowena's top windows was open.

'By gosh!' shouted an astonished Stephen. 'Bravo, Rowena!'

It wasn't long before four flashing police cars screamed up and carted Vladimir and Yuri off. It turned out that Vladimir Kirillov was very well known to them.

'You've just taken a very dangerous man off the street, gentlemen,' the police officer told Benedict and Klaus.

Afterwards, the residents of Montague Mews gathered in Caro and Benedict's living room. Velda offered to put the kettle on, but Benedict had pulled a bottle of single malt whisky out of the drinks cupboard.

'I think we need something a bit stronger.'

Caro's hands were still shaking violently. The room was filled with frightened eyes and faces; it was starting to sink in just how badly things could have ended.

Stephen pulled a handkerchief out of his top pocket and dabbed his eyes. 'I thought I was going to lose you,' he told Klaus, voice trembling.

Klaus put a strong arm around him. 'I vos always going to be fine, Stephen.'

'Where did you learn that roundhouse kick?' Saffron asked. 'It was wicked!'

'You learn a lot of things growing up in the country that runs with wolves,' the enigmatic Klaus replied.

Chapter 56

To: Caro Towey
From: Clementine Standington-Fulthrope
Subject: Russian henchmen

*Caro? Are you there? I know we've just spoken, but
I wanted to write and let you know that everyone in
Churchminster sends their love and best wishes. Oh,
Caro, what a horrible experience! If any harm had
come to any of you, I don't know what I would have
done. Thank goodness Benedict was there, and who
would have known Klaus was a black belt in karate?
Although I can't say I'm really surprised, he was
awfully supple when he helped me cut back the apple
trees in the orchard last summer.*

*Darling, I've been thinking. It's not for me to say,
but don't you think it'd be safer for you all to come
home? Of course, we've been having a few problems
here with the boy racers from Bedlington, but I soon
found out, from Stacey Turner, where they lived and
drove over there to give the little oiks a ticking-off.
You should have seen them cowering behind their
mothers in the doorway! Errol Flynn gave them his*

most fearsome bark for good measure, and fingers crossed, they haven't been back since.

Anyway, do think about it, I know it would make your parents feel better, too.

All my love, Granny Clem xxxxx

A few days after the drama at Montague Mews, Velda came round to see Caro, clutching a potted plant.

'I thought you needed something bright in your home to banish any trace of those horrible men. I made the pot myself.'

'It's lovely, you are sweet,' said Caro. Then she gasped. 'Oh!' She took Velda's hand and placed it on her stomach. 'Can you feel the baby kicking?'

'There it goes! How marvellous!'

'He – or she – has been kicking like David Beckham at a Wembley final. Poor Benedict hasn't had a good night's sleep all week, what with me getting up for the loo every five minutes.'

'I shouldn't think he minds too much,' smiled Velda. 'Pregnancy is such a wonderful thing.'

'Did you ever think about having children?' Caro asked.

Velda looked wistful. 'Oh yes. I would have loved to, but unfortunately I found out early on I wasn't able to.'

Caro was mortified, but Velda smiled reassuringly. 'Don't worry; I came to terms with it many years ago. Besides, I've got Saffron.'

'How is she? She was jolly brave getting hold of that knife the other night.'

Velda looked a little nervous. 'That's the other reason I came round to see you. Saffron's on her way to Churchminster . . . to see her mother.'

*   *   *

445

If Velda was feeling anxious, it was nothing to the trepidation Saffron was feeling. She'd borrowed her aunt's Beetle for the journey, and had made good time to the country.

It was a completely different landscape to the one Saffron had seen on her first visit. Spring was waking up all over the Cotswolds, and vibrant greens, reds and yellows were flourishing across hedgerows, woodlands and the rolling fields. For someone more familiar with the concrete landscapes of London, she marvelled at how much a place could change in a relatively short period of time.

Saffron still didn't know if she was doing the right thing. Her conversation with Tom had really got her thinking. In fact, he was part of the reason she was heading out to the Cotswolds today. They'd been for secret drinks a few times since their first ones in the Frog and Stoat, and Saffron couldn't believe the funny, honest character she enjoyed talking to so much was the same mumbling, withdrawn person that had been working at *Soirée* for the past six months. Tom's clothes and hair were terrible, but for the first time Saffron was seeing past how cool someone's wardrobe was, or how many friends they had on Facebook. She wasn't sure if she fancied him, but he definitely made her see things – and people – in a very different way. Like her mother.

The recent scare in Montague Mews had helped her to make the decision. Everyone had been so emotional afterwards, and Saffron had realized for the first time how precious life really was. She had thought she hated her mother, but now she realized that love and hate sat close to each other on the emotional spectrum. She had to have it out with Babs if they had any chance of repairing their relationship.

Saffron hadn't wanted to call her mother, so Velda had rung Babs to tell her she was on her way. When Saffron pulled up outside Hardwick House, Babs was already at the front door. It was a pretty little place, with two bay windows looking out on to a rather overgrown garden. Blankets of ivy crept up the wall, almost obscuring one of the upstairs windows. The gate creaked loudly as Saffron pushed it open; it obviously hadn't been oiled for quite some time.

Babs was wearing a turquoise turban and matching scarf. Reassuringly, she looked as nervous as Saffron felt. 'Darling!' she exclaimed, rushing forward and kissing Saffron on both cheeks. Instinctively Saffron jerked her head back, and Babs was left rather clumsily kissing the air. She quickly recovered. 'Come in, come in!' she cried, leading Saffron into a long, narrow corridor. It was completely filled with paintings, piled up against the walls and radiators.

Saffron followed her mother to the back of the house, where a large conservatory looked out on to an even wilder back garden. It was obviously Babs's studio, living room and kitchen all rolled into one. At one end was a huge easel, with what looked like mud splatters all over it. Tins of paint and jam jars filled with brushes were stacked up on every surface. In the middle of the room was a battered-looking sofa furnished with bright pink cushions, while at the other end was a small kitchen area littered with empty wine bottles. A rickety table stood off to one side with two chairs round it.

One of the walls was completely covered in what looked like magazine features. As Saffron got closer, she realized they were *her* articles. Everything she had ever written was up there. Some had paint swatches next to them, or unintelligible scribbles written in the margin.

'What's this?' she gasped.

Babs flushed. 'That's my inspiration wall. I've cut out everything you've ever done. Whenever I need a surge of creativity I come over here and reread one of your articles.' An expression a little like pride crept on to her face. 'You really are a marvellous writer, Saffron. Your interview with Savannah Sexton was spellbinding!'

Saffron didn't know what to say. 'How long have you been doing this?'

'Since the beginning of your career.' Babs looked at her. 'It was my only way into your life, darling, I couldn't see how else I could get to know you.'

'Don't start that again,' replied Saffron angrily, her emotion at seeing the wall quickly extinguished. 'You knew where I bloody was, you could have come and seen me any time.'

'What – and had the door slammed in my face?' Babs wrung her hands anxiously. 'I really don't want to argue with you. Please, Saffron, can't we just sit down and talk? I'm so tired of fighting.'

Saffron sank down in one of the chairs. 'So am I,' she admitted.

The kettle whistled. 'Would you like a coffee?' asked Babs. 'Or something stronger?' she added hopefully.

'Coffee's fine,' said Saffron as she watched Babs fish out two dirty cups from the washing-up bowl and rinse them under the tap. Domesticity clearly wasn't one of her mother's strong points.

A few minutes later they were sitting round the little table drinking scalding hot cups of coffee. Saffron was sure she could taste white spirit in hers. After a few attempts to drink it, she put it back down on the table. This was so surreal. She half-expected Jeremy Kyle to pop up and wave a microphone in her face at any moment. Talk about fucked-up families!

Babs looked at her sorrowfully. 'I know I've let you down.'

'That's a fucking understatement.'

Babs flinched. 'I've made mistakes, and heaven knows, I'm paying for them. But you have to understand that through a child's eyes, as you were at the time, you see things differently. Your father and I had, well, issues.'

Saffron raised a cynical eyebrow. 'What kind of "issues"?'

Babs hesitated. 'I fell in love with your father because he was so romantic and dashing. I really loved him, and for a time, I thought he loved me. But Harry was never going to settle down with one woman.'

Saffron's face was pale. 'Not even when I came along?'

Babs shook her head sadly. 'Your father was a serial womanizer. I wasn't the first woman he charmed, and I certainly wasn't the last.'

There was a long pause. 'I didn't know,' said Saffron eventually. Her voice had become duller. 'I thought he left you because you were so awful to live with. That's the impression he gave me.'

Babs gave a small smile. 'Of course he did, he knew what a hero he was to you. You were the only good thing he produced in his life, and he couldn't bear to smash the illusion. That's why I didn't tell you the truth, either. You already hated me, what good would it have done to have felt the same way about your father?'

Saffron tried to swallow the lump in her throat. 'I know I haven't been the easiest daughter,' she admitted.

Babs put her hand over Saffron's. This time she didn't

pull away. 'Darling, will you forgive me?' she asked. 'I so badly want to be a proper mother to you again.'

Despite her heartfelt plea, Saffron wasn't going to let her off the hook that easily. 'You can't just waltz back into my life after all these years and claim that right. Velda's been so much more of a mother to me than you have.' Babs looked crushed. When Saffron spoke again, her voice was gentler. 'Let's start off as friends and see how we get on, shall we?'

Babs bit her lip. 'Whatever makes you happy. I really am so pleased you came down today.'

As Saffron drove past the entrance to the Maltings some time later, Ash King was lying spreadeagled on the double bed in the granny annexe. Angie had done his washing again, and the beautifully pressed clothes were laid out on the back of a chair. The first time she'd done it, Ash had felt a bit awkward. He was used to doing his own washing at home, and besides, he didn't want some woman he hardly knew going through his boxers. Angie, however, wouldn't hear of it.

'Ash, it's really no problem. I can throw them in with our stuff.' Secretly she liked doing it, it made her feel like she still had a role as a mother.

Ash put his hands behind his head and looked up at the ceiling. That conversation seemed like such a long time ago, and so much had happened since then. Angie and Freddie had gone out of their way to make him part of the family. They were so easy and, well, normal, to be around. Ash knew he'd been lucky. But the more settled he felt in Churchminster, the more guilt he felt about his dad.

If anything, his close relationship with the Fox-Titts – and especially Angie – only highlighted how fucked-up his and his dad's was. Would his dad ever put him before the drink? Because that, deep down, was the root of Ash's anger.

He sighed. His brain was hurting from all this shit.

Once an alcoholic . . . he told himself, reaching for the TV remote.

It was dark by the time Saffron got back to Montague Mews. Velda was lying on the sofa watching television, but clicked it off and sat up expectantly when her niece walked in.

'How did it go?'

Saffron sat down in the chair opposite her. 'Better than I thought, actually. It pains me to say it, but I now realize my mother isn't exactly the Wicked Witch of the West I'd built her up to be.'

Surprise and hope flooded Velda's face. 'Does this mean you're friends?'

Saffron sighed. 'Friends are what we're aiming for. She wanted to slip into the doting mother role straight-away, but I've told her she has to work harder than that.'

Velda gave a small smile. 'She really does love you, Saffron. It's just that my sister has never been able to deal with real life. The moment it gets too hard, she retreats into her world of paint and watercolours.'

Saffron's eyebrows shot up. 'Christ! I hate to think what her state of mind is like. Have you seen those things?'

'Belle has got a rather unusual style,' said Velda tactfully.

'You can say that again! Who *buys* that stuff?'

They both burst into laughter. 'I needed that,' said Velda, wiping her eyes a few moments later.

APRIL

Chapter 57

At *Soirée*, it was a time of highs and lows. The Savannah Sexton interview had been picked up all over the world, and the issue was simply flying off the shelves. Savannah had begun a whirlwind round of red-carpet appearances for the premiere of *Power Trip*, and barely a day went past without her being plastered across a newspaper or magazine. As expected, her performance received rave reviews, and critics were hailing it as Oscar-worthy. At that moment in time, Savannah Sexton was the most famous woman on the planet, and the public couldn't get enough of her.

Not that any of this really mattered in the scheme of things, thought Catherine. If she had to listen to Adam moan one more time: 'If only we'd got Savannah for the March issue we could have saved the magazine,' she was going to scream.

For the second month running, the sales figures had not been released to her, but when she emailed the head of sales, she received an apologetic reply informing her that it was the express wish of Sir Robin Hackford to keep the final figures private until further notice. Catherine felt more like she was working for the FBI than a bloody publishing company. She hated being left hanging on like this, it was almost as if 'Hatchet' Hackford was milking it as much as he could, just to add to her discomfort.

It didn't help that Adam was as much in the dark as she was. The penny seemed to have finally dropped that they were in real trouble, and he'd taken to hanging around in her office like a grey cloud. It wasn't helping Catherine's state of mind.

'Thomasina has just put Cosmo's name down for Eton, I don't know how the hell we're going to afford the fees if this all goes tits up,' he told her gloomily one afternoon.

'You could always try sending him to a comprehensive,' Catherine pointed out. Adam looked at her as if she'd just projectile-vomited on his Tod's loafers.

'Do *you* think we've done it?' he asked.

Irritated by his pleading expression, Catherine didn't pull any punches.

'Added 45,000 sales on in a month? No, I don't actually Adam, if you want my honest opinion. Not that Sir Robin seems in any rush to put us out of our misery.'

Adam sighed. 'Christ, if we'd only got Savannah a month earlier . . .'

Catherine resisted the urge to bury her staple gun in his head. 'Well, we didn't, Adam, and we probably *are* going to fold, and there's fuck all I can do about it!'

Her publisher looked up, astonished, then stood up awkwardly. 'I think I'll leave you to it.'

A short while later, the email Catherine had been dreading came through from him.

Sir Robin's secretary just phoned. It doesn't look good. The board want to see you tomorrow morning at Martyr House at 11.30. I'll meet you there.

Catherine reread it. She felt strangely empty. She had failed them all. There was nothing more she could do now.

That evening Catherine was due to attend the annual Vision Unite charity gala. She didn't know if this was a blessing or a curse. The last thing she felt like doing was going out and facing people, but at the same time, she knew it would be easier than staying home alone, tormented by her thoughts. Besides, tickets had been extremely hard to come by and Catherine had been looking forward to it.

An extremely high-profile event, Vision Unite was one of the rare occasions when the world of magazines and newspapers came together to raise money for the charity World Vision. The newspapers added a frisson of energy and edge to the proceedings that was sometimes lacking in the world of monthly magazines.

Catherine looked across the office at the stunning Valentino dress hanging on the back of the door. She had bought it especially for the occasion, and it had cost her an arm and a leg, even with Alexander's discount. Catherine pursed her lips resolutely. God knows she needed a night out. Sod Sir Robin Hackford, he wasn't going to ruin this for her as well.

With bittersweet irony, congratulations for *Soirée* flooded in all evening. Savannah Sexton had been the one front page every editor, magazine or newspaper had desperately wanted, and the fact that she had only talked to *Soirée* had left them full of grudging admiration. By the time the gala had finished, and tens of thousands of pounds had been raised, Catherine was beginning to feel she'd received the same amount of compliments. It was getting exhausting keeping a smile fixed to her face, knowing that by tomorrow afternoon she wouldn't have a job.

'What's the matter, darl? For someone who's the belle of the ball you don't look very happy.' Fiona MacKenzie eyed Catherine wisely across the table as their dinner companions headed for the bar.

Catherine played with the stem of her wine glass. 'I've been summoned in front of the board tomorrow.'

Fiona pulled a face. 'Ouch. The preposterous "Project 300".'

Catherine sighed. 'I don't think we've done it, Fi, and I can't tell you how much I'm dreading telling my staff they haven't got jobs any more.'

'Are you sure?' asked Fiona sympathetically.

Catherine shrugged. 'Rancid Robin is holding the latest sales figures back, the sadistic old git. I expect he'll want to humiliate me with them in front of everyone.'

Fiona looked genuinely upset. 'Oh, darl, I really am sorry. And to think that everyone is green with jealousy at the Savannah exclusive.' She sighed. 'Life's a bastard, isn't it? If it's any consolation, I'm bored off my B cups at *Teen Style*.'

As if on cue, a well-known media magnate staggered up, his dinner jacket gaping open.

'Catherine, love your latest issue!' he bellowed drunkenly. 'If that doesn't win you Magazine of the Year I'll eat my hat!'

Catherine smiled falsely as he swayed back into the crowd. She stood up. 'Come on, Fi, I need a drink.'

The bar was packed, mostly with hacks talking noisily. Fiona winked at Catherine. 'Let's go and swim with the sharks. I must pop to the loo quickly first, will you be OK?'

Catherine smiled. 'I'll survive. See you in a minute.' She pushed her way through the crowd, but not before several people had slapped her on the back with more congratulations.

'Two glasses of champagne, please,' she told the barman.

The short, shifty figure of the *Daily Mercy*'s editor, Drew Summers, appeared beside her. 'Get one more in will you? After all, we're not paying.' As usual Drew was smoking furiously, eyes darting around the room.

'Hey, Drew.' He was the last person Catherine felt like talking to, and in a moment of paranoia she wondered if he'd overheard her conversation with Fiona, and come to sniff around. She didn't trust Drew as far she could throw his twitching little body.

Drew inhaled on his B&H deeply, ignoring the dirty looks from everyone around him. He'd staunchly ignored the anti-smoking law ever since it had come in, and regularly ran bits of gossip in his paper on the unfortunate ministers who had imposed it.

His beady eyes bored into Catherine's. 'Well, you've pulled it out of the bag.'

No congratulations from Drew, then, she thought. He looked around him and leaned in towards her. 'You've got a way in with her people, then? Let's say you pass it on to us and we'll do you a favour in return.'

Catherine smiled pleasantly. 'No thanks, Drew.'

His dark little eyes became sly. 'Come on, you scratch our back and all that . . .'

Their conversation was interrupted by the arrival of Fiona and, to Catherine's disgust and horror, Isabella Montgomery.

'Look who I bumped into,' said Fiona half-heartedly.

Isabella looked straight at Catherine, her face more

pinched than ever, lips twisted into a ghastly ruby smile. 'I've been looking for you, my dear!' Turning her back on Drew, she pulled Catherine towards her.

'We've got so much to catch up about!'

'Not as far as I'm concerned.'

Isabella's smile turned even more malicious.

'Oh, darling! There's nothing more unbecoming than a bad loser, but John had to follow his heart. I gather he took you to his special little place as well.' Her mouth widened into a red slit. 'Men! Of course, with *me* it really meant something.'

Behind Isabella, Drew's ears had pricked up.

'What are you talking about?' Catherine said, trying to keep her emotions in check. She couldn't bear the thought of John making love to Isabella in his bed, just as he'd done with her.

Isabella's eyes glinted like a crocodile's caught on a night-vision camera. 'A certain Lord Fairfax's house? The view from the attic room window? That's where John and I first got intimate, you know, nothing like the romantic history of a house to bring out a true attraction!'

Isabella leant forward as if they were old friends sharing a confidence. 'I must say, I've never had a lover like it! You know, darling, sometimes two people are just *so* sexually compatible.' She looked triumphantly at the hurt on Catherine's face. 'Oh, silly, you know it would never have worked between you two! John was just waiting for a real woman to come along, someone who could satisfy him properly. Not like you, darling. From what I can gather it was like sleeping with an ironing board! Men really don't like a frigid shag, do they?'

A little piece of Catherine died inside. She now knew that she had never known John Milton at all.

She'd obviously wounded his male pride and he'd taken revenge by spouting off to Isabella. She had the urge to ask Isabella where she and John had met, how long it had been going on, what on earth they had in common, but instead she turned to Fi, who was hovering uncertainly at her side, trying to decipher the tension between the two women.

'Come on, let's go,' Catherine said through gritted teeth. There was no way she was going to stand here and let Isabella rub her nose in it in front of Drew. It would be all over the *Daily Mercy*'s gossip pages tomorrow. She turned away from the bar.

'Oh, I'm sorry!' Isabella called out. 'Aren't I good enough for you, Catherine Connor? That's a bit of a joke.'

Several people turned round at her raised voice.

'After all, darling, I'm the one who should be dubious about being in *your* company.' Isabella raised her voice still louder, making sure every pair of eyes in the place were fixed on her.

'What with you being a cold-blooded murderer!'

Chapter 58

Catherine felt like her world had suddenly ground to a halt.

'What did you say?' she gasped, spinning around. Isabella was almost beside herself with malevolent pleasure.

'You heard, darling, or should I say, *Cathy Fincham.*' She spat the two words out. 'That's your real name, isn't it? Of course, your mother went down for the crime, but everyone knew you did it really.' She exhaled gleefully. 'Who would have thought it? Catherine Connor, darling of the industry and feted magazine editor, is really Cathy Fincham, disgraced daughter of the notorious Crimson Killer!'

'Catherine, what's going on?' Fiona asked in confusion. 'Who's Cathy Fincham?'

Beside them Drew Summers was muttering under his breath, trawling his encyclopaedic memory. 'Cathy Fincham, Cathy Fincham . . .' His head whipped up, eyes bulging in shock. 'That's you?' His mouth dropped open as realization dawned. 'Fuck me! I see it now! You're the spitting image of her!'

Through the crashing in her head, Catherine could almost hear the whirr of tape-recorders being switched on as the eavesdropping crowd, smelling blood, drew closer.

Isabella was positively revelling in having such an appreciative audience. 'Of course, you were quick to put the blame on your mother, weren't you? And people were ready enough to believe it at first. After all, who would have thought such a mouse of a fifteen-year-old schoolgirl was capable of such a terrible thing?'

'That's not how it happened!' Catherine could feel the hysteria building, out of control. She didn't care who was looking.

Isabella smiled evilly, in complete, calculated control. 'I don't know how you live with it, darling, I really don't. Sending your own mother to prison for a murder *you* committed!'

Loud gasps echoed round the room. Catherine was moments from being sick, and blindly pushed her way through the crowd. She needed to get out, away from those people.

On the street Catherine bent over, great racking heaves sweeping her body.

'I say, are you all right?' asked a passer-by.

'Leave me alone,' she sobbed. She could see a crowd had followed her out, including a worried-looking Fiona. Oh Christ, someone had a camera . . .

As if by a miracle, a cab pulled up. Without thinking Catherine pushed past the couple who'd flagged it down and threw herself into it. A flashbulb went off in her face, temporarily blinding her.

'Oi! What do you think you're doing?' a woman cried angrily.

The cabbie looked round. 'You can't push in like that luv . . .'

He trailed off as he saw Catherine's tear-streaked

face and the advancing pack of people behind her, and then he put his foot down and sped away.

Somehow Catherine made it home. As she fell into her flat, she couldn't stop sobbing. It was almost too much to bear. John Milton had obviously told Isabella about her past. The sheer force of his betrayal made her legs buckle, and she slid down against the wall.

'How could you?' she wept. 'I trusted you.'

Somewhere in the background her mobile was ringing. She pulled it out of her bag. Fiona's name flashed up. Catherine threw it away down the hall, and the phone fell silent. She couldn't speak to Fiona now, she couldn't speak to anyone. Isabella had picked her moment perfectly; it would be all over the papers again tomorrow, just as it had been twenty years ago. 'I'm finished,' Catherine sobbed to herself. 'I'm finished.'

Chapter 59

Angie was worried. It had been Ash's day off today, but normally he came to the house for dinner in the evening. Tonight, however, he hadn't turned up, despite telling Angie he would be there. *And* Liverpool were playing Arsenal; Ash would never miss out on that. Leaving Freddie with his feet up watching the soccer, she went to investigate.

At the granny annexe the windows were dark, and there was no movement inside. She knocked at the door. No answer. After trying again Angie went round to peer through the kitchen window. A dirty plate and cup stood in the sink, and an empty milk carton had been left out on the draining board. She'd already tried ringing his mobile, but it was off. '*This is Ash,*' his voice-mail had recited back to her, the sound of loud techno music in the background. '*Leave a message, yeah? And I'll get back to you.*'

Angie frowned, where could he have got to? It wasn't as if Ash had a car, and besides, he didn't really know any other people in the village. Could he be in the Jolly Boot? Angie very much doubted it. An awful thought struck her: *what if he'd fallen over and knocked himself out, and had been lying there unconscious for hours*? His laces were always trailing out of his trainers; Freds had even said it was an accident waiting to happen.

Angie stood on tiptoe, and looked through the window again. Thankfully she couldn't see a body lying anywhere, but what about upstairs? He could have fallen over in the bedroom. She agonized for a moment. She was loath to disturb Ash's privacy and just go barging in there, but she didn't know what else to do. Feeling for the spare set of keys in her Barbour waistcoat pocket, she got them out and opened the door.

'Ash? Are you there?'

She was met by a resounding stillness. Something wasn't right. Making her way through the little open-plan kitchen and living area, she paused at the foot of the stairs. 'Hello?'

Nothing. She reached for the light switch and flicked it on. Tentatively Angie put a hand on the rail and started making her way up the stairs. If he was asleep he really wasn't going to appreciate her bursting in on him like this.

Angie got to the top and peered round the corner into the bedroom. The large bed was made, but it looked as though it had been done in a hurry. To her relief, Ash wasn't lying unconscious on the floor, blood streaming from a ghastly head wound.

Angie stepped in, feeling slightly relieved. But where *was* he? The wardrobe doors were open and she couldn't help but notice it was half-empty. Angie looked for Ash's favourite baseball cap, a distinctive red and black colour, but she couldn't see it. Nor his ruck-sack, mobile phone or wallet . . .

Two minutes later she flew back into the main

house, making Freddie spill his nightcap all over his chest.

'Good Lord, what on earth's the matter?'

Angie looked at her husband, lower lip wobbling.

'Oh, darling, I think Ash has gone!'

Chapter 60

As she sank to the floor in the hall, Catherine's past washed over her like a waking nightmare.

She had never known her father. He was a travelling salesman who'd been passing through the area, and once he'd met sweet, pretty twenty-two-year-old Annie Fincham, decided to stay a little bit longer. It was love at first sight for the impressionable Annie, but then she unexpectedly fell pregnant. Her lover, who had neglected to tell her that he already had a family in another part of the country, couldn't get out of there quick enough.

Annie's mother, a hard-faced woman with a nature to match, declared her daughter had brought shame on the family and promptly threw her out. Devastated, Annie was forced to live in an unmarried mothers' home, but from the moment Cathy entered the world, she fell head over heels with her smiling, chubby-cheeked bundle of joy.

Eventually Annie found them a council flat, and she and her infant daughter had their first home. It wasn't easy for them, but Annie took a job as a low-paid secretary, leaving her daughter with her kindly next-door neighbour, who was like the grandmother Cathy never had. When Cathy was nine, old Mrs Ainsworth died, and when she wasn't at school Cathy started to take care of the day-to-day running of their home. She didn't mind: by then her mother had worked her way up in the firm she had started in and was earning good money.

'I'm doing this for us, Cathy,' she used to say. 'I want to give you the life I never had.'

But their happy existence quickly came to an end once Ray entered their lives. Annie met him in a bar on a rare night out, and fell in love all over again. Cathy was fourteen when he came to live with them, and it didn't take long for his true colours to come out.

Ray was a control freak, a lazy manipulative slob who lay around the house all day dictating how Annie's money should be spent. Cathy grew to hate him and the way his eyes lingered on her legs when she came home from school. Often, she would walk into the kitchen to find her mother quietly crying after yet another one of their rows.

'Kick him out, Mam!' Cathy would urge. She hated to see her mum like this, but Annie, who had been alone since Cathy's dad had left her, kept giving Ray more chances.

'Ray's just had a bad day, Cathy,' she'd plead, taking her daughter's hands in hers. 'He's a good man, really.'

Then the beatings started. The first time Annie got a black eye she tried to tell Cathy she'd walked into something, but as the rows got louder and more physical, it was impossible to ignore. Cathy begged her mum to go to the police, but her mum wouldn't hear of it. This was a tough estate in Newcastle where men still ruled, and domestic violence was a hidden, dirty secret. In some misguided way, Annie thought it was all her fault.

'I need to try harder,' she'd say. 'Ray's told me he'll never marry someone like me unless I sort myself out. No wonder he gets so angry.'

The house became a war zone, and night after night Cathy would lie awake in her narrow bed, pillow wrapped around her head, trying to drown out the rowing. She got used to blocking it out. Until one night.

Cathy had just started to doze off to sleep when a fearsome row erupted downstairs in the kitchen, before spilling out into the hallway. Cathy sat up alert, for once it sounded like her mother was giving as good as she got.

'I've had enough, Ray! All this fighting – it's not fair on Cathy.'

An angry bellow, then Annie shouted again. Her voice was shaking.

'I mean it! I want you out of here tomorrow. This is no good for any of us.'

Cathy heard her mother's softer footsteps on the stairs, and breathed a sigh of relief. But suddenly they were followed by louder, heavier ones. There was a thump, as if someone had fallen to the floor, and Annie gave a loud scream. It was so terror-struck it sent a chill down the teenager's spine.

'No Ray! Get off me! *I can't breathe!*'

Cathy jumped out of bed and pulled open the door. Just a few feet away on the landing at the top of the stairs, Ray was lying on top of her mother. With a sickening jolt, Cathy saw his hands round her throat.

'Don't you fucking tell me you're kicking me out, woman! I make the decisions round here. You got that?' He was almost incoherent with anger.

Annie couldn't speak. Her face had gone violently red, eyes popping out from their sockets as Ray slowly squeezed the life out of her. Somehow her gaze fixed on to Cathy's, struck dumb with terror in the doorway.

Annie's gaze was pleading. *Help me*, she was saying, *I'm dying.*

Something went off in Cathy's head. Leaping forward, she frantically tried to pull Ray off her mother. But he was a burly man, and his grip held.

'Get off her, get off her!' Cathy screamed hysterically, trying to claw at him, but Ray threw her against the wall, pain searing across her back.

'Stay out of it, you little bitch! I'll deal with you in a minute.'

Annie's face was turning purple and she had stopped thrashing about. Cathy knew she had to do something; she just needed Ray to stop. In a blind panic she scrabbled around, her fingers chancing across the ornamental vase that stood on the top of the landing. As if in a dream, she picked it up, and brought the vase down on Ray's head, smashing it into pieces.

He dropped her mother like a bag of rubbish, and tried to get up, rubbing his head. He looked at Cathy in disbelief, eyes black with fury.

'Now you're for it.' He lunged towards her groggily.

'Get away from me!' Cathy screamed, and with all her strength, pushed him away. Ray stumbled back, losing his footing as he fell backwards. Eyes wide with shock, he looked at Cathy, grabbing out for the banister. But it was too late. As if in slow motion, he started to tumble backwards down the stairs, his head descending in a terrible arc. There was a loud *crack* as it hit a stair halfway down.

Cathy's hands flew over her eyes, but it still didn't stop the sound of Ray's body slithering heavily downwards. After what seemed an eternity an eerie silence settled on the house, punctuated only by Annie's gasping breaths and crying.

'Mam! Are you OK?' Cathy knelt down beside her. Annie nodded and grabbed on to her, struggling to sit up.

'Ray? What's happened?' she croaked.

Cathy forced herself to look down the stairs at that dreadful lifeless heap. Ray's eyes were open and staring, his neck bent at an impossible angle.

'He's dead, Mum,' Cathy moaned again and again. 'I pushed him and now he's dead. It's my fault, I killed him.'

The police arrived quickly, alerted by the neighbours. Annie told her daughter not to say it was she that had pushed Ray, sending him to his death down the stairs.

'I'll say I did it in self-defence, Cathy,' Annie said, her face a swollen mass of tears and bruises. 'They'll believe me, of course they will, with a face like this.'

Unfortunately, they didn't. Annie's own mother, still bitter over her daughter's 'betrayal', denounced her and publicly announced to anyone who would listen that she had always known Annie was a bad egg. Rumours started circulating wildly on the estate that Annie, who had always been thought of as 'stuck up' by others, just because she didn't socialize at the pub or bingo, had murdered Ray in cold blood and sworn her daughter to secrecy.

Weeks later in court, Annie told the packed room she'd never meant to kill him and had only hit him once in self-defence. But the victim's lawyer had already painted her as a loose, morally corrupt woman who had snared a man once by falling pregnant, and would stop at nothing to get what she wanted again. Once it turned out that Ray had had substantial life savings, mainly due to the different women he'd lived off, Annie stood no chance. Certain parts of the press jumped on the story, crassly labelling her the 'Crimson Killer', a name that stuck after her pink lipstick was found on the dead man's face.

After a two-week trial, the jury of eight men and four women found Annie guilty of manslaughter. She was given an eight-year jail sentence and sent to a tough women's prison far away in Norfolk.

The day Cathy had gone to see her mother in prison had been the worst day of her life. Gone was the vivacious, warm woman she had known. All that was left was an empty shell.

For Cathy, who had already been carrying round the unimaginable burden of their secret pact, it was too much.

'I should be in here, Mam!' she sobbed. 'I can't let you do this.'

It was the one time Annie showed any of her former strength.

'No, Cathy!' Her voice was urgent. 'You must never tell anyone.' She reached across the table in the visiting room and took Cathy's hands in hers.

'You were only protecting me, the way I should have protected you. I let you down, Cathy. I jeopardized your happiness for my own. I should have listened to you from the start, seen Ray for what he really was.'

Cathy looked down at the table, not knowing what to say. Annie laughed to herself bitterly. 'What a mother I've turned out to be! I know what people are saying about me, maybe they're right after all . . .'

'No, Mam, don't think like that!' Cathy was close to tears.

'Pet, you're better off without me, now. As far as the

world's concerned, I'm the Crimson Killer.' Her voice caught. 'How can I carry on being any sort of mother to you?'

Cathy didn't like the way her mum was talking. 'Don't say that, you're scaring me.'

Annie gripped her daughter's hand. 'I may have ruined my life, but don't let it ruin yours, Cathy.' She smiled through her tears. 'I've always known you're going to make something of yourself.'

'Time's up.' The prison warden was standing over them. Annie gave Cathy's hand one final squeeze.

'Promise me, Cathy!' Her voice was insistent again. 'You've got potential, don't waste it!'

Cathy couldn't answer for a moment, then she squeezed her mum's hands in return. 'I promise. You'll be out of here one day, and I'll have a nice big house by then, you wait and see. Just you and me, away from everything.' She gulped away the tears, trying so hard to stay strong. 'I love you, Mam.'

Annie Fincham smiled back sadly. 'I love you too, sweetheart.'

Cathy watched her mother being led off, like a butterfly that had been trapped and had its wings broken. It was the last time she ever saw her alive.

Desolate with grief and shame, Annie Fincham lasted exactly two weeks and three days before she hung herself in her cell with a bed sheet, a tragedy that further convinced the public of her guilt.

Aside from the prison chaplain and a prison officer, Cathy was the only one at her mother's funeral. Annie Fincham's ashes were buried in an unmarked grave at an unmarked location.

Cathy, now sixteen, was taken in by her reluctant grandmother, and she never let Cathy forget the scandal her mother had brought upon them. Cathy, who was devastated, guilt-stricken and betrayed by her mother's death, was left to deal with her grief alone.

But the nightmare was by no means over. A bent copper who'd worked on the case and needed money to clear his debts had sold a story to one of the most salacious tabloids, asserting his conviction that Annie and Cathy had plotted to kill Ray Barnard for months. Claiming that something about Annie's story hadn't added up, the policeman was convinced she was lying to protect the real perpetrator of the crime, Cathy. An injunction was brought out, but by then the damage was done. The whispers didn't take long to start, and before long they had degenerated into downright finger-pointing. At school and at home, Cathy was shunned and taunted. 'Killer!' the kids would shout at her in the street as their mothers ushered them away from her. 'There goes the murderer, walking free!' It seemed as if the whole world had turned against her.

During that dreadful time, when Cathy didn't know how she got out of bed in the mornings to face yet another day of hatred and hostility, the only person who wanted to know her was John Milton. Cathy wouldn't, couldn't talk about what had happened, and amazingly John hadn't pried. She brought it up just once, when her head felt like it would explode if she didn't let out some of the emotion trapped in there.

'What if I had done it?' They were sitting on the playing fields at the rec, sharing the spoils of John's trip to the newsagents.

John shrugged. 'Done what?'

'Killed my mam's boyfriend.' Cathy pulled at the grass, trying to sound nonchalant.

John propped his head on one elbow and looked at her perceptively.

'I'd say you did whatever you had to do, Cathy. It wouldn't make you a murderer.'

The meaning had been implicit, and it had taken all her self-control to not break down and tell John everything. But she couldn't; it was the only thing left that she could do for her mother. She made the decision there and then never to get close to anyone again.

Soon after that conversation, Cathy stopped taking John's calls and started avoiding him at school. And then she'd had the defining moment that changed her life for ever.

As she passed the doctor's surgery on her way home one day, Cathy noticed copies of *Tatler* and *Soirée* dumped outside the dustbin. Looking around to see if anyone was watching, she quickly crammed as many into her bag as possible. Back in the tiny second bedroom at her grandmother's, she was entranced by the vibrant, intoxicating pages full of glamorous, exciting people and fabulous locations. They soon became her only escape, and Cathy would spend ages in the newsagents reading each one from cover to cover until she was ordered out by irate shopkeepers.

On the morning of her seventeenth birthday, and halfway through her uninspired choice of A-Levels, Cathy walked out of her grandmother's house and never went back. With only a small bag containing her meagre wardrobe, and all her savings from the building society, she bought a one-way coach ticket to London, hidden away under a big hat and bulky coat. At Victoria Station, she went straight into the toilets and hacked off her long hair into a short crop. As she stared at herself in the mirror afterwards, she was startled

476

by the transformation. It wasn't just the hair, she just looked . . . different. The name was the next thing to go, and suddenly Cathy Fincham had disappeared, replaced by a more sophisticated-sounding Catherine Connor. Suddenly it was as if her former life had never existed.

Catherine Connor found the capital to be a different world, a place where people were more interested in their own lives than in others'. In those early months she was terrified at the thought of someone recognizing her, but somehow they never did. Despite her lack of experience her determination paid off, and it wasn't long before Catherine landed a job as a junior writer at a small women's weekly. The pay was crap, and the hours shitty, but from that moment on Catherine felt like she had a second chance at life. She'd been unhappy for so long, but now it was time to put her anguish and heartache – along with the memory of her mother and John Milton – away in a box she swore never to open again. Catherine told herself it was the only way, a clean break.

Although people occasionally remarked that her face looked familiar, Catherine would casually brush them off. The press had moved on to other things by then, and although her mother's case was still reported on occasionally, the fate of the Crimson Killer's kid had slowly faded out of public consciousness and Catherine hadn't been found out.

Until now.

The implications hit Catherine again as she sat, weak from crying. Her life had been ruined, irrevocably. It was a savage irony that the one person who had been her saving grace all those years ago had proved her downfall in the end. How else could Isabella have found out?

Bile rose in her throat and Catherine rushed for the toilet. She would be sacked from *Soirée* on the spot, and would lose her home, her belongings, everything. As she retched into the bowl, Catherine Connor realized she was now nothing more again than miserable, scared, hated Cathy Fincham.

Chapter 61

Caro had just put the kettle on when the phone rang. She glanced at the clock on the kitchen wall. It was still early, who could be calling at this time?

Her grandmother was talking even as she picked the receiver up.

'Darling, you'll never guess what's happened! Angie's just been round; young Ashley has taken off, just like that! Angie has no idea where, and she can't get hold of him. She's awfully upset.'

'Oh, the poor thing!' Caro really felt for her friend, she knew how fond Angie had grown of her new protégé.

'Freddie has done a thorough check of the estate, just to make sure he hadn't gone off for a walk and fallen in a ditch or something,' said Clementine. 'Remember that awful time when Archie came off his quad bike and they didn't find him under the hedge for hours? Luckily it was only minor concussion, but one can never be too prudent about these things.'

Clementine sighed. 'Of course, he's obviously decided to throw the towel in and hotfoot it straight back to London. *So* unfair on poor Freds and Angie, they've worked wonders with that boy. His spots had even started to clear up.' Clementine made a cross noise. 'Young people! They just don't have the commitment these days. When I was in the Land Girls . . .'

Caro could feel one of her grandmother's diatribes coming on. Absent-mindedly she walked over and switched on the small television that stood on the corner of the worktop. As the morning news flickered to life, Caro frowned. That face looked familiar . . . With Granny Clem still talking in the background, she reached across for her new copy of *Soirée*. On the first page was the editor's letter, and Caro gasped in recognition. It *was* Catherine Connor! She reached for the remote control and turned the sound up. The newsreader was just starting her piece.

The Crimson Killer case was one of the most infamous cases of the eighties. Many thought at the time that Annie Fincham was not to blame for the death of forty-three-year-old Ray Barnard. Annie's teenage daughter Cathy, who was at the scene of the killing, went to ground shortly after her mother committed suicide in her prison cell. The whereabouts of Cathy Fincham have always remained a mystery until now, and the shocking revelation that she is high-flying magazine editor Catherine Connor, who was named one of the most influential women in British media by the Guardian *two years ago . . .*

Caro nearly dropped the remote. She remembered that case, it had been huge! On the other end of the line in Churchminster, Clementine was still in full flow.

'The government just haven't got the backbone these days, that's the problem. We could sort out this ASBO problem once and for all by bringing back national service . . .'

Caro interrupted. 'Sorry to be rude, Granny Clem, but can I call you back?' She had to talk to Harriet.

At some point Catherine must have cried herself to sleep, curled up on the bathroom floor, because the doorbell woke her with a jump. She looked round confusedly, a few seconds of merciful respite before the horror of her situation hit home. The doorbell went again, this time whoever it was was keeping their finger on the buzzer. Still groggy from sleep and crying, Catherine got up to answer.

No sooner had she opened the door, than a flash went off in her face, momentarily blinding her. A babble of voices started, and as the stars faded from Catherine's eyes, she could see the jostling crowd of reporters, shouting and shoving their microphones in her face. Another flash went off, making her eyes water. Through the melee, she saw the concierge standing at the back, wringing his hands.

'They just pushed past me!' he shouted. 'Your intercom is off, I've been trying to get hold of you all night!'

Somehow, Catherine forced the door shut. She thought she might be sick again. Someone had thrown in a copy of the *Daily Mercy*, and along the top screamed the headline of her nightmares.

'WE'VE FOUND THE CRIMSON KILLER'S KID! FULL SHOCKING STORY PAGES 4, 5, 6 & 7.' Shaking like a leaf, nausea almost drowning her, Catherine opened the paper. Inside, it was even worse: 'FROM GUTTER TO GLAMOUR – HOW THE CRIMSON KILLER'S KID FOOLED THE WORLD!' There was a small, grainy photograph of Annie Fincham with Ray Barnard in happier times, but the main photo was a very unflattering one of Catherine, taken a few years ago at an awards ceremony. She was holding a glass of champagne and had obviously blinked at the flash, her eyes half-closed. The accompanying caption claimed that she was known in the industry for liking a drink.

The main story was attributed to Isabella's friend Henrietta Lord-Wyatt, but the words were straight from the mouth of the *Grace* editor herself. The tone was breathy, bitchy and went straight for the jugular.

To many, Soirée's *ageing editor Catherine Connor . . .*

'Bitch!' shouted Catherine furiously, briefly roused from her misery.

. . . has climbed to the top of the tree in the jungle of Britain's glossy magazines. Designer wardrobes, prestigious parties, there wasn't an invite this attention-seeking woman would ever turn down. But for all her desperate attempts at living the dream, Catherine Connor has been hiding a scandalous secret – she is the daughter of the notorious 1980s Crimson Killer, Annie Fincham. It has always been widely speculated that Annie had assistance in committing her grisly crime – with some even convinced that fifteen-year-old Catherine was the one behind the killing of Ray Barnard, 43.

'I always thought she had a dark side,' one extremely well-respected editor told the Daily Mercy.

'Read that as Isabella,' Catherine said through gritted teeth.

'One could never put one's finger on it, but there was definitely something "off" about Catherine Connor. One can just sense bad blood. And all along, she was

482

the Crimson Killer's daughter. Of course, I'm convinced that Annie Fincham covered up her daughter's crime. Catherine Connor is a woman capable of anything – even murder.'

And so it went on. Vitriolic sentence after vitriolic sentence. Catherine retched several times as she read it, but made herself finish. Then she ripped it into shreds and didn't stop until the living room floor was covered with paper.

When she finally collapsed on the sofa, arms shaking from exertion, Catherine waited for an avalanche of fresh tears. But this time none came. Instead, she was left with an overwhelming emptiness. In one single article, Isabella had bulldozed away two decades of hard work and recognition. If Sir Robin needed any more ammunition to shut *Soirée* down, this was it, taking *Soirée* Sponsors – and the future of thousands of young kids – along with it. As far as she was concerned, Isabella and John Milton had blood on their hands. Bitter bile rose up at the back of Catherine's throat. She was feeling anger now, a heat that burned through her veins and raced round her head.

'Fuck you both!' she shouted. 'Go to hell!'

An hour later the concierge looked up from his desk and his mouth fell open. Striding out of the lift, the stunning woman in the fitted red dress and killer heels was a world away from the red-eyed, bewildered person he'd seen a short time earlier. Catherine glanced briefly outside, where a media pack had already assembled. As soon as they saw Catherine, they went wild.

'Your cab's outside,' stuttered the concierge. 'Would you like me to walk you to it?'

Catherine shook her head. 'Thanks, but I can

manage,' she said and walked off into the eye of the storm.

Watching from the other side of the road, beneath a large oak tree, John Milton couldn't help but smile. Catherine Connor was some woman. He didn't know why he'd come really. For a moment he thought about whether to run over, see if she really was OK, but John knew there was no way she'd speak to him. As far as she was concerned, he'd done the worst thing imaginable. His face dropped as the cab drove Catherine away and out of his life. Not for the first time, John cursed that he had ever set eyes on Isabella Montgomery.

There was another pack of reporters outside Valour, but Catherine kept her head down and strode through them, blocking out the shouts in her ears. She'd half-expected to be barred from the building; her phone had been switched off from last night, so she didn't know if Adam had left a voicemail telling her not to come back. But to her surprise, instead of blocking her entrance with folded arms, the security guard was there to pull the door open and usher her in. 'Morning, Miss Connor,' he said almost reverentially, ushering her towards the lifts.

Catherine was astonished, hadn't he read the papers? By the time she approached the door to *Soirée*, she'd never felt so nervous in all her life. Taking a deep breath, she pushed it open, not looking left or right, aware everyone had stopped talking. Harriet tried to meet her eyes as she swept past, but Catherine didn't falter until she had pulled her office door closed behind her. She let the blinds down and sank into her seat. Her heart was hammering. Catherine had sworn she wouldn't slink away as Isabella wanted her to, but now she'd made it to work, her resolve was faltering. What on earth was she to do now, wait for Adam to come and fire her on the spot?

Suddenly there was a loud bang on the door. He hadn't wasted his time. Steeling herself, Catherine sat up.

'Come in.'

To her surprise it was Alexander, looking extremely excited.

'Darling!' he exclaimed. 'You never told me! How thrilling!' He checked himself. 'Of course, I'm not making light of your misfortunes; you must have suffered dreadfully. I was almost *hysterical* with tears reading it.'

Catherine couldn't quite believe what she was hearing. 'You're not disgusted?'

One of Alexander's eyebrows shot up. 'Heavens, no! Why on earth would you think that?'

Catherine thought he must be winding her up. 'Al, haven't you seen the *Daily Mercy*?'

Alexander's top lip wrinkled distastefully. 'Oh that. Everyone knows it's just a spite-filled old rag. They've made quite a fool of themselves. That revolting little rat Drew Summers must be spitting.'

Still Catherine didn't understand. 'What are you talking about?'

Alexander threw a bundle of newspapers down on her desk, his eyes shining. '*You*, darling! You're the new Diana!'

Catherine's face was on every front page she could see. Hands shaking, she picked up a copy of Britain's biggest tabloid, the *Scoop*. 'CLEAR THEM!' the headline shouted.

The glamorous world of magazines is today reeling after the discovery that renowned Soirée *editor Catherine*

Connor is in fact Cathy Fincham, daughter of Annie 'Crimson Killer' Fincham, jailed in 1988 for the manslaughter of her boyfriend, 43-year-old Ray Barnard. At the time the case caused uproar, especially when tragic Annie hung herself just three weeks into her 15-year sentence. 15-year-old Catherine, then just a vulnerable schoolgirl, was also implemented in the crime, with hate-mongers claiming it was SHE who was responsible for the death of Ray Barnard.

Catherine gulped and read on.

But far from being cold-blooded killers, Annie and Catherine Fincham were the victims of a terrifying regime of domestic violence inflicted on them by Barnard. Today, after uncovering fresh evidence, the Scoop brings you the TRUE tragic story of the Crimson Killer. Including:

- *Far from being a victim, Barnard was a VILE and ABUSIVE drunk.*
- *The FATAL blow – which some still believe was delivered by Catherine – was an act of SELF DEFENCE.*
- *How BRAVE Catherine REBUILT her life, becoming one of the country's TOP campaigners for TEENAGE charities.*

Catherine couldn't speak. How had they got this? They may not have got hold of Catherine herself, but the paper had done a thorough job. The piece was extensive, and the *Scoop* had spoken to several people who still lived on Catherine's old estate, who'd been too scared to reveal at the time that Ray Barnard had a history of being a wife-beater. 'That poor little girl and her mother,' said one neighbour, who declined to be named. 'It was a witch-hunt that went on here, people should be ashamed of themselves.'

'The *Scoop* does love a campaign,' Alexander said happily.

It wasn't just the tabloids: an influential broadsheet had devoted their front page and two spreads inside to the Crimson Killer case, saying it had been a pivotal point in reassessing the British justice system. A retired policeman who'd worked on the case was interviewed, revealing his unease when Annie Fincham had been charged with manslaughter on what should have been a domestic-violence case. Another tabloid, perhaps somewhat crassly, had called Catherine and her mother the 'Real Life Jordaches', referring to the infamous Brookside storyline in which Anna Friel's character Beth Jordache and her mother Mandy had killed violent dad Trevor Jordache and buried his body under the garden patio. Catherine cringed when she read that comparison, but the message coming through was loud and clear. Her mother's imprisonment had been one of the worst miscarriages of justice the country had ever seen, and the entire British press had gone gaga over the story.

Harriet's head suddenly appeared round the door. 'Sorry to disturb you, Catherine, but you've got messages from the *Sun*, *Daily Mirror*, *Daily Telegraph* and the *New York Post* to call them. *Sky News* are ringing every five minutes, and I've also had seven book publishers ring up in the last hour wanting to talk to you urgently. What shall I say to them?'

Catherine gave herself a mental shake, trying to clear her head. 'Tell them they'll have to wait.' In the madness of the last few hours, she had forgotten what this day was really about.

It was time for her meeting with the board.

*   *   *

It was 11.15 a.m. as Catherine arrived at Martyr House, inside a blacked-out people carrier. She'd spent the journey in quiet reflection, her mobile still switched off. She'd deal with all that later. As the car sat in the slow London traffic, passing pedestrians had no idea that behind the glass was that day's most talked-about woman in Britain.

There was a new girl in reception, and her eyes widened in surprise at the sight of Catherine. 'Oh, it's you!' she gasped.

Catherine tried to smile. 'I'm here to see Sir Robin Hackford.'

Without taking her eyes off Catherine, the girl picked up the phone. Catherine felt rather like an exotic specimen in a museum. 'The board aren't ready for you yet,' the girl said apologetically. 'Can I get you anything, tea, coffee, sparkling water?'

'I'm fine, thanks.'

Catherine took a seat. The waiting area was empty, the only sound a giant clock ticking loudly overhead. It felt symbolic, like it was counting down her final moments with the company. Catherine noticed her palms were sweating.

Eventually the receptionist smiled reverentially. 'You can go up now.'

On the top floor Catherine stepped out on to the thick carpet. As before, the wide corridors were empty, the air strangely lifeless. 'Boardroom' read the sign in ornate gold letters. As if in a dream, Catherine lifted her hand and knocked on the heavy wooden door.

'Enter,' commanded the voice of Sir Robin Hackford.

A room of solemn faces greeted her, including Fiona MacDonald-Scott, the woman Catherine had sent a

488

ranting email to by mistake. Ms MacDonald-Scott's lips were pursed disapprovingly.

'Sit down,' said Sir Robin. It wasn't an invitation but an order. He looked more like a silvery fox than ever; white hair brushed back, high feline cheekbones.

'So,' he announced, an unpleasant smile curling at the edge of his mouth. 'I had no idea we had such a *celebrity* in our midst.' Fiona MacDonald-Scott let out a thin titter. The chief executive played unhappily with his cufflinks. Beside him sat Adam, looking every bit like a rabbit caught in the headlights. He clearly had no idea what was going on, still.

Catherine ignored Sir Robin's jibe as she sat upright in her chair, ankles neatly crossed and hands clasped in her lap where no one could see them. 'You wanted to see me?'

Her nemesis stared at her, relishing the power he held. His voice was slow and deliberate. 'Six months ago I set you the biggest challenge of your career, Miss Connor, the "Project 300" campaign. The idea was that you were to improve *Soirée*'s falling sales, and push them over the 300,000 mark.'

'I am aware of this,' she said acidly. Sir Robin stared at her as if she had just crawled out of a hole in the ground.

'I have been monitoring your progress *extremely* carefully.' He looked down at a single piece of paper.

'Here, in front of me, are the final sales figures.'

No one said anything. It was so quiet Catherine could only hear the air conditioning and the laboured breathing of one of the more elderly directors.

'Have you got anything to say before I read them out?' asked Sir Robin.

Her gaze was just as cold as his tone. 'What do you want me to say? That we haven't reached our target and

Soirée is finished? Oh, not to forget about the dreams of about ten thousand kids with fuck-all in life who were looking to us for a better start.'

Around the table, all eyes turned to him. His lips had turned white with anger, and when he eventually spoke, his voice was barely controlled.

'Miss Connor, it is no secret that I think you do this company more harm than good, and never more so than over the last twenty-four hours.' He peered at her disgustedly, over his half-moon glasses. 'In the circumstances, it might also have been prudent to inform the company beforehand of your *controversial* background.'

Humiliated, Catherine flushed.

'I say, I'm not sure what that's got to do with anything,' protested the chief executive.

Sir Robin flashed a contemptuous look at him and turned back to Catherine. 'You are a loose cannon who consistently flouts authority, someone who thinks with her heart and not with her head. In business, this is not the way we do things.' He smiled at her for the first time. It reminded Catherine of a frozen lake cracking up. 'As the final figures have shown.'

She stuck her chin out defiantly. 'I'm not an idiot, Sir Robin. I know we've suffered another drop.'

'Indeed.' Sir Robin laboured over every word, maximizing his pleasure. 'The final sales figure you reached by the end of last month was . . .' he paused, savouring the moment, '273, 876.'

All Catherine heard were the first two digits. Her mind went into a blur as the last bit of hope was extinguished.

'A long way short, by anyone's reckoning,' said Sir Robin, rubbing salt into the wound. 'You have failed to meet the "Project 300" Ms Connor.'

If he was expecting a reaction, he didn't get one. Catherine slumped back in her chair, utterly defeated.

It was over. She'd known it all along, really, and she had known that he had set her an impossible task. But instead of anger, she just felt sadness. She had filled people with false hope, and now she had let so many down, including herself.

For thirty seconds Sir Robin just looked at her. Catherine had had enough.

'For God's sake, say something!' she cried. 'What, do you want us out of the building by the end of the day? So who's got the swinging great bollocks to come down and tell my team they haven't got a job any more?'

To her surprise, the chief executive let out a burst of laughter.

'It wasn't that funny,' said Catherine in astonishment.

'Bloody was,' he chuckled, ignoring a death stare from Sir Robin.

Catherine looked round at the others. 'What's going on?'

The chief executive leaned in. 'She needs to know, Robin. Stop dragging this out.'

Catherine's eyes darted between them. 'Know what? *Soirée* is closing down, isn't it?'

Silence, as everyone waited for Sir Robin to speak.

'What the hell is going on?' repeated Catherine.

Sir Robin cleared his throat. Suddenly, he looked as sick as a pig. '*Soirée* has failed to meet its targets. Therefore, theoretically, it *should* close.'

'Get on with it, man!' The chief executive was almost shouting now.

On the other hand, it looked like it was physically painful for Sir Robin to talk. 'However, certain things that I – we – were not expecting to happen, have happened. This Savannah Sexton issue looks to outsell the entire monthly market put together.'

'How many?' asked Catherine.

Sir Robin forced the words out. 'It's early days, but if we carry on selling like this, we're predicted to sell over one million.'

Anyone would think he'd just told everyone someone had died, not that *Soirée* had just made magazine history.

'Oh my God!' shrieked Catherine, jumping up. The chief executive did the same, and they high-fived each other over the desk, whooping loudly.

Fiona MacDonald-Scott's mouth virtually disappeared at this display of over-exuberance. Catherine couldn't have cared less.

Sir Robin looked equally disapproving. 'I'm confident it's a one-off, something *Soirée* will never achieve again, and I know many of the board agree with me.' Several suits mumbled their agreement.

'However,' he swallowed hard. 'It appears I have been overruled on this occasion. The latest developments have attracted a wave of new interest from advertisers and company investors, and new recent reader research has also proved extremely favourable. Therefore I have been advised by certain key figures in the company that it is not in our best interests to close the magazine. Despite it not reaching its intended target,' he added venomously.

Catherine couldn't quite take it in. 'We're not closing?'

The chief executive broke into a broad smile. 'We're not closing! Catherine, this is a new era for *Soirée*.'

'What about *Soirée* Sponsors?' Catherine could hardly bring herself to hear the answer.

'Safe as houses! Even with the current economic

climate, we know we're on to a winner here. The company is investing millions of pounds in the *Soirée* brand, across all areas.'

Catherine put her head in her hands, trying to keep the tears from coming. 'Thank God,' she muttered. 'Thank God.' After a moment she regained her composure, stood up and smoothed her dress down.

'I have an announcement of my own to make.'

She looked down at them all.

'I would like to take this opportunity to hand in my resignation.'

Around the table, everyone's mouth fell open. 'Y-y-you can't!' stuttered Adam Freshwater.

Catherine looked at him with something like pity. 'Yes, I can. I'm proud to have brought *Soirée* to the top of its game again. But I've got nothing left. I need to do something else while I've still got the chance.'

She looked pointedly at the chief executive. 'I would like to take this opportunity to thank those of you who have always supported me, and I would like to recommend Fiona MacKenzie of *Teen Style* for my position. She is an exceptionally talented editor and journalist.'

'What are you going to do?' gasped the chief executive.

Catherine smiled wryly. 'Apart from get a life and face the demons I've been running from all these years? I'm going to go straight down to *Soirée* Sponsors and ask them for a job.'

Despite his shock, the chief executive looked impressed. 'Good on you, Catherine.'

Sir Robin Hackford wasn't so complimentary. 'Give up all this prestige and power under some self-deluded notion of being the next Mother Teresa? You're mad, woman!'

Catherine looked down at his cold, unpleasant face.

'Oh, back in your box, Robin. You're the one who needs help.'

And with that, she swept out.

Two industry announcements were sent out that afternoon. The first was news that Sir Robin Hackford was leaving Valour's board of directors by 'mutual agreement', and that more resignations were expected to follow. The other, announced by Valour's rival publishing company Signet, was that following a catastrophic fall in sales, *Grace* editor Isabella Montgomery was standing down, with immediate effect.

Chapter 62

Angie was standing at the kitchen sink when she saw the taxi coming up the drive. Instantly, she knew who it was. She rushed out, Avon and Barksdale trotting close behind.

'Oh, darling, where have you been?' she cried, as Ash climbed out of the cab. 'I've been so worried.'

Ash looked contrite. Despite her concern, Angie noticed how much his skin had cleared up; he really did have a lovely bone structure.

'Sorry, I should have called. It's just all been a bit mental.'

'Are you OK?' she persisted, ushering him inside to the kitchen. Freddie looked up from reading the racing pages of the newspaper.

'Hello there, young fellow! We were beginning to think you'd fallen down a great big hole or something.' Although he'd stopped his wife phoning the missing person helpline, Freddie was relieved to see Ash back again.

'Darling, give the poor boy a chance to put his bag down!' he added.

Ash put his Adidas holdall on the floor, and Avon

pounced on it, his wet nose snuffling around in a pocket open at one end.

Ash turned to the Fox-Titts, his face serious. 'I've been in London. Dad's in hospital, he had an accident.'

Angie's hand flew to her mouth. 'Oh no! Is he all right?'

Ash grimaced. 'He's broken two ribs and his collar-bone. It could have been worse, he was piss . . .' He stopped himself. 'He was drunk again, fell down two flights of stairs in our block of flats.'

Freddie glanced at his wife. 'Poor fellow.'

Angie's kind brown eyes looked at Ash. 'Are *you* OK, darling? It must have been dreadfully upsetting for you.'

Ash felt a lump rise in his throat. Angie's concern always got to him a bit.

'Yeah, I'm cool. The thing is, I've realized I need to be there for my dad if he's going to get better. We're all each other has got.' He trailed off.

Angie knew what was coming. 'You're going back to live with him,' she prompted gently.

Ash was silent for a moment. 'Yeah,' he said finally. 'I'm sorry.'

Angie smiled. 'Oh, darling, you've got nothing to be sorry about. Family is so important, Freds and I understand that.' Despite her resolve to be stoical, her voice wobbled. 'I'll just miss you dreadfully, though, you're my star pupil!'

To her surprise, Ash loped over and gave her a hug. 'Don't be upset, Angie. This whole *Soirée* Sponsors thing has been a wicked experience, and you and Freddie have been great to me. Y'know, for the first time in my life, I really feel like I'm going somewhere.'

Freddie handed his wife a piece of kitchen roll. She blew her nose loudly. 'Freds and I are very proud of the way you've dealt with everything, aren't we, darling?'

'Absolutely,' agreed Freddie. 'You know you're always welcome here,' he added.

Ash grinned, an easy genuine smile that reached every inch of his face.

'I'll come and visit, I promise.'

'I'll keep you to that!' laughed Angie. 'When are you off?'

Ash looked awkward again. 'Tomorrow.'

'Oh! So soon?'

'I've gotta pick Dad up from the hospital.'

'Of course.' Angie looked fondly at him for a moment, then pulled herself together. 'Seeing as it's such a nice evening, will you do Avon, Barksdale and myself the honour of one final walk?'

Ash grinned. 'Nice one.'

A few days later interest in the Annie Fincham case hadn't waned. Harriet had even been stopped by a reporter in the street and asked what it was like working with the '*Soirée* Saviour'. The *Scoop*'s campaign had received nationwide support, and there was talk of going to Downing Street with a petition. Domestic violence charities came out in support of Catherine and her mum, highlighting other similarly controversial cases, while survivors of abuse themselves told their stories. They were old, young, rich and poor; it seemed no part of society was unaffected. The Crimson Killer case had finally made everyone sit up and take notice.

Inside the four walls of the *Soirée* office, however, the staff could be forgiven for not having a clue what was happening. Ever since the story had broken, Catherine had been huddled away in her office, or off having mysterious meetings.

Saffron couldn't bear the suspense. 'I mean, is she going to say anything?' she whispered loudly, as she and Harriet made hot drinks in the kitchen one morning. 'I know she's always kept her private life separate, but this is ridiculous. The whole country's talking about it!'

Harriet pulled a face. 'I know, it must be awfully difficult for her. She's had a terribly sad life.'

Since Catherine hadn't publicly said otherwise, Saffron asked the question that was on everyone's lips, but that they were too afraid to ask.

'Do you think it was her, and not her mother? The one who pushed him down the stairs, I mean. They're saying it could even have been an accident; that he tripped and fell.'

Harriet was quiet for a minute. 'I don't know,' she admitted. 'But if I was in Catherine's position and my mother's life was in danger, I honestly think I'd do anything I could to save her.'

Saffron thought about Babs. Would she put her own life in danger to save her mother's? It made her feel unexpectedly emotional, and she changed the subject.

'What's going to happen now?' she asked, stirring her coffee furiously. 'We still don't know if we've met this stupid "Project 300". Everyone is on tenterhooks.' She sighed. 'I can't take this much longer. Have we all still got jobs or not?'

Saffron didn't have to wait long. That afternoon Catherine gathered them together in the middle of the office. The tension was palpable.

'As you are probably aware, it's been an extraordinary few days. I'm sorry I haven't had the chance to talk to you all earlier; I know you're all anxious to know if we've met the "Project 300" target.'

Even Alexander looked nervous, his face nearly as pale as his newly dyed white-blonde hair.

Catherine wasn't going to play it out like Sir Robin Hackford. She looked round before breaking into a big smile.

'I'm delighted to tell you we have smashed our target.'

It was true, give or take a month. She wasn't going to bother them with the nitty-gritty, all they needed to know was what a fantastic job they'd done, and that their own jobs were safe.

Everyone started cheering and hugging each other. One of the beauty girls burst into tears and ran off to find her eye make-up remover pads, as mascara trailed down her face.

'That's bloody brilliant!' shouted Saffron.

'There's more,' said Catherine, once the noise had died down. 'Because of the Savannah Sexton issue, *Soirée* has become the highest-selling women's magazine . . . in *history*. In fact, I found out this morning we have just passed the one million mark.'

No one spoke for a moment as the news sank in.

'One million?' the chief sub eventually repeated.

Catherine grinned.

'Fuck a duck!' he gasped. Everyone hooted with laughter. The chief sub never swore.

'So we're not closing?' someone asked, still a little tentative.

'Definitely not,' said Catherine. 'In fact, I am just in the process of sorting out the bonuses everyone is going to get for working so hard. It may not be six figures but it will pay for a well-deserved holiday.'

Everyone whooped again, and Saffron found herself flinging her arms around Tom Fellows. They jumped apart, embarrassed, but in the carnival atmosphere no one noticed.

'There is one more thing,' called Catherine, straining to be heard above the noise.

'Quiet!' someone shouted.

'We have made *Soirée* the best monthly magazine in Britain, and it's down to each and every one of you. I know I've pushed you over the past six months but you've risen to the challenge admirably. You are an exceptionally talented team of people, and it has been a privilege to work with you. I know *Soirée* is going on to even bigger and better things . . .' She gave a sad smile. 'But unfortunately, it won't be with me.'

Alexander looked shocked. 'Darling, you're leaving?'

Catherine tried to reassure the worried faces. 'Hey, you'll be fine. And I'm confident that whoever becomes editor next will do a great job.' She continued. 'The good news is that I'm still going to be involved with the *Soirée* brand. Yesterday Gail Barker from *Soirée* Sponsors very kindly offered me a job on her team. I'm going to be working to make us even bigger and better, with plans to go nationwide in the next two years.' Catherine gave a wry grin. 'Of course, most of you know by now that I always like to have more than enough on my plate. Three hours ago, I also signed a book deal with Starlight Publishing to write a story about my life. If anyone does feel like reading it, all profits from the sales will be going to charity.'

'I'm going to buy ten copies, darling!' Alexander shouted out, as others murmured their agreement.

Catherine smiled at him. 'You haven't read it yet!' Her tone grew more serious. 'It's not going to be an easy journey, but I'm the only one who can set the record straight about what happened that night. My mother was a wonderful person and I haven't had the chance to grieve for her properly because I've always shut out the past. I'm hoping this book will clear her name and give me the peace I've been looking for all these years. And if it helps even one woman who is suffering domestic violence to get out of her situation, then it's all been worth it.' Catherine looked around, slightly embarrassed, at the spellbound faces. 'Well, that's all folks,' she added awkwardly.

Saffron started clapping softly, and everyone joined in, louder and louder, their faces etched with admiration. Catherine's candour had touched them all. They'd never work for anyone as inspirational again.

Catherine felt overwhelmed at the show of solidarity. Alexander rushed over and planted two emotional kisses on her cheeks. 'How we will miss you! What on earth is the world of magazines going to do without Catherine Connor?'

Catherine choked back the tears. 'It will survive, Al, just like we all have.'

It was past seven o'clock by the time Catherine left work. It had been a funny day: everyone was delighted the magazine was safe, but at the same time sad their boss was leaving. The only solution to the conflicting emotions seemed to be going to the pub, but Catherine eschewed the invite. She'd celebrate properly with them at her leaving party, and besides, she had pressing things to be getting on with: drafting out her official resignation letter to Adam, for one thing. She wondered how long he'd last without her.

Spring was definitely in the air as Catherine left the building. She thought about walking home, but then looked ruefully at her feet, encased in a pair of pointed Gucci slingbacks. That was going to be one of the things she definitely wouldn't miss about *Soirée*.

His voice made her stop dead in her tracks.

'Catherine?'

Fighting to keep control, she turned round. And hated how she felt.

Even now, after everything that had happened, her stomach still flipped as she found herself facing John Milton. He was wearing a simple white T-shirt and jeans, his hair as thick and black as ever. The olive-green eyes, normally so penetrating, were almost opaque with an emotion Catherine couldn't decipher.

Her reaction was instinctive. Marching over, she slapped him hard across the face.

John Milton didn't even flinch. His eyes looked into hers, a red mark from her hand already starting to form on his cheek.

Catherine stared back defiantly: she wasn't going to fall for his shit again. 'What the fuck are you doing here? Come to finish off what you and your girlfriend started?'

The emotions she'd been trying so desperately to keep down bubbled over and Catherine lifted her hand to strike him again. She wanted to hurt him like he'd hurt her. She *needed* him to feel that physical pain.

This time John caught her wrist and held it in a steel grip.

'Get off me!' she hissed furiously.

He released her. 'I wanted to see if you were OK.'

Catherine couldn't believe his audacity. 'Are you having a fucking laugh?'

Not for the first time, they were attracting the attention of passers-by. There was a little coffee shop next door.

'Can we go somewhere more private?' John asked, tilting his head in that direction.

'I think you've already taken my privacy away from me,' Catherine responded icily.

He sighed. 'Please, Catherine. Let me explain.'

Something in his voice made Catherine think twice about walking away. 'Five minutes.'

Inside the tiny coffee shop, there was only a cramped table for two. Catherine leaned against the wall, trying to keep as much distance between them as possible, but she could still feel the heat from John's body, and smell the familiar scent of his aftershave. 'Shoot,' she said, in her most businesslike tone.

John looked at her with his steady gaze. 'Isabella and I have never once been an item.'

Catherine gave a derisive snort. 'Oh, please! She wasted no time in telling me how into each other you both were.'

Confusion flashed across John's face. 'I honestly have no idea why she would say that. You might, as you seem to know her better, but God's honest truth, Catherine, is that the only contact I've had with Isabella has been in a business capacity.'

Catherine raised an unimpressed eyebrow, but couldn't help but ask. 'Why were you together at Duvalls?'

John looked at her. 'It was a rather weird chain of events that led to us being there at all, and I certainly wouldn't have agreed to go if I'd known you two knew each other, or what she was capable of.' He sighed. 'I'd been to pick up some paperwork from one of my clients, an American guy named Teddy Barsmann. I met Isabella at his office. I take it they're some kind of couple or something – she was certainly all over him when I arrived. Anyway, Teddy suddenly had to work at the last minute, and Isabella made a scene about him not taking her out. So he asked if I would go in his place. I must admit, I was pretty shocked, but Teddy seemed keen to get her out of there. I didn't want to, but I felt I couldn't say no. He's one of our biggest clients.'

'You looked very cosy together,' Catherine shot back.

'It was the worst evening of my life! Isabella isn't my kind of person, anyway, but as soon as she found out I knew you, she wouldn't stop talking about you and asking questions. I just said we were old school friends but she kept quizzing me if we'd had any kind of relationship. I told her it was none of her business. The woman is obsessed with you. She's clearly jealous.' John smiled. 'And so she should be.'

Catherine ignored the compliment. 'So you didn't sleep together?'

He looked angry now. 'Of course not! When I saw you leaving, it took all I had not to follow you.' John frowned. 'And anyway, what about that guy you were with?'

Catherine flushed guiltily at the memory of waking up next to Tolstoy. 'He took me home,' she said quickly. 'He's just a work friend.'

John wouldn't take his eyes off her, and she tried not to get drawn into those impossibly dark-green pools.

'What about the house you're doing up, the one that Lord Fairfax used to own? Isabella practically told me you had sex in the attic room.'

John looked disgusted. 'For God's sake! Teddy Barsmann has just bought it, that's who I'm working for at the moment! Isabella dropped round out of the blue one day, and asked if I'd give her a tour. I couldn't very well turn down the client's girlfriend.' John smiled grimly. 'Although, from what I hear, she's not his only girlfriend. I'm sure they've met their match in each other.'

Catherine was feeling more thrown by the minute.

'So you're telling me you told Isabella *nothing* about my background? About who my mother was?'

'Catherine, do you really have such a low opinion of me?' A passing waitress heard John's raised voice and glanced over. 'Isabella must have found out some other way, but I can assure you it wasn't through me.'

'Why should I believe you?' she demanded, but her voice had lost some of its hard edge.

'Because it's the truth!' John sighed in exasperation. 'Will you give me a break? You never gave me the chance to explain. I know you've been through a tough time, but everything you blame me for is entirely in your imagination.'

Suddenly, Catherine felt hugely embarrassed. She knew he was right. She had so little trust in people that she had jumped the gun and automatically thought the worst. As she looked at John, she saw for the first time how weary he looked, the fine worry lines at his temples. 'Maybe I should be the one apologizing,' she admitted. 'I shouldn't have just assumed . . .' She started again. 'I guess I've got so little confidence in myself it was easier to believe her over you.' She shook her head helplessly, trying to take it all in. 'How did Isabella find out, John? I should have listened to my friend Fiona. She warned me Isabella was a troublemaker.' Catherine gave a small smile. 'I just didn't realize how much trouble.'

John reached over and put his hand over hers. She let it stay there.

'These past weeks must have been terrible for you,' he said gently. 'When I saw the papers and the news . . .' He smiled at her. 'I turned up at your apartment, you know, the day the story broke in the papers. You looked amazing in that red dress.'

Catherine looked shocked. 'You were there? I didn't see you!'

John smiled wryly. 'I was keeping a low profile. I wanted to see you, but I honestly didn't know what reaction I'd get.'

'Probably an even worse one than I gave you earlier.' She gave him a small smile. 'Sorry for hitting you.'

He grinned crookedly. 'Nothing worse than you've done to my heart already.'

His comment hung heavy in the air. Catherine looked at him. 'I've left my job. I've got a book deal to write my life story.' She shook her head in disbelief. 'I still can't believe it. The thing I was most afraid of happened, and nothing but good seems to be coming out of it.'

'I think it's a really brave thing you're doing.'

She looked thoughtful. 'Let's see. But as well as setting the record straight, it will be a proper chance for me to say goodbye to Mum. We had so much unfinished stuff between us. I want to get it all out, otherwise I'm never going to be able to move on.'

John squeezed her hand hard. 'She'd be very proud of you.'

Tears pricked the back of Catherine's eyes. 'I hope so,' she whispered.

Another moment passed before John spoke. 'Where does this leave us, Catherine?'

She sighed, trying to find the right words. 'Oh, John. You really do mean the world to me.'

He cocked an eyebrow. 'But?' He was smiling but his hand had clenched hers even more tightly.

Catherine hesitated, willing herself to say the words that would set their lives on different paths again. 'I think you and I just met at the wrong time. Too much water has passed under the bridge.'

John's voice was thick with emotion. 'Let *me* be the judge of that. Don't write me off because of the past, I've never cared about that. I want to look after you, Catherine.'

Catherine looked down at his hand wrapped over hers. 'That's just it, John, I need to do this on my own. I'm going to have shit days, and it's not going to be pretty, and I don't want to put you through it all again. It sounds clichéd, but I need to find out who I am. I need to be *me*, not just a person who is shaped by secrets and tragedy. Once I've dealt with it all, a fresh start is the only way forward. Do you understand?'

John Milton's broad shoulders sank. He knew now that he'd lost her.

Catherine gently took her hand from beneath his and reached across to stroke his face. 'Goodbye, John.'

His handsome features were filled with pain. 'You don't always have to run away.'

Catherine stood up and smiled. 'I know. And for the first time in my life, I've stopped running.'

Chapter 63

Saffron was meeting Tom in a new bar in Notting Hill. It was one of those minimalist, glass-fronted places where everyone sat poised in cliques, eyes constantly on the door to see who had come in.

As she sat on a stool at the bar, Saffron wondered if it had been a good idea to meet Tom here. He was going to stick out like a sore thumb; this was the kind of place where outfit was everything. Tom had had a few days off, and the last time she'd seen him at work, he'd just sat on his glasses by accident and was sticking them back together with silver masking-tape. Saffron hoped fervently he'd managed to visit the optician's.

Twenty minutes later he still hadn't arrived. Saffron looked at her watch. This wasn't like him. Normally she would be the one who was late, and Tom would be at the bar, waiting with her vodka and cranberry. She'd called earlier to check they were still on for tonight, and his phone had gone straight through to voicemail. He hadn't called her back. The knot of anxiety growing in her stomach surprised Saffron; she never normally worried about people being late, especially Tom Fellows. She ordered another drink and got her BlackBerry out, playing with it to kill time.

A few minutes later her mobile went. Tom! But it was her mother. Saffron felt a mixture of pleasure and annoyance. Despite Babs promising to take things slowly, she had been calling Saffron almost every day. Saffron found Babs's neediness claustrophobic, but the more she backed off, the more desperate her mother became.

'Hi, Babs.'

'Darling! Please call me Mummy, you know how it upsets me if you don't.'

Saffron sighed.

'Hi, Mum.' This felt so weird.

'Where are you? It sounds very noisy.' Before Saffron had a chance to answer, Babs was off and away.

'I'm simply *exhausted*! I've been working on this new exhibition; I swear I haven't slept in weeks. Will you come and see it with me, darling? I'd love to know what you think.'

Saffron winced, that would be a tricky one.

'I'd love to, Babs. I mean, Mum . . .'

'Excellent! So, where did you say you were?'

'I didn't. I'm in a bar waiting to meet someone.'

Babs took a dramatic intake of breath. 'Might this someone be a *gentleman*?'

'Might be,' Saffron replied shortly. She wasn't going to get into this now. 'I've got to go.'

'Are you using protection?' Babs cried.

'*What*? Look. I'm not talking to you about this! I'll call tomorrow, OK?'

'Promise me you will, darling!'

Saffron promised and hung up. Her mother left her feeling so confused! Part of her wanted to welcome Babs back with open arms, but the other part wanted to punish her and make her feel crap, the way she herself had felt all these years. She sighed again; why weren't mother-daughter relationships ever easy?

Out of the corner of her eye, the bar door had opened, and the beautiful crowd started chattering wildly. Saffron turned to see a face and body that had graced just about every advertising board in the land. Dark hair cropped fashionably short framed the heavenly cheekbones, inky black eyes and full lips. The famous torso with wide shoulders and narrow hips was shown off casually in a thin silk John Smedley jumper, and dark jeans. He wore no jewellery, apart from a discreet silver identity bracelet glinting at his wrist – sexy, stylish but not overdone.

'Oh my God, it's Rex Sullivan!' cried the rail-thin woman next to Saffron.

Saffron gasped. Rex Sullivan! Put simply, he was the hottest male model the industry had seen since nineties phenomenon Markus Schenkenberg. Armani, Calvin Klein, Ralph Lauren . . . everyone wanted a piece of the British-born model.

Despite the stares in his direction, it seemed Rex Sullivan was heading straight for Saffron. Confused, she looked around to see if Kate Moss or some other model was sitting behind her.

She couldn't believe it when he stopped right in front of her. Up close, his looks were magnetic, but there wasn't a hint of arrogance. In fact, an almost shy expression crossed the model's face. Hang on, those eyelashes looked familiar . . .

'Er, hi there,' said Tom Fellows.

Saffron's mouth fell open.

'Tom?'

'Sorry I'm late, they took ages in the hairdressers.'

'But how . . . what?' In shocked wonder, Saffron put her hand up to touch his new haircut.

Tom looked bashful. 'I got contacts instead, thought it was about time. And Alexander took me clothes shopping.' Saffron couldn't speak. Tom had gone the same colour as Saffron's red nail varnish. 'What do you think?' he asked shyly.

She looked him up and down. Even his feet looked smaller, dressed as they were in a pair of elegant tan leather shoes.

'I think, I think . . .' Saffron tried to find the right words. What she really thought was Tom Fellows looked fit as anything, but there was no way she was going to say that. 'I think you look really nice.'

Tom looked disappointed at her lukewarm reaction. 'Really? You don't think it's too much?'

Saffron laughed. 'If you want the real truth, you look like Rex Sullivan's doppelgänger, and that *definitely* isn't a bad thing.'

Tom grinned. 'I should think so, too. He is my twin brother, after all.'

Saffron nearly fell off her stool, as did the woman next to her, who was leaning over trying – and failing – to listen in. 'Rex Sullivan is your brother?'

Tom chuckled, settling down on the seat next to her. 'Hard to believe, isn't it? Growing up we were like two peas in a pod. Then Rex discovered girls and partying, while I was happy to stay in with my computer. He got spotted at university by a talent scout, and it all took off from there, really. Rex decided to use my mother's maiden name because he thought it sounded better.'

Saffron was seriously impressed. 'Why didn't you ever say anything?'

Tom glanced at her. 'Why, would it have made me cooler?'

Now it was her turn to go red. 'That's not what I meant,' she mumbled, realizing that was exactly what she'd meant. What a shallow cow she'd been!

Tentatively, as if he were David Bellamy about to

511

touch a rare butterfly, Tom put his hand up to one of her fake diamanté earrings.

'I like these, they make your eyes stand out even more.'

Saffron felt her stomach flip. Suddenly, it was as though they were the only two people in the bar. Without really stopping to think what she was doing, she leaned over, and kissed Tom Fellows. His lips were surprisingly soft and warm. In fact they seemed to be getting hotter by the second. Saffron's stomach did another somersault.

'Ooh, Julianne's not going to like that!' the woman next to them exclaimed loudly. Julianne French was a Victoria's Secret model Rex had been going out with for two years.

They both pulled back and laughed.

'Shall we get out of here before I totally destroy my brother's love life?' chuckled Tom. 'Julianne's got quite a temper on her.'

They stood outside just staring at each other, hands entwined. Saffron noticed Tom was breathing as heavily as she was. 'Where shall we go next?' It was a loaded question.

Tom glanced up the road. 'I only live round the corner.' He looked at her with liquid brown eyes. 'I don't suppose you . . . ?'

Saffron smiled saucily. 'You bet I do.'

Somehow she managed to keep her hands off him all the way into the communal hallway of his flat. As he fumbled with the key to his front door, she pressed herself against him, her mouth searching for his.

'Not here,' he mumbled. 'The neighbours might see.'

'Don't be so boring,' Saffron murmured, but moments later she was forced to eat her words. As the door shut

512

behind them, Tom turned and slammed Saffron against the wall. She gasped with surprise and pleasure. He was suddenly wild, groaning and moaning, frenzied hands running over her breasts, across her mouth, through her hair. Tom pulled her top down, exposing Saffron's pert, bra-less breasts as his other hand moved roughly between her legs. Saffron felt completely overwhelmed and powerless.

She loved it.

'You're an animal!' she gasped, as Tom half carried her down the corridor and kicked open another door. Saffron just had a chance to see an electric guitar leaning against the wall, and a computer in the corner, before Tom threw her down on the double bed. She lay there, watching in fascination as Tom pulled his shirt and trousers off. Saffron had a moment to reflect that it certainly was true what they said about men with big feet, before Tom advanced on her, his eyes dark with lust.

With one deft movement, he pulled her jeans and G-string off. Saffron put her arms over her head and wriggled out of her T-shirt and lay back, naked. Tom stood there looking at her for a moment, as if he couldn't quite believe what he was seeing. Saffron barely registered him putting the condom on before he was on top of her again, almost crushing her with his weight; kissing, licking and caressing every inch of her body . . .

Saffron couldn't take it any longer. She had never been so turned on in her life.

'Fuck me. *Now!*'

Tom didn't need any more encouragement. Eyes on hers, he gently eased himself into her. Saffron felt a momentary stab of pain – my God, he was enormous! 'Ow!' she yelped.

'Are you alright?' he breathed.

'It was just the going in part. Oh, do that, it's lovely,' she gasped as he started to move back and forth. After a few moments Tom pulled out and turned her over.

'I want to watch us in the mirror,' he said, pulling her hips high up to meet his enormous erection. He thrust into her, but Saffron felt like someone had just driven a truck up her. 'Too much!' she winced.

Tom withdrew immediately. 'What shall I do? I don't want to hurt you . . .'

Saffron smiled wickedly, back in control again. 'Let's try this.' Pushing him back on the bed, she straddled his lap and sat on him.

'Fuck, that's good,' she murmured. She was just getting into the rhythm when Tom suddenly picked her up, his arms around her legs. 'Hey, I was enjoying that!'

'You'll enjoy this more.'

As if she was feather light, he carried her across the room and pushed her on to the dressing table. Bottles of deodorant and contact-lens solution went flying. Slowly, they started grinding together, tongues in each other's mouths, tasting each other. Saffron could feel the mirror behind her grow wet with condensation.

'Oh, Tom,' she gasped, 'this is amazing!' He pumped harder, still kissing her. Gradually Saffron felt that wonderful feeling building up from her toes, and up her legs, until her orgasm exploded throughout her body, a delicious tingling resonating from the backs of her arms to her scalp.

They stayed there for a moment, giving short, loud breaths, each soaked in sweat. Tom looked deep into her eyes. 'Was that OK?' he asked hesitantly.

Saffron laughed and kissed him deeply. 'That wasn't

OK,' she told him. 'That was bloody brilliant! Where did you learn to do that?'

Tom blushed, suddenly back to his normal self.

It's always the quiet ones, Saffron thought blissfully, as he covered her face with little kisses, then gently picked her up and carried her back to the bed.

MAY

Chapter 64

It was a time for new beginnings, and in the *Soirée* office, changes were afoot already. Catherine was sad to be leaving the team and the magazine, but the thought of what lay ahead filled her with an excitement she had never experienced before, not even when she first got the *Soirée* editorship.

After several meetings with her book publishers, Catherine had delivered a synopsis to them. They were thrilled with it, declaring to Catherine it was going to be a bestseller. Catherine felt rather daunted now. She had to write it! There would no doubt be tears along the way, but it was going to be the most important thing she had ever done in her life.

Meanwhile, Catherine had something else to take care of. The person she was about to sack had finally returned to their desk. Catherine picked up her phone.

'I'd like to see you in my office, please.'

Moments later the unseemly bulk of Annabel Trowbridge lumbered through the door. She sat down heavily in a chair, looking very pleased with herself as usual. 'Before you say anything, can I just say I think it's my finest work yet?' she breathed. 'I'd like to put myself up for Interviewer of the Year at Valour's next awards ceremony.'

Catherine frowned. 'I don't follow.'

Annabel smiled fulsomely. 'My Naomi Campbell interview! I'm sure you're as pleased with it as I am.'

Catherine was grim-faced. 'Actually, I'm not. I thought you let her get away with murder, and your writing was very weak in parts. It won't be happening again.'

Annabel's mouth fell open. 'Well, *I* thought it was brilliant.'

'Well *I* didn't. And I'm still in charge here, in case you hadn't noticed.'

Annabel began to protest, but thought better of it. 'Was there anything else?' she huffed.

'That's not the reason I called you in here.'

Annabel heard the note of steel in Catherine's voice, and started looking rather uncomfortable. 'Do you like moles, Annabel?' Catherine asked suddenly.

Shock and confusion flooded the moonlike face. 'I don't know what you mean.'

'Oh, I think you do.' Catherine's gaze was unflinching, and Annabel looked away. 'You see, I've been rather concerned about the amount of interviews and features we've done over the last few months that have ended up in *Grace*. Something happening once is an unfortunate coincidence, but anything more than that and I start to be suspicious.'

Annabel's bulbous eyes flickered as she stared at the wall.

Catherine continued. 'I had a nasty hunch someone was hacking into my email account, so I asked the IT guys to look into it. I've also been looking at the CCTV footage from the cameras we had installed back after those computer thefts. Did you forget about those?'

Annabel made a great show of examining her nails.

'How long have you been feeding stuff to Isabella Montgomery, Annabel? And worst of all, revealing to her the contents of my private files? It's the only way she could have discovered my true identity.'

Annabel looked up. 'How dare you accuse me . . .'

'Enough!' Catherine slammed her hand down on the desk. She reached across to her in-tray and held up a dossier.

'I have all the evidence. As of this moment you are suspended on full pay pending an inquiry.'

Annabel stared belligerently at Catherine. 'Fine! I don't want to work here, anyway.' She stood up and stormed over to the door.

Catherine stopped her. 'Your reputation will be irreparably damaged, and I doubt you'll work in this industry again. Why on earth did you do it?'

Annabel turned back, looking miserable for the first time. 'Isabella promised to make me deputy editor at *Grace*, said I could have her job in a few years' time.' She looked at Catherine. 'She never meant it, did she?'

Catherine shook her head wearily. 'You've got fifteen minutes to clear your desk.'

Her last day at *Soirée* came all too quickly. It felt strange, putting on her power suit for the last time and climbing into the cab waiting outside the apartment. As they pulled up at Valour Publishing, Catherine had a momentary wobble. She was kissing goodbye to a steady six-figure salary, and the chance to take the magazine on to even greater things. 'It's too late now, girl,' she muttered to herself. Chin stuck out resolutely, she walked into the building.

The security guard had a bunch of flowers ready for

her, and so did the post-room boys, so that by the time Catherine reached her office she felt like a walking florist's shop. More bouquets greeted her, along with pink balloons and a bright, 'Sorry You're Leaving!' banner hung across the door. Catherine picked up the nearest card on a stunning bunch of lilies.

To the best editor I know. You've got bigger balls than all of them! Thank you so much for putting me forward for the job, it means the bloody world. Good luck and keep in touch darl,
Fi xx

Her PA knocked on the open door. 'Harriet, you shouldn't have!' Catherine smiled, gesturing at the balloons.

Harriet smiled warmly. 'It was the least we could do.' She giggled. 'I think Saffron's a bit puffed out, though, she blew up thirty-nine by herself.'

Catherine looked out to where Saffron sat at her desk, being fanned back to life by one of the beauty team. Saffron raised a hand in weak salute.

Catherine laughed. 'Is everything OK for later?' Valour had hired a swanky cocktail bar for her leaving party. It promised to be quite a do.

Harriet nodded. 'Moët and Chandon have just called to say they're donating four extra cases!'

Catherine had barely switched on her computer when Alexander came in, dressed in what seemed to be some sort of green and orange striped flying suit. He was brandishing a copy of the *Daily Mercy*.

'You are going to fucking LOVE this!' he shrieked, shoving the newspaper under her nose.

Catherine blinked. She was looking at a picture of a woman dressed in top-to-toe bondage gear, one of her

522

spiked black boots resting on a naked elderly gentleman who was on all fours in front of her. The woman had the man on a leash as she leered into the camera. Catherine blinked again – surely it wasn't . . . Isabella?! Mouth open, Catherine recognized the old man as a prominent MP in the House of Commons.

'LONDON ELITE CAUGHT IN SEX SCANDAL!' said the headline.

With a quick glance at Alexander, who was hopping excitedly from foot to foot, Catherine began to read.

*Lord Belfry's campaign to become the next Mayor of London has been left in tatters after he was caught taking part in a sordid S&M party. Our intrepid undercover reporter infiltrated the perverted proceedings after a tip-off, and found Lord Belfry strung up on a rack in the basement of his grace-and-favour apartment, along with a number of influential society figures. A dominatrix whipping the willing 'victims' with a six-foot leather whip turned out to be ex-*Grace *editor, Isabella Montgomery, who stepped down from her position in disgrace several weeks ago after disastrous sales figures. When confronted, Ms Montgomery turned violent and tried to attack the* Daily Mercy *with a metal nipple-clamp. The police were called, and Ms Montgomery was arrested and taken to Kensington Police Station. She was charged with assault, and was bailed to appear before a west London magistrates' court next month.*

Disbelievingly, Catherine read on. It seemed Isabella had tried to finish the reporter off by ramming a butt plug (unused, the paper added helpfully), down his throat. It was later revealed that Lord Belfry had put the cost of the DIY work on the dungeon, and his sex toys, down on his expenses. The article went on and on, every excruciating detail laid out for all to see.

Catherine sat back in her seat, stunned. Alexander did a gleeful little jog round the room. 'Hoisted by her own petard! Talk about bad karma, that witch has had it coming to her for a long, long time.'

Catherine looked at him sternly. 'Alexander, stop it! I mean, how awful . . .' They stared at each other for five seconds before collapsing into gales of laughter.

'I'll never look at a butt plug in the same way again,' said Alexander, finally recovering.

Chapter 65

'My dear! And how is Montague Mews's fragrant mother-to-be today?' Caro had opened the front door to Stephen, who was looking as immaculate as ever in a lemon-yellow shirt, matching cravat, and paisley smock.

'Like someone who is about to give birth! I can't remember the last time I saw my feet.' She smiled. 'Come in, I've just brewed a fresh pot of coffee.'

Caro's due date was still two weeks away, although she had been ten days late with Milo. She was convinced the same thing was going to happen with this one.

In the kitchen, Stephen appraised her huge stomach. 'If you don't mind, darling, I'll forgo the actual grand event and make my appearance afterwards, with a wildly extravagant bunch of flowers.'

Caro laughed. 'Flowers sound good enough to me. And chocolates, don't forget those. I was ravenous after having Milo.'

'Fortnum & Mason Champagne Truffles?'

'Fabulous!'

As Caro turned to pour the coffee, she felt a twang

deep inside her, like an elastic band snapping. Suddenly, warm fluid soaked her trousers. Stephen looked at her in horror. 'Oh God,' Caro wailed. 'I think my waters have broken!'

He leapt up from the table. 'But you're not due yet!'

'Babies don't care about that sort of thing.' Caro leaned against the work surface, desperately trying to think. She'd had stomach cramps all morning, but had put them down to indigestion.

She felt a tightening cramping sensation again, much stronger than before. 'I'm having contractions!' she gasped.

White-faced, Stephen put his hand in his chinos and pulled out a highly polished pocket watch. 'Shall I start timing them?' He shuddered. 'Oh, dear Lord, I'm not going to be very good at this.'

Caro held her arm out. 'Just get me on to the sofa.'

It all happened so quickly. By the time Amelia, who had been having lunch with friends nearby, had run home, Caro was having regular contractions. Benedict was on his way back from work. Stephen was sitting in an armchair, his eyes pinned to his pocket watch, as Amelia mopped Caro's brow.

Meanwhile Velda, who had been summoned round by Stephen, was upstairs filling Caro's hospital bag. From the sofa, Caro shouted instructions.

'My new pyjamas are in the wardrobe! Oh, and can you pack the Evian face spritzer that's in the bathroom cupboard? Oww!'

A car screeched to a halt outside, and moments later Benedict rushed in. 'Darling! Are you OK?'

'I think so,' she said and winced. 'Oh, there's another one.'

'Contractions are every five minutes now,' announced Stephen.

'We need to get you to hospital,' said Benedict. He and Amelia helped Caro to her feet.

'I'll ring Tink and Clementine,' Amelia said.

'What about Milo . . .'

'I'll pick him up from nursery. Don't worry. Go!'

'Good luck!' cried Velda, thrusting a bag into Benedict's hand. 'Remember the deep breathing exercises we practised together.'

As their car drove off in a squeal of rubber, Stephen took out his handkerchief and wiped his forehead. 'I don't know about you, but I need some reviving. Care to join me?'

From the hidden vantage point at her landing window, Rowena Elgin was thoughtful. She hoped Caro would be all right, she seemed like a nice woman. And as for the husband! Rowena chuckled, she hadn't seen anyone as handsome in a long time. He had provided inspiration for her latest piece of work.

Rowena went back into her office. It was a light airy room covered with canvases of stunning landmarks around the world. She was thinking hard: maybe she could even put the pregnancy in; the Russian henchmen drama had already added a useful twist.

She sat down at her laptop and opened the document. The first page came up.

'*Close Comforts*, by Valentina Black.'

Rowena smiled and started typing.

Oblivious to the fact that she lived only a couple of doors down from her literary heroine, Caro was getting severely panicky. The traffic was awful, and they had come to yet another standstill. Benedict had phoned ahead on the hands-free to let the hospital know they were coming, but she was starting to think they might not make it in time. Another crippling contraction gripped her body, and she let out an animal groan.

Benedict turned round in alarm. 'Not long now.'

'I really think the baby's coming!' she gasped.

Benedict's jaw set decisively. 'Right, that's it.'

Indicating left, he pulled out into the empty bus lane. A barrage of angry hoots sounded from other drivers. Putting his foot down, Benedict flew past the queues of stationary traffic.

'We're almost there,' he told her. 'Hang on.'

Suddenly, there was a flash of blue lights behind them. Benedict looked into the rear-view mirror and cursed as he slowed to pull over.

Moments later, a uniformed police officer with a *Magnum, P.I.* moustache knocked on the window. 'You've just broken the law, sir,' he said pompously.

'My wife's in labour,' Benedict said, as calmly as he could. 'I need to get her to Chelsea and Westminster.'

The officer peered into the back seat, where Caro was sweating and pale-faced. 'Aargh,' she moaned, slightly louder than was strictly necessary.

The officer shouted to his partner. 'All right Colin, put the siren on. We've got a woman about to give birth here.'

The police escort safely delivered Caro and Benedict into the waiting arms of the medical team. A short while later, at 6.31 p.m., the midwife safely delivered Rosanna Sophia Clementine Towey into the world. The little girl weighed a healthy eight pounds and six ounces, and both mother and daughter were healthy and happy.

By the time Amelia had arrived with Milo, Caro was sitting up in bed sipping a celebratory glass of champagne. Benedict was next to her, cradling his newborn daughter as though she was made of glass.

'Mummy!' Milo ran over and jumped on Caro.

'Ouch, careful, darling,' she said. 'Mummy's got a bit of a sore tummy.'

'Where's your bump gone?'

'She's there. Milo, say hello to Rosanna. She's your new sister.'

They all watched as Milo peered into the blanket.

'Hello, Rosanna,' he said cheerfully, patting her on the head.

Benedict gently stopped him. 'Be careful, Milo, she's only little. You'll have to look after her from now on.'

Milo clambered up on the bed beside Caro. 'Is Errol Flynn coming to see Rosie-anna?'

'I don't think they'll let dogs in here, darling,' Caro told him.

Milo digested the information, frowning. 'I miss him. When are we going back?'

Caro thought of Churchminster, of the winding country lanes and glorious walks, of evening G and Ts in the sun-dappled garden at Fairoaks. Her heart filled up with yearning.

She and Benedict looked at each other. As the business was going so well, they'd discussed staying on another year at the mews. Benedict raised his eyebrows questioningly.

Caro kissed the top of Milo's head. 'Not just yet, darling, we've got lots more adventures to have in London, and we can visit Errol Flynn soon.'

Milo shrugged cheerfully and started playing with the racing car he'd brought with him.

'Thank you,' mouthed Benedict.

Caro smiled, she knew how important his work was to him. As long as they were all together, she was happy.

Chapter 66

Harriet laced up her trainers and stood up to look in the mirror. She was definitely a bit trimmer. Admittedly, it was easier to go running in the summer months, but this year, Harriet was determined to carry on once the evenings drew in again. Maybe she would even get a personal trainer with rock-hard thighs and a wonderful bedside manner, someone who fancied her even when she was beetroot-faced and doing star jumps. Harriet smiled wistfully as she adjusted the bobbles on the back of her trainer socks. She could always dream.

She headed for the local park. She'd planned to do five laps tonight, her furthest distance yet. After the busy days at *Soirée*, running cleared Harriet's mind and gave her time to think. Over the last week she had decided to do a painting course, join the Samaritans and replace the Max Factor mascara that had been languishing in the bottom of her make-up bag for years. The only thing that was still missing was a boyfriend. Harriet hated herself for sounding so desperate, but she really did want someone to share her life with. Most of all, she wanted the chance to get good at sex!

Harriet picked up her stride. Another one of the downsides of being single was that it did get rather lonely, especially at weekends. Everyone was always off doing 'couply' things, like visiting one set of parents or going on romantic walks along the Thames. Harriet had spent last Sunday in front of the television watching *Ugly Betty* re-runs. A rather alarming thought had struck her halfway through – was that how she'd been viewed when she first joined *Soirée*? She was so deep in thought as she rounded the corner by a large rhododendron bush that she didn't hear the warning shout.

'Watch out!'

Before Harriet knew it, she was sprawled flat on her back on the path.

'I say! Are you all right?' said a deep voice. Harriet blinked. Standing over her was the most gorgeous man she had ever seen. Tall and capable-looking, he had puppy-dog eyes and curly brown hair that curled in little bits round his neck. If Harriet had still been standing, she would have swooned right back over again.

The man pulled her up. He was wearing a running kit as well, that showed off an impressive pair of thighs.

'My f-fault . . .' she stuttered. 'I wasn't looking where I was going, as usual.'

He smiled. 'You *were* going at quite a pace! You must be jolly fit.'

Harriet blushed. He really was dashing. 'I normally get a stitch after five minutes.'

'Well, you look fit enough to me.' The man stuck out a hand. 'I'm Bruce.'

Before she had the chance to take it, another runner came sprinting round the corner and ran straight into Harriet, sending her flying into the rhododendron bush. The runner jogged on the spot, glanced at the

Casio watch on his wrist, and cried, 'Sorry, can't stop! Trying to beat my PB!'

Bruce shook an angry fist after him. 'You scoundrel!' He turned back to the bush, where Harriet was trying to struggle out. 'Hold on, you've got your hair caught.' Carefully he extracted a frizzy curl and pulled her up again. Harriet winced: she was sure she'd twisted her knee. 'You're having quite a time of it! What's your name, by the way?'

'Harriet,' she gasped.

She tried to put weight on her leg, but it gave way, and Bruce quickly reached out and caught her.

'I say, Harriet,' he murmured, looking into her eyes. 'This is awfully forward, considering we've only just met, but would you do me the honour of having dinner with me?'

At this both of Harriet's knees went weak, and this time it was entirely pleasurable.

'Oh, Bruce,' she gasped. 'I'd love to!'

Epilogue

Six months later, off the island of La Gomera, the Canaries

Catherine stretched out on her lounger, savouring the heat of the sun. The stillness of the afternoon was only broken by the gentle hum of the motor, and the 'tap tap' of buoys bobbing against the side of the yacht. Endless blue sky filled the horizon, sending an occasional breeze brushing over her body. Soon they would be docking again.

A shadow fell across her. Catherine put a hand up to shield her eyes. A young, good-looking man in pristine white shorts and T-shirt smiled easily at her, revealing milk-white teeth. 'Can I get you anything, Miss Connor?'

'A fresh juice would be great. And, Diego, I've told you, call me Catherine.'

Diego bowed fluidly and slipped away.

Catherine lay back and looked out to sea. This cruise, a treat to herself after finishing the book, had been a perfect idea. She couldn't believe how stunning it was. High above the deep blue waters of the Atlantic, the isolated island of La Gomera reared proudly upwards, magnificent with its soaring mountains and densely forested peaks. Beneath the dramatic valleys and plunging ravines, whitewashed villages with terracotta red roofs nestled amongst olive groves, vineyards and banana groves. It was wild, rugged and undeniably romantic.

Catherine sighed and sank back into her thoughts. It was a few moments before she was aware Diego was back, one glass of chilled orange juice in the centre of a silver tray.

This time, though, he looked concerned. 'Miss Connor . . . I mean, Catherine,' he corrected himself in heavily accented English. 'Forgive me, are you all right? I hear you sigh . . .'

Catherine laughed at his worried expression. 'Diego, I'm fine! Who couldn't be happy in a place like this?'

Diego looked wise. 'But perhaps even better to have someone to share it with?'

Catherine took a sip of juice. 'Maybe.'

He bowed again, 'Captain says we are arriving soon.'

Ten minutes later, they had moored in a secluded bay, nestled between two rocky outcrops. The little restaurant where they were going to have lunch stood a few hundred feet back from the waterfront. Barefoot, Catherine made her way down the gangplank on to the sun-warmed wooden jetty, flip-flops in one hand and camera in the other.

If her old work colleagues had seen her now, they wouldn't have recognized her. Gone were the ball-breaking power suits, to be replaced by a vest and pair of faded cut-off denim shorts, which showed off her long brown legs. Her hair, longer and streaked blonde round the hairline, was pulled back in a casual ponytail. Catherine looked around at her surroundings, savouring the moment. Every part of her felt renewed and rested, and yet . . .

The sun was in her eyes, so Catherine didn't see the figure at the end of the jetty until she was just feet away. Disbelieving, she stopped in her tracks and pulled off her sunglasses. Standing close enough to reach out and touch, in shorts and white linen shirt, a pair of Ray-Bans tucked in his chest pocket, was John Milton.

Catherine finally found the power of speech. 'What on earth are you doing here?' she gasped.

John grinned, green eyes almost luminous against the backdrop of his tan.

'Let's just say you have a very efficient ex-PA.'

He took a step forward, his face full of emotion.

'I've given you six months, Catherine, I can't stay away any longer.'

He lifted his strong hand to caress her face and suddenly nothing else mattered.

'Catherine, I—'

'Sssh,' she said tenderly, and reached up on tiptoe to kiss him.

THE END

Acknowledgements

It goes without saying I am forever in gratitude to my brilliant editor, Sarah Turner at Transworld, and my fab agent, Amanda Preston. Beyond that I'd like to thank Fran Babb and Kate Mulloy for letting me poke around their enchanting mews house, also Emma Fowler for her own experience of mews life – who'd have imagined the things that get picked up on baby monitors? Sounding boards Joe Towns and Kay Ribeiro for their counsel and creativity (the lift sex scene will make it in there soon, Kay, I promise), along with Kay's fellow *Heat* colleague, reviews editor Karen Edwards, for her support and kind words. Another thank you to my Cotswold tour guide Julian Linley and his faithful sidekick Buster. Also Sam Haddad for coming up with the name for this book, Sally Marsh from the Prince's Trust, and Dr Barnaby Wright, curator at the Courtauld Gallery in London, for his expertise and eloquence. A big show of gratitude to fashionistas Ellie Crompton and Bronagh Meere, and my mum, Aunty Barbie and Aunty Pam for making sure I know my gardenias from my gladioli. My dad in a million Neil, who is probably responsible for 90% of my book sales in East Anglia. Finally, Lucie Barboni and Kate Aslett for guiding me through the adventures of pregnancy. Oh, and I can't forget bookseller maestro Jeff Towns, for without his flat-pack assembly skills, I wouldn't have been able to write this thing in the first place.

Country Pursuits

JO CARNEGIE

The gorgeous women of Churchminster know exactly
what they want – a constant flow of champagne and the
love of a good man. But faced with the likes of beer-
guzzling farmer Angus, foul-tempered Sir Fraser and
conceited banker Sebastian, their attentions are drawn to
more *attractive* possibilities . . .

Meanwhile, when a part of their beloved village comes
under threat from a villainous property developer,
the villagers are united by a different kind of passion.
Can they raise enough money to save Churchminster?
Will Mick Jagger turn up to the charity ball?
Will good (sex) overcome bad?

**Introducing a glamorous and unforgettable cast,
Country Pursuits is Jo Carnegie's raunchy, rip-roaring,
gloriously romantic début.**

'Pacy, racy and enormous fun!'
TASMINA PERRY

'Carnegie gives Jilly Cooper a run for her money...A racy read
that'll have you snorting with laughter'
Glamour

9780552157063

Don't forget to look out
for the fabulous new novel from

Jo Carnegie

ROLE PLAY

Out Spring 2010
in Corgi paperback